Alexander Thom and Co.

Irisch Land Commission

Return of judicial rents

Alexander Thom and Co.

Irisch Land Commission
Return of judicial rents

ISBN/EAN: 9783742806086

Manufactured in Europe, USA, Canada, Australia, Japa

Cover: Foto ©Andreas Hilbeck / pixelio.de

Manufactured and distributed by brebook publishing software
(www.brebook.com)

Alexander Thom and Co.

Irisch Land Commission

Irish Land Commission.

The Land Law (Ireland) Act, 1881, 44 & 45 Victoria, ch. 49

RETURN

ACCORDING TO PROVINCES AND COUNTIES

OF

JUDICIAL RENTS

FIXED BY

SUB-COMMISSIONS

AND

CIVIL BILL COURTS,

AS NOTIFIED TO THE IRISH LAND COMMISSION DURING THE MONTH OF

JULY, 1883,

SPECIFYING DATES AND AMOUNTS RESPECTIVELY OF THE LAST INCREASES OF RENT WHERE ASCERTAINED,

ALSO

RENTS FIXED UPON THE REPORTS OF VALUERS APPOINTED BY THE IRISH LAND COMMISSION ON THE JOINT APPLICATIONS OF LANDLORDS AND TENANTS.

Presented to both Houses of Parliament by Command of Her Majesty.

DUBLIN:
PRINTED BY ALEX. THOM & CO., 87, 88, & 89, ABBEY-STREET,
THE QUEEN'S PRINTING OFFICE.

To be purchased, either directly or through any Bookseller, from any of the following Agents, viz.:
Messrs. Hansard, 13, Great Queen-street, W.C., and 32, Abingdon-street, Westminster;
Messrs. Eyre and Spottiswoode, East Harding-street, Fleet-street, and Sale Office, House of Lords;
Messrs. Adam and Charles Black, of Edinburgh;
Messrs. Alexander Thom and Co., or Messrs. Hodges, Figgis, and Co., of Dublin.

1883.

[C.—3827.] *Price 2s. 7d.*

INDEX.

COUNTY.	Page
ANTRIM, ...	4
ARMAGH, ...	14
CARLOW, ...	101
CAVAN, ...	28 and 234
CLARE, ...	171 and 228
CORK, ...	186 and 230
DONEGAL, ...	30
DOWN, ...	34
DUBLIN ...	104
FERMANAGH, ...	61 and 234
GALWAY, ...	114, 226, and 236
KERRY, ...	200
KILKENNY, ...	104
LEITRIM, ...	128
LIMERICK, ...	213 and 230
LONDONDERRY, ...	74
LONGFORD, ...	108
LOUTH, ...	110
MAYO, ...	112
MEATH, ...	110 and 234
MONAGHAN, ...	51
QUEEN'S, ...	114
ROSCOMMON ...	168 and 276
SLIGO, ...	170
TIPPERARY, ...	230 and 236
TYRONE, ...	66
WEXFORD, ...	116

SUMMARY.

Showing, according to Counties and Provinces, the Number of Cases in which Judicial Rents have been Fixed by Sub-Commissions during the Month of July, 1883; and also the Acreage, Tenement Valuation, Former Rents, and Judicial Rents of the Holdings.

	Number of Cases in which Judicial Rents have been fixed.	Acreage.	Tenement Valuation.	Former Rent.	Judicial Rent.
		Statute Acres.	£ s. d.	£ s. d.	£ s. d.
ULSTER—					
Antrim, ...	108	6,121 0 31	2,848 6 8	3,633 3 7	2,798 19 10
Armagh, ...	207	2,613 1 3	1,691 18 4	1,847 13 8	1,304 16 6
Cavan, ...	176	3,913 0 25½	3,070 15 0	3,610 14 6	3,094 12 0
Donegal, ...	331	13,351 0 7	2,059 16 0	2,613 19 6½	2,123 10 8
Down, ...	161	3,693 3 33	3,286 8 8	3,641 15 1	3,070 11 3
Fermanagh, ...	173	4,961 2 6	2,120 10 7	2,847 3 5	2,172 0 0
Londonderry, ...	173	3,911 0 7	3,181 17 6	3,534 11 5	3,140 5 3
Monaghan, ...	36	568 2 27	407 7 0	500 0 4½	680 12 6
Tyrone, ...	311	9,654 1 38	3,656 10 7	4,307 19 4½	3,184 15 6
Total, ...	1,726	49,275 1 29¼	21,600 3 8	28,039 2 1½	20,850 8 5
LEINSTER—					
Carlow, ...	5	161 1 33	83 0 0	119 0 0	109 8 0
Dublin, ...	3	112 1 23	93 15 0	130 10 2	106 15 2
Kilkenny, ...	7	629 1 5	350 14 0	466 1 8	343 7 0
Longford, ...	84	3,030 1 25	2,044 3 0	2,689 18 0	2,236 3 1
Louth, ...	6	231 3 19	228 15 0	274 4 8	233 17 8
Meath, ...	66	2,297 3 19	1,715 13 0	2,290 13 3	2,083 0 11
Queen's, ...	1	30 0 27	30 3 0	34 9 4	38 0 4
Wexford, ...	4	166 3 30	89 15 9	108 15 7	91 0 0
Total, ...	170	6,700 3 11	4,654 3 0	6,129 12 9	5,277 1 1
CONNAUGHT—					
Galway, ...	174	5,059 1 16	1,726 8 11	2,330 6 5½	2,115 3 4
Leitrim, ...	373	6,730 2 33½	2,366 11 0	3,735 18 3	3,208 16 10½
Mayo, ...	480	6,292 1 37½	2,009 0 10	2,520 0 6½	2,286 9 8
Roscommon, ...	37	700 1 3½	266 7 0	420 6 0	276 3 0
Sligo, ...	56	1,630 2 16	616 13 0	784 11 6	680 12 6
Total, ...	936	20,431 1 39	7,106 5 9	10,557 8 6	8,828 4 4½
MUNSTER—					
Clare, ...	199	7,663 0 21	2,830 15 6	4,188 8 7	3,431 9 11
Cork, ...	237	10,626 0 3	4,163 10 10	6,094 3 7	5,439 6 11
Kerry, ...	193	10,378 1 38	1,433 11 0	3,029 17 0	2,330 6 0
Limerick, ...	167	6,290 0 31¼	5,050 4 6	7,689 11 7	6,443 0 9
Total, ...	778	34,886 3 31¼	13,330 10 10	21,439 19 9	17,644 8 0

IRELAND.

ULSTER, ...	1,726	49,275 1 29¼	21,600 3 8	28,039 2 1½	20,850 8 5
LEINSTER, ...	170	6,700 3 11	4,654 3 0	6,129 12 9	5,277 1 1
CONNAUGHT,	936	20,431 1 39	7,106 5 9	10,557 8 6	8,828 4 4½
MUNSTER, ...	778	34,886 3 31¼	13,330 10 10	21,439 19 9	17,644 8 0
TOTAL, ...	3,610	111,297 3 30¾	46,691 3 3	64,159 3 3½	52,094 16 10½

NOTE.—For Civil Bill Court and Valuers' [illegible], see pp. [illegible]

PROVINCE OF

COUNTY OF

Names of Assistant Commissioners by whom Cases were decided	No.	Name of Tenant.	Name of Landlord.	Townland
Assistant Commissioners—				
Edward Greer (Legal). J. R. Meadows. J. H. McKeever. F. O'Callaghan. John Lowe.	1912	Samuel McAlister, ...	Robert N. Batt, ...	Small Quarter, ...
	1913	William Scott, ...	Theodosia E. Scott, ...	Mason Ward, ...
	1914	James K. Scott, ...	do.	do. ...
	1915	Robert Lake, ...	James H. Crummie, ...	Carrowreagh, ...
	1916	John Crossley, ...	do.	Umbinagh, ...
	1917	Robert Gill, ...	do.	do. ...
	1918	John Gill, ...	do.	do. ...
	1919	John Hamill, ...	do.	do. ...
	1920	William Rogers, ...	do.	do. ...
	1921	William Clarke, ...	Chas. J. H. Todd-Thornton, ...	Ballyvally, ...
	1922	Robert Carson, ...	John L. Burns, ...	Artifinal, ...
	1923	Patrick Fronie, ...	Sir R. H. Harvey, Bart., ...	Ballymaconnelly,
	1924	Sarah McGahan, ...	do.	Gortnagihy, ...
	1925	John Kilbride, ...	do.	Maghernahey, ...
	1926	David Robinson, ...	do.	Tamlaght, ...
	1927	William Logan, ...	do.	Drumnamb, ...
	1928	Thomas Killough, ...	do.	Garvagher, ...
	1929	James Elder, ...	do.	Gortnaghey, ...
	1930	Alexander McKinley, ...	do.	Drum, ...
	1931	James McCaughern, ...	do.	Ballydonnelly, ...
	1932	Oliver Coleman, ...	do.	Maghernahey, ...
	1933	William Black, ...	do.	Moneydig, ...
	1934	John Stewart, ...	do.	Maghernahey, ...
	1935	John McFerran, ...	do.	Craigagh, ...
	1936	Mary Ann Glasgow, ...	do.	Lisnagrot, ...
	1937	Robert Rea, ...	do.	Ballydonnelly, ...
	1938	John Wilson, ...	do.	Tamlaght, ...
	1939	Arthur Brennan, ...	do.	Oldmore, ...
	1940	James Boag, ...	do.	Lisnagrot, ...
	1941	Arthur Moore, ...	do.	Tamlaght, ...

ULSTER.

ANTRIM.

Extent of Holding. Statute.	Poor Law Valuation.	Former Rent.	Judicial Rent.	Observations.	Value of Tenancy.
A. R. P.	£ s. d.	£ s. d.	£ s. d.		£ s. d.
23 2 20	18 5 0	17 10 0	16 10 0	By consent.	
23 2 3	12 8 0	17 10 0	11 0 0	do.	
25 0 13	11 0 0	17 10 0	15 0 0	do.	
7 2 0	3 18 0	7 13 0	4 10 0	do.	
30 1 5	13 0 0	18 9 0	12 10 0	do.	
19 1 10	13 10 0	14 1 0	11 7 0	do.	
33 1 20	22 5 0	28 10 0	22 0 0	do.	
11 0 10	5 15 0	8 0 0	5 15 0	do.	
14 2 20	7 0 0	8 18 6	7 0 0	do.	
27 1 5	20 10 0	30 0 0	23 0 0	do.	
44 0 0	20 18 0	34 0 0	20 15 0	£ s. d.	
14 3 10	9 15 0	11 3 3	9 10 0	Rent changed in 1870 from . . . 8 11 0	
23 2 11	14 12 0	26 18 7	13 10 0		
25 3 20	18 5 0	19 10 0	13 2 0	do. 15 0 0	
15 3 26	7 10 0	9 8 3	6 10 0		
31 1 20	15 8 0	14 8 7	11 5 0		
47 1 0	27 15 0	28 18 8	23 15 0	do. 21 17 0	
8 3 30	5 15 0	6 4 0	4 18 0		
7 2 10	6 0 0	6 15 11	5 5 0		
22 0 0	12 5 0	17 8 8	13 15 0	do. 16 0 3	
48 3 0	16 10 0	18 0 0	14 10 0	do. 13 0 0	
27 0 0	11 10 0	12 6 6	10 0 0		
14 2 0	9 0 0	11 11 6	8 0 0		
38 3 25	14 18 0	18 3 1	15 12 0		
31 2 25	25 0 0	34 5 8	18 6 0	do. 20 0 0	
33 0 10	18 15 0	23 0 6	17 18 0	do. 18 5 0	
41 3 20	33 10 0	35 0 0	34 16 0	do. 30 0 0	
25 0 30	18 5 0	18 1 8	14 8 0		
15 0 0	11 8 0	11 18 6	9 10 0	do. 9 12 6	
8 3 20	8 10 0	3 18 9	6 18 0		

COUNTY OF

Names of Assistant Commissioners by whom Cases were decided.	No.	Name of Tenant.	Name of Landlord.	Townland.
Assistant Commissioners—				
EDWARD GREER (Legal). J. R. HEADECH. J. H. MCDEVITT. F. O'CALLAGHAN. JOHN LOWE.	1942	Mary McDonnell, ...	Sir R. B. Harvey, Bart., ...	Carnwighey, ...
	1943	Samuel Pinkerton, ...	James S. Moore, ...	Bann Mea, ...
	1944	Samuel Pinkerton, jun.,	do.	do. ...
	1945	James McLaughlin, ...	William F. Hutchinson, ...	Gruelaghs, ...
	1946	Anne Shaw, ...	do.	Dunaghey, ...
	1947	Mary McGregor, ...	Earl of Antrim, ...	Newhill, ...
	1948	Denis McIlravick, ...	Alexander Dunlop, ...	Ardagh, ...
	1949	Thomas Stevenson, ...	Alexander Patterson, ...	do. ...
	1950	David McAleavy, ...	Daniel H. S. McKay, ...	Cabbell, Upper, ...
	1951	James Conghlin, ...	Rev. T. L. Nash, ...	Drumlin, ...
	1952	Henry Hume, ...	Thomas Montgomery, ...	Ellmonda, ...
	1953	William Moore, ...	James G. Moore, ...	Lisnisk, ...
	1954	James Stevenson, ...	Alexander Boyd, ...	Kinnahan, ...
	1955	Patrick Martin, ...	Robert N. Gait, ...	Artiferrall, ...
	1956	Nancy McKeown, ...	The Misses Moore, ...	Lisbragan, ...
	1957	John McIlwaine, ...	Samuel B. Greenfield, ...	Dunglo, ...
	1958	Mary McAlambridge, ...	Alexander Macaulay, a Minor, and another,	Lisnagh, ...
	1959	Robert McMullan and another,	James E. Leslie, ...	Ballyrennald, ...
	1960	Benjamin McAfee, ...	Colonel S. D. Leslie, ...	do. ...
	1961	Samuel Crawford, ...	John Graham, ...	Drumnagoon, ...
	1962	Andrew McLaughlin, ...	Robert Woodside, ...	Carninneen, ...
	1963	Archibald McCurdy, ...	Sadleir E. Givens, ...	Lisnarioch, ...
	1964	James Dobbs, ...	Henry H. McNeill, ...	Kilmandore [illegible],
	1965	Hugh McGowan, ...	Robert Howard, ...	Parkmore, ...
	1966	Anne McAuley, ...	do.	do. ...
	1967	Patrick McIlheron, ...	Colonel White, ...	Barnmore, ...
	1968	William Fleming, ...	J. Todd Thornton, ...	Moneycannon, ...
	1969	John Christie, ...	Alexander McNeill, ...	Drumaduff, ...
	1970	James Reilly, ...	do.	do. ...
	1971	Michael McAleese, ...	do.	do. ...
	1972	Neal McNeill, ...	A. and H. Johnston, ...	Carnanagh, ...
	1973	William Brown, ...	do.	Feigh, ...
	1974	William Wilson, ...	do.	do. ...
	1975	James MacKenzie, ...	do.	do. ...
	1976	Hugh McDougall, ...	do.	Prolusk, ...

ANTRIM—*continued.*

Extent of Holding. Statute.	Poor Law Valuation.	Former Rent.	Judicial Rent.	Observations.		Value of Tenancy.
A. R. P.	£ s. d.	£ s. d.	£ s. d.		£ s. d.	£ s. d.
10 3 5	7 10 0	5 0 0	6 0 0			
34 0 0	31 0 0	38 0 0	27 15 0			
28 0 0	25 15 0	35 0 0	27 15 0			
22 2 10	23 0 0	12 0 0	18 0 0	Rent changed in 1839 from . . .	16 13 10	
34 1 27	27 10 0	34 0 0	31 10 0			
11 3 04	16 0 0	15 0 0	18 10 0			
63 2 14	11 17 0	19 14 10	13 10 6	1871	10 3 7	
20 3 10	20 0 0	28 0 0	20 14 0			
23 2 35	16 5 0	18 17 0	15 0 0	By consent.		
20 0 6	17 15 0	21 0 0	18 0 0			
28 3 0	28 5 0	35 0 0	34 0 0			
137 3 0	84 5 0	93 0 0	87 0 0	Rent changed in 1877 from . . .	84 5 0	
78 1 7	43 5 0	65 0 0	60 0 0			
0 3 30	0 5 0	1 0 0	1 0 0			
20 3 26	15 10 0	16 0 0	11 10 0			
20 0 8	14 10 0	17 11 0	14 0 0	1878	19 0 0	
10 3 4	7 5 0	8 0 0	5 6 0	1877	7 6 5	
14 1 10	9 15 0	12 0 0	8 17 0			
11 0 0	9 10 0	6 12 0	7 8 0			
16 2 0	10 12 0	14 0 0	8 10 0	1870	11 0 0	
17 2 28	16 15 0	28 10 0	20 5 0			
64 3 20	43 0 0	60 10 6	64 10 0	1853	39 11 10	
8 1 35	16 0 0	14 7 1	18 5 0			
40 3 34	—	14 0 0	13 10 0			
27 0 26	13 0 0	10 0 0	18 0 0			
20 0 16	13 14 0	16 0 0	12 0 0			
73 3 0	38 0 0	63 0 0	41 0 0	By consent.		
11 0 0	10 10 0	12 3 6	8 16 0			
21 0 0	10 0 0	23 6 3	18 10 0			
24 0 6	18 10 0	32 0 0	16 16 0			
40 3 10	37 0 0	42 0 0	35 10 0	Rent changed in 1848 from . . .	31 0 0	
88 0 0	83 0 0	56 0 0	45 0 0	1859	37 13 8	
47 1 10	67 10 0	65 10 0	61 13 0			
61 3 18	71 13 0	85 0 0	63 0 0	do.	80 0 0	
58 3 20	30 0 0	34 0 0	31 10 0	1879	38 0 0	

COUNTY OF

Names of Assistant Commissioners by whom Cases were decided.	No.	Name of Tenant.	Name of Landlord.	Townland.
Assistant Commissioners—				
Edward Greer (Legal). J. R. Hamilton. J. H. McKerrow. F. O'Callaghan. John Love.	1977	Alexander McClelland,	Rev. James O'Hara,	Breckenagh,
	1978	Hamilton McArthur,	do.	Cabragh,
	1979	Alexander Hunter, junr.,	Sir Frederick Boyd, Bart.,	Ballyreagh,
	1980	Ann Baillie,	do.	Craigfad,
	1981	Patrick McGlone,	do.	Broughanlea,
	1982	John Donnelly,	Alexander George Fullerton,	Knocklayde,
	1983	Patrick Hanna,	do.	Knocknagarvan,
	1984	Hugh McKay,	do.	Ballinlea Demesne
	1985	James Wilson,	John McGildowney,	Tornaroan,
	1986	Hugh Moore,	do.	Ballyvoy,
	1987	Alexander McCormick,	do.	Bonamargy,
	1988	Alexander Ferguson,	do.	Drumavoley,
	1989	John McLaughlin,	do.	do.
	1990	Do.	do.	Fairview,
	1991	John McDowell,	do.	Carrymill,
	1992	Robert Mant,	do.	Turiff,
	1993	Alexander Parnell,	Alexander G. Fullerton,	Losnagh More,
	1994	James McLernon,	do.	Losnagh Beg,
	1995	Thomas McCloskey,	do.	Lagavara,
	1996	Hugh O'Kane,	Conway R. Dobbs & another, Trustees of Alex. Cuppage.	Lecky,
	1997	James McCloskey,	do.	Tenaxe,
	1998	Daniel Kearney,	do.	Glenaghan,
	1999	Daniel McGill,	do.	Broughindrumnill
	2000	John McMahon,	do.	do.
	2001	James Kane,	do.	do.
	2002	John McKeown,	Elizabeth S. Moore,	Moyarget, Upper,
	2003	Samuel Smiley,	do.	do.
	2004	Mary McGaw,	Rev. Adam Cuppage,	Craiganorthy,
	2005	William Hill,	do.	Ardboy,
	2006	William McCurdy,	do.	[illegible]
	2007	John Fleming,	do.	do.
	2008	Alexander McCaw,	do.	Craiganorthy,
	2009	John McCurdy,	do.	Tobarbuugh,
	2010	Alexander McCurdy,	do.	do.
	2011	William Hill,	do.	[illegible]

ANTRIM—*continued.*

Extent of Holding (Statute).	Poor Law Valuation.	Former Rent.	Judicial Rent.	Observations.	Value of Tenancy.
A. R. P.	£ s. d.	£ s. d.	£ s. d.	£ s. d.	£ s. d.
27 1 30	24 0 0	25 0 0	22 12 6		
8 1 0	1 18 0	5 4 0	8 10 0		
32 3 3	7 18 0	10 0 0	5 5 0		
38 3 31	15 10 0	19 0 0	18 0 0		
16 0 24	10 10 0	23 0 0	18 12 0	Rent changed in 1873 from . . . 15 19 0	
29 2 23	38 10 0	24 10 0	29 10 0		
27 0 28	17 10 0	17 5 5	16 0 0	1883 14 0 0	
18 0 0	20 5 0	32 11 7	27 10 0		
80 1 0	18 16 0	22 15 8	32 0 0		
38 3 28	29 5 0	33 14 0	31 0 0		
8 2 0	7 0 0	4 6 0	7 6 0		
84 0 0	17 5 0	32 0 0	18 0 0	1847 18 12 0	
29 0 0	23 6 0	23 1 10	22 18 0		
38 0 0	16 10 0	13 4 10	12 1 10		
6 3 25	8 15 0	7 1 5	5 6 0		
14 0 0	11 13 0	13 11 10	8 0 0		
28 3 7	17 5 0	23 0 0	17 10 0		
71 0 28	17 0 0	21 3 7	37 0 0		
10 0 0	10 15 0	18 0 0	10 15 0		
31 3 26	17 0 0	17 10 0	18 0 0		
36 0 11	17 5 0	16 0 0	14 5 0		
40 1 30	17 0 0	19 10 0	18 10 0		
16 0 5	6 3 0	7 12 0	6 12 0		
16 1 0	5 5 0	7 5 0	6 3 0		
7 2 0	3 6 0	3 11 6	2 6 0	1854 3 10 0	
68 1 25	28 5 0	25 0 0	29 0 0	1860 27 0 0	
3 3 7	2 5 0	4 0 0	6 0 0		
18 0 10	13 1 0	18 5 0	13 10 0		
86 1 30	18 0 0	17 16 0	10 4 0		
23 1 14	19 10 0	32 12 0	18 0 0	1877 21 17 5	
24 0 36	18 0 0	24 4 0	18 10 0	1875 11 17 8	
8 1 20	0 15 0	8 10 0	7 0 0		
18 5 0	15 5 0	17 0 0	13 10 0	1861 16 5 0	
19 1 2	12 10 0	17 0 0	13 10 0	1863 15 3 0	
10 3 0	10 10 0	18 7 3	9 5 0	1878 5 7 10	

COUNTY OF

Names of Assistant Commissioners by whom Cases were decided.	No.	Name of Tenant.	Name of Landlord.	Townland.
Assistant Commissioners—				
Edward Greer (Legal). J. B. Heagney. J. H. McEntyre. F. O'Callaghan, John Love.	2012	Francis McAuley,	Earl of Antrim,	[illegible],
	2013	Denis McCormick,	do.	Glenmakeeran,
	2014	Hugh McMullan,	do.	[illegible],
	2015	William McCambridge,	do.	Ballynagard,
	2016	Catherine McBride,	do.	East Torr,
	2017	John Black,	do.	Glenmakeeran,
	2018	Denis McKinley,	do.	Glenmakeeran,
	2019	Robert Kirkpatrick,	Sir Robert B. Harvey, Bart.,	Cortober,
	2020	James Thom,	Lieutenant-Colonel J. H. Todd Thornton,	Ballyvelly,
	2021	John McKay,	James Crommie,	Unshinagh,
	2022	William Gait,	do.	do.
	2023	James Henderson,	Sir Robert B. Harvey, Bart.,	Ballydonnelly,
	2024	Robert Jamieson,	do.	Cortrighey,
	2025	James H. Ferguson,	Ralph Smith & another, Trustees of C. G. Macartney,	Moyarget, Upper,
	2026	Henry Chesnutt,	Alex. Jameson and another, Reps. of James Watson,	Irish Omerbane,
	2027	Andrew Gregg,	Thomas Montgomery,	Ballyhagin,
	2028	James Coppin,	do.	do.
	2029	Matthew Graham,	do.	Inisloughan,
	2030	William Parr,	do.	Ballyhagin,
	2031	David Watson,	do.	do.
	2032	Thomas Ewart,	James and George Gray, Trustees of Major Gray,	Tullygarvey,
	2033	Hiro Rainey,	do.	Ormskill,
	2034	Andrew Gatton,	do.	Dunmurry,
	2035	John and Alexander Mulvenna,	Anne Wiley,	Killinaraggy,
	2036	John Davison,	do.	do.
	2037	William and Alexander Davison,	do.	do.
	2038	James Davison,	do.	do.
	2039	Matthew Culverwell,	Thomas Craig,	Killyfinnelly,
	2040	Robert McConaghy,	Richard Dyatt,	Cortaheran,
	2041	John Norris,	do.	do.
	2042	John Kenny, senior,	do.	Ballykeenan,
	2043	Mary Mulholland,	William Miller and another,	Gilgad,
	2044	William Graham,	Francis McCord,	do.
	2045	William Barton,	Robert J. Alexander,	Lismolesky,
	2046	James Wilson,	Francis G. Rowan,	Ballyloughan,

ANTRIM—*continued.*

Extent of Holding. Statute.	Poor Law Valuation.	Existing Rent.	Judicial Rent.	Observations.		Value of Tenancy.
a. r. p.	£ s. d.	£ s. d.	£ s. d.		£ s. d.	£ s. d.
178 3 20	37 5 0	30 0 0	27 0 0	Rent changed in 1864 from	30 0 0	
47 0 0	10 15 0	14 13 10	11 5 0			
30 0 0	30 0 0	33 11 0	30 0 0			
17 3 35	13 10 0	15 5 0	13 0 0			
23 3 20	10 0 0	7 11 6	9 0 0			
25 2 0	18 0 0	18 5 0	16 10 0			
25 1 0	13 0 0	16 0 0	14 0 0			
38 0 0	22 0 0	23 19 11	19 12 0	1870	20 2 0	
61 0 0	35 5 0	33 10 0	37 10 0	By consent.		
33 2 0	12 15 0	18 18 6	12 0 0	do.		
30 3 0	19 0 0	21 2 0	17 7 6			
13 2 10	10 3 0	11 5 11	8 10 0			
63 0 0	54 15 0	83 11 3	69 0 0			
64 3 0	39 0 0	63 0 0	63 0 0			
18 0 0	10 0 0	13 0 0	13 6 0			
30 1 0	30 10 0	38 17 9	33 10 0			
36 2 0	25 10 0	42 18 3	30 10 0			
53 3 20	25 10 0	43 0 0	35 0 0			
30 2 34	23 15 0	20 1 9	23 10 0			
60 0 27	23 10 0	49 13 0	42 0 0			
65 3 24	20 0 0	33 0 0	25 0 0			
14 0 0	13 15 0	15 15 0	14 10 0			
17 2 22	10 10 0	17 5 0	14 13 0			
371 2 20	33 10 0	70 0 0	35 0 0			
81 0 0	11 10 0	5 5 0	6 5 0	Rent changed in 1875 from . . .	5 16 7	
189 1 17	81 10 0	17 0 9	16 0 0			
380 1 0	37 5 0	43 0 0	33 10 0			
21 2 0	11 4 0	17 0 0	13 6 0	1860	10 0 0	
11 2 11	8 15 0	11 0 0	9 0 0			
19 3 0	16 0 0	18 0 0	14 4 0	1862	13 3 0	
5 0 30	8 0 0	5 0 0	4 10 0			
16 0 31	11 15 0	11 0 0	12 10 0			
11 0 0	8 10 0	14 0 0	10 0 0			
31 2 28	24 15 0	27 7 6	21 0 0			
6 2 10	7 5 0	13 15 0	9 6 0	1860	11 8 0	

COUNTY OF

Names of Assistant Commissioners by whom Cases were decided.	No.	Name of Tenant.	Name of Landlord.	Townland.
Assistant Commissioners—				
Edward Greer (Legal). J. B. Heasman. A. H. McEntyre. F. O'Callaghan. John Love.	2047	William McVicker, ...	John Ward, — —	Dunmbaning, —
	2048	John Elliott, ... —	do. — —	do. —
	2049	Hugh McCullough, —	F. A. (G. M. Steel), —	—
	2050	William Kennedy, ...	John Given, — —	Ballyclose, —
	2051	William Stevens, —	William Baker, ... —	Dunnyvaddan, —
	2052	Andrew Lackey, ...	Jane Dunnevah, — —	Carnstown, —
	2053	William Tinsam, —	do. — —	Killowney, —
	2054	Thomas Pickon, —	Henry H. MacNeill, ...	Craigs, —
	2055	James Kennedy, —	The Misses Dickey, —	Ballynagh, —
	2056	James Fleming, —	do. — —	do. —
	2057	David McCreight, ...	James S. Moore, ...	Drumagrove, —
	2058	Alexander Stewart, ...	do. — —	Glenkeile, —
	2059	Isabella Dickson, —	do.	do. —
	2060	James Crawford, ...	do. ... —	do. —
	2061	Daniel Kyle, —	do. ... —	do. —
	2062	Andrew McCleery, —	do. ... —	do —
	2063	Thomas Dickson, —	do. ... —	do. —
	2064	John Hogg, ...	do. ... —	do. —
	2065	Mary Gordon, ...	do. — —	do. —
	2066	Mary Jane Hutchinson,	do. ... —	do. —
	2067	Thomas Hollingsley, ...	do. — —	do. ...
	2068	William Gregg, ...	do.	do. —
	2069	John McAteer, —	do.	do. —
	2070	James Barr, ... —	do. ... —	do. —
	2071	Robert McIntyre, ...	do. — —	do. —
	2072	John Dennis, ... —	do. — —	Lower Tullykittagh.
	2073	Ellen O'Raw, —	do. — —	do. —
	2074	Daniel Higgins, —	do. — —	do. —
	2075	John Casey, ... —	do. — —	do. —
	2076	William Crawford, —	do.	Upper Tullykittagh.
	2077	Hugh McCambridge, —	do. — —	do. —
	2078	William McCreight, —	do. — —	Drumagrove, —
	2079	Patrick O'Loan, —	do. — —	do. —
				Total, —

ANTRIM—*continued.*

Extent of Holding. Statute.	Poor Law Valuation.	Former Rent.	Judicial Rent.	Observations.		Value of Tenancy.
A. R. P.	£ s. d.	£ s. d.	£ s. d.		£ s. d.	£ s. d.
23 1 0	23 0 0	34 16 0	30 0 0			
31 0 15	20 8 0	31 4 6	25 10 0			
6 1 20	7 5 0	8 1 3	5 10 0			
1 2 38	5 10 0	10 0 0	0 10 0	Rent changed in 1850 from . .	8 0 0	
30 3 23	8 5 0	18 0 0	13 0 0			
33 1 25	13 5 0	20 4 0	19 0 0			
30 0 0	27 0 0	29 0 0	28 10 0			
10 0 0	7 10 0	13 0 0	8 0 0	1878	6 10 0	
7 3 30	6 5 0	8 13 10	6 10 0			
19 0 23	16 0 0	21 18 0	15 0 0			
31 3 0	22 0 0	27 0 0	23 10 0	1870	14 0 0	
20 2 0	11 10 0	17 10 0	13 13 0			
28 1 0	10 15 0	22 0 0	17 10 0			
16 0 10	7 10 0	13 0 0	8 5 0			
42 0 0	18 0 0	23 10 0	18 10 0			
18 2 15	6 0 0	10 0 0	6 10 0	1879	5 10 0	
13 3 0	0 15 0	10 10 0	7 10 0			
8 1 0	2 0 0	2 16 0	3 15 0			
20 0 0	6 15 0	13 0 0	9 5 0	1863	9 6 0	
8 1 0	3 5 0	3 16 0	3 13 0			
64 0 13	30 0 0	30 0 0	28 0 0	1878	37 0 0	
42 2 0	35 15 0	35 0 0	27 18 0	do.	15 19 6½	
8 2 8	6 10 0	8 0 0	6 0 0			
30 0 0	10 15 0	16 0 0	16 18 0	do.	15 0 0	
14 2 25	0 0 0	8 0 0	6 0 0			
5 2 0	4 10 0	5 16 0	4 10 0			
42 0 0	12 15 0	19 0 0	14 10 0	do.	18 0 0	
41 0 0	31 10 0	30 0 0	22 10 0			
45 0 0	24 10 0	31 0 0	26 0 0	1880	19 0 0	
20 0 10	10 0 0	14 10 0	10 13 0	1877	10 0 0	
26 0 5	5 10 0	6 0 0	5 5 0			
23 0 0	21 0 0	28 0 0	21 10 0			
44 0 0	34 0 0	40 0 0	36 10 0	1880	21 6 6	
6,157 0 31	3,686 0 0	3,633 5 7	[illegible] 13 10			

COUNTY OF

Names of Assistant Commissioners by whom Cases were decided.	No.	Name of Tenant.	Name of Landlord.	Townland.
Assistant Commissioners,—				
James G. Wylie (Legal). T. Nevin. G. O. Kenney. Wm. Davison. A. Ferguson.	2547	James Callaghan & anor.,	F. W. Wilkinson, ...	Drumnahunshin,
	2548	Catherine Carvey, ...	Robert John McGeough, ...	Ummericam, ...
	2549	Patrick McGeough, ...	do.	Cashel, ...
	2550	John Fyme, ...	do.	Aughnaskeagh, ...
	2551	Lawrence Caffly, ...	do.	Ummericam, ...
	2552	Catherine Murphy, ...	do.	Aughnaskeagh, ...
	2553	Owen Small, ...	do.	do. ...
	2554	Patrick Callaghan, ...	do.	do. ...
	2555	Patrick T. Callaghy, ...	do.	do. ...
	2556	Bridget Mackeer, ...	do.	do. ...
	2557	Sarah Ley, ...	do.	Ummericam, ...
	2558	Owen McVarry, ...	do.	do. ...
	2559	Patrick Gunn, ...	do.	Cashel, ...
	2560	Patrick Small, Reps. of James Small,	do.	Aghnaskeagh, ...
	2561	Bridget Mackin, ...	do.	Ummericam, ...
	2562	James Johnston & anor., Reps. of Arthur Johnston,	do.	do. ...
	2563	James Cavanagh, ...	do.	Aghnaskeagh, ...
	2564	Henry Ley, ...	do.	Ummericam, ...
	2565	Ann Ley, ...	do.	do. ...
	2566	James Gunn, Rep. of Mary Magee,	do.	Ummericam, ...
	2567	James McGeough, ...	do.	Cashel, ...
	2568	John Hanratty, ...	do.	do. ...
	2569	James McGeough, ...	do.	do. ...
	2570	Thomas McGeough, ...	do.	Ummericam, ...
	2571	James McEvoy, minor,	do.	Cashel, ...
	2572	James Carry, ...	do.	Darvey Forge, ...
	2573	Michael Powers, ...	do.	Aghnaskeagh, ...
	2574	Mary McGeough, ...	do.	Cashel, ...
	2575	James McKeown, ...	do.	Ummericam, ...
	2576	Neill Quillan, ...	do.	Cashel, ...
	2577	Alice Quillan, ...	do.	Aghnaskeagh, ...
	2578	Alice McGeough, ...	do.	Tullyvaughan,
	2579	Mary Magee, Rep. of Michael Magee,	do.	Ummericam, ...
	2580	Michael McGeough, ...	do.	Cashel, ...
	2581	John McVarry, ...	do.	do. ...

ARMAGH.

Content of Holding. Statute.	Poor Law Valuation.	Former Rent.	Judicial Rent.	Observations.	Value of Tenancy.
A. R. P.	£ s. d.	£ s. d.	£ s. d.	£ s. d.	£ s. d.
6 2 19	9 0 0	8 16 2	6 6 0		
23 0 0	0 15 0	7 17 3	5 0 0	Rent changed in 1871 from . . . 6 3 0	
5 1 20	5 10 0	5 18 0	4 14 0	1879 5 0 0	
29 3 0	10 10 0	13 0 3	7 17 0	1873 9 0 0	
16 3 9	8 10 0	9 1 3	6 7 6	do. 8 6 0	
31 2 20	10 0 0	13 10 0	9 8 0	1876 10 11 0	
18 1 26	7 5 0	11 7 3	7 0 0	1871 7 7 0	
6 3 1	2 10 0	3 1 6	3 8 0		
14 3 12	6 15 0	6 14 0	3 9 0		
7 2 20	3 5 0	4 3 0	2 18 0		
9 2 2	4 5 0	6 3 5	3 10 0	do. 4 11 0	
13 0 0	8 16 0	9 15 0	7 17 6	1861 8 14 0	
9 1 9	7 15 0	6 8 0	4 15 0		
13 0 10	7 0 0	7 13 7	5 15 0	1871 6 14 0	
17 2 0	6 0 0	0 15 3	4 10 0		
38 1 35	11 15 0	17 8 10	12 10 0		
15 0 30	5 10 0	8 7 8	6 12 0		
13 1 30	6 5 0	7 6 0	5 6 0		
1 0 37	1 8 0	1 10 0	0 18 0	1876 0 10 0	
6 3 38	8 0 0	6 14 11	5 0 0	do. 3 5 0	
8 1 30	8 10 0	3 9 0	1 17 6	do. 2 2 0	
4 2 0	3 8 0	4 10 0	2 15 0		
7 3 16	5 5 0	8 0 0	6 10 0		
33 0 10	14 15 0	18 16 1	11 13 6	1873 14 12 0	
4 1 20	5 5 0	6 0 0	3 7 6		
11 3 10	6 18 0	6 19 0	6 2 6		
18 1 33	5 16 0	6 7 6	4 17 6		
11 0 0	7 5 0	6 11 0	5 15 0	1882 6 18 0	
17 3 10	4 10 0	5 10 0	8 15 0	1871 4 18 0	
3 2 0½	5 0 0	5 7 0	4 5 0		
9 1 31	8 18 0	3 17 5	8 12 6		
80 3 9	27 5 0	37 16 4	20 0 0	1878 22 4 6	
23 1 08	15 10 0	15 16 9	10 5 0	do. 19 10 0	
10 3 28	8 15 0	6 15 0	5 5 0		
16 2 0	9 5 0	10 9 5	7 10 0		

Names of Assistant Commissioners by whom Cases were decided.	No.	Name of Tenant.	Name of Landlord.	Townland.
Assistant Commissioners—				
James O. Wylie (Legal). T. Smith. G. C. Henry. Wm. Davidson. A. Paterson.	[illegible]	Anne Gallogly, ...	Robert John McAlonagh, ...	Cashel, ...
	[illegible]	James Gallogly, ...	do.	do. ...
	[illegible]	Patrick McCoy & another, Reps. of Ewen McCoy.	do.	[illegible] ...
	[illegible]	Patrick Grant, Rep. of Michael Grant.	do.	Cashel, ...
	[illegible]	John McCreash, ...	do.	do. ...
	[illegible]	Mary Mooney, ...	do.	do. ...
	[illegible]	Patrick McCann, Rep. of James McCann.	Miss Margaret Johnston, Rep. of R. K. Johnston.	[illegible] ...
	[illegible]	Patrick McCully, ...	Charlotte Patton, ...	Tullyvallen, ...
	[illegible]	William McKelvey, ...	James Jenkins, ...	do. ...
	[illegible]	Mary McCullagh, ...	do.	do. ...
	[illegible]	William McKelvey, ...	do.	do. ...
	[illegible]	John McCullagh, ...	do.	do. ...
	[illegible]	James McKeown, ...	William Reid and another, ...	[illegible] ...
	[illegible]	Mary [illegible], ...	do.	do. ...
	[illegible]	[illegible] Mullin, ...	do.	do. ...
	[illegible]	Elizabeth Mullin, ...	do.	do. ...
	[illegible]	Peter Hughes, ...	Philip McArdle, ...	[illegible] ...
	[illegible]	Patrick Bennett, ...	do.	do. ...
	[illegible]	Thomas Morris, ...	do.	do. ...
	[illegible]	Andrew Kinnear, ...	Mrs. Rhoda Barton & another,	Tullyvallen. ...
	[illegible]	Elizabeth Clarke, ...	do.	do. ...
	[illegible]	William Harvey, ...	do.	do. ...
	[illegible]	Hugh Milligan, ...	Captain R. [illegible] D. [illegible],	Altnamackan, ...
	[illegible]	James Jenkins, ...	do.	do. ...
	[illegible]	Thomas Gordon, ...	do.	do. ...
	[illegible]	Andrew McKee, ...	do.	do. ...
	[illegible]	James Bell, ...	do.	do. ...
	[illegible]	Alexander Reid, ...	do.	do. ...
	2810	The Reps. of John Carroll, deceased.	do.	do. ...
	2811	John Evans, ...	do.	do. ...
	[illegible]	Adam Meek, ...	do.	do. ...
	[illegible]	William Milligan, ...	do.	do. ...
	2814	Joseph Carroll, ...	do.	do. ...
	[illegible]	Reps. of William McKee, deceased,	do.	do. ...
	2816	Reps. of John Allen, decd.	do.	do. ...

ARMAGH—*continued.*

Extent of Holding. Statute.	Poor Law Valuation.	Former Rent.	Judicial Rent.	Observations.		Value of Tenancy.
A. R. P.	£ s. d.	£ s. d.	£ s. d.		£ s. d.	£ s. d.
30 1 20	9 0 0	8 18 0	7 10 0	Rent changed in 1846 from	7 0 0	
8 0 18	5 6 0	5 6 3	3 15 0			
23 1 38	12 10 0	14 8 11	10 15 0	1874	13 19 0	
11 1 20	7 15 0	6 4 8	6 0 0	1873	7 9 6	
10 2 0	6 16 0	7 14 0	5 12 6			
7 2 16	1 5 0	5 6 3	4 0 0			
13 1 18	8 0 0	6 18 0	4 10 0			
12 1 18	3 15 0	6 12 0	4 0 0	1873	4 11 3	
6 2 13	3 0 0	5 9 4	3 15 0			
0 0 6	3 0 0	5 0 0	3 10 0			
2 0 25	1 0 0	2 0 0	1 10 0			
12 3 6	7 15 0	13 0 0	7 10 0			
16 2 5	9 10 0	8 13 4	7 0 0			
14 3 25	8 15 0	7 18 10	7 5 0			
22 0 30	13 0 0	15 13 8	10 0 0			
8 3 20	6 10 0	6 5 4	8 0 0			
22 0 29	13 10 0	16 14 10	11 5 0			
10 2 4	6 5 0	8 17 0	6 0 0			
10 3 22	7 0 0	6 18 9	6 0 0			
8 1 0	4 5 0	5 3 3	3 18 0	1867	8 9 8	
34 2 20	17 10 0	31 13 5	16 0 0			
31 0 25	13 10 0	19 6 1	10 0 0	do.	6 16 2	
32 3 20	22 0 0	34 3 11	19 0 0	1875	33 18 6	
37 2 25	28 10 0	28 19 0	20 0 0	do.	31 0 0	
23 0 30	10 15 0	16 15 3	15 0 0	1876	18 6 4	
8 0 0	3 5 0	4 13 9	2 18 0	1875	3 7 6	
6 3 0	3 16 0	3 13 6	2 15 0	do.	2 18 1	
3 3 8	2 0 0	1 17 10	2 3 6	1876	2 8 6	
10 2 20	6 10 0	8 8 0	6 0 0			
1 3 28	1 0 0	1 9 2	0 18 0	1876	1 0 0	
2 0 19	1 10 0	1 19 8	1 0 0	do.	1 8 0	
16 1 26	10 0 0	10 17 6	8 10 0			
23 1 26	17 0 0	18 9 2	13 15 0	do.	18 8 0	
15 0 7	9 5 0	9 6 8	7 0 0	1876	7 8 0	
20 2 10	13 0 0	18 14 4	12 10 0	do.	13 13 0	

COUNTY OF

Names of Assistant Commissioners by whom Cases were decided.	No.	Name of Tenant.	Name of Landlord.	Townland.
Assistant Commissioners—				
J. G. Wylie (Legal). T. Mayne. G. G. Kelly. William Davidson. A. Ferguson.	2617	Abraham McMahon,	Capt. R. M'G. R. Stuart,	Altnamackin,
	2618	Andrew Cunn,	James Murphy,	Tullyvallen,
	2619	Frank Irwin,	Mary McBeth and others,	do.
	2620	Andrew Cunn,	Mary Shaw,	do.
	2621	James Paxton,	William Hughes,	do.
	2622	Patrick McElroy,	Robert Hughes,	do.
	2623	Thomas McVey,	Joseph W. M'C. Reed,	do.
	2624	John Lennerty,	Robert Hughes,	do.
	2625	Patrick McElroy,	Mrs. Jane Douglas,	do.
	2626	Thomas Morris,	James Hanratty,	Rathkeeland,
	2627	Samuel Andrews,	A. H. Synge,	Newtownhamilton
	2628	Mary Mulkeeny,	Frances C. Johnston & another, Reps. of James Johnston.	Umerigan,
	2629	Arthur Hughes,	do.	do.
	2630	Michael McArdle,	do.	do.
	2631	John Haggard,	Capt. R. M'G. R. Stuart,	Altnamackin,
	2632	Joseph Carroll,	do.	do.
	2633	Reps. of James Carroll,	do.	do.
	2634	Sarah McConnell,	James Jenkins,	Tullyvallen,
	2635	Andrew Cunn,	John Shaw,	do.
	2636	David Hardy,	Rev. John White Bell,	Ballinlea,
	2637	Stephen Mallon,	John Q. Henry and others,	Lisle,
	2638	James Hewitt & another, Reps. of Daniel Hewitt,	Rev. R. Johnston,	Redhill,
	2639	Elizabeth Garvey, Reps. of John Garvey.	H. F. Thorp and another,	Ballyhenry Up.
	2640	Charles Grant,	Mrs. Margaret Thompson,	Ayallage,
	2641	Mary O'Neill,	Charlotte F. Digges,	Cregganduff,
	2642	James Magill,	do.	do.
	2643	Terence Larkin,	do.	do.
	2644	Michael Henry,	do.	do.
	2645	Peter Hughes,	Joseph Bell,	Clonlum,
	2646	Bernard Hanlon,	do.	do.
	2647	Arthur Toal,	Meredith Henry and another,	Ballintemple,
	2648	Thomas Carr,	do.	do.
	2649	Owen Mackin,	do.	do.
	2650	Patrick Mackin,	do.	do.
	2651	James Rice,	do.	do.

ARMAGH—*continued.*

Extent of Holding. Statute.	Poor Law Valuation.	Former Rent.	Judicial Rent.	Observations.	Value of Tenancy.
A. R. P.	£ s. d.	£ s. d.	£ s. d.	£ s. d.	£ s. d.
11 2 15	5 0 0	8 16 4	6 15 0	Rent changed in 1870 from . . . 7 5 5	
10 0 25	6 5 0	14 0 0	8 10 0		
20 2 23	17 10 0	20 0 0	13 0 0	1873 10 0 0	
13 3 15	9 10 0	14 0 0	11 0 0		
6 1 8	—	4 10 0	4 10 0		
5 3 0	—	7 15 0	1 0 6		
6 3 0	3 12 0	4 0 0	2 17 5		
3 3 18	—	5 0 0	3 0 0	1875 4 10 0	
4 0 10	4 10 0	9 0 0	6 0 0		
19 3 28	15 17 6	17 15 6	15 0 0		
5 1 10	5 18 0	7 0 0	5 0 0	1870 3 6 2	
5 1 30	2 10 0	3 10 0	1 17 6		
9 3 30	3 15 0	5 0 0	3 2 6		
6 0 10	2 10 0	3 0 0	2 1 0		
15 3 30	11 5 0	15 11 2	6 0 0	1876 5 5 10	
5 2 0	12 0 0	16 6 5	7 0 0	do. 8 1 0	
17 0 30	12 10 0	13 7 5	11 0 0	1873 12 0 10	
4 1 23	—	4 11 0	3 0 0		
5 3 30	4 15 0	7 0 0	5 0 0		
3 1 30	4 0 0	3 15 6	3 0 0		
17 1 10	13 15 0	17 1 3	13 0 0		
11 2 0	14 5 0	16 17 8	12 0 0		
37 0 30	29 7 0	17 0 0	33 15 0	1854 15 0 0	
15 3 34	10 5 0	13 18 2	5 10 0	1853 13 16 0	
10 3 0	6 0 0	8 15 10	5 0 0		
5 0 34	5 15 0	6 3 6	2 15 0		
27 1 30	13 0 0	16 10 10	11 0 6		
20 2 0	18 0 0	21 3 5	14 6 0	1870 22 14 8	
6 1 30	6 10 0	8 3 10	4 5 0	1865 7 15 3	
4 1 5	3 5 0	5 3 6	3 0 0		
15 1 0	15 0 0	22 5 0	12 0 0		
6 3 35	4 0 0	8 0 0	3 0 6		
17 0 25	5 5 0	10 10 0	1 0 0		
2 2 0	1 5 0	5 0 0	1 0 0		
10 0 30	6 10 0	10 11 5	6 10 0		

COUNTY OF

Names of Assistant Commissioners by whom Cases were decided.	No.	Name of Tenant.	Name of Landlord.	Townland.
Assistant Commissioners—				
J. O. Wylie (Legal). T. Smith. G. C. Kenny. William Davidson. A. Ferguson.	2652	Daniel Hardy & another, Exors. of Michael Elkins,	Meredith Henry and another,	Ballintemple,
	2653	Henry Cranney,	do.	do.
	2654	Thomas Teal,	do.	do.
	2655	Daniel Rice,	do.	do.
	2656	Edward Rice,	do.	do.
	2657	Bridget Teal,	do.	do.
	2658	Sarah O'Hare,	do.	do.
	2659	Bernard Henry,	do.	do.
	2660	Patk. Carragher (Frank),	James W. McC. Bond,	[illegible] Treanor,
	2661	Bridget McElderry,	do.	do.
	2662	Bridget Carragher,	do.	do.
	2663	Peter Carragher (Frank),	do.	do.
	2664	Neal Carragher,	do.	do.
	2665	Peter Carragher (John),	do.	do.
	2666	Bridget Carragher (Vinny),	do.	do.
	2667	Michael McVerry,	do.	do.
	2668	Michael Carragher,	do.	do.
	2669	do.	do.	do.
	2670	Patrick McVerry,	do.	do.
	2671	John Carragher,	do.	do.
	2672	Samuel Montgomery,	The Commissioners of Education in Ireland.	Belton,
	2673	Hugh Slack,	do.	Brackagh,
	2674	Jane Porter,	do.	Killeen,
	2675	Ellen Vesey,	do.	do.
	2676	Terence McCrink and another,	Earl of Gosford,	Carnagrally,
	2677	Mary Byrne,	do.	[illegible],
	2678	Michael Byrne,	do.	do.
	2679	James McShane,	do.	Ballenk,
	2680	Owen O'Callaghan,	do.	do.
	2681	James McParland,	do.	do.
	2682	Peter Boyle,	do.	Drumsheilly,
	2683	Owen O'Hare,	do.	Corrinagallaghly,
	2684	Thomas Hoskins,	do.	Greyhillan,
	2685	John Hoskins,	do.	Cregans Lower,
	2686	Edward McParland,	John T. Henry and others, Trusts. of Thomas G. Henry.	Leslie,

ARMAGH—*continued.*

Extent of Holding. Statute.	Poor Law Valuation.	Former Rent.	Judicial Rent.	Observations.		Value of Tenancy.
A. R. P.	£ s. d.	£ s. d.	£ s. d.		£ s. d.	£ s. d.
6 1 14	4 0 0	8 1 4	6 13 0			
5 3 7	3 10 0	6 6 0	3 10 0			
7 3 30	7 10 0	11 10 4	9 10 0			
8 0 29	5 15 0	9 5 0	4 17 6			
3 1 0	3 0 0	7 9 1	4 0 0			
4 0 38	4 0 0	6 7 8	3 7 6			
10 3 33	11 5 0	15 3 3	8 16 0			
5 1 5	4 15 0	7 9 1	4 0 0			
8 1 20	4 15 0	5 3 8	4 0 0	Rent changed in 1868 from	4 8 0	
15 1 30	11 15 0	14 1 10	10 5 0	1872	12 18 1	
8 3 20	8 10 0	7 7 10	5 5 0	do.	6 4 6	
14 3 15	12 5 0	14 7 1	10 8 0	do.	15 7 0	
16 1 0	10 15 0	11 0 0	8 17 6			
3 1 20	3 0 0	3 0 6	2 5 0	1840	2 9 0	
6 1 37	3 0 0	6 17 9	3 7 6	1871	4 11 8	
7 3 0	3 5 0	3 17 1	3 8 0	1873	3 [illegible] 0	
5 3 0	4 10 0	6 8 0	5 10 0			
19 0 30	10 0 0	11 7 7	7 12 0			
6 3 30	3 0 0	3 15 3	2 0 0	1871	3 12 0	
8 0 30	4 12 0	4 9 5	0 8 0	do.	3 18 6	
66 1 11	66 5 0	51 3 5	41 10 0			
30 1 1	21 10 0	31 13 5	17 10 0			
9 1 36	10 5 0	8 4 7	7 10 0			
7 2 19	7 10 0	7 13 5	6 18 0			
31 2 10	16 15 0	17 6 6	15 15 0	1873	8 11 6	
29 2 20	15 10 0	17 1 4	11 5 0			
27 0 16	15 10 0	16 18 6	12 10 0	1860	4 1 0	
19 3 20	9 0 0	7 11 6	5 5 0	1867	6 0 8	
30 3 5	25 10 0	10 5 6	28 10 0	1858	14 17 6	
39 3 31	16 5 0	10 0 2	18 0 0	1866	10 10 0	
11 5 20	18 5 0	5 17 6	3 5 0			
10 1 5	8 0 0	7 15 9	6 0 0	1863	8 11 11	
81 2 13	27 0 0	23 10 6	16 0 0			
91 2 36	30 5 0	43 15 8	24 15 0			
15 1 16	13 5 0	18 5 0	13 5 0			

Names of Assistant Commissioners by whom Cases were decided.	No.	Name of Tenant.	Name of Landlord.	Townland.
Assistant Commissioners—				
J. O. Wylie (Legal). T. Hayes. G. G. Kenny. William Gaynor. A. Fleming.	2687	Bridget McElroy, ...	Earl of Gosford, ...	Carrowmaiaun,
	2688	Michael McAnulty, Rep. [illegible] McAnulty.	Margaret O'Hagan, ...	[illegible], ...
	2689	Patrick McGeough, ...	do.	do. ...
	2690	Patrick McAnulty, Rep. David McAnulty.	do.	do. ...
	2691	Stephen McCoy, ...	do.	do. ...
	2692	Thomas Conway, ...	do.	do. ...
	2693	John Mullen, ...	do.	do. ...
	2694	James McAnulty, ...	do.	do. ...
	2695	Patrick Clarke, ...	do.	do. ...
	2696	Edward McCoy, ...	do.	do. ...
	2697	John McAleer, ...	do.	do. ...
	2698	Owen Cassidy, ...	do.	do. ...
	2699	Patrick Conroy, ...	do.	do. ...
	2700	Joseph McNamee, ...	do.	do. ...
	2701	Lawrence Murphy, Rep. Owen Murphy.	do.	do. ...
	2702	Anne O'Hanlon, ...	do.	do. ...
	2703	Alice McCoy, ...	do.	do. ...
	2704	Stephen McKeever, ...	do.	do. ...
	2705	Bernard McGinnity, ...	do.	do. ...
	2706	Mary Boyle, Rep. of Terence Boyle.	do.	do. ...
	2707	Margaret, Rep. of Patrick Mullen.	do.	do. ...
	2708	Bridget McCoy, ...	do.	do. ...
	2709	Rose McNamee, ...	do.	do. ...
	2710	Margaret Cassidy, Admx. of Patrick Cassidy.	do.	do. ...
	2711	Rose Hanlon, ...	do.	do. ...
	2712	Catherine McAnulty, Admx. of Philip McAnulty.	do.	do. ...
	2713	James McGeough, ...	do.	do. ...
	2714	Patrick Mullen, ...	do.	do. ...
	2715	Thomas Murphy, ...	do.	do. ...
	2716	Stephen McQuaid, ...	do.	do. ...
	2717	Peter McCoy, ...	do.	do. ...
	2718	Michael McNamee, ...	do.	do. ...
	2719	Nancy McAleer, ...	do.	do. ...
	2720	Ellen McAnulty, Rep. of Patk. Henry McAnulty.	do.	do. ...
	2721	John McAnulty, Rep. of Mathew McAnulty.	do.	do. ...

ARMAGH—*continued.*

Extent of Holding Statute.	Poor Law Valuation.	Former Rent.	Judicial Rent.	Observations.		Value of Tenancy.
A. R. P.	£ s. d.	£ s. d.	£ s. d.		£ s. d.	£ s. d.
14 3 13	7 10 0	8 0 0	7 0 0			
15 0 28	9 15 0	10 0 0	7 7 6			
6 1 30	4 0 0	4 10 2	3 13 6			
6 3 18	5 5 0	6 10 0	4 0 0			
14 3 30	8 0 0	11 0 0	7 0 0			
6 2 8	4 5 0	5 8 0	3 7 6			
4 0 0	4 15 0	5 7 9	3 18 6			
3 0 35	2 10 0	2 18 6	1 15 0			
3 1 8	1 0 0	2 10 6	1 8 0	Rent changed in 18[illegible] from	1 0 0	
10 0 20	8 15 0	7 0 0	6 0 0			
3 0 0	2 10 0	3 6 6	2 2 6			
6 2 15	3 15 0	4 3 4	2 18 0			
8 0 30	0 15 0	2 7 0	1 0 0	1863	1 10 0	
2 3 30	1 0 0	2 15 0	1 0 0			
16 5 0	10 5 0	18 0 0	6 5 0			
6 0 8	3 16 0	6 0 0	3 5 0			
6 0 8	4 15 0	4 0 6	3 12 6			
9 2 15	8 0 0	8 11 0	6 0 0	1860	6 18 0	
9 2 8	5 15 0	8 10 0	5 0 0	1856	5 0 0	
5 2 10	4 15 0	6 0 0	3 5 0			
13 3 18	5 5 0	18 0 0	6 10 0			
6 1 10	5 0 0	6 15 0	3 15 0			
5 3 35	6 10 0	7 15 6	5 0 0			
6 1 20	6 0 0	5 13 4	4 0 0			
6 0 17	—	4 5 0	8 8 0			
30 1 30	16 0 0	15 7 6	13 6 8			
13 2 3	10 5 0	11 10 0	7 18 8	1856	9 18 0	
6 3 0	3 10 0	3 10 0	2 15 0			
6 0 5	4 15 0	5 17 6	3 18 0	1855	4 3 4	
5 0 25	5 15 0	4 6 0	2 18 0			
8 0 25	8 10 0	3 18 0	2 10 0	do.	3 5 0	
6 1 5	8 0 0	6 6 0	3 10 0			
15 0 35	7 18 0	9 18 7	6 3 6	do.	8 12 7	
7 1 5	3 15 0	4 16 0	3 13 6			
3 8 0	3 10 0	5 0 0	3 8 0			

Names of Assistant Commissioners by whom Cases were decided.	No.	Name of Tenant.	Name of Landlord.
Armagh, Crossmaglen—			
James G. Wylie (Legal). Z. Smith. G. G. Kenny. Wm. Davidson. A. Ferguson.	2722	Anne McKeown, ...	Margaret O'Hagan,
	2723	Mary Daly, ...	do. ...
	2724	Do., ...	do. ...
	2725	Catherine McGuigan, ...	do. ...
	2726	Thomas McAlister, ...	do. ...
	2727	Patrick Duncan, ...	do. ...
	2728	Mathew Mallaney, ...	do. ...
	2729	Stephen McIlear, ...	do. ...
	2730	Margt. McDonagh, Rep. of Peter McDonagh.	do. ...
	2731	Thomas McDonagh, ...	do. ...
	2732	Bridget McAnulty, ...	do. ...
	2733	Mary McAliney, ...	do. ...
	2734	Michael Murphy, ...	Maxwell G. Close,
	2735	James Mooney, ...	do. ...
	2736	Mary McFarland, ...	Mark Seton Synnott,
	2737	Michael Lee, ...	do. ...
	2738	John Hoyes, ...	do. ...
	2739	Catherine Rice, ...	Thomas Wilson, ...
	2740	Henry McAbe, ...	do. ...
	2741	Edward Mullen, ...	do. ...
	2742	Michael Larkin, ...	Thomas Irwin, ...
	2743	Michael Humphrey, ...	Mrs. Thompson, ...
	2744	Anne Colgan, ...	do. ...
	2745	Sarah McAteer, Rep. of Thomas McAteer,	do. ...
	2746	James S. Brannigan, ...	W. R. Bristow, ...
	2747	Bridget McNelly, ...	Kendrick Jones, ...
	2748	Mary M. Rice, ...	do. ...
	2749	Thomas McFarland, ...	do. ...
	2750	John Magenty, ...	do. ...
	2751	Neal O'Hare, ...	do. ...
	2752	Charles Digney, ...	do. ...
	2753	Catherine Mulholland,	do. ...

ARMAGH—*continued.*

Extent of Holding. Statute.	Poor Law Valuation.	Former Rent.	Judicial Rent.	Observations.		Value of Tenancy.
A. R. P.	£ s. d.	£ s. d.	£ s. d.		£ s. d.	£ s. d.
7 1 28	8 0 0	6 8 8	1 0 0			
6 2 28	4 10 0	5 0 0	3 10 0			
6 1 0	—	2 18 2	1 13 6			
4 3 5	8 0 0	8 5 5	4 0 0	Rent changed in 1844 from . .	6 18 0	
6 1 15	3 10 0	4 5 1	2 16 0			
6 1 15	4 10 0	3 0 0	5 17 6			
8 1 8	5 5 0	6 19 9	3 10 0			
5 0 35	3 15 0	4 18 8	7 0 0			
5 8 10	4 18 0	4 12 0	5 8 0			
9 3 10	3 5 0	3 0 0	1 16 0			
3 0 10	3 10 0	3 16 0	1 12 0	1856	3 10 6	
8 3 30	1 0 0	3 0 0	1 0 0			
11 0 17	11 15 0	15 8 3	9 10 0			
15 3 24	20 5 0	16 8 0	13 10 0	1873	14 17 3	
8 0 8	5 0 0	1 12 6	1 12 6			
19 0 22	17 10 0	14 3 0	11 5 0			
12 3 30	7 15 0	8 0 0	6 0 0			
11 1 8	7 0 0	10 8 0	7 18 0	1853	6 0 0	
19 0 31	6 5 0	9 8 0	5 0 0	1848	7 0 0	
9 3 6	5 8 0	6 12 0	1 0 0	1863	4 5 0	
3 3 14	4 8 0	8 7 6	3 10 0	By consent.		
6 3 16	6 0 0	7 5 8	3 15 0	do.		
3 3 12	7 5 0	8 16 10	7 0 0	do.		
6 0 8	3 0 0	4 8 3	3 8 0	do.		
15 3 28	16 0 0	14 12 0	11 0 0	do.		
8 1 10	3 5 0	3 13 0	2 16 8	do.		
9 3 30	6 0 0	6 0 0	5 0 0	do.		
6 3 8	7 0 0	9 7 6	7 6 0	do.		
1 2 1	—	1 15 0	1 7 6	do.		
6 8 23	4 16 0	9 1 3	4 13 6	do.		
3 8 0	1 18 0	3 3 8	1 15 0	do.		
8 1 6	9 13 0	13 3 9	9 16 6	do.		
3,493 1 3	1,801 13 6	1,847 18 6	1,328 14 8			

COUNTY OF

Names of Assistant Commissioners by whom Cases were decided.	No.	Name of Tenant.	Name of Landlord.	Townland.
Assistant Commissioners—				
L. Doyle (Legal). J. Horgan. J. J. Gerety. J. T. Hayes. G. H. Mitchell.	615	James Brennan,	William Black,	Tunagh,
	616	Thomas Brady,	do.	do.
	617	John Kelly,	do.	do.
	618	James McLaughlin,	William Parke,	Bran,
	619	William O'Donnell,	do.	do.
	620	John Dunne,	Matthew Caffrey,	Drumarow,
	621	Thomas Morahan,	Ferguson Cunningham,	Aghavoran,
	622	Hugh & Anne McEnroe,	do.	do.
	623	Charles Reilly,	do.	do.
	624	Michael Rogers,	do.	do.
	625	Bryan Flanagan,	do.	do.
	626	Martin Mahon,	William Hogg,	Killygreagh,
	627	Matthew Ferguson,	Stewart Hogg,	do.
	628	Patrick Ferguson,	do.	do.
	629	Thomas Galligan,	Mrs. Anne Brady,	Drumcassidy,
	630	Peter McElvoy,	Miss Rose A. Brady,	do.
	631	Michael Donohoe,	Lord Farnham,	Cappagh,
	632	Hugh Reilly,	do.	Clontarra,
	633	Patrick Dolan,	do.	do.
	634	John Fitzpatrick,	do.	do.
	635	Philip Fitzpatrick,	do.	do.
	636	Rose Clarke,	Matthew Smith,	Mullaw,
	637	Bernard Smith,	do.	do.
	638	Mary Smith, Admix. of Owen Smith,	do.	do.
	639	James Smith,	do.	do.
	640	Rose Smith,	do.	do.
	641	Michael Clarke,	do.	do.
	642	Michael Treacy,	do.	Killygreagh,
	643	Bernard Smith,	do.	do.
	644	Patrick McCabe,	do.	do.
	645	James Brady,	do.	do.
	646	James Smith,	do.	do.
	647	Bernard Smith,	do.	do.
	648	Laurence Walker,	do.	Drumagh,
	649	Terence Gannon,	W. B. Cuney,	Drumerill,

CAVAN.

Extent of Holding (Statute).	Poor Law Valuation.	Former Rent.	Judicial Rent.	Observations.	Value of Buildings.
A. R. P.	£ s. d.	£ s. d.	£ s. d.	£ s. d.	£ s. d.
15 0 1	18 5 0	13 0 0	9 15 0		
16 0 34	11 10 0	15 0 0	11 5 0	Rent changed in 1856 from 13 10 0	
27 0 19	31 0 0	32 0 0	18 17 4	1871 34 0 0	
33 2 0	31 0 0	33 0 0	33 0 0	1880 34 0 0	
13 2 25	14 10 0	35 0 0	21 3 6		
0 3 0	0 10 0	5 0 0	3 7 5	By consent.	
36 3 9	23 18 0	33 0 0	30 0 0	do.	
33 1 23	39 0 0	37 15 0	33 0 0	do.	
34 1 6	18 0 0	18 0 0	18 0 0	do.	
34 1 19	23 10 0	38 0 0	30 0 0	do.	
30 0 11	19 15 0	31 0 0	19 0 0	do.	
5 3 0	4 5 0	6 5 5	4 15 0	do.	
17 0 34	7 10 0	9 15 0	7 10 0	do.	
19 0 24	7 10 0	9 13 0	7 10 0	do.	
9 2 3	6 10 0	7 10 0	6 6 0	do.	
0 3 10	1 10 0	3 0 0	3 0 0		
30 1 35	30 10 0	38 3 6	18 10 0		
33 3 33	30 7 0	16 15 0	10 10 0		
16 3 12	6 10 0	11 11 8	8 7 0	do.	
10 0 29	6 1 0	7 14 0	6 16 0	do.	
29 0 3	13 3 0	15 9 4	12 0 0	do.	
8 0 15	6 16 0	5 18 0	5 0 0		
13 3 33	10 5 0	8 18 0	8 0 0		
18 1 30	8 16 0	13 11 8	9 10 0		
3 3 13	3 0 0	3 3 0	1 15 0		
24 3 34	18 15 0	19 16 6	14 0 0		
8 0 15	4 5 0	5 0 0	3 15 0		
10 2 4	7 0 0	7 13 3	6 10 0		
18 1 16	6 10 0	8 13 0	7 10 0	Rent changed in 1850 from 5 0 0	
8 0 15	5 18 0	5 13 8	4 12 6		
6 0 16	3 15 0	5 11 7½	4 5 0		
37 1 3	8 16 0	13 6 8	10 11 8	do. 5 13 4	
16 3 31	7 10 0	10 1 0	8 12 6	do. 8 1 0	
4 0 8	2 0 0	9 10 0	3 0 0		
33 1 17	17 5 0	15 15 0	14 0 0		

COUNTY OF

Names of Assistant Commissioners by whom Cases were decided.	No.	Name of Tenant.	Name of Landlord.	Townland.
Assistant Commissioners—				
L. Doyle (Legal). J. Howley. J. J. Gorey. J. T. Davys. G. H. Mitchell.	850	Owen Heraghty, —	W. R. Cherry, — —	Drumcon, —
	851	Thomas Reilly, —	do. — —	do. —
	852	Thomas Parker, —	do. — —	do. —
	853	Thomas Gormley, ...	do. — —	Drumrush, —
	854	John Reilly, ...	do. — —	do. —
	855	James Hatton, —	Mr. Walker, — —	Tully, —
	856	Lawrence Masterson, —	George Clarke, — —	Clough, —
	857	John Phair, ... —	do. — —	do. —
	858	James Brennan, —	do. — —	Clough Glebe, —
	859	John Ellis, ... —	do. — —	do. —
	860	Walter Tully, —	do. — —	do. —
	861	Richard Weir, —	do. — —	do. —
	862	Patrick Minagh, —	do. — —	do. —
	863	Peter McDonald, —	Incumbered Townlands v. Hamilton, In Chancery Division of High Court of Justice in Ireland.	Drumlin, —
	864	Hugh McDonald, —	do. — —	do. —
	865	Charles Clarke, —	do. — —	do. —
	866	James McMahon, —	do. — —	do. —
	867	John Leavy, —	do. — —	do. —
	868	Patrick Brady, —	Martin Cochrane, —	Killycannon and another.
	869	John Daniel, ... —	do. — —	do. —
	870	Patt Gaffney, —	Robert F. Mullins, —	Middletown, —
	871	John Gibbons, —	do. — —	do. —
	872	Edward Brady, —	do. — —	do. —
	873	Patt Campbell, —	do. — —	do. —
	874	Patrick Reilly, —	do. — —	do. —
	875	Anne Brady, ... —	Michael Leary, — —	Killyfana, —
	876	Patrick Smyth, —	Trustees Tatlow, —	Drumsnagh, —
	877	Thomas Smith, —	Lewis Dunlevy, — —	Tulaghan, —
	878	Thomas Dolan, —	do. — —	do. —
	879	Charles Brewster, —	James McCann, — —	Bane Glebe Kilsherdany.
	880	Mary Reilly, —	Col. H. W. Bromford & others, Reps. of John Bromford.	Cornacleigh —
	881	Ellen Smyth, —	do. — —	do. —
	882	Charles Bird, —	do. — —	do. —
	883	Margaret Gorman, —	do. — —	do. —

CAVAN—*continued.*

Extent of Holding. Statute.	Poor Law Valuation.	Former Rent.	Judicial Rent.	Observations.		Value of Tenancy.
A. R. P.	£ s. d.	£ s. d.	£ s. d.		£ s. d.	£ s. d.
30 2 22	14 10 0	13 10 4	12 10 4			
17 1 8	13 15 0	12 14 10	11 5 4			
23 2 30	17 15 0	18 5 4	14 2 6			
10 1 37	8 10 0	7 14 11	7 0 0	Rent changed in 1879 from . . .	5 10 0	
3 0 14	3 0 0	3 14 2	3 3 6			
16 1 35	13 0 0	17 1 4	14 15 0			
25 3 5	30 0 0	31 18 2	25 2 6			
13 1 33	9 0 0	18 16 0	13 0 0			
10 [illegible] 36	7 5 0	9 16 5	8 0 0	1850	8 7 2	
18 1 29	12 3 0	17 1 0	14 0 0			
24 3 22	17 10 0	21 10 0	16 15 0			
4 3 16	5 10 0	6 2 5	5 0 0			
16 0 5	12 5 0	15 18 0	13 10 0			
1 2 3	0 10 0	2 10 0	1 7 6			
7 3 25	1 18 0	10 0 0	6 10 0			
2 1 18	1 0 0	3 0 0	1 17 6			
20 1 21	15 10 0	23 0 0	15 18 0			
1 0 34	—	2 0 0	1 0 0			
10 2 18	3 15 0	6 0 0	4 5 0			
20 0 34	14 0 0	17 0 0	18 10 0			
6 0 16	5 10 0	7 0 0	6 0 0			
15 3 5	10 10 0	12 0 0	10 0 0			
20 1 34	17 10 0	18 12 2	16 0 0	1877	1 10 0	
6 1 31	1 5 0	3 0 0	2 0 0			
6 1 6	4 0 0	4 13 0	3 0 0			
34 0 14	13 18 0	14 0 0	13 0 0	1866	12 5 0	
8 0 27½	7 5 0	9 4 0	6 15 0			
22 2 38	19 10 0	20 0 0	22 10 0			
18 2 21	10 5 0	14 16 0	20 10 0	1858	10 12 2	
37 0 34	37 0 0	43 15 7	30 5 0			
19 1 34	9 0 0	10 5 0	8 7 4			
18 2 18	8 5 0	11 10 0	9 12 6			
18 0 37	14 18 0	18 0 0	14 15 0	do.	15 12 6	
11 0 27	7 0 0	8 0 0	7 5 0			

COUNTY OF

Names of Assistant Commissioners by whom Cases were decided.	No.	Name of Tenant.	Name of Landlord.	Townland.
Assistant Commissioners—				
J. Dwyer (Legal). J. Heron. J. J. Gunn. J. T. Davis. G. H. Mitchell.	884	Patrick Campbell, ...	Col. H. W. Beresford & others, Reps. of John Beresford,	Cornaclagh, —
	885	Owen Lynch, —	do.	do. —
	886	Bridget Bird, —	do. — —	do. —
	887	Patrick Duel, —	do. — —	do. —
	888	James Smyth, ...	do. — —	do. —
	889	Mary Gatmore, —	do. — —	do. —
	890	Charles Brady, ...	do.	do. —
	891	Anne Cusack, ...	do. — —	do. —
	892	Edward Cusack, —	do. — ...	do. —
	893	Michael Hughes, Admor. of Charles Hughes & ors.	Lord Annesley, —	Drumnaweigh, —
	894	Michael Hughes, —	do. ... —	do. —
	895	Thomas Clarke, —	do. — —	do. —
	896	William Jennings, —	do. — ...	do. —
	897	John Brady, —	John W. Humphreys, —	Derrygarra, —
	898	Do. — —	do. — —	Aughkeef, —
	899	James Ryan, —	Lord Farnham, —	Corraugrow, —
	900	George Hunt (Ronald) —	Reps. of Lord Michael Sheridan,	Drumcarbin, —
	901	George Hunt (Buck), —	do. — —	do. —
	902	James Weir, —	do. — —	do. —
	903	Jane Kenneday, —	Somerset H. Maxwell, —	Killydoon, —
	904	Arthur McCann, —	do. — —	Lisduff, —
	905	Do. — —	do. — —	Tullyloy, —
	906	John Wilson, ...	James McCreight, ...	Drumkeeldrin, —
	907	Ellen McCaffrey, —	do. — ...	do. —
	908	Patrick Maguire, —	do.	do. —
	909	James Lee, —	do.	do. —
	910	Hugh McCaffrey, —	do. — ...	do. —
	911	John Brady, —	John and Frederick Gillespie,	Dunaun, —
	912	Patrick Kennedy, ...	do. ... —	do. —
	913	Patrick Walker, Admor. of William Walker.	do.	do. —
	914	Patrick Dunden, —	do.	do. —
	915	Patrick Galligan, senior,	Rev. Richard Booth, —	Cordeff, —
	916	Mathew Galligan, —	do. ... —	do. —
	917	Patrick Galligan, junior,	do.	do. —
	918	Mathew Galligan, —	do. ... —	do. —

CAVAN—*continued.*

Extent of Holding. Statute.	Poor Law Valuation.	Former Rent.	Judicial Rent.	Observations.		Value of Tenant's
A. R. P.	£ s. d.	£ s. d.	£ s. d.		£ s. d.	£ s. d.
31 2 20	16 0 0	17 0 0	13 0 0	Rent changed in 1858 from . . .	16 4 0	
6 3 1	6 0 0	6 10 6	5 3 8			
9 2 8	6 15 0	8 0 8	6 12 8	do.	7 10 1	
16 1 23	11 0 0	14 0 0	13 17 0			
6 0 25	4 13 0	5 4 0	4 9 6	do.	5 9 0	
31 1 26	17 0 0	20 0 0	20 2 6	do.	18 3 2	
20 1 8	12 15 0	16 0 6	14 17 6			
9 0 1½	6 10 0	8 8 0	6 15 6			
31 3 37	16 5 0	21 0 0	18 13 0			
20 0 2	12 0 0	13 16 3	11 3 6			
23 0 3	13 10 0	16 5 6	11 13 6	1854	10 14 0	
18 1 0	8 5 0	10 2 10	6 18 6			
31 1 2	17 10 0	20 16 6	15 18 0			
38 0 0	20 18 0	37 0 0	23 12 6	1850	12 18 0	
47 1 20	33 15 0	44 8 6	40 10 0			
18 0 0	—	12 0 0	4 10 0			
13 3 20	8 10 0	9 17 6	7 19 6			
9 0 7	6 5 0	7 6 3	8 0 0			
6 1 10	4 15 0	6 9 3	5 0 0			
26 0 20	16 5 0	13 8 6	12 0 0	1863	12 0 0	
65 2 3	18 0 6	28 19 2	24 16 0			
63 0 16	33 0 0	34 12 2	33 17 6			
9 0 31	7 18 6	8 6 9	6 13 6			
12 0 24	6 18 0	10 16 7	8 0 0			
19 1 31	13 5 0	18 18 10	15 10 0			
12 2 0	7 18 0	11 8 0	9 12 6			
16 3 12	12 0 0	14 8 1	11 5 6			
12 0 14	6 0 0	10 5 0	7 17 6			
6 3 2	6 0 0	5 0 0	4 13 6			
22 1 27	9 8 0	19 16 10	16 8 6	1864	14 5 0	
20 0 19	9 10 0	15 8 5	12 6 0			
17 2 1	12 5 0	12 8 8	10 0 0			
17 0 8	16 5 0	12 12 6	10 0 0			
12 3 8	9 0 0	8 1 10	8 0 0			
9 2 9½	8 19 0	8 16 6	6 12 6			

COUNTY OF

Names of Assistant Commissioners by whom Case was adjudicated.	No.	Name of Tenant.	Name of Landlord.	Townland.
Assistant Commissioners—				
L. Irvine (Legal). J. Howlin. J. J. Hanly. J. T. Davys. G. H. Mitchell.	919	Daniel Smith, ...	Rev. Richard Booth, ...	Corlurgan, ...
	920	Patrick and Hugh Kelly,	William Collins, ...	Bakersely, ...
	921	Patrick Fleming, ...	do.	do. ...
	922	Philip Gaffney, ...	James H. Webster, ...	Drumlelly, ...
	923	John Finnegan, ...	R. B. De Burgh, ...	Drumrora, ...
	924	Michael Sheridan, ...	do.	do. ...
	925	Widow and Mary Reilly,	do.	do. ...
	926	Peter Young, ...	do.	do. ...
	927	John Sheridan, ...	do.	do. ...
	928	Charles McCormick, ...	do.	do. ...
	929	Edward Reilly, ...	do.	do. ...
	930	Peter Hylton, ...	do.	do. ...
	931	Patrick Reilly, ...	Peter Carr, ...	Legaghory, ...
	932	James Cusack, ...	do.	do. ...
	933	Thomas Clarke, ...	William Hague and another, Trustees of James McFadden,	Mullyaaley, ...
	934	John McCabe, ...	do.	do. ...
	935	Daniel Fitzpatrick, ...	do.	Corlismore, ...
	936	John Hughes, ...	do.	Mullyaaley, ...
	937	John McKiernan, ...	do.	Mullyaaley and others.
	938	Margaret Neill, ...	do.	Corlismore, ...
	939	Thomas Brady, ...	Mr. Wallace, ...	Tully, ...
	940	Thomas Reilly, ...	John Fay, ...	Ballytrust, ...
	941	Judith Galligan, ...	do.	Cam, ...
	942	Marianne Lee, ...	Charles B. Morley, ...	Drumshillagh, ...
	943	Patrick McCabe, ...	Mathew W. O'Connor, ...	Lanagh, ...
	944	Michael Reilly, ...	Trustees of C. B. Lloyd, ...	Drumcrowland, ...
	945	Daniel Wheelan, ...	Philip Lowry, ...	Tonymoile, ...
	946	Andrew McCann, ...	William and M. Adams, ...	Drumalee, ...
	947	Philip Smith, ...	Alexander Nesbitt, ...	Artonagh, ...
	948	James Anderson, ...	Rev. Thomas Moore, ...	Killeter, ...
	949	Patrick Sheridan, ...	Benjamin S. Adams, ...	Lisdrugher, ...
	950	Owen Fay, ...	Miss Bridget Fitzsimons, ...	Tullyunder, ...
	951	Pat Brennan, ...	William Black, ...	Kevagh, ...
	952	Patrick Walsh, ...	Cecil W. Lowry, ...	Mullagher, ...
	953	Matthew Sheridan, ...	S. B. De Burgh, ...	Drumcrow, ...

CAVAN—*continued.*

Extent of Holding. Statute.	Poor Law Valuation.	Former Rent.	Judicial Rent.	Observations.		Value of Tenancy.
A. R. P.	£ s. d.	£ s. d.	£ s. d.		£ s. d.	£ s. d.
12 3 0	9 16 0	12 9 0	9 0 0			
40 0 35	33 0 0	26 17 0	20 0 0	Rent changed in 1834 from . .	24 17 0	
22 3 24	18 0 0	18 17 1	18 0 0			
0 2 7	5 0 0	0 5 11½	5 2 0	1865	6 0 0	
36 3 20	21 18 0	23 2 0	20 15 0	1857	18 3 4	
11 0 9	9 5 0	16 1 4	8 17 0	1878	9 0 0	
20 0 15	15 5 0	16 18 4	16 7 6			
5 1 26	7 12 0	7 18 10	7 0 0	1863	7 0 0	
36 2 3	31 6 0	27 15 5	31 0 0	1878	24 16 5	
11 0 7	10 0 0	18 3 1	13 3 4	1857	10 0 0	
6 3 13	5 5 0	6 6 6	6 1 10			
10 2 28	6 0 0	9 11 2	6 0 0	do.	7 3 0	
11 2 1	3 13 0	7 8 6	6 0 0	1863	8 18 8	
16 3 3	5 12 0	8 0 0	5 2 6			
25 0 11	11 10 0	16 16 6	13 0 0			
6 1 8	6 5 0	8 5 6	6 7 6			
25 3 37	22 8 0	28 3 6	25 0 0			
12 0 25	5 15 0	7 12 6	5 12 6			
16 3 9	11 8 0	14 18 6	11 10 0			
7 1 28	6 16 0	8 13 4	5 0 0			
18 3 17	19 6 0	16 14 0	15 17 6			
24 3 24	19 16 0	18 19 0	14 0 0			
28 2 24	18 10 0	24 3 6	19 10 0			
15 0 0	9 6 0	10 0 0	7 15 0	1876	11 0 0	
16 3 10	27 10 0	28 6 4	18 0 0			
20 1 30	11 0 0	18 0 0	13 1 0	1877	18 6 0	120 0 0
87 2 24	71 15 0	100 0 0	66 1 0			
22 0 8	18 5 0	16 17 6	13 5 0			
127 2 29	73 10 0	100 0 0	67 0 0	1861	45 0 0	
10 2 6	7 0 0	8 0 0	6 3 0			
9 1 8	6 10 0	8 11 3	4 0 0			
15 0 20	8 10 0	16 0 0	13 0 0	1820	17 10 0	
16 0 34	10 10 0	14 0 0	11 11 0			
34 2 11	25 10 0	29 10 0	25 7 6			
8 3 35	5 4 0	8 17 0	6 10 0	1860	6 0 0	

COUNTY OF

Names of Assistant Commissioners by whom Cases were decided.	No.	Name of Tenant.	Name of Landlord.	Townland.
Assistant Commissioners—	954	Margt. Cumiskey, Admx. of John Cumiskey.	Robert Foster Mollan,	Middletown,
L. Doyle (Legal).	955	Bernard Flood,	Lord Southwell,	Clones,
J. Howley	956	Peter Smith,	Matthew Smith,	Killyvagan,
J. J. Gubey.	957	Thomas Kemp,	Cornwall Maddan & another,	Drumsnade,
J. T. Davis.	958	James McMahon,	James McCreight,	Drumshiddan,
G. H. Mitchell.	959	Farrell Smith,	Lord Farnham,	Drumbuck,
	960	Mary Anne Williams,	Lord Cremorne,	Braddock,
	961	Thomas Henderson,	William Parks,	Rann,
	962	Hampden Fitzpatrick,	Earl Annesley,	Derryvalsel,
	963	Michael Lawler,	Andrew C. Montgomery,	Cornacrum,
	964	Mary Smith,	do.	Fortown,
	965	Dan Cunagh,	Col. M. W. Beresford & others, Reps. of John Beresford, decd.	Crumcrilagh,
	966	Peter Haddan,	do.	do.
	967	Thomas Thornton,	do.	do.
	968	Owen Lee,	George Stewart Smith,	Drummurry,
	969	Bernard Duggan,	do.	do.
	970	Hugh McElhenny,	Reps. of George Adams,	Mullaghard,
	971	Mary Martin,	do.	do.
	972	James Greenan,	do.	do.
	973	Patt Costello,	do.	do.
	974	Denis Macmahon,	do.	do.
	975	James Murphy,	do.	do.
	976	Thomas Connolly,	Isabella Smith and others, Exors. of Edward Smith, decd.	Corclam,
	977	Samuel Dale,	do.	Drum,
	978	David Dale,	do.	Magheraveely,
	979	John Connolly,	do.	Corclam,
	980	William Elliot,	do.	do.
	981	William McVeagh,	do.	Quintow,
	982	Patrick Maclean,	do.	Clonghelcale,
	983	Andrew Mackey,	do.	Quintow,
	984	Daniel Mackey,	do.	do.
	985	John Mackey, senior,	do.	do.
	986	Daniel Fay,	do.	Lisboe,
	987	Mary Gillan, Rep. of Philip Gillan,	Reps. of George Adams,	Mullaghard,
	988	Mary Reilly,	Col. M. W. Beresford & others, Reps. of John Beresford, decd.	Crumcrilagh,
				Total,

CAVAN—*continued.*

Extent of Holding. Statute.			Poor Law Valuation.			Former Rent.			Judicial Rent.			Observations.	Value of Tenancy.
A.	R.	P.	£	s.	d.	£	s.	d.	£	s.	d.	£ s. d.	£ s. d.
6	1	33	5	10	0	6	10	0	5	5	6		
16	2	11	11	10	0	15	15	0	11	2	6		
17	0	31	10	0	0	12	15	8	10	7	6		
24	1	14	8	0	0	16	2	0	13	7	6		
8	2	9	8	10	0	7	17	6	5	12	6		
6	1	32	3	10	0	4	2	6	4	10	0	Rent changed in 1870 from . . . 3 18 0	
18	3	3	11	10	0	13	1	11	10	2	6		
18	2	19	17	16	0	23	0	0	23	0	0	1851 26 0 0	
31	3	17	27	15	0	27	13	0	22	16	0		
15	1	5	13	10	0	18	15	0	11	15	6		
28	3	6	20	16	0	21	11	0	18	10	0		
20	1	1	12	10	0	17	7	0	16	0	0	1854 17 6 7	
18	0	0	14	15	0	18	5	6	15	0	0		
10	2	23	5	5	0	7	15	0	7	0	0		
18	1	9	10	10	0	11	10	6	8	17	6	1856 6 15 0	80 0 0
27	0	24	17	18	0	20	0	0	18	0	0	do. 15 10 0	140 0 0
24	2	11	13	6	0	16	18	0	13	13	6		
16	1	30	11	10	0	14	16	5	11	2	0		
27	0	20	7	18	0	13	3	8	9	8	0		
9	1	31	5	10	0	6	10	0	5	0	0		
17	1	17	10	0	0	13	16	10	10	12	6		
13	3	33	7	15	0	0	7	0	7	3	0		
14	2	14	9	10	0	14	1	8	11	8	6	1879 18 13 0	
20	2	17	12	0	0	17	1	8	13	18	6		
8	2	20	7	15	0	8	3	2	6	10	0		
11	3	22	7	17	0	10	13	4	8	15	0		
24	0	8	20	0	0	23	13	4	18	0	0		
8	3	18	6	10	0	8	0	0	5	17	6	1878 6 18 0	
11	2	6	5	10	0	7	18	4	5	15	0		
15	0	18	5	9	0	10	3	0	8	10	0		
9	0	17	5	10	0	7	13	4	5	15	0		
10	2	26	5	6	0	7	17	0	6	3	0		
30	3	18	35	0	0	47	1	3	33	0	0	1860 30 0 0	
5	1	9	3	5	0	4	13	3	3	8	0		
19	1	34	9	0	0	10	8	8	8	7	4		
3,515	0	26½	2,070	13	0	2,810	14	0	2,094	18	0		

Names of Assistant Commissioners by whom Cases were decided.	No.	Name of Tenant.	Name of Landlord.
Assistant Commissioners—			
Ulick Bourke (Legal). R. Reynolds. William Gray. Thomas Hynes. R. R. Graves.	2142	Ross Byrne, ...	John and James Musgrave,
	2143	Thomas Leonard, ...	do. ...
	2144	Thomas Fawcett, ...	do. ...
	2145	Mary McDevitt, ...	do. ...
	2146	Neil O'Donnell, ...	do. ...
	2147	Anne Fawcett, ...	do. ...
	2148	John Byrne, ...	do. ...
	2149	Patrick Doherty, ...	do. ...
	2150	Owen Byrne (Pat), ...	do. ...
	2151	Patrick Cunningham, ...	do. ...
	2152	Patrick Sweeney, ...	do. ...
	2153	Daniel Doherty, ...	do. ...
	2154	Elizabeth Doherty, ...	do. ...
	2155	Cicely Boyle, ...	do. ...
	2156	Hugh Boyle, Admor. of Patrick Boyle.	do. ...
	2157	Owen Byrne (Steve), ...	do. ...
	2158	Doherty Doherty, Admor. of Catherine Doherty.	do. ...
	2159	John Cunningham, ...	do. ...
	2160	Mary Cunningham, ...	do. ...
	2161	John Byrne, ...	do. ...
	2162	Bridget Gallagher, ...	do. ...
	2163	Peggy Ward, ...	do. ...
	2164	Rose McElhinney, Rep. of Robert McElhinney.	do. ...
	2165	Susan Byrne, ...	do. ...
	2166	Frank Cunningham, ...	do. ...
	2167	Widow Dan Murray,	do. ...
	2168	Widow Susan Murray,	do. ...
	2169	Hugh Mooney, ...	do. ...
	2170	Frank Haughey, ...	do. ...
	2171	Biddy Cunningham, ...	do. ...
	2172	Edward Gannon, ...	do. ...
	2173	Anne Peyton, ...	do. ...
	2174	James Hegarty, ...	do. ...
	2175	James Carr, ...	do. ...
	2176	Catherine Kelly, ...	do. ...

DONEGAL.

Extent of Holding. Statute.	Poor Law Valuation.	Former Rent.	Judicial Rent.	Observations.	Value of Tenancy.
A. R. P.	£ s. d.	£ s. d.	£ s. d.	£ s. d.	£ s. d.
7 2 30	3 17 0	3 12 6	1 15 0		
13 1 30	8 2 0	8 7 6	6 2 6		
13 3 18	6 18 0	7 10 0	5 13 8		
11 3 30	4 15 0	6 0 0	4 17 6		
13 1 30	5 2 0	6 7 6	5 7 6	Rent changed in 1853 from . . . 4 18 0	
18 2 13	5 3 0	6 7 0	5 0 0	do. 5 18 0	
12 3 0	4 18 0	6 0 0	4 15 0	do. 5 10 7	
4 8 0	2 0 0	2 18 0	1 5 0		
11 3 31	1 10 0	2 4 7	1 17 6	1880 1 10 8	
4 3 34	1 10 0	3 4 7	1 17 6		
6 1 8	2 10 0	3 14 0	2 18 6		
8 1 17	3 0 0	2 18 0	1 5 0	do. 1 17 11	
6 3 0	2 0 0	2 18 0	2 5 6	do. 1 10 11	
7 0 10	3 0 0	3 4 10	2 13 6		
6 3 17	3 0 0	3 18 0	3 7 6		
7 0 28	1 10 0	2 4 7	1 0 0	do. 1 10 0	
6 1 0	3 17 0	6 16 0	5 3 6	do. 1 16 0	
36 3 6	13 10 0	18 19 6	13 19 0		
6 3 25	2 13 0	3 15 0	6 2 6	1853 3 10 0	
19 1 15	3 17 6	8 8 6	6 17 6		
17 3 15	2 16 0	4 0 0	3 10 0	do. 0 15 0	
10 3 27	3 17 0	8 8 6	6 3 6	do. 4 5 9	
16 0 25	4 11 0	6 18 0	5 16 0		
17 3 30	5 15 6	7 0 0	5 11 8		
11 0 0	8 10 0	4 8 6	3 18 0		
13 1 31	2 15 0	8 5 0	6 8 0		
8 0 0	1 15 6	3 13 3	1 0 0		
4 0 0	3 10 0	8 18 3	3 0 0		
67 0 0	8 10 0	8 2 4	5 8 0		
10 1 30	3 0 0	4 8 0	8 17 6		
30 2 10	3 4 0	4 18 0	5 0 0		
10 3 11	3 0 0	3 15 0	1 10 0		
14 3 30	3 0 0	4 13 0	4 0 0	do. 3 4 7½	
24 3 0	4 4 0	5 3 0	4 13 6	do. 4 8 9	
6 1 0	1 12 0	3 0 0	3 0 0	do. 1 13 4	

2180	Unity Morton,	...
2181	Michael McGroarty,	...
2182	Patrick Cunningham,	...
2183	Mary Gallagher,	...
2184	James O'Hara,	...
2185	Cherry Byrne,	...
2186	James Beatty,	...
2187	Bryan Byrne,	...
2188	Michael Gallagher, Admr. of Francis Gallagher.	
2189	Mary Mundy,	...
2190	James Doherty,	...
2191	John Gallagher,	...
2192	Barney O'Donnell,	...
2193	James Byrne,	...
2194	Thomas McGlone,	...
2195	Owen McGroarty,	...
2196	John Byrne, ...	...
2197	John Morrison,	...
2198	George Beatty,	...
2199	Denis Dorrian,	...
2200	Connell McGroarty,	...
2201	Stephen Dunlevy,	...
2202	Anne McFadden,	...
2203	Patrick Boyle,	...
2204	Jas. Cunningham, Admr. of Alice McGroarty.	
2205	Alice Gallagher,	...

DONEGAL—*continued.*

Extent of Holding. Statute.	Poor Law Valuation.	Former Rent.	Judicial Rent.	Observations.		Value of Tenancy.
A. R. P.	£ s. d.	£ s. d.	£ s. d.		£ s. d.	£ s. d.
11 3 15	3 0 0	3 14 0	2 8 0	Mean charge 1 in 18 to form .	3 0 0	
10 3 23	1 16 0	3 5 0	2 5 0	do.	1 13 4	
15 3 3	2 18 0	4 4 0	3 3 0	do.	3 0 8	
8 3 25	3 0 0	3 10 0	2 0 0	do.	3 0 4	
22 0 18	1 10 0	2 10 0	2 10 0	do.	1 19 7	
24 3 13	4 15 0	7 0 0	5 0 0	do.	3 0 10	
28 3 3	4 15 0	8 10 0	6 7 8	do.	4 0 8	
8 3 30	5 0 0	7 0 0	4 10 0			
15 1 18	3 4 0	4 5 0	3 10 0	do.	3 0 1	
3 3 20	3 10 0	5 5 0	3 0 0			
9 1 20	8 10 0	8 3 0	3 15 0			
3 3 10	1 10 0	5 3 0	1 17 6	do.	1 5 0	
4 0 20	3 0 0	5 0 0	2 0 0	do.	3 1 0	
8 3 27	3 10 0	4 15 0	3 17 6	do.	2 11 0	
3 3 13	1 13 0	2 1 3	2 12 6	1860	1 16 0	
7 3 14	2 5 0	4 1 6	3 10 0			
8 0 0	4 5 0	6 8 8	5 0 0			
30 0 27	8 10 0	15 3 0	8 0 0			
8 3 34	4 5 0	6 0 0	4 7 6			
60 0 45	8 0 0	11 17 0	8 10 0			
15 0 31	8 10 0	8 10 0	7 3 6	1855	9 4 6	
16 0 35	6 5 0	9 10 0	6 12 6	1850	9 4 0	
8 0 25	3 3 0	4 16 0	3 10 0	1858	4 13 3	
18 3 34	8 10 0	10 10 0	7 15 0			
9 0 16	3 5 0	4 16 0	4 0 0			
10 0 6	4 10 0	5 17 0	5 0 0	do.	5 13 6	
380 0 0	3 14 0	6 13 0	5 10 0	do.	3 10 9	
9 3 16	4 15 0	8 2 0	4 15 0			
11 1 0	4 15 0	6 3 0	4 18 0	do.	3 19 0	
10 3 27	4 10 0	6 5 0	4 15 0			
6 3 16	4 0 0	5 0 0	3 15 0			
18 3 22	8 19 6	6 7 6	3 5 0			
14 0 3	3 14 0	4 4 0	3 10 0	do.	2 17 11	
23 0 22	8 10 0	6 10 0	5 10 0	do.	8 11 7	
7 1 16	3 0 0	1 13 0	1 11 0			

COUNTY OF

Names of Assistant Commissioners by whom Cases were decided.	No.	Name of Tenant.	Name of Landlord.	Townland.
Assistant Commissioners—				
Ulick Bourke (Legal).	2312	Francis Lough,	H. G. Murray Stewart,	Bunlevy,
E. Spencer.	2313	Neil Kenny,	Miss Prudence Hale,	Bellion,
William Gray.	2314	John Meighan,	do.	do.
Thomas Meek.	2315	Mary Campbell,	do.	Drumberry,
R. E. Gibson.	2316	James Leslie,	do.	do.
	2317	Patrick Waugh,	Elizabeth Walker,	Ballyjagan,
	2318	Patrick Byrne,	do.	do.
	2319	Lanty Hanlon,	John H. Dunsley,	Meenagowan,
	2320	Charles Kelly,	do.	Farangan,
	2321	Pat Sweeny,	do.	Bunny,
	2322	James Gallagher,	do.	Derry,
	2323	Mary Gallagher,	Marquess of Conyngham,	Cunningland,
	2324	Charles McDevitt,	do.	Meenacarragh,
	2325	John Gildea,	do.	Drumnacillagh,
	2326	Bridget McGrath,	do.	Ballyvoodan,
	2327	Rebecca Brennan,	do.	Lackagh,
	2328	William Harkin,	do.	Bunbeg,
	2329	William Gallagher,	do.	Castleguard,
	2330	James Gallagher,	do.	Meenamore,
	2331	John Gallagher,	do.	Meenamore, West,
	2332	Henry Doherty, Rep. of Patrick Doherty, decd.	do.	Addervale,
	2333	John Doherty,	do.	do.
	2334	Hugh Ward,	do.	do.
	2335	Owen Cannon,	do.	Lackagh,
	2336	Francis Sharkey,	do.	Sandfield,
	2337	William Toorish,	do.	Lackagh,
	2338	Edward Early,	do.	Drumnacillagh,
	2339	Manus Brearty	do.	do.
	2340	Charles Brearty,	do.	do.
	2341	Patrick Boyle,	do.	Meenanahin,
	2342	James Ward,	do.	Kelly,
	2343	William McDevitt,	do.	Greffy,
	2344	Bernard McDermott,	do.	Drumnacillagh,
	2345	Catherine Boyle,	do.	Meenamore, West,
	2346	John McGee,	do.	do.

DONEGAL—*continued.*

Extent of Holding. Statute.	Poor Law Valuation.	Former Rent.	Judicial Rent.	Observations.	Value of Tenancy.
A. R. P.	£ s. d.	£ s. d.	£ s. d.		£ s. d.
13 3 38	3 0 0	3 10 0	3 2 8		
70 0 0	3 10 0	5 16 8	4 10 0		
80 0 0	1 0 0	7 0 0	5 7 6		
3 0 0	3 0 0	5 0 0	3 7 6		
1 3 0	1 0 0	3 18 0	3 0 0		
31 3 0	5 13 0	4 13 7	7 6 0		
6 0 8	3 5 0	4 9 5	3 18 0		
50 0 0	84 5 0	61 3 0	30 0 0	By consent.	
18 3 16	3 0 0	3 13 0	2 15 0	Rent changed in 1867 from £1 13 0	
17 1 20	1 10 0	1 18 0	1 10 0	do. 0 6 0	
18 1 18	3 15 0	4 7 4	4 0 0	do. 3 10 0	
189 3 7	63 6 0	44 0 0	30 0 0		
310 1 3	31 0 0	16 0 0	16 0 0		
82 3 20	31 10 0	18 13 0	13 0 0		
48 0 15	8 10 0	9 0 0	6 10 0		
70 1 30	15 0 0	23 0 0	17 0 0	1860 13 15 0	
38 1 30	6 10 0	7 7 6	4 0 0		
77 1 20	87 0 0	38 0 0	27 0 0		
157 1 16	1 15 6	8 10 0	3 10 0		
157 1 16	1 18 0	2 10 0	2 16 0		
65 3 0	1 13 0	2 0 0	3 10 0		
65 3 0	1 18 0	3 0 0	3 10 0		
86 3 35	3 5 0	3 0 0	3 0 0		
18 3 10	5 18 0	4 10 0	6 0 0		
38 1 25	3 15 0	5 0 0	4 0 0	1880 4 0 0	
12 3 0	3 10 0	5 0 0	5 18 0	do. 3 8 8	
10 0 0	1 8 0	3 0 0	1 18 6	1865 1 10 0	
25 0 5	6 0 0	10 0 0	7 10 0		
8 1 5	3 0 0	5 0 0	4 13 6		
76 1 33	4 10 0	8 10 0	6 2 6	1820 4 0 0	
40 1 30	8 18 0	3 13 0	2 18 6		
60 1 16	6 15 0	8 8 0	7 8 0		
64 3 10	6 16 0	14 0 0	10 15 0		
58 2 6	3 0 0	8 10 0	2 10 0	1868 1 15 0	
63 0 35	1 17 0	3 10 0	3 0 0		

2257	John Ward, ...
2258	Simon Gallagher,
2259	Patrick McGrath,
2260	Patrick Quigley,
2261	Edward Gallagher,
2262	John Gibbon,
2263	Sarah McElwey,
2264	Denis McIlmough,
2265	Philip McIlmough,
2266	William Mannix,
2267	Patrick Boyle,
2268	Patrick Gallagher,
2269	John Brown,
2270	Edward McGrath,

DONEGAL—*continued*.

Extent of Holding—Statute.	Poor-Law Valuation.	Former Rent.	Judicial Rent.	Observations.		Value of Tenancy.
A. R. P.	£ s. d.	£ s. d.	£ s. d.		£ s. d.	£ s. d.
20 1 19	3 10 0	5 10 0	5 0 0			
63 3 20	2 0 0	2 10 0	2 10 0			
48 3 10	1 18 0	3 10 0	2 18 0	Rent changed in 1853 from	1 11 0	
65 0 0	8 10 0	11 0 0	6 18 0	1866	0 0 0	
16 0 20	1 18 0	3 0 0	2 10 0			
14 2 15	5 15 0	9 0 0	6 0 0	do.	7 0 0	
18 2 13	4 2 0	6 0 0	4 7 0			
31 0 0	2 18 0	3 0 0	5 0 0			
185 0 38	23 15 0	33 1 6	27 0 0			
71 1 0	1 15 0	3 10 0	2 10 0	1880	1 0 3	
80 1 0	1 18 0	3 10 0	2 10 0	do.	1 8 3	
180 3 0	4 8 0	4 10 0	3 3 6	do.	4 7 6	
41 0 20	6 1 0	6 16 3	5 0 0			
60 3 10	8 0 0	7 18 4	4 10 0			
37 2 0	5 10 0	8 0 0	6 10 0			
62 2 30	10 8 0	10 0 0	11 0 0			
240 0 0	3 5 0	3 13 0	4 0 0			
100 0 0	1 16 0	3 10 0	2 10 0			
45 3 20	1 18 0	3 10 0	2 18 0			
34 0 30	3 0 0	4 0 0	3 18 0			
38 0 20	12 5 0	13 0 0	10 10 0			
284 3 0	42 0 0	50 0 0	42 10 0			
53 3 34	8 15 0	13 13 0	9 8 0			
69 3 17	17 18 0	17 0 0	17 0 0			
87 1 25	4 0 0	5 0 0	4 7 8			
23 2 30	4 18 0	5 0 0	3 18 0			
16 3 20	1 0 0	2 18 6	2 15 0			
41 0 0	6 10 0	7 0 0	5 0 0	1880	6 10 0	
17 2 20	2 10 0	4 7 6	3 5 0	do.	5 17 6	
16 2 0	1 18 0	2 18 0	2 3 4	do.	1 13 0	
158 1 25	18 0 0	16 0 0	13 10 0			
118 3 37	13 8 0	18 0 0	13 0 0	1883	17 8 0	
116 1 30	10 8 0	15 0 0	12 0 0	do.	17 8 0	
17 0 30	4 15 0	7 14 0	5 17 6	1880	6 0 0	
8 3 22	6 0 0	6 10 8	2 10 0	do.	3 3 0	

COUNTY OF

Names of Assistant Commissioners by whom Cases were decided.	No.	Name of Tenant.	Name of Landlord.	Townland.
Assistant Commissioners—				
Ulick Bourke (Legal).	2282	Cundy Pain, ...	Marquis of Conyngham, ...	Tullydouganon, ...
B. Heddle.	2283	Bryan Boyle, ...	do.	do. ...
William Gray.	2284	James Gallagher, ...	do.	do. ...
Thomas Meath.	2285	Edward Gallagher, ...	do.	Mullaghderg, ...
E. B. Curling.	2286	Owen Glenn, ...	do.	Mullaghmulgin,
	2287	Manus Byrne, ...	do.	Letterilly, ...
	2288	Denis Molloy, ...	do.	Stroboy, ...
	2289	Patrick Kennedy, ...	do.	Keeraun, ...
	2290	Manus McHugh, ...	do.	Cornamarkilagh,
	2291	Patrick Boyle, ...	do.	Drumnacartagh, ...
	2292	Patrick McMonagle, ...	do.	Derries, ...
	2293	Teague Boyle, ...	do.	Derries and another,
	2294	Charles McHugh, ...	do.	Dunmoreville, ...
	2295	Peter Gallagher, ...	do.	Meenabolady, ...
	2296	Edward O'Shea, ...	do.	Cloughgart, ...
	2297	James McGroarty, ...	do.	Dobbin, ...
	2298	Patrick Cunningham, ...	do.	Stroboy, ...
	2299	Neal Campbell, ...	do.	Derrylagan, ...
	2300	Owen Doherty, ...	do.	do. ...
	2301	James Boner, ...	do.	Ashbrook, ...
	2302	Shane Molloy, ...	do.	Cornagilla and another,
	2303	Teague Gallagher, ...	do.	Drimnacraig, ...
	2304	Margaret McInerney, ...	do.	Meenacladdy and another,
	2305	William McNelis, ...	do.	do. ...
	2306	John Boyle, ...	do.	Stroboy, ...
	2307	James McGlinchey, ...	Miss Prudence Hale, ...	Drumkerrig, ...
	2308	Michael Cannon, ...	John and James Musgrave, ...	Kill, ...
	2309	Hannah O'Shea, ...	William Wilson, ...	Loughros, ...
	2310	John Quinn, ...	do.	do. ...
	2311	Connell McMonagle, ...	do.	do. ...
	2312	Connell Timony, ...	do.	do. ...
	2313	John Harkin, ...	do.	do. ...
	2314	Michael McLaughlin, ...	do.	Meenymore, ...
	2315	James Ward, ...	do.	do. ...
	2316	Fanny McGarrigle, ...	do.	Meenmore, ...

DONEGAL—*continued.*

Extent of Holding. Statute.	Poor Law Valuation.	Former Rent.	Judicial Rent.	Observations.	Value of Property.
A. R. P.	£ s. d.	£ s. d.	£ s. d.	£ s. d.	£ s. d.
20 0 0	1 7 6	2 10 0	2 10 0	Rent changed in 1850 from 1 10 0	
17 0 30	3 5 0	3 0 0	4 18 0	do. 2 16 0	
20 0 8	3 15 0	6 0 0	5 10 0	1850 3 18 0	
46 2 31	6 5 0	7 10 0	8 15 0		
33 1 0	2 18 0	3 5 0	3 5 0	1850 1 18 0	
74 1 20	3 15 0	4 10 0	3 17 6		
38 3 30	1 18 0	1 13 0	1 18 0	do. 4 0 0	
41 1 35	2 10 0	6 0 0	3 18 0		
14 3 35	2 0 0	3 0 0	2 15 0		
13 3 20	2 5 0	3 10 0	2 5 0	1860 2 1 0	
31 3 25	5 2 0	5 17 6	5 10 0		
36 1 25	7 16 0	10 6 0	8 15 0		
64 0 25	7 13 0	18 12 6	8 15 0		
46 3 10	7 15 0	8 18 0	7 13 0		
78 0 5	6 10 0	8 5 0	7 5 0		
113 3 30	4 0 0	4 8 0	3 7 6		
15 3 20	3 15 0	4 8 3	3 10 0		
70 0 30	4 10 0	6 10 0	5 6 6		
127 3 17	4 10 0	5 4 6	5 5 0		
87 0 0	8 10 0	5 10 0	3 10 0		
28 2 25	6 17 0	5 17 0	4 15 0		
137 3 17	7 5 0	8 0 0	7 8 0		
226 1 13	18 5 0	23 8 6	20 0 0		
80 0 0	10 7 0	18 15 0	12 0 0	do. 10 10 0	
51 0 20	3 4 0	8 13 6	7 15 0		
6 2 0	8 0 0	2 5 1	3 10 0		
37 3 20	6 15 0	7 6 0	4 16 0	1856 7 3 0	
80 2 20	5 16 0	3 5 0	5 0 0	1867 3 14 0	
196 3 24	2 16 0	6 5 0	4 0 0		
344 1 30	8 6 0	15 18 0	12 0 0	do. 3 8 0	
33 3 27	3 5 0	6 18 0	8 10 0		
4 1 0	2 0 0	7 0 0	5 10 0	1878 5 0 0	
16 1 10	1 16 0	3 7 6	2 15 0	1867 1 9 0	
84 2 25	5 0 0	3 0 6	4 5 0	do. 7 10 0	
60 0 20	2 0 0	2 17 0	2 17 0	do. 3 3 0	

Names of Assistant Commissioners by whom Cases were decided.	No.	Name of Tenant.	Name of Landlord.	Townland.
Assistant Commissioners—				
Ulick Bourke (Legal).	2317	Patrick McGlynn,	William Wilson,	[illegible],
[illegible]	2318	John Matthews,	do.	[illegible],
William Gray.	2319	James Tierney,	do.	do.
Thomas [illegible].	2320	John Gallagher,	do.	do.
R. D. [illegible].	2321	Patrick D. Ward,	do.	do.
	2322	Connell Boyle,	do.	do.
	2323	Neil Browne,	do.	do.
	2324	Lawrence Hutchinson,	do.	do.
	2325	Myles Tierney,	do.	do.
	2326	Charles Browne,	do.	do.
	2327	Mary McHugh,	do.	do.
	2328	Margaret Boyle,	do.	do.
	2329	Patrick Brown,	do.	do.
	2330	Connell Tierney,	do.	do.
	2331	Bridget Doherty,	Neil McLaine,	[illegible],
	2332	James Byrne,	do.	[illegible],
	2333	Patrick Farrey,	do.	do.
	2334	Bridget Byrne,	do.	[illegible],
	2335	John Byrne,	do.	do.
	2336	Mary McMenamin,	do.	[illegible],
	2337	Patrick Cannon,	do.	do.
	2338	James Byrne,	do.	do.
	2339	Bridget Campbell,	do.	do.
	2340	Mary Greene,	do.	do.
	2341	Mary McMonigle,	do.	do.
	2342	William Doherty,	do.	do.
	2343	Bryan Cunningham,	Frances [illegible],	[illegible].
	2344	John Haskin,	do.	do.
	2345	Denis Lynam,	do.	[illegible],
	2346	Margaret [illegible],	do.	do.
	2347	James Gillespie,	do.	do.
	2348	John Lynam,	do.	do.
	2349	James Haskin,	do.	[illegible] and [illegible].
	2350	John Lynam,	do.	[illegible],
	2351	John McConyngham,	do.	do.

DONEGAL—*continued*.

Extent of Holding, Statute.	Poor Law Valuation.	Former Rent.	Judicial Rent.	Observations.		Value of Tenancy.
A. R. P.	£ s. d.	£ s. d.	£ s. d.		£ s. d.	£ s. d.
133 1 30	8 13 0	11 0 0	6 15 0	Rent changed in 1867 from	7 19 0	
14 1 20	3 5 0	3 17 0	3 13 8	do.	3 5 0	
30 1 0	3 8 0	4. 3 8	3 15 0	do.	3 6 0	
9 0 0	3 0 0	3 17 0	3 5 0	do.	3 8 0	
11 1 8	1 10 0	3 5 0	3 0 0	do.	1 14 6	
30 0 0	3 10 0	6 3 0	3 10 0	do.	3 10 0	
120 2 30	4 0 0	5 18 0	4 10 0	do.	4 4 0	
76 3 30	4 0 0	15 18 0	6 0 0			
33 0 00	5 5 0	6 ·5 0	6 5 0	do.	3 7 0	
23 3 10	3 5 0	4 5 0	3 17 6	do.	3 14 0	
12 1 10	3 10 0	4 6 0	3 15 0	do.	3 14 0	
13 0 00	3 10 0	3 13 0	3 0 0	do.	3 1 0	
67 8 0	4 0 0	6 10 0	6 10 0	do.	4 1 0	
19 1 30	1 15 0	6 9 0	3 15 0	do.	3 6 0	
5 2 0	8 10 0	6 8 0	3 10 0			
15 9 5	—	3 8 0	3 0 0			
16 1 [illegible]	3 15 0	4 [illegible] 0	3 10 0			
25 1 37	3 15 0	4 18 0	3 [illegible] 0			
14 2 33	1 10 ·0	3 8 0	3 8 0			
1 0 0	1 5 0	1 0 0	0 15 0			
8 0 0	8 10 0	6 10 0	5 0 0			
5 8 0	3 16 0	4 12 0	5 0 0			
3 1 13	1 0 0	1 13 0	1 11 0			
7 0 0	4 15 0	7 14 0	3 15 0	1848	6 10 0	
7 3 18	3 0 0	3 0 0	3 7 0			
5 1 0	1 13 0	8 8 0	0 15 0			
8 8 33	3 15 0	5 0 0	4 0 0	1850	4 0 0	
8 3 30	7 10 0	5 0 0	6 0 0			
6 0 5	4 5 0	3 17 0	3 10 0			
6 1 36	3 15 0	3 0 0	5 0 0			
11 0 35	6 0 0	6 3 0	3 17 6			
8 6 15	6 0 ·0	4 19 0	4 0 0			
6 0 36	4 10 0	4 ·0 5	4 0 8			
13 0 5	5 0 ·0	5 5 0	4 16 0			
14 3 27	5 15 0	7 0 0	5 0 0			

Names of Assistant Commissioners by whom Cases were decided.	No.	Name of Tenant.	Name of Landlord.
Assistant Commissioners—			
Ulick Bourke (Legal). E. Spragle. William Gray. Thomas Maher. S. E. Gibson.	2352	Jane Maxwell,	Frances McBride,
	2353	James McElhinney,	do.
	2354	Edward Malloy,	do.
	2355	Edward Boyle,	do.
	2356	Ellen Kenny,	do.
	2357	Peter Hoskin,	do.
	2358	Denis McNelis,	do.
	2359	James McGinley,	do.
	2360	Andrew McNelis,	do.
	2361	Mary O'Clery,	do.
	2362	James Boyle,	do.
	2363	James Gillespie,	do.
	2364	John Gorm,	do.
	2365	William Boyle,	do.
	2366	Denis McCoy,	Thomas Colquhoun,
	2367	Bernard Hume,	do.
	2368	James McGinley,	Sir W. H. Boyle, Bart,
	2369	Patrick McNulty,	do.
	2370	Hugh Boner,	do.
	2371	Bridget Bonner,	do.
	2372	Owen McBrearty,	do.
	2373	Edward Scanlan,	do.
	2374	Peter Scanlan,	do.
	2375	Charles Gallagher,	do.
	2376	James Gallagher,	do.
	2377	Peter Scanlan,	do.
	2378	John Boyle,	do.
	2379	Neil McMenamin,	do.
	2380	Patrick Foy,	do.
	2381	Neil Doherty,	do.
	2382	James Foy,	do.
	2383	John Quin,	do.
	2384	Charles Boner,	do.
	2385	Daniel Gallagher,	do.
	2386	John McGildea,	do.

DONEGAL—*continued.*

Extent of Holding. Statute.			Poor Law Valuation.			Former Rent.			Judicial Rent.			Observations.
A.	R.	P.	£	s.	d.	£	s.	d.	£	s.	d.	
23	0	29	7	15	0	7	15	8	6	7	6	
7	0	19	2	0	0	2	4	6	2	0	0	
16	0	16	4	10	0	0	4	8	4	10	6	
6	1	30	3	15	0	6	0	0	3	15	0	
2	1	11	1	10	0	1	18	3	1	10	0	
6	1	35	5	10	0	6	2	6	3	2	6	
2	3	28	1	10	0	2	6	3	1	13	6	
99	3	4	2	18	0	3	19	6	2	11	6	
7	0	20	4	5	0	3	19	0	5	0	0	
1	1	25	2	10	0	2	18	6	2	17	6	
1	1	30	5	15	0	8	9	9	5	15	0	
8	3	10	2	18	0	3	2	6	2	10	0	
3	3	30	2	18	0	3	8	0	2	18	0	
3	1	8	1	10	0	5	2	0	1	15	0	
13	1	20	3	5	0	3	4	0	3	0	0	By consent.
87	2	0	3	5	0	4	10	0	3	15	0	do.
29	0	3	2	18	0	2	10	0	2	2	0	
16	3	8	2	0	0	3	0	3	3	0	3	
16	0	0	3	0	0	3	6	6	3	0	0	
41	2	20	3	18	0	5	0	6	5	10	0	
69	0	0	4	15	0	5	8	9	4	5	0	
71	3	10	4	5	0	5	2	6	5	1	6	
47	1	19	4	5	0	4	18	0	4	7	6	
43	3	0	3	6	0	3	10	8	3	0	0	
182	1	25	5	0	0	8	8	0	3	18	0	Rent changed in 1850 from - - - £ 5 s. 0 d. 0
93	1	38	6	10	0	6	12	1	5	0	0	
71	3	30	5	15	0	6	6	10	5	10	0	
19	2	13	3	8	0	3	4	6	3	8	0	
41	1	26	4	0	0	4	14	0	4	8	6	
18	2	16	7	18	0	8	10	0	7	15	0	
21	0	30	2	0	0	2	3	8	2	17	6	
11	2	16	2	5	0	3	16	2	3	5	0	
23	0	0	7	0	0	7	9	0	7	9	0	
30	1	0	4	0	0	4	15	0	4	5	0	
98	3	29	13	0	0	14	15	6	13	0	0	

COUNTY OF

Names of Assistant Commissioners by whom Cases were decided.	No.	Name of Tenant.	Name of Landlord.	Townland.
Assistant Commissioners— Ulick Holmes (Legal). R. Hewson, W. William Gray. Thomas Muir. R. B. Carden.	2387	James Mason, ...	Sir W. H. Style, Bart., ...	Ballyherrigan, ...
	2388	Patrick Mason, ...	do.	do. ...
	2389	John Magee, ...	do.	do. ...
	2390	James Carlin, ...	do.	do. ...
	2391	Betty McElroy, ...	do.	Drumderryglass,
	2392	Do. ...	do.	Crossroads, ...
	2393	John McMenamin, ...	do.	Tamnagh, Tamnagh...
	2394	Patrick McHugh, ...	Sir Frederick Heygate, Bart.,	Stripy, ...
	2395	James and Patrick McIntyre,	Marquis of Conyngham, ...	Mass, ...
	2396	Sarah Brown, ...	Susan Brown, ...	Fern, ...
	2397	Hugh Kelly, ...	Sir Frederick Heygate, Bart.,	Gorly, ...
	2398	Joseph Crean, ...	do.	Raws, ...
	2399	Samuel and Edward Corrigan,	do.	Drumbagh, ...
	2400	Michael Breslin, ...	do.	do. ...
	2401	Samuel Nelson, ...	do.	Drumkeel, ...
	2402	William J. Stewart, ...	William J. Stewart, ...	Castlefin, ...
	2403	Mathew Patterson, ...	Robert Sproule, ...	Ballyboe and another.
	2404	Bryan Mackee, ...	Mary C. Barton, ...	Drumardart, ...
	2405	Susan McBride, Rep. of Charles McBride,	do.	Drumardart and another.
	2406	Pat Francis, ...	do.	Carnhill, ...
	2407	Bryan McQuaid, ...	do.	do. ...
	2408	Patrick McGuigan, ...	do.	do. ...
	2409	Patrick McElhinney, ...	Thomas Colquhoun, ...	Legacurry, ...
	2410	Catherine Harraghy, ...	do.	Drumore, ...
	2411	Edward Breslin, ...	do.	do. ...
	2412	Connell Haughey, ...	do.	do. ...
	2413	Michael Harraghy, ...	do.	do. ...
	2414	Mary Brogan, ...	do.	do. ...
	2415	John Murphy, ...	Rev. John Hamilton, ...	Drumendoney, ...
	2416	James McGlinchy, ...	do.	Tullyvast, ...
	2417	Patrick Murphy, ...	do.	Drumendoney, ...
	2418	Susan Harraghy, ...	do.	Lighaney, ...
	2419	James McMullin, ...	do.	Magherabrew, ...
	2420	James Murphy, ...	do.	Lighaney, ...
	2421	Francis Gillespie, ...	Mary C. E. Johnston, Rep. of Joseph Johnston, deceased.	Cappry, ...

DONEGAL—*continued.*

Extent of Holding (statute).	Poor Law Valuation.	Former Rent.	Judicial Rent.	Observations.		Value of Tenancy.
A. R. P.	£ s. d.	£ s. d.	£ s. d.		£ s. d.	£ s. d.
22 2 0	4 0 0	4 4 8	3 17 6			
29 0 28	6 0 0	6 3 8½	5 15 0			
21 1 18	4 0 0	4 10 3	4 10 2			
6 3 27	4 10 0	4 10 2	4 0 8			
60 2 30	4 10 0	4 7 0	3 10 0			
23 1 38	11 0 0	11 9 8	9 0 0			
16 2 33	4 0 0	3 10 0	4 0 0	Rent changed in 1850 from	2 15 1	
61 2 33	31 15 0	36 10 8	30 0 0	By consent.		
108 3 10	14 3 0	18 18 0	14 10 0			
20 3 4	8 3 0	7 7 8	6 10 8	do.		
7 3 0	6 0 0	8 0 0	7 0 8			
48 0 0	26 0 0	29 0 0	22 10 0	Rent changed in 1870 from	6 0 0	
82 1 20	34 10 0	41 0 0	34 0 0	1877	33 0 0	
80 3 10	27 8 0	33 10 0	30 0 0	do.	19 19 0	
60 3 31	30 0 0	38 0 0	30 0 0			
8 2 6	12 10 0	18 0 0	14 18 0			
15 0 30	16 8 0	13 4 8	18 0 0			
18 1 15	7 18 0	7 18 0	6 10 0	1850	7 18 0	
75 3 20	10 5 0	15 6 0	10 8 0			
9 1 20	3 15 0	4 10 0	3 15 0	do.	3 10 0	
18 1 38	5 3 0	4 13 0	4 8 8	do.	3 10 0	
6 1 8	3 3 0	3 0 0	2 12 0	do.	2 10 0	
4 2 31	1 10 0	1 1 0	1 3 6	1876	1 3 6	
8 3 28	3 3 0	4 13 6	3 13 0	1874	3 10 7	
8 1 25	3 15 0	3 2 3	4 2 6	1878	6 1 0	
3 3 20	8 3 0	3 15 10	3 7 6	1874	2 8 0	
10 2 0	4 1 8	6 4 6	3 10 0	1871	3 12 6	
14 0 30	3 11 0	3 15 0	3 3 0	do.	4 7 3	
13 2 28	6 8 0	6 2 0	6 0 0	1860	6 16 0	
11 2 0	5 15 0	8 0 0	6 10 0	1860	4 3 6	
18 1 25	6 15 0	6 16 0	6 0 0			
9 0 13	3 13 0	4 10 0	3 10 0	1860	3 14 0	
6 2 23	3 5 0	4 0 0	3 16 0	1870	3 11 6	
63 0 27	10 5 0	11 10 0	11 5 0	1860	10 5 0	
6 0 0	1 7 0	3 0 0	1 7 6			

COUNTY OF

Names of Assistant Commissioners by whom Cases were decided.	No.	Name of Tenant.	Name of Landlord.	Townland.
Assistant Commissioners—				
Ulick Bourke (Legal). [illegible]. William Gray. Thomas [illegible]. R. R. [illegible].	2422	Robert Graham, ...	Mary G. F. Johnston, Rep. of Joseph Johnston, deceased.	Tullyvaal, ...
	2423	John Key, ...	do.	Hayes, ...
	2424	Francis Gillespie, ...	do.	Aughlin, ...
	2425	Donald Toland, Rep. of Denis Toland,	Robert George Montgomery,	Kellogs, ...
	2426	John Gallagher, ...	do.	Castlegoe, ...
	2427	Michael Gallagher, ...	do.	do. ...
	2428	John Daly, ...	William Atkinson, ...	Ballymacarrick and another.
	2429	Phelix Timony, ...	Colonel George Knox, ...	Bennett, ...
	2430	William Taylor, ...	do.	Killybegs Bay and another,
	2431	John Timony, ...	do.	Bennett, ...
	2432	James McCadden, ...	do.	Bay of Ballymacarrick.
	2433	Hugh McCafferty, ...	do.	do. ...
	2434	Peter McGlinchy, Admr. of John McGlinchy.	do.	do. ...
	2435	George Thompson, ...	do.	Bernah, ...
	2436	Patrick Gallagher, ...	do.	Drumlaine, ...
	2437	James Gayle, ...	do.	Killybegs Bay,
	2438	William McGinn, ...	do.	Bernah, ...
	2439	Catherine Clarke, ...	do.	Killybegs Bay,
	2440	William Clarke, ...	do.	do. ...
	2441	Robert Pinkerton, ...	do.	Killybegs Bay and another.
	2442	James McIntyre, ...	do.	do. ...
	2443	Do.	do.	do. ...
	2444	John Crawford, ...	do.	Bennett, ...
	2445	John Porter, ...	do.	Ballymacarrick, ...
	2446	James Gallagher, ...	do.	[illegible] ...
	2447	John Dinsmore, ...	do.	[illegible], ...
	2448	Owen Timony, ...	do.	Bennett, ...
	2449	Mary Porter, ...	do.	Ballymacarrick, ...
	2450	Michael Diver, ...	do.	Bern, ...
	2451	William Wilson, ...	do.	Killybegs Bay,
	2452	Robert Ellis, ...	do.	Ballymacarrick, ...
	2453	James Allen, ...	do.	Bernah, ...
	2454	John McGonigle, ...	do.	Killybegs Bay and another.
	2455	John Porter, ...	do.	do. ...

Extent of Holding. Statute.	Poor Law Valuation.	Former Rent.	Judicial Rent.	Observations.		Value of Tenancy.
A. R. P.	£ s. d.	£ s. d.	£ s. d.		£ s. d.	£ s. d.
9 3 35	7 15 0	10 0 0	8 0 0	Rent changed in 1865 from . .	7 10 4	
10 2 7	8 10 0	11 0 0	9 0 0			
16 1 35	7 0 0	12 10 0	8 0 0	do.	9 10 3	
9 3 0	3 5 0	5 10 0	4 0 0	1850	6 18 11	
16 0 10	3 0 0	8 0 0	2 12 8			
22 3 8	8 0 0	6 0 0	6 10 0			
16 3 6	10 15 0	27 10 0	23 0 0	By consent.		
35 1 35	10 10 0	25 0 0	18 10 0			
19 1 7	14 14 0	18 6 8	13 0 0			
23 1 10	15 15 0	20 7 6	9 10 0			
63 1 23	4 0 0	5 1 8	3 15 0			
74 0 30	5 0 0	8 0 0	5 0 0			
135 1 16	8 5 0	6 6 8	4 15 0			
103 0 0	40 15 0	52 2 4	40 0 0			
10 1 27	7 10 0	8 0 0	5 15 0			
24 2 8	14 8 0	17 10 0	15 0 0			
23 0 16	10 0 0	10 18 0	7 10 0			
28 0 35	19 10 0	14 18 4	13 10 0			
25 0 35	13 10 0	16 11 4	11 10 0			
34 0 23	15 7 6	16 7 0	15 10 0			
65 0 0	23 18 0	31 19 0	23 0 0			
39 1 0	20 5 0	25 5 0	18 0 0			
49 0 1	23 0 0	27 7 0	21 0 0			
81 3 11	12 0 0	14 0 0	12 0 0			
8 1 0	4 15 0	8 9 0	4 15 0			
28 0 16	18 0 0	20 14 3	19 0 0			
5 0 15	3 5 0	4 5 0	3 17 6	Rent changed in 1850 from . .	8 9 0	
13 0 25	8 0 0	10 3 10	8 10 0	By consent.		
16 0 24	9 0 0	13 15 6	10 10 0	do.		
7 3 20	4 10 0	6 18 0	8 0 0	do.		
7 0 23	5 15 0	8 10 0	5 0 0	do.		
18 3 8	13 15 0	16 0 0	13 10 0	do.		
15 1 8	8 10 0	13 5 0	10 0 0	do.		
30 3 0	20 0 0	25 16 0	21 0 0	do.		
9 0 0	6 16 0	11 17 6	10 0 0	do.		

COUNTY OF

Names of Assistant Commissioners by whom Cases were decided.	No.	Name of Tenant.	Name of Landlord.	Townland.
Assistant Commissioners—				
[illegible] (Legal).	3457	Mary Carson, Rep. of Wm. Carson, deceased,	Colonel George Knox, —	Sessagh, —
R. [illegible].	3458	Margaret McCoy, —	do. — —	do. —
William Gray.	3459	Ellen Hagan, —	do. — —	[illegible]
Thomas [illegible].	3460	Philip Kelly, —	H. G. Stuart, —	Drumnamoh, —
R. M. [illegible].	3461	Philip Kelly, —	do. — —	[illegible], —
	3462	Daniel McIlwain, —	do. — —	Drumgarran, —
	3463	John Kelly, — —	do. — —	Ballydavitting, —
	3464	Edward Kennedy, —	Thomas [illegible], — ...	[illegible], —
	3465	Edward Kennedy, senr.,	do. — ...	do. —
	3466	James Kerry, —	do. — ...	do. —
	3467	James Stewart, —	Marquis of Conyngham, ...	[illegible], —
	3468	[illegible] Doyle, — ...	do. — ...	[illegible], —
	3469	Thomas Kerrigan, ...	do.	Drumgre, ..
	3470	Hugh Martin, ...	Sir John Leslie, Bart., ...	[illegible], —
	3471	Lewis McIlwee, ...	do.	Middletown, —
	3472	Charles Fitzpatrick, —	do. .. —	[illegible], —
				Total, —

COUNTY OF

[illegible] Commissioners—				
[illegible] (Legal).	2725	Alexander Johnston, —	[illegible], — ...	Ballydrain, —
[illegible].	2726	Michael McCarron, —	Colonel C. [illegible], —	[illegible], —
[illegible].	2727	Sarah Lowther, —	do. — —	do. —
[illegible].	2728	Agnes McClorian, Admix. of Felix McClorian,	do. — —	do. —
[illegible].	2729	Mary Whiteside, —	Earl Annesley, — —	[illegible], —
	2730	Thomas [illegible], —	do. — ...	[illegible], —
	2731	Robert [illegible], —	do. — —	[illegible], —
	2732	John Grey, — —	J. J. White, — —	Tullyrat, —
	2733	William Price, —	do. — —	Tullydown, —
	2734	Thomas [illegible], —	do.	Dunglory, —
	2735	Samuel Arnold, —	do. — —	do. —
	2736	Andrew [illegible], —	do. — —	Tullyrat, —
	2737	Samuel Thompson, —	do. — —	Dunglory, —
	2738	Patrick O'Hagan, —	do. ... —	Tullyrat, —

DONEGAL—continued.

Extent of Holding. Statute.	Poor Law Valuation.	Former Rent.	Judicial Rent.	Observations.	Value of Tenancy.
a. r. p.	£ s. d.	£ s. d.	£ s. d.		£ s. d.
16 1 32	14 10 0	18 8 0	15 0 0	By consent.	
13 1 25	4 15 0	5 5 0	4 10 0	do.	
20 2 0	1 10 0	5 0 0	3 0 0	do.	
37 1 15	23 15 0	26 0 0	25 10 0		
14 0 6	8 15 0	12 4 0	10 0 0		
15 3 32	7 15 0	10 0 0	8 10 0	Rent changed in 1877 from . . . 1860 £ s. d. 8 10 0 / 3 10 0	
9 3 8	8 10 0	9 12 0	8 5 0		
113 0 0	8 15 0	8 0 0	7 0 0		
873 1 10	8 8 0	10 18 0	8 8 0	1863 9 10 0	
62 3 2	8 10 0	6 0 0	8 10 0	do. 3 2 0	
34 1 32	13 0 0	19 0 0	17 10 0	1850 13 12 0	
100 3 20	6 8 0	7 10 0	6 10 0		
113 1 8	14 5 0	13 10 0	12 0 0	1859 11 16 6	
23 8 4	9 12 0	12 5 0	10 0 0		
5 1 31	6 0 0	8 0 0	4 0 0	1858 6 10 0	
17 3 21	4 8 0	8 0 0	5 5 0		
13,361 0 7	2,030 14 0	2,812 14 8½	2,122 10 8		

DOWN.

40 2 37	71 5 0	77 12 0	73 14 0		
16 1 25	14 15 0	16 3 0	13 10 0		
13 3 0	11 5 0	13 6 0	10 10 0		
12 2 23	14 15 0	16 3 0	13 0 0		
23 1 3	21 5 0	17 16 0	20 0 0		
23 0 16	15 10 0	9 4 0	11 0 0		
20 1 8	12 0 0	14 6 0	12 0 0		
9 2 23	17 5 0	13 3 6	10 10 0		
31 3 6	20 10 0	61 5 3	25 0 0		
25 1 12	31 0 0	26 8 11	23 10 0		
11 1 10	15 0 0	15 6 0	14 0 0		
8 3 23	10 0 0	11 11 8	10 10 0		
75 0 21	31 10 0	87 18 0	82 0 0		
10 0 0	—	13 2 2	18 0 0		

COUNTY OF

Names of Assistant Commissioners by whom Cases were decided.	No.	Name of Tenant.	Name of Landlord.	Townland.
Assistant Commissioners—				
F. O. Harrison (Legal). J. M. Wynn. J. E. Bergin. J. Gleeson. F. Fitzgerald.	2739	Andrew Porter, ...	J. J. White, ...	Dougherty, ...
	2740	Robert J. Hill, ...	do.	Tullyear, ...
	2741	John Stevenson, ...	do.	do. ...
	2742	James Gordon, ...	do.	Dougherty, ...
	2743	Robert Cromie, ...	do.	do. ...
	2744	Hugh McIlveen, ...	do.	Colmanow, ...
	2745	Samuel Martin, ...	do.	Ballydown, ...
	2746	Thomas Coburn, ...	do.	Tullyear, ...
	2747	James Lorby, ...	do.	Colmanow, ...
	2748	William Merlin, ...	do.	Ballydown, ...
	2749	James McClean, ...	do.	Ballyrainey, ...
	2750	Thomas McBride, ...	do.	Tullyear, ...
	2751	Sarah Jane Ratcliffe, ...	do.	do. ...
	2752	Ellen Dale, ...	do.	Ballyrainey, ...
	2753	John Porter, ...	do.	Ballydown, ...
	2754	Robert McElborough, ...	do.	Colmanow, ...
	2755	James Hutchinson, ...	do.	Tullyear, ...
	2756	William Barr, ...	do.	Ballydown, ...
	2757	Thomas Purvey, ...	do.	Tullyear, ...
	2758	Rachel Davis, ...	do.	do. ...
	2759	William Hare, ...	do.	do. ...
	2760	Robert McIlwraith, ...	do.	do. ...
	2761	John Stevenson, ...	do.	do. ...
	2762	John Gordon, ...	do.	Dougherty, ...
	2763	Hugh Mannion, ...	do.	Tullyear, ...
	2764	Samuel McClean, ...	do.	do. ...
	2765	Samuel Adams, ...	do.	Ballydown, ...
	2766	Charles Morgan, jun., ...	do.	Dougherty, ...
	2767	James Nelson, ...	do.	Ballydown, ...
	2768	James Hughes, junior, ...	do.	Dougherty, ...
	2769	Mary Graham, ...	James G. Stewart, ...	Castlereagh, ...
	2770	David Stewart, ...	do.	do. ...
	2771	Alexander Murray, ...	do.	do. ...
	2772	Mary Doyle, ...	do.	do. ...
	2773	John McKevitt, ...	do.	Ballyrainey, ...

DOWN—continued.

Extent of Holding. Statute.	Poor Law Valuation.	Former Rent.	Judicial Rent.	Observations.	Value of Tenancy.
A. R. P.	£ s. d.	£ s. d.	£ s. d.	£ s. d.	£ s. d.
27 3 [illegible]	21 0 0	[illegible] 7 7	[illegible] 0 0	Rent changed in 1876 from . . . [illegible] 10 0	
6 2 [illegible]	6 6 0	6 14 6	7 15 6		
11 1 27	16 10 0	18 8 3	[illegible] 10 0		
12 0 0	13 5 0	13 [illegible] 2	11 10 0		
35 3 13	37 15 0	43 [illegible] 6	[illegible] 7 6		
31 3 [illegible]	34 13 0	[illegible] 4 5	34 0 0		
29 3 20	35 10 0	41 3 6	[illegible] 0 0		
[illegible] 0 [illegible]	34 5 0	[illegible] 1 1	34 [illegible] 0		
4 3 10	4 15 0	5 [illegible] 0	4 15 0		
5 0 13	4 5 0	6 11 3	6 0 0		
61 1 20	61 15 0	41 17 4	[illegible] 0 0		
15 0 15	17 10 0	18 12 7	15 15 7		
7 3 0	18 6 6	14 7 8	11 10 0		
5 3 25	5 10 0	6 1 0	6 1 4		
6 5 20	7 10 0	6 13 3	7 1 0		
44 3 [illegible]	[illegible] 0 0	43 5 10	37 10 0		
[illegible] 3 15	94 10 0	[illegible] 4 0	[illegible] 0 0		
46 1 21	[illegible] 15 0	107 17 0	96 0 0	do. 120 0 0	
31 9 [illegible]	41 0 0	40 0 0	27 0 0		
4 3 17	6 0 0	6 6 6	6 10 0		
4 5 17	5 5 0	6 6 0	5 0 0	1873 5 0 0	
13 1 16	13 10 0	13 6 6	13 6 5		
15 0 7	17 10 0	20 9 0	17 15 0		
43 0 15	[illegible] 0 0	46 13 6	45 15 0		
7 5 0	6 0 0	6 10 6	5 0 0		
11 1 6	12 10 0	23 1 9	15 0 0		
4 5 5	6 10 0	8 15 6	7 5 0		
10 0 [illegible]	16 0 0	17 5 11	12 0 0		
15 1 [illegible]	16 15 0	19 6 5	[illegible] 10 0		
16 1 15	[illegible] 10 0	[illegible] 7 6	20 10 0		
16 1 [illegible]	15 0 0	16 5 10	13 3 0	By consent.	
[illegible] 1 15	16 0 0	16 11 6	14 0 0	do.	
19 1 20	17 15 0	[illegible] 4 6	17 3 0	do.	
6 2 [illegible]	6 15 0	6 1 2	4 10 0	do.	
3 3 0	5 0 0	5 1 2	3 10 0	do.	

Names of Assistant Commissioners by whom Case was decided.	No.	Name of Tenant.	Name of Landlord.	Townland.
Assistant Commissioners: —				
F. G. Hughes (Legal). J. M. Weir. J. F. Hamilton. J. Cunningham. P. Fitzpatrick.	2774	David Gowan, ...	James G. Stuart, ...	Ballywaltyman,
	2775	Roger Flanigan, .	do.	do. ...
	2776	William Martin, ...	do.	Castlequarter, ...
	2777	Bernard McCracken, ...	do.	Ballealyman, ...
	2778	Bernard McElroy, ...	do.	[illegible], ...
	2779	Edward Flanigan, ...	do.	Ballealyman, ...
	2780	Alexander Kelley, ...	do.	do. ...
	2781	David Maxwell, ...	do.	do. ...
	2782	Bernard Flanigan, ...	do.	do. ...
	2783	James Gray, ...	do.	do. ...
	2784	Ellen Magrath, ...	do.	do. ...
	2785	Hugh McGrath, ...	do.	Castlequarter, ...
	2786	Robert McGrath, ...	do.	do. ...
	2787	Arthur O'Hare, ...	do.	Ballealyman, ...
	2788	Patrick Hagan, ...	do.	do. ...
	2789	James Hamilton, ...	do.	do. ...
	2790	Andrew Ewart, ...	do.	do. ...
	2791	Anne Morgan, ...	do.	do. ...
	2792	Patrick Diamond, ...	do.	do. ...
	2793	Sarah J. Maxwell, ...	do.	do. ...
	2794	Michael O'Hare, ...	do.	do. ...
	2795	John Reid, ...	Lady [illegible], ...	[illegible], ...
	2796	Mary Orr, ...	W. R. McDonnell, ...	Ballyeaglan, ...
	2797	David McKey, ...	Robt. and W. D. McCullough,	[illegible] ...
	2798	James Courtney, ...	do.	do. ...
	2799	Isaac Shaw, ...	do.	do. ...
	2800	Agnes Todd, ...	do.	do. ...
	2801	Daniel O'Hare, ...	J. W. E. Macartney & others,	Ballytobit, ...
	2802	Patrick Toomby, sen.,	do.	do. ...
	2803	Patrick Toomby, jun.,	do.	do. ...
	2804	William and Thomas Murray,	do.	do. ...
	2805	John McIlroy, ...	do.	do. ...
	2806	Anne O'Hare, ...	do.	do. ...
	2807	Alexander Murray, ...	do.	do. ...
	2808	Robina Murray, ...	do.	do. ...

DOWN—*continued.*

Extent of Holding. Statute.	Poor Law Valuation.	Former Rent.	Judicial Rent.	Observations.	Value of Tenancy.
A. R. P.	£ s. d.	£ s. d.	£ s. d.		£ s. d.
23 0 5	22 18 0	25 12 0	19 10 0	By consent.	
9 1 10	9 5 0	11 7 0	8 0 0	do.	
39 1 30	27 10 0	30 7 5	24 0 0	do.	
5 0 35	5 10 0	5 11 6	4 15 0	do.	
14 0 35	16 15 0	14 5 4	13 0 0	do.	
5 0 20	6 15 0	8 9 8	6 0 0	do.	
26 3 30	20 0 0	28 5 6	19 0 0	do.	
30 0 10	41 15 0	65 12 0	43 0 0	do.	
9 0 37	8 10 0	9 6 6	7 5 0	do.	
10 3 15	13 0 0	12 1 9	10 0 0	do.	
4 1 15	5 5 0	6 16 7	3 15 0	do.	
20 1 10	15 0 0	18 13 5	16 14 0	do.	
35 3 15	33 0 0	30 0 0	30 0 0	do.	
30 0 30	18 10 0	23 8 9	19 0 0	do.	
16 0 20	15 13 0	15 18 9	13 0 0	do.	
19 3 30	25 5 0	30 9 7	16 0 0	do.	
18 0 30	14 0 0	20 9 3	11 0 0	do.	
16 3 15	15 5 0	17 18 7	15 0 0	do.	
35 3 35	21 15 0	35 4 7	27 15 0	do.	
6 2 20	6 5 0	7 8 8	4 0 0	do.	
19 1 30	10 0 0	21 10 9	18 10 0	do.	
8 1 18	7 5 0	7 9 7	6 5 4	do.	
12 0 0	11 15 0	11 7 6	10 0 0	do.	
70 0 38	—	30 0 4	30 17 0	do.	
17 1 30	17 5 0	34 5 0	13 4 10	do.	
22 0 35	24 10 0	30 11 5	22 10 0	do.	
17 0 30	15 18 0	24 10 10	17 16 0	do.	
13 1 10	10 10 0	13 18 8	10 0 0		
8 1 15	—	10 6 5	8 0 0		
6 3 30	4 15 0	5 10 6	5 5 0		
10 0 30	15 5 0	10 13 5	15 5 0		
4 0 0	6 0 0	6 16 10	3 10 0		
11 1 27	9 15 0	15 16 1	9 13 6		
34 0 0	38 10 0	47 18 8	33 10 0		
11 0 30	5 5 0	15 0 10	9 10 0		

COUNTY OF

Names of Assistant Commissioners by whom Cases were decided.	No.	Name of Tenant.	Name of Landlord.	Townland.
Assistant Commissioners—				
F. G. Hamilton (Legal). J. M. Wynne. J. F. Barrowes. J. Cunningham. F. Fitzpatrick.	2809	Eliza Burns, Admx. of Patrick Burns,	J. W. H. Montray & others,	Ballybrick, ...
	2810	James O'Hara, ...	do.	do. ...
	2811	Do.	do.	do. ...
	2812	John Doyle, ...	do.	do. ...
	2813	George Erwin, ...	do.	do. ...
	2814	Patrick Connor, ...	Edward McCartan, ...	Ballymoley, ...
	2815	Thomas McKay, ...	Stewart B. Douglas, ...	Ballandare, ...
	2816	Samuel Anderson, ...	do.	do. ...
	2817	Patrick McAlinden, ...	William C. Heron and ors., Trustees of John Heron.	Corbally, ...
	2818	Bernard McAlinden, ...	do.	do. ...
	2819	John McAlinden, ...	do.	do. ...
	2820	Henry Fairs, ...	William G. Heron, ...	Tullyhinny, ...
	2821	Arthur McCormick, ...	Patrick Murphy, ...	Ballyanesy, ...
	2822	George Henley, ...	do.	do. ...
	2823	John Craig, ...	do.	do. ...
	2824	Robert Stewart, ...	do.	do. ...
	2825	Ann Morgan, Admx. of Arthur Devlin,	William Maie and others, ...	Balmakeyrane, ...
	2826	Robert Osborne, Exor. of William J. Osborne,	Francis Chipps, ...	Carlecht, ...
	2827	Edward Hillen, ...	do.	do. ...
	2828	Joseph Flock, ...	do.	do. ...
	2829	James & William Wrain,	W. G. Baron, ...	Ballintaggart, ...
	2830	William Copeland, ...	Colonel C. Maguire, ...	Kilmore, ...
	2831	John McDowell, ...	do.	do. ...
	2832	James Porter, ...	J. J. White, ...	Dungorey, ...
	2833	William J. Hamilton, ...	do.	do. ...
	2834	George Osborne, ...	James C. Stuart, ...	Balnakeyrane, ...
	2835	Ruth Linton, ...	do.	Carrickwater, ...
	2836	Hugh McCleery, ...	do.	Balnakeyrane, ...
	2837	John Thompson, ...	do.	Castelreagh, ...
	2838	Wm. James McKelvey,	George Allen, ...	Ballyknaghlin, ...
	2839	John Moore, ...	Hugh Kelso, ...	Leggagh, ...
	2840	Alexander Woods, ...	Patrick Murphy, ...	Ballyanesy, ...
	2841	Robert Davison, ...	William C. Heron, ...	Ardkeen, ...
	2842	William Dalzell, ...	George Vaughan, ...	Ballylaunderry,
	2843	W. B. Mitson, ...	Mrs. Mary Vaughan, ...	do. ...

DOWN—continued.

Extent of Holding. Statute.	Poor Law Valuation.	Former Rent.	Judicial Rent.	Observations.		Value of Tenancy.
A. R. P.	£ s. d.	£ s. d.	£ s. d.		£ s. d.	£ s. d.
3 0 30	4 0 0	4 15 0	4 0 0			
6 3 33	5 15 0	10 0 5	7 15 0			
6 0 10	5 13 0	7 0 4	5 10 0			
7 0 [illegible]	7 10 0	8 10 10	5 10 0			
6 2 15	6 13 0	6 6 6	6 10 0			
12 0 5	13 15 0	15 5 0	11 10 0			
45 0 [illegible]	41 15 0	47 15 3	41 0 0			
85 1 14	85 13 0	85 18 4	87 10 0			
29 0 25	86 0 0	38 0 0	86 5 0			
13 1 25	7 15 0	12 12 0	8 0 0			
16 0 8	11 5 0	17 0 0	8 10 0			
64 1 20	61 0 0	67 3 0	40 0 0			
3 0 35	6 10 0	6 12 3	3 10 0			
6 0 3	3 0 0	6 14 0	1 5 0			
15 2 15	17 0 0	20 10 0	17 0 0			
18 1 20	16 15 0	15 1 8	13 0 0			
13 0 3	16 8 0	18 0 0	15 0 0			
16 0 25	13 10 0	16 13 10	16 0 0			
10 1 0	19 15 0	23 15 0	10 0 0	Rent changed in 1875 from . .	20 1 6	
87 0 35	65 0 0	65 13 0	87 0 0			
15 0 17	15 5 0	18 18 0	15 5 0	By consent.		
18 2 25	20 13 0	21 3 6	10 0 0			
17 1 30	18 3 0	14 0 4	11 3 0			
41 0 16	43 10 0	53 8 1	45 10 0			
31 2 0	25 3 0	26 18 1	36 0 0			
40 1 18	60 0 0	58 10 11	44 0 0	do.		
15 0 5	16 5 0	15 15 1	13 0 0	do.		
20 0 25	25 3 0	38 6 3	13 0 0	do.		
24 3 20	73 0 0	36 6 5	27 5 0	do.		
183 1 0	170 0 0	203 17 8	175 0 0			
80 1 3	33 0 0	37 1 4	38 0 0			
60 2 16	64 5 0	55 8 5	50 0 0			
36 3 21	38 15 0	42 18 0	34 0 0			
13 0 0	60 10 0	73 0 0	63 0 0			
4 0 7	7 0 0	5 0 1	5 10 0			

Names of Assistant Commissioners by whom Cases were decided.	No.	Name of Tenant.	Name of Landlord.	Townland.
Antrim Commissioners—				
F. G. Hemans (Legal). J. M. Wynn. J. F. Barrows. J. Cunningham. F. Fitzgerald.	2844	John Young,... ...	James Black, ...	Ballyvasey, ...
	2845	Laurence Fitzsimons, ...	Sarah Nicholson, ...	Drumnamoney, ...
	2846	George W. White and another,	George G. Lindsay, ...	Ballydown, ...
	2847	John McClelland, ...	Thomas Brown, ...	Ballinry, ...
	2848	James McMullan, ...	Walter Waugh, ...	do. ...
	2849	Mary Devlin, ...	Mrs. Ellen Moore, ...	Ballinlymara, ...
	2850	Francis Beckett, ...	Colonel C. D. Waddell, ...	Islandderry, ...
	2851	Samuel Gardiner, ...	do.	do. ...
	2852	William Copeland, ...	Alexander J. R. Stewart, ...	Lessdrug, ...
	2853	Alexander Magee, ...	do.	Ringlishgon, ...
	2854	Mary Jane Forsythe, ...	George Waugh, ...	Tullyrusky, ...
	2855	David Keenan, ...	do.	do. ...
	2856	Robert Creighton, ...	do.	do. ...
	2857	Robert M'Gh, ...	do.	do. ...
	2858	Richard Hammond, ...	do.	do. ...
	2859	John Young, ...	do.	do. ...
	2860	Robert Gaiven, ...	do.	do. ...
	2861	James Mills, ...	do.	do. ...
	2862	Patrick Brennan and another,	Mrs. Mary Vaughan, ...	Ballyvicmalally, ...
	2863	William Brennan, ...	do.	do. ...
	2864	James Gibson, ...	Viscount Bridport, & another, Trustees of Marquis of Londonderry,	Tervally, ...
	2865	James A. Dowell, ...	do.	Tullyvaine, ...
	2866	Patrick McAvoy, ...	do.	Lisnadiggan, ...
	2867	John Lusk, ...	do.	Ballylally, ...
	2868	Thomas McKelvey, ...	do.	Lisnakyan, ...
	2869	Ann McMahon, ...	do.	do. ...
	2870	William Carlson, ...	J. R. Crow, ...	Aughnaskeagh, ...
	2871	Alexander Carlson, ...	do.	do. ...
	2872	Richard Copeland and another,	do.	do. ...
	2873	Samuel Davison, ...	do.	do. ...
	2874	John Martin, ...	do.	do. ...
	2875	Gawn Anderson, ...	Alexander J. R. Stewart, ...	Clew, ...
				Total, ...

DOWN—continued.

Extent of Holding. Statute.	Poor Law Valuation.	Former Rent.	Judicial Rent.	Observations.	Value of Tenancy.
a. r. p.	£ s. d.	£ s. d.	£ s. d.		£ s. d.
[illegible] 3 [illegible]	[illegible] 15 0	[illegible] 7 6	[illegible] 8 0		
12 0 35	16 5 6	[illegible] 0 0	20 0 8		
6 1 [illegible]	11 0 0	14 15 0	11 0 0		
7 7 1	8 0 0	10 0 0	8 5 0		
[illegible] 2 14	20 10 0	[illegible] 0 0	[illegible] 0 0		
6 0 5	3 5 0	4 13 10	5 0 0		
17 0 0	19 0 0	21 6 0	11 0 0		
20 0 0	24 0 0	[illegible] 0 0	21 5 0		
6 0 10	9 0 0	8 15 0	7 6 0		
7 3 0	9 5 0	6 6 8	7 10 0		
6 5 18	7 0 0	7 5 0	6 15 0		
16 0 10	18 10 0	17 6 9	11 10 0		
6 3 18	7 0 0	7 8 0	5 15 0		
12 0 30	15 15 0	16 3 0	12 10 0		
[illegible] 2 15	15 10 0	51 0 0	[illegible] 10 0		
65 3 5	60 10 0	45 6 3	[illegible] 0 0		
44 1 20	45 0 0	36 10 3	44 0 0		
[illegible] 0 6	34 0 0	[illegible] 9 3	[illegible] 0 0		
[illegible] 3 10	[illegible] 0 0	[illegible] 17 6	[illegible] 0 0		
[illegible] 0 35	[illegible] 10 0	[illegible] 15 3	[illegible] 10 0		
9 3 39	14 5 0	10 0 0	8 10 0		
[illegible] 1 34	78 0 0	[illegible] 6 10	[illegible] 6 14		
11 0 12	13 15 0	11 10 0	10 5 0		
[illegible] 1 37	20 12 0	31 13 6	[illegible] 0 0		
14 3 25	17 10 0	13 13 0	13 15 0		
5 3 12	6 5 0	3 10 0	5 0 0		
53 0 0	[illegible] 18 0	[illegible] 7 11	53 0 0		
19 5 16	16 0 0	14 0 0	18 0 0		
34 2 34	[illegible] 0 0	[illegible] 11 0	[illegible] 10 0	By consent.	
10 0 12	11 15 0	10 0 0	8 0 0		
62 1 15	34 0 0	[illegible] 17 0	[illegible] [illegible] 0		
5 1 [illegible]	4 15 0	[illegible] 14 6	6 5 0		
3,081 5 16	3,375 8 0	3,648 16 1	3,070 11 8		

COUNTY OF

Names of Assistant Commissioners by whom Cases were decided.	No.	Name of Tenant.	Name of Landlord.	Townland.
Assistant Commissioners—				
M. T. O'Brien (Legal). Stephen Moynihan. Richard Garland. J. A. O'Keeffe, E. Bland-Smith.	798	William Dagnis,	Irvine Wilson and another,	Mongale,
	799	John Crawford,	do.	Coleshill,
	800	Robert Rainford,	do.	do.
	801	Patrick Donaghue,	Thomas G. Collins and others, Minors	Unterss,
	802	Catherine McHugh,	do.	Aghnale,
	803	Joseph Maguire,	do.	Aghnaskeagh,
	804	Edward Martin,	Sir Victor A. Brooke, Bart.	Tonna,
	805	Peter Crudden,	Kate McKnight,	Knockbeg & anr.
	806	Elizabeth Renwick,	John Brady,	Derrybrusk,
	807	Edward Maguire,	Samuel Gilmary,	Tully,
	808	Bartholomew Sweeney, Rep. of Roger Sweeney.	do.	do.
	809	Robert Monaghan,	Lord Rathdonnell,	Derrynakan,
	810	James Treanor,	do.	Tolmhoff,
	811	Reps of William Atwell,	do.	Derrynahinch,
	812	Hugh Fitzpatrick,	do.	Galloon,
	813	Samuel Clifford,	Earl of Erne,	Gortgarvan,
	814	Christopher Conlon,	do.	Clonmurphy,
	815	Martha Conlon,	do.	Ballinamallard,
	816	Michael McIlroy,	do.	do.
	817	Martha Conlon,	do.	Clonmurphy.
	818	Edward Brown,	do.	Gargivan,
	819	Christopher Conlon,	do.	Ballinamallard,
	820	John Carey,	do.	Gortgarvin & anr.
	821	Do.,	do.	Ballinamallard,
	822	James McVitty,	do.	Gortgarvan,
	823	Do.,	do.	Ballinamallard,
	824	James Maguire,	Thomas Dickson and others,	Fallow,
	825	Peter Maguire,	do.	do.
	826	Henry McCabe,	do.	Gortalum
	827	John McCabe,	do.	do.
	828	James Beatty,	do.	do.
	829	Redmond Cadden,	do.	Fallow,
	830	Hugh McCabe,	do.	do.
	831	Edward Brown,	William K. Blair,	Lenney,
	832	George Downey,	do.	Cloghmullin,

FERMANAGH.

Extent of Holding Statute.	Poor Law Valuation.	Former Rent.	Judicial Rent.	Observations.	Value of Tenancy.
A. R. P.	£ s. d.	£ s. d.	£ s. d.	£ s. d.	£ s. d.
16 0 0	7 13 0	13 0 0	11 0 0		
[illegible] 1 1	[illegible] 6 0	14 0 0	13 10 0		
[illegible] 3 0	24 13 0	[illegible] 0 0	[illegible] 0 0		
5 1 12	4 0 0	6 6 0	4 7 0	Rent changed in 1874 from . . . [illegible]	
25 0 0	4 0 0	5 10 0	4 0 0		
12 0 2	6 5 0	10 0 0	7 7 0		
31 0 [illegible]	31 0 0	35 0 0	31 0 0	1880 [illegible]	
40 3 [illegible]	19 10 0	[illegible] 15 0	25 11 0	Provision has been made in this case to [illegible] a labourer.	
44 2 11	37 0 0	45 0 0	35 0 0	do.	
43 1 0	39 10 0	35 18 0	35 10 0		
19 0 20	16 18 0	21 0 0	20 0 0		
10 5 0	11 10 0	10 18 5	8 10 0		
13 3 35	8 0 0	5 10 10	7 12 6		
[illegible] 3 25	13 10 0	13 15 0	11 0 0		
17 1 25	10 10 0	11 3 0	9 10 0		
8 0 0	7 5 0	8 14 5	7 10 0		
22 1 30	20 10 0	18 7 0	15 2 0		
4 1 30	1 15 0	4 0 0	3 10 0		
[illegible] 0 0	16 15 0	15 0 4	14 17 0		
16 3 13	14 5 0	13 17 0	11 0 0		
10 0 21	15 15 0	20 5 10	13 10 0		
67 0 0	[illegible] 5 0	57 1 6	45 0 0		
5 0 30	2 15 0	3 15 6	2 5 0		
16 1 30	10 0 0	16 0 4	15 10 0		
[illegible] 0 20	[illegible] 10 0	[illegible] 4 4	[illegible] 11 0		
45 1 16	24 5 0	40 0 0	35 10 0	do.	
15 0 37	6 10 0	8 10 0	7 10 0		
10 2 [illegible]	7 10 0	7 7 0	7 7 0		
9 2 37	5 15 0	6 5 0	5 0 0		
10 0 6	6 16 0	5 0 0	6 10 0		
27 1 0	9 10 0	5 0 0	8 10 0		
6 1 24	8 0 0	3 1 3	2 15 0		
[illegible] 1 16	5 10 0	5 0 0	5 0 0		
19 0 10	10 10 0	13 [illegible] 0	11 15 0		
48 3 0	17 5 0	16 0 0	16 0 0		

COUNTY OF

Names of Assistant Commissioners by whom Cases were decided.	No.	Name of Tenant.	Name of Landlord.	Townland.
Assistant Commissioners—				
E. T. Crean (Legal). Stephen Maunsell. Edward Gahan. J. A. O'Kelly. J. Bellingham.	633	William Nixon, ...	William H. Lowry, ...	Raleigh, ...
	634	Margaret Downey, ...	do.	Lisnamallard, ...
	635	Ann Buchanan, ...	do.	Rathmore, ...
	636	James McCaffrey, ...	do.	Tattymoyle, ...
	637	Thomas Boggan, senior,	do.	Garvallagh, ...
	638	Andrew Cassidy, ...	do.	do. ...
	639	Thomas Tierney, ...	do.	Tattymoyle, ...
	640	John McDonald, ...	do.	do. ...
	641	James Tierney, ...	do.	Clodmoyle, ...
	642	William Devers, ...	do.	Lisnamallard, ...
	643	Bernard Graham, ...	do.	Lowry, ...
	644	William Carroll, ...	James Moutray and others,	Killynaley, ...
	645	John Smith, ...	do.	do. ...
	646	Patrick Cassidy, ...	James Walsh, ...	Knockaleenet, ...
	647	James Quigley, ...	Col. J. G. Irvine, ...	Stranadariff, ...
	648	Felix Monaghan, ...	do.	Barragh, ...
	649	James O'Hara, ...	do.	Mannaghbeg, ...
	650	Margaret Markey, ...	do.	Drumbughey, ...
	651	William Watson, ...	do.	do. ...
	652	James Brown, ...	do.	Glenn, ...
	653	John Connolly, ...	do.	do. ...
	654	Pat Monaghan, ...	do.	Drumummery, ...
	655	James McNulty, ...	Anderson H. Irvine, ...	Aghavaddan, ...
	656	Andrew Kerr, ...	Edward Armstrong, ...	Drumcaravastin,
	657	James Chisick, ...	Henry L. St. George, ...	Drumnamarin, ...
	658	Francis Maguire, ...	do.	do. ...
	659	Thomas Sproule, ...	do.	Kedrim, ...
	660	John Swift, ...	do.	Drumnaclard, ...
	661	Christopher Carey, ...	William D'Arcy Irvine, ...	Drumclain, ...
	662	Isabella Gray, ...	do.	Drumnahinlaing,
	663	John Maxwell, ...	do.	Drumbee, ...
	664	Robert Reid, ...	do.	Drumclabble, ...
	665	Robert Hughes, ...	do.	Drumclain, ...
	666	John Maguire, ...	W. Johnston, ...	Mongarlan, ...

FERMANAGH—continued.

Extent of Holding, Statute.	Poor Law Valuation.	Former Rent.	Judicial Rent.	Observations.	Value of Tenant-right
A. R. P.	£ s. d.	£ s. d.	£ s. d.	£ s. d.	£ s. d.
130 0 5	71 10 0	98 11 5	72 0 0		
19 [illegible] 6	14 15 0	26 12 8	16 4 0		
23 3 1	20 10 0	25 6 10	21 0 0		
30 1 15	28 5 0	31 13 5	27 17 6		
30 1 20	7 10 0	11 18 4	10 10 0		
19 0 [illegible]	11 6 8	18 0 0	15 15 0		
88 2 20	—	30 0 0	25 0 0	Rent changed in 1877 from . . . . 28 0 0. Provision has been made in statement as regards a labourer.	
17 1 20	12 0 0	13 0 0	13 7 0		
16 3 10	7 10 0	8 8 6	7 12 0		
23 0 20	20 0 0	29 16 7	26 8 0		
18 2 20	16 0 0	14 0 0	12 0 0		
8 0 15	7 8 0	10 0 0	[illegible]		
8 2 18	7 6 8	10 10 0	8 10 0		
23 0 0	3 3 0	5 0 0	5 0 0		
20 3 10	13 8 0	15 0 0	13 10 0	Rent changed in 1850 from . . . £ s. d. 16 0 0	
13 2 20	8 0 0	10 0 0	8 0 0		
22 1 28	14 15 0	18 0 0	15 0 0		
31 2 0	20 5 0	23 10 0	17 10 0	1870 20 0 0	
30 0 13	20 10 0	30 0 0	23 10 0	Provision has been made as regards a labourer.	
[illegible] 2 77	10 10 0	10 0 0	1 0 0	Rent changed in 1853 from . . . £ s. d. [illegible] 10 0	
13 0 26	6 10 0	12 0 0	5 12 0		
180 0 0	20 10 0	80 0 0	60 0 0	Provision has been made as regards a labourer.	
16 1 24	6 15 0	10 0 0	6 0 0	Rent changed in 1857 from . . . £ s. d. 8 3 0	
23 1 20	14 0 0	16 0 0	15 10 0		
16 2 25	13 5 0	17 6 0	16 7 0	1864 9 19 4	
85 3 19	63 18 0	85 16 0	56 0 0		
28 1 30	21 10 0	25 5 0	16 0 0	do. 10 13 0	
16 0 0	13 8 0	16 12 0	13 10 0		
33 2 10	31 15 0	33 0 0	32 15 0	1862 27 0 0	
44 0 10	42 10 0	46 0 0	41 0 0		
71 0 20	30 13 0	31 7 0	30 5 0	1858 18 4 6	
27 0 0	23 0 0	27 4 0	24 0 0		
8 0 10	7 0 0	7 14 0	9 8 0		
21 3 16	16 5 0	23 2 0	18 0 0		

COUNTY OF

Names of Assistant Commissioners by whom Cases were decided.	No.	Name of Tenant.	Name of Landlord.	Townland.
Assistant Commissioners— M. T. Cullan (Legal). Stephen M'Farlane, Richard Garland, J. A. O'Kelly. J. Blennerhassett.	867	John Wilson, —	Simon Lowry, — —	Lowry, —
	868	William M'Cann, —	Captain Barton, — —	Springtown, —
	869	Do. —	do. — —	Lowry, —
	870	James Ballard, —	Margaret Rounke, —	Cabbraun, —
	871	John Hennessy, —	John B. M'Crudy, —	Brookhill, —
	872	James Mullin, —	Miss Janet Barton, —	New Island, —
	873	Arthur O'Neill, —	Margaret A. Given, —	Brookhill, —
	874	Alexander Owens, —	do. — —	do. —
	875	Ellen Humphreys, —	Anne Jane Keys, — —	Rossnole, —
	876	Roger M'Hugh, —	do. — —	Killanewgan, —
	877	Do. — —	do. — —	Rossnole, —
	878	John Foster, —	Charles Barton, — —	Mullins, —
	879	James Foster, —	do. — —	do. —
	880	Anne M'Cabe, —	do. — —	do. —
	881	James Swanston and another,	do. — —	Rushin, —
	882	Thomas Brandon, —	Miss Anne Johnston and another, Guardians of James C. Johnston, a Minor.	Gortnagallon, —
	883	Roland Burge, —	do. — —	Drumhurry, —
	884	William Wood, —	do. — —	Drumnagreshal, —
	885	Terence M'Ardle, —	do. — —	Gortnagallon, —
	886	John Cahan, —	do. — —	Edenaquereranin,
	887	John Moore, —	do. — —	Derrygunna, —
	888	John Reid, — —	do. — —	Gortnagallon, —
	889	John M'Hugh, —	Edward Barton — —	Lergandoy, —
	890	Arthur Keenan, —	William Bird, — —	Killyhappy, —
	891	Thomas M'Cusker, —	Sir Alexander Armstrong, Bart.	Conglass, —
	892	James Burns, —	Charles W. Irvine, —	Gortgonnan, —
	893	Stephen Keon, —	Major F. Dacey, — —	Drumlasset, —
	894	Mary Lindsay, —	George C. Lendrum, —	Magheraboy, —
	895	John M'Hugh, —	Sir John Leslie, Bart., —	Drumaghmore, —
	896	William Johnston, —	do. — —	Dunagh, —
	897	John Reilly, —	Captain Mervyn Archdale, —	Gortacurra, —
	898	Terence Donnelly, —	do. — —	Rossan, —
	899	Robert Gray, —	do. — —	Whitehill, —
	900	James M'Elroy, —	do. — —	Bohill, —
	901	Robert Porter, —	do. — —	Kesnakeen, —

FERMANAGH—continued.

Extent of Holding. Statute Measure.	Poor Law Valuation.	Former Rent.	Judicial Rent.	Observations.	Value of Tenancy.
A. R. P.	£ s. d.	£ s. d.	£ s. d.		£ s. d.
43 1 30	26 10 0	40 0 0	30 0 0	By consent.	
13 3 36	—	12 7 0	10 0 0		
20 1 5	13 0 0	14 0 0	11 13 5		
40 1 20	22 10 0	28 0 0	22 0 0		
6 1 12	7 15 0	4 4 0	3 10 0		
9 0 35	3 0 0	4 0 9	4 0 0		
17 1 2	4 0 0	13 13 0	9 15 0		
18 1 13	9 15 0	11 14 0	8 0 0	Rent changed in 1871 from £ s. d. 5 0 0	
14 3 35	10 18 0	13 13 0	11 10 0		
19 3 10	6 10 0	13 13 0	10 16 0		
30 2 13	17 18 0	30 0 0	23 0 0		
14 0 9	6 5 0	8 2 0	7 10 0		
27 3 10	13 0 0	15 4 0	15 10 0		
32 0 30	19 10 0	14 7 2	14 0 0		
44 0 33	30 10 0	33 0 0	33 0 0	Lump 16 16 0	
67 0 31	24 10 0	27 2 0	27 1 0		
46 0 30	18 0 0	14 5 0	12 1 2		
27 0 30	10 0 0	11 6 0	10 0 0		
16 0 10	8 15 0	8 16 0	5 17 4		
22 1 17	8 15 0	12 0 0	8 0 0		
31 1 31	11 10 0	13 0 0	11 0 0		
38 0 10	14 5 0	18 0 0	16 15 0		
31 0 0	20 0 0	22 0 0	18 15 0	By consent.	
14 0 0	9 15 0	18 0 0	10 15 0	do.	
11 3 25	10 5 0	16 7 0	10 5 0		
25 3 15	15 0 0	17 11 0	14 10 0		
15 1 0	5 10 0	7 10 0	7 10 0		
29 1 30	20 0 0	21 8 11	17 0 0		
34 1 35	16 0 0	10 19 0	16 0 0		
30 1 10	15 0 0	17 0 5	15 15 0		
70 3 30	27 5 0	21 0 0	24 10 0		
19 1 26	6 15 0	9 0 0	7 0 0	do.	
61 1 5	20 10 0	33 0 0	25 0 0	do.	
16 3 20	7 5 0	8 13 0	6 15 0		
68 3 31	33 0 0	40 0 0	37 0 0		

COUNTY OF

Names of Assistant Commissioners by whom Cases were decided.	No.	Name of Tenant.	Name of Landlord.	Townland.
Assistant Commissioners—				
M. T. Crean (Legal). Stephen Mowbray. Richard Garland. J. A. O'Reilly. J. Blood-Smyth.	902	Archibald McFarland, ...	Charles R. James and ors., Assignees of John Allen.	Aghafad, ...
	903	Bernard McElroy, ...	do.	Raw, ...
	904	Andrew Kerr, ...	do.	do. ...
	905	John McFarland, ...	do.	do. ...
	906	Alexander McFarland,	do.	Aghafad, ...
	907	Philip Martin, ...	do.	do. ...
	908	Rachel McQuade, ...	W. Johnston, ...	[illegible], ...
	909	Thomas McQuade, ...	do.	do. ...
	910	Neal McQuade, ...	do.	do. ...
	911	John Kerr, ...	Edith C. Johnston, and anor., Guardians of Jas. C. Johnston.	[illegible],
	912	James Gallagher, ...	Benjamin M. Bloomfield, ...	[illegible], Lower,
	913	Owen Gallagher, ...	do.	do. ...
	914	John & Hugh Gallagher,	do.	do. ...
	915	Patrick Gallagher, ...	do.	do. ...
	916	[illegible] Gallagher, ...	do.	do. ...
	917	Edward [illegible], ...	do.	[illegible], ...
	918	Ann, Rep. of Denis Gallagher.	do.	[illegible] Lower.
	919	Denis [illegible], ...	do.	do. ...
	920	Michael [illegible], ...	do.	do. ...
	921	John McLoughlin, ...	do.	do. ...
	922	Felix Kerr, ...	do.	[illegible], ...
	923	Michael, Rep. of Andrew Early.	do.	[illegible], ...
	924	John Lennon, junior, ...	do.	do. ...
	925	John O'Brien, ...	William Johnston, ...	[illegible].
	926	William Johnston, ...	do.	do. ...
	927	[illegible] Johnston, ...	Marquis of Ely, ...	[illegible] and [illegible]
	928	James, Rep. of Patrick Gallagher.	do.	Carry, ...
	929	Patrick Campbell, ...	do.	[illegible], ...
	930	Do.	do.	do. ...
	931	James, Rep. of John [illegible].	do.	[illegible], ...
	932	Robert [illegible], ...	Captain M. Archdale, ...	[illegible].
	933	Andrew Kerr, ...	do.	[illegible], ...
	934	James [illegible], ...	do.	[illegible].
	935	George [illegible], ...	do.	do. ...
	936	Robert [illegible], ...	do.	do. ...

FERMANAGH—*continued.*

Extent of Holding. Statute.	Poor Law Valuation.	Former Rent.	Judicial Rent.	Observations.		Value of Tenancy.
A. R. P.	£ s. d.	£ s. d.	£ s. d.		£ s. d.	£ s. d.
18 3 20	11 18 0	15 8 0	11 0 0	(Rent changed in 1877 from		
30 3 31	15 11 0	16 18 9	10 0 0	1856	11 3 5	
4 3 17	3 10 0	6 17 6	5 7 6	do.	4 0 0	
18 1 0	10 15 0	16 0 0	11 10 0	do.	5 4 4	
10 0 30	5 18 0	17 13 4	11 10 0	1873	7 6 8	
7 3 10	6 0 0	7 3 4	5 0 0	1871	7 10 4	
3 0 32	1 10 6	1 3 4	1 10 6			
7 3 10	6 10 0	7 0 0	6 10 0			
6 0 0	6 15 0	8 0 0	8 10 0	1857	6 0 0	
35 1 30	19 5 0	19 12 0	15 0 0			
17 0 0	—	6 0 0	8 10 0			
16 0 16	6 10 0	5 0 0	6 10 0	1850	3 13 0	
64 0 31	—	4 10 0	4 10 0	1853	3 11 0	
17 2 37	—	6 7 0	6 0 0	do.	3 12 0	
24 1 31	3 15 0	6 10 0	6 10 0	do.	6 0 0	
18 2 0	4 18 0	6 10 0	6 11 0			
20 3 37	4 10 0	6 0 0	5 0 0			
3 1 13	—	1 0 0	1 0 0			
7 3 25	3 0 0	9 11 0	8 10 0			
2 0 0	1 0 0	1 7 6	1 7 6			
19 0 0	1 10 6	6 0 0	8 15 0			
15 1 10	3 5 0	3 18 0	5 0 0			
18 1 3	3 18 0	4 12 4	4 0 0			
14 0 0	4 0 0	6 0 0	4 0 0	do.	9 15 0	
87 3 20	22 10 0	30 0 0	17 10 0			
65 2 1	20 18 0	30 15 4	18 0 0			
18 1 20	8 0 0	11 10 0	6 10 0			
87 1 25	20 0 0	30 0 0	25 11 0			
32 0 5	20 10 0	30 0 0	18 7 5			
64 0 30	33 5 0	35 0 0	30 0 0			
5 1 13	3 0 0	4 0 0	3 0 0			
17 2 13	3 10 0	6 0 0	4 6 0			
17 0 0	5 5 0	10 15 0	5 5 0			
3 2 5	—	3 10 0	3 0 0			
44 0 0	11 10 0	16 0 0	13 15 0			

COUNTY OF

Names of Assistant Commissioners by whom Cases were decided.	No.	Name of Tenant.	Name of Landlord.	Townland.	
Assistant Commissioners— M. T. Crean (Legal). Stephen Mowbray. Richard Garland. J. A. O'Kelly. J. Blennerhassett.	937	William Ferguson, jun.,	Captain M. Archdale, ...	Clonglaw,	—
	938	John Kerr, ...	do.	Urvanbeg,	—
	939	Bridget Burns, Rep. of John Burns,	Benjamin [illegible],	Larkhill, Castlecaldwell Estate,	
	940	William Gallagher, ...	do.	Garvary,	—
	941	Mary Muldoon, ...	do.	Castlecaldwell Estate.	
	942	Mary Monaghan, Rep. of James Monaghan,	do.	Schaids, Upper,	
	943	Bridget Burns, Rep. of Felix Burns,	do.	Larkhill,	—
	944	Bridget Gallagher, ...	do.	Scardans, Lower,	
	945	Michael Burns, ...	do.	Castlecaldwell Estate.	
	946	Denis Flanagan, ...	Marquis of Ely, ...	Magheramenagh,	
	947	Pat Campbell, ...	do.	do.	—
	948	James Elliott, ...	do.	Mangro,	—
	949	William Breen, ...	do.	Glen, West,	—
	950	Robert Carson, ...	Rev. George V. Dowell, ...	Garrison,	—
	951	James Haldane, ...	do.	do.	—
	952	Owen Elms, ...	Edith G. Johnston & another, Guardians of James G. Johnston, a Minor,	Tawnymanus,	—
	953	Patrick Davis, ...	do.	Drumskiller,	—
	954	Pat Burns, ...	do.	Corgolagh,	—
	955	Thomas Gallagher, ...	Archibald Collum, ...	Keenaghan,	—
	956	Michael Duffy, ...	Claudius Morris, ...	—	
	957	Edward Berry, ...	do.	Ballinamallard,	—
	958	Thomas Elliott, ...	do.	Brittonsbay,	—
	959	Irvine Wilson, ...	Robert Collum, ...	Cranaroragh,	—
	960	James Corrigan, ...	do.	do.	—
	961	Hugh Leamy & Bernard Leamy,	do.	Ballintemple,	—
	962	John Muldoon, ...	do.	do.	—
	963	Francis Clegg, ...	do.	Drumkeen,	—
	964	Terence McKenna, ...	do.	Carrowmacnagh,	—
	965	Terence Maher, ...	do.	do.	—
	966	John Monaghan, ...	do.	Oakleigh,	—
	967	James Crawford, ...	do.	Tamlaght,	—
	968	Robert Beatty, ...	Rupert F. Collum, ...	Clonaghan,	—
	969	Archibald Carrothers, ...	George Barton and Hannah Barton,	Whitehigue Glebe,	
	970	John Carrothers, ...	J. G. V. Porter, ...	Farnaught,	—
				Total,	—

FERMANAGH—*continued.*

Extent of Holding Statute.	Poor Law Valuation.	Former Rent.	Judicial Rent.	Observations.	Value of Tenancy.
A. R. P.	£ s. d.	£ s. d.	£ s. d.	£ s. d.	£ s. d.
83 0 20	87 8 0	42 0 0	35 5 0		
49 0 10	30 0 0	36 0 0	12 15 0		
18 0 10	3 5 0	3 10 0	4 8 0		
11 0 1	4 10 0	7 10 0	4 10 0		
8 2 36	5 5 0	5 10 0	8 15 0		
8 1 23	3 0 0	3 11 7	3 10 0		
3 3 32	8 8 0	2 0 6	1 18 0		
17 3 32	3 7 0	3 15 0	3 7 0		
3 2 0	8 0 0	2 0 8	1 10 0		
84 1 30	18 10 0	17 10 0	11 0 0		
187 2 20	58 10 0	82 0 0	35 0 0		
16 3 13	5 0 0	8 3 4	0 15 0	Rent changed in 1857 from . . . 8 0 0	
81 0 35	10 18 0	13 10 2	9 15 0	1859 7 10 0	
18 0 6	7 0 0	6 0 6	7 5 0		
37 0 20	21 0 0	10 10 7	9 5 0		
16 0 25	8 10 0	6 8 0	6 8 6		
86 3 34	17 0 0	20 16 0	17 0 0		
8 2 4	1 15 0	8 8 0	0 0 0	1861 6 0 0	
86 3 21	63 0 0	100 0 0	88 15 0	1870 90 10 [illegible]	
31 0 0	10 10 0	13 0 0	10 10 0		
8 0 30	6 10 0	10 15 0	7 14 0		
83 2 29	26 0 0	29 5 0	24 10 0	1830 17 [illegible] 0	
85 0 17	9 5 0	18 0 0	12 0 0		
82 3 0	85 0 0	30 0 0	28 0 0		
85 0 15	20 18 0	38 0 0	27 5 0		
20 2 35	24 10 0	30 0 0	20 0 0		
64 3 8	30 10 0	41 0 0	38 0 0		
36 1 0	14 15 0	23 10 0	16 0 0		
17 1 27½	10 10 0	13 10 0	10 10 0		
19 2 36	10 5 0	13 0 0	14 0 0		
8 3 5	8 0 0	10 10 0	8 0 0		
87 3 10	14 10 0	22 10 0	18 5 0		
57 2 19	15 10 0	18 0 0	18 10 0		
12 1 10	25 10 0	56 10 10	33 10 0		
4,201 2 8	1,420 10 7	3,967 2 8	2,472 0 0		

Names of Assistant Commissioners by whom Cases were decided.	No.	Name of Tenant.	Name of Landlord.	Townland.
Assistant Commissioners— H. J. Hanlan (Legal). James Hewn. Hugh Johnston. Andrew Hemphill. G. A. Pringle.	1309	Samuel Jackson, ...	Jacob Jackson, ...	Beraw, ...
	1310	Jacob Turkitt, ...	William Tillie, ...	Drumsdery, ...
	1311	Elizabeth Kerr, ...	Captain R. Olpherts, ...	Ballyrenney, ...
	1312	Margaret McCloskey, ...	do.	do. ...
	1313	John Thompson & others,	Elizabeth Twigg and others,	Dreenagh, ...
	1314	Michael Hallen, ...	William Osborne, ...	Ballyhargan, ...
	1315	Samuel Young, ...	Andrew Ogilvy, ...	Drumraighland,
	1316	John Blair, ...	Richard King, ...	Little Derry, ...
	1317	James Boyle, ...	Stewart H. Bruce, ...	Magheramore, ...
	1318	John Mullan, ...	Robert Proctor and another,	Templemoyle, ...
	1319	Patrick Hampson, ...	do.	do. ...
	1320	Patrick Sharvey, ...	John McCoy, ...	Ballyhargan, ...
	1321	Robert Devlin, ...	do.	do. ...
	1322	James Kerr, ...	Adam Wray, ...	Derryfloe, ...
	1323	William Irwin, ...	Isabella Jackson, ...	Hill Head and another.
	1324	Joseph Quigley, ...	James Wray and another, ...	Bovane, ...
	1325	Charles Rainey, ...	George Cather and others, Trustees of William Cather,	Leck, ...
	1326	John Conway, ...	John Semple, ...	Rannabough, ...
	1327	John Orr, ...	do.	do. ...
	1328	Henry Mallon, ...	Robert James Cook and another.	Templemoyle, ...
	1329	Do.	do.	do. ...
	1330	John McMann, ...	do.	do. ...
	1331	John Moorhead, ...	William Tillie, ...	Tullygarran and another.
	1332	Hamilton McMaster, ...	do.	Ardkelly, ...
	1333	Samuel Mullan, ...	do.	Tullygarran, ...
	1334	William Adams, ...	do.	Tullygarran and another.
	1335	Robert Dysart, ...	do.	do. ...
	1336	Mathew McElhenny, ...	do.	Streeborough, ...
	1337	William Henry, ...	do.	Dirtagh, ...
	1338	John Irwin, ...	do.	Drumsdery, ...
	1339	Robert Stewart, ...	do.	Tullygarran and another.
	1340	Henry Stewart, ...	do.	Lismagrill, ...
	1341	Josiah McClenaghan, ...	Marquis of Waterford, ...	Drumachose, ...
	1342	James McLenaghan, ...	do.	do. ...
	1343	Edward McCloskey, ...	do.	Gortgarn, ...

LONDONDERRY.

Extent of Holdings. Statute.	Poor Law Valuation.	Former Rent.	Judicial Rent.	Observations.	Value of Tenancy.
A. R. P.	£ s. d.	£ s. d.	£ s. d.		£ s. d.
21 1 20	8 0 0	27 0 0	11 0 0		
39 3 16	26 0 0	41 3 6	[illegible] 0 0		
41 1 18	18 9 0	18 13 0	18 10 0		
49 3 8	11 5 0	16 16 7	15 0 0		
51 3 14	22 0 0	20 10 0	[illegible] 10 0		
25 0 0	10 0 0	13 7 10	13 0 0		
36 1 10	4 15 0	8 1 0	0 0 0		
32 0 3	12 15 0	23 0 0	29 0 0		
137 0 0	43 18 0	46 0 0	47 0 0		
453 3 10	18 10 0	21 0 0	[illegible] 0 0		
129 3 11	18 10 0	25 0 0	17 10 0		
16 2 15	7 5 0	11 8 8	9 10 0		
6 3 0	4 8 0	4 10 0	3 15 0		
8 1 3	3 15 0	7 0 0	8 0 0		
7 0 6	3 5 0	13 0 0	9 15 0		
36 0 0	6 10 0	12 0 0	20 10 0		
67 0 0	1 10 0	5 0 0	5 0 0		
14 0 30	10 0 0	18 0 0	11 10 0		
85 3 6	22 15 0	36 0 0	28 10 0		
30 0 0	7 15 0	18 0 0	19 0 0		
85 0 0	8 13 0	19 16 4	15 0 0		
35 0 0	8 15 0	15 0 0	13 0 0		
85 3 34	30 0 0	45 6 4	37 0 0		
47 3 15	40 0 0	57 14 0	40 10 0		
15 1 10	13 0 0	17 1 0	13 0 0		
35 0 0	23 3 0	28 16 8	27 0 0		
30 0 0	23 0 0	28 3 1	23 0 0		
47 0 8	16 10 0	17 17 9	16 10 0		
43 3 28	37 0 0	30 16 8	24 0 0		
57 1 29	63 0 0	61 12 8	[illegible] 0 0		
61 0 18	39 10 0	73 0 4	61 0 0		
71 2 30	49 10 0	60 4 8	44 0 0		
38 3 28	14 15 0	15 0 0	11 10 0		
36 0 20	7 5 0	7 10 0	7 10 0		
32 3 10	19 0 0	28 0 0	18 0 0		

COUNTY OF

Names of Assistant Commissioners by whom Cases were decided.	No.	Name of Tenant.	Name of Landlord.	Townland.
Assistant Commissioners—				
G. H. Garstin (Legal). James Ross. Hugh Jefferson. Andrew Spencer. G. A. Fenwick.	1344	Neal McHenry, ...	Marquis of Waterford, ...	Gortgarn, ...
	1345	Edward Conway, ...	do.	do. ...
	1346	Patrick Farrell, ...	do.	[illegible], ...
	1347	Henry Irwin, ...	do.	Ballyrum, ...
	1348	Patrick Farrell, ...	do.	do. ...
	1349	Johnstone Love, ...	do.	Ballyrum, ...
	1350	James White, ...	do.	Drumtamm, Upper,
	1351	James Logan, ...	do.	[illegible], ...
	1352	John Kelly, ...	do.	Drumgrowny, ...
	1353	John Kyle, ...	do.	[illegible] Walks,
	1354	Hugh O'Connor, ...	do.	Drumnaw, Upper
	1355	Patrick Dougherty, ...	G. V. McCausland, ...	Tawnn, ...
	1356	James Harkness, ...	do.	Drumramdale, ...
	1357	John McLeod, ...	do.	Ranky, ...
	1358	Do.	do.	Drummamore and another.
	1359	Do., ...	do.	Glenkeen, ...
	1360	Samuel Steward, ...	do.	Carrowclare, ...
	1361	John Martin, ...	do.	Drumore, ...
	1362	Frederick Arbuckle, ...	do.	Mulbrough, ...
	1363	Bradford T. Arbuckle,	do.	Tully, ...
	1364	Thomas Smith, ...	do.	Drummond, ...
	1365	Anne Shannon, ...	do.	Bratcock, ...
	1366	Joseph Mullen, ...	do.	Ballymully, ...
	1367	Joseph White, ...	do.	do. ...
	1368	James McLeod, ...	do.	Drummond, ...
	1369	George Neely, ...	do.	Carran, ...
	1370	Alexander McCorkell and another.	do.	Drumalarney, ...
	1371	William Mitchell, ...	Miss Anne Henderson and others.	Tamnymullan, ...
	1372	Robert Whiteside, ...	H. F. Lloyd and another, Trustees of James Darbishire.	Kilcronaghan,
	1373	Marshall M. Craig, ...	do.	Fallaward, ...
	1374	Henry Hegan, ...	do.	Gorteeny, ...
	1375	Do., ...	do.	do. ...
	1376	John Boyd, ...	do.	Muff, ...
	1377	Do., ...	do.	do. ...
	1378	James Thompson, ...	do.	Muff and another,

LONDONDERRY—*continued.*

Extent of Holding. Statute.	Poor Law Valuation.	Former Rent.	Judicial Rent.	Observations.		Value of Tenancy.
A. R. P.	£ s. d.	£ s. d.	£ s. d.		£ s. d.	£ s. d.
16 3 16	9 0 0	11 0 0	8 15 0			
43 0 0	19 5 0	20 12 0	16 15 0			
20 0 0	7 10 0	6 10 0	5 0 0			
43 1 13	14 15 0	20 10 0	15 10 0			
61 3 3	40 0 0	44 0 0	35 0 0			
31 2 31	15 10 0	20 14 6	16 5 0			
20 3 15	11 10 0	14 0 0	11 11 0			
46 1 35	20 10 0	22 10 0	16 0 0			
18 3 36	12 0 0	11 0 0	9 5 0			
39 1 20	30 0 0	61 10 0	41 10 0			
43 3 0	26 5 0	30 0 0	25 0 0			
24 0 0	7 15 0	10 0 0	7 7 6			
68 3 10	37 6 0	81 5 6	50 10 0			
50 1 24	40 5 0	60 7 0	55 5 0			
106 3 0	32 5 0	37 0 0	30 0 0	Rent changed in 1875 from . .	31 4 11	
17 0 8	45 15 0	45 0 0	45 0 0			
96 0 0	37 10 0	64 2 0	55 0 0			
24 2 0	6 5 0	0 0 0	6 10 0			
65 0 0	37 0 0	37 10 0	35 0 0			
20 1 20	14 15 0	18 10 0	15 10 0			
8 1 16	5 0 0	4 12 0	4 0 0			
30 3 30	25 0 0	48 0 0	34 0 0			
31 3 0	14 3 0	20 7 6	16 11 0			
20 3 20	11 0 0	19 1 0	16 0 0			
80 3 18	90 0 0	80 10 9	65 0 0			
47 2 0	63 15 0	73 0 0	63 0 0			
19 0 12	33 10 0	46 0 0	37 0 0			
8 0 0	4 8 0	0 16 0	5 10 0			
16 1 20	18 0 0	18 0 0	10 0 0			
47 0 14	35 15 0	34 0 0	31 0 0	1856	20 0 0	
14 3 10	12 10 0	17 0 0	15 0 0			
33 1 4	33 5 0	31 0 0	27 0 0			
8 1 18	12 14 0	15 0 0	11 0 0			
41 1 25	20 15 0	33 2 0	18 0 0	1863	20 0 0	
43 1 8	57 3 0	31 0 0	25 0 0			

COUNTY OF

Name of Assistant Commissioners by whom Case was decided.	No.	Name of Tenant.	Name of Landlord.	Townland.
Assistant Commissioners—				
G. H. Gamble (Legal). James Ross. Hugh Jamieson. Andrew Brechin. G. A. Fowler.	1379	Joseph Henry, ...	R. P. Lloyd and another, Trustees of James Davidson,	Moss, ...
	1380	John Acheson, ...	William F. Bigger, ...	Glenarland, ...
	1381	John Robinson, ...	do.	Derryallen, ...
	1382	Robert McCloskey, ...	do.	Derryallen, Upper and Lower
	1383	James Holmes, ...	James Stevin, ...	Lurgyvagh, ...
	1384	Robert James Irwin, ...	G. T. McCausland, ...	Glenaragh & other,
	1385	Thomas Smith, ...	do.	Gabery, ...
	1386	John G. Allison, Executor of George McIlreen,	John and Robert J. Irwin, ...	Terrydrum, ...
	1387	Thomas McClelland, ...	do.	do. ...
	1388	Brian Mitchell, ...	John Walls, ...	Rossgarran, ...
	1389	Daniel Diamond, ...	Dr. Andrews Beathers, Trustees of John O'Neill, deceased.	Gorragh, ...
	1390	Felix McLaren, ...	do.	do. ...
	1391	Patrick Lowery, ...	do.	do. ...
	1392	Douglas Kennedy, ...	James Adams, ...	Lisnagleeve, ...
	1393	James Lowder, ...	do.	Altnagelvin, ...
	1394	William McCrory, ...	do.	do. ...
	1395	Alexander Mitchell, ...	John McCloskey, ...	Upper Gallagh,
	1396	Rose O'Kane, ...	The Skinners' Company, ...	Altinderry, ...
	1397	Susan Brown, ...	do.	do. ...
	1398	Mathew Chambers, ...	do.	Ardground, ...
	1399	Do.	do.	do. ...
	1400	Henry Dempsey, ...	do.	Roughery Hill and another,
	1401	William Robinson, ...	Edward Stevenson, ...	Loughagh, ...
	1402	Samuel Mitchell, ...	do.	do. ...
	1403	James Moulden, ...	Campbell Cameron & another, Trustees of Mrs. Elizabeth Hall, otherwise McIntyre	Ballynagvigan, ...
	1404	Patrick Walls, ...	do.	do. ...
	1405	Bridget McErlean, ...	do.	do. ...
	1406	Michael McKeown, ...	do.	do. ...
	1407	John Conlon, ...	do.	do. ...
	1408	John McEldowney, ...	do.	do. ...
	1409	Michael O'Neill, ...	do.	do. ...
	1410	James McKay, ...	Patrick O'Connor, ...	Derrymadore, ...
	1411	John Hattick, ...	Robert Stevenson, ...	Carnafern, ...
	1413	Hugh McHenry, ...	Marquis of Waterford, ...	Gortgarn, ...
	1415	John Given, ...	George Kerr, ...	Carrowdy, ...

LONDONDERRY—*continued.*

Extent of Holding. Statute.	Poor Law Valuation.	Former Rent.	Judicial Rent.	Observations.	Value of Tenancy.
A. R. P.	£ s. d.	£ s. d.	£ s. d.	£ s. d.	£ s. d.
[illegible] 3 [illegible]	33 0 0	40 0 0	41 0 0	Rent changed in 18[illegible] from 47 10 0	
[illegible] 3 [illegible]	60 10 [illegible]	84 [illegible] [illegible]	[illegible]		
61 1 0	30 [illegible] 0	[illegible] 0 0	43 [illegible] 0	18[illegible] 46 0 0	
[illegible] 3 25	34 5 0	71 [illegible] [illegible]	18 10 [illegible]		
[illegible] 3 15	16 [illegible] 0	[illegible] 0 0	13 [illegible] 0		
34 [illegible] 10	33 10 0	78 15 0	73 13 [illegible]		
125 0 0	31 [illegible] 0	1[illegible] 0 0	16[illegible] 0 0		
4 3 30	1 5 0	[illegible]	4 16 [illegible]		
36 [illegible] 10	15 0 [illegible]	27 10 [illegible]	16 15 [illegible]		
7 3 [illegible]	5 0 0	[illegible] [illegible] 0	[illegible]		
1 [illegible] 0	0 10 0	2 [illegible] [illegible]	1 3 [illegible]		
[illegible] 3 [illegible]	—	1 17 [illegible]	1 3 5		
3 1 20	—	3 [illegible] 0	1 [illegible] [illegible]		
[illegible] 1 22	57 0 0	71 1 [illegible]	[illegible] 0 0		
[illegible] 3 [illegible]	[illegible] 0 [illegible]	47 16 6	[illegible]	1871 [illegible] 12 11	
13 0 36	11 10 0	[illegible] [illegible] 0	33 [illegible] [illegible]		
17 [illegible] 0	[illegible] 10 0	[illegible]	36 10 0		
[illegible] 0 [illegible]	11 [illegible] 0	18 [illegible] [illegible]	11 [illegible] [illegible]		
16 [illegible] 15	[illegible] 5 0	10 [illegible] [illegible]	7 [illegible] [illegible]		
61 1 0	[illegible] 10 0	[illegible] [illegible] 0	30 0 [illegible]		
63 1 20	[illegible] 10 0	[illegible] [illegible] 0	[illegible] 10 0		
71 0 [illegible]	[illegible] 4 0	61 12 0	[illegible] [illegible] 0		
5 0 18	—	[illegible]	1 10 [illegible]		
14 0 [illegible]	—	10 0 0	[illegible] 0 [illegible]		
3 3 10	1 10 0	3 0 [illegible]	1 7 [illegible]		
11 [illegible] 0	13 5 [illegible]	15 [illegible] 4	10 16 [illegible]		
1 [illegible] 26	1 5 0	[illegible] [illegible] 6	1 [illegible] [illegible]		
[illegible] [illegible] 16	3 10 0	3 10 [illegible]	1 14 [illegible]		
4 [illegible] 0	1 [illegible] [illegible]	4 0 5	[illegible] 3 0		
7 3 [illegible]	5 10 0	7 14 10	5 0 [illegible]		
[illegible] 3 35	[illegible] [illegible] 0	[illegible] 10 6	3 5 [illegible]		
11 0 0	5 16 0	[illegible] [illegible] 0	5 [illegible] 0		
16 3 33	11 5 0	13 0 0	13 [illegible] [illegible]		
[illegible] 0 0	14 1 0	17 0 0	15 5 [illegible]		
[illegible] 1 20	13 0 0	17 10 0	15 [illegible] 0		

Names of Assistant Commissioners by whom Cases were decided.	No.	Name of Tenant.	Name of Landlord.	Townland.
Assistant Commissioners—				
G. H. Gamble (Legal). James Ross. Hugh Jefferson. Andrew Spiers. G. A. Pringle.	1414	Patrick McCafferty, ...	George Ross, ...	Gortnagy, ...
	1415	John McMillan, ...	do.	Sellan, ...
	1416	Daniel Gallagher, ...	do.	do. ...
	1417	Edward Lynch, ...	do.	Fedan, ...
	1418	Betty McElhinney, ...	do.	Stranagalwilly, ...
	1419	Denis McCafferty, ...	do.	Dunsilly, ...
	1420	James Morrison, ...	do.	Lisnaharney, ...
	1421	Ann Brown, ...	George Crawford, ...	Aughnaglaveny, ...
	1422	Samuel Reay, ...	Frederick Browne and ors., Trustees of Col. H. F. Browne,	Derrygarve, ...
	1423	James Gribben, ...	do.	Creagh, ...
	1424	John Meekle, ...	do.	do. ...
	1425	Robert Chalmers, ...	do.	Derrygarve, ...
	1426	Mary Ann Lawrence, ...	do.	do. ...
	1427	James O'Neill, ...	do.	Creagh, ...
	1428	John Logan, ...	Julia [illegible], ...	Moyagall, ...
	1429	Edward McAtamney, ...	do.	do. ...
	1430	James Kennedy, ...	William J. Hutchinson, ...	Ballymaguigan, ...
	1431	William Taggart, ...	do.	do. ...
	1432	James Boyle, ...	John S. [illegible], ...	Gulladuff, ...
	1433	William J. [illegible], ...	do.	do. ...
	1434	John Houston, ...	do.	do. ...
	1435	Do., ...	do.	do. ...
	1436	Charles Quin, ...	William H. Harris, ...	Lemnaroy, ...
	1437	William Martin, ...	James McQuillan, ...	Lisduff, ...
	1438	James Kealey, ...	David S. Kelly, ...	Ballymacombs [illegible],
	1439	Charles Bradley, ...	do.	do. ...
	1440	Robert Taylor, ...	John Johnston, ...	Slaghtneill, ...
	1441	James Alexander, ...	Robert William Newton, ...	Tyanee, ...
	1442	John Lennox, ...	The Mercers' Company, ...	[illegible], ...
	1443	Robert Bailey, ...	Joseph Marshall, ...	Curragh, ...
	1444	William Hogg, ...	Sir Thomas Bateson, Bart., and another,	Ballymaguigan, ...
	1445	Peter Kelly, ...	Edward H. C. [illegible], ...	Hockery, ...
	1446	John Walkinshaw, ...	do.	Mullagh, ...
	1447	John Nelson, ...	do.	[illegible], ...
	1448	Robert Kerr, ...	General William Stuart, ...	Mullaghboy, ...

LONDONDERRY—*continued.*

Extent of Holding. Statute.	Poor Law Valuation.	Former Rent.	Judicial Rent.	Observations.	Value of Tenancy.
A. R. P.	£ s. d.	£ s. d.	£ s. d.		£ s. d.
36 1 21	17 0 0	20 0 0	18 0 0		
12 2 36	14 5 0	18 0 0	15 10 0		
18 0 16	12 5 0	18 0 0	15 0 0		
8 3 10	8 5 0	10 0 0	7 12 0		
7 1 20	6 10 0	8 10 0	6 0 0		
60 0 19	28 15 0	41 0 0	33 0 0		
15 2 18	10 10 0	15 0 0	11 0 0		
11 3 0	8 5 0	10 0 0	10 10 0		
8 3 20	3 0 0	3 15 0	2 5 0		
6 0 16	5 5 0	6 13 0	6 10 0		
30 1 0	20 0 0	25 0 0	18 0 0		
27 0 0	15 0 0	18 7 0	14 0 0		
11 1 20	10 0 0	11 5 0	8 0 0		
3 0 0	—	5 0 0	1 10 0		
14 3 5	10 15 0	13 10 4	10 10 0		
9 0 14	8 10 0	8 13 8	6 15 0		
3 1 0	—	7 10 0	5 12 6	By consent.	
2 0 20	—	7 5 0	5 0 0	do.	
19 3 0	15 5 0	22 0 0	13 10 0		
16 3 0	6 10 0	9 11 0	6 10 0		
22 1 5	6 12 0	11 0 0	8 0 4		
18 2 20	17 0 0	19 0 3	14 5 0		
9 1 0	5 5 0	8 6 10	6 15 0		
3 0 0	—	6 0 0	4 10 0		
10 0 0	5 15 0	11 15 0	7 10 0		
6 2 5	5 0 0	5 5 0	5 5 0		
19 1 20	12 0 0	10 0 0	12 0 0		
3 3 16	3 10 0	5 10 0	5 10 0		
16 0 26	11 5 0	12 1 0	8 15 0		
13 3 23	8 13 0	12 0 0	8 0 0		
83 0 0	23 15 0	23 0 0	19 0 0		
13 0 0	8 13 0	13 10 0	9 5 0		
5 0 0	2 0 0	9 8 8	5 10 0		
20 0 0	17 10 0	10 15 0	9 0 0		
6 2 20	6 10 0	9 10 0	1 0 0		

Names of Assistant Commissioners by whom Cases were decided.	No.	Name of Tenant.	Name of Landlord.	Townland.
Assistant Commissioners—	1449	James Mitchell, ...	Robert Blair, ...	Ballyquigley, ...
G. H. Bartley (Legal). James Ross. Hugh Johnston. Andrew Spencer. C. A. Fitzgerald.	1450	Richard Hughes, ...	Charlotte A. Howard, ...	Rossgarron, ...
	1451	Edward Wade, ...	do.	do. ...
	1452	John Lowther, ...	Captain David Boyd, ...	Lisdillon, ...
	1453	Margaret Murphy, ...	Charlotte A. Howard, ...	Rossgarron, ...
	1454	James Douglas, ...	William Tillie, ...	Stonyburgh, ...
	1455	David Doole, ...	Jane Doole, ...	Lurgy, ...
	1456	Elizabeth Hood, ...	William Palmer, ...	Dungorough, ...
	1457	Bernard Wade, ...	John Dougherty, ...	Mayoglass, ...
	1458	Patrick Carr, ...	Robert Hughes, ...	Tullyveston, ...
	1459	James Fallon, ...	do.	Gortmore, ...
	1460	William Lister, ...	Sir Frederick W. Heygate, Bart.	Ballyrushlecky,
	1461	William Lister, Exor. of John Lister, deceased.	do.	Oughtymoyle and another,
	1462	Samuel Aitken, ...	do.	do. ...
	1463	John McDonald, ...	do.	Tamlaght & c.,
	1464	John Henderson, ...	John Elliott, ...	Fortwilliam, ...
	1465	James McLaughlin, ...	Isabella Harbison, ...	Ballyholly, ...
	1466	James Crossley, ...	The Salters' Company, ...	Moyamshinney,
	1467	Joseph Longbarge & others,	do.	Ballygillmoore,
	1468	Margaret Eakin, ...	do.	Ballygillmoore and another.
	1469	Robert Brown, ...	do.	Ballygillmoore,
	1470	Mary Cleary, ...	James S. Sheriff, ...	Moyard, ...
	1471	William Logan, ...	Robert Wright, ...	Mawillian, ...
	1472	Robert Whiteside, ...	do.	do. ...
	1473	John Johnston, ...	do.	do. ...
	1474	Samuel McCleery, ...	do.	do. ...
	1475	James Roe, ...	do.	do. ...
	1476	Thomas Hutchinson, ...	do.	do. ...
	1477	John Smillie, ...	William Smith, ...	Drumballyhagan,
	1478	Dorothy Palmer, ...	Richard Gilmore, ...	Lettrey, ...
	1479	Thomas Laycock, ...	F. Augustus St. G. Nicoll, ...	Glenmaquill and others.
	1480	William Miller, ...	Richard King and others, Trustees of Sir Samuel Martin.	Lisnamorrow, ...
	1481	Robert J. Gilmour, ...	do.	do. ...
	1482	John McElhone, ...	Rev. Canon Ball, ...	Ballynacross, ...
	1483	Samuel Brown, ...	Margaret Allen, ...	Londonderry, ...
				Total, ...

LONDONDERRY—continued.

Extent of Holding. Statute.			Poor Law Valuation.			Former Rent.			Judicial Rent.			Observations.	Value of Tenancy.
A.	R.	P.	£	s.	d.	£	s.	d.	£	s.	d.		£ s. d.
1	0	0	—			5	0	0	4	3	0		
30	0	30	37	10	0	34	14	0	27	0	0		
14	0	18	8	15	0	14	0	0	9	0	0		
30	0	0	13	10	0	30	10	0	24	10	0		
6	1	30	5	0	0	7	0	0	5	10	0		
167	0	0	11	10	0	14	17	10	11	17	10		
11	2	34	4	15	0	14	0	0	11	0	0		
5	1	0	7	0	0	10	0	0	7	10	0		
18	1	0	5	15	0	11	0	0	10	0	0		
17	1	20	9	0	0	8	18	6	8	10	0		
11	1	30	4	10	0	6	10	0	6	10	0		
30	1	36	17	10	0	22	0	0	17	0	0		
68	0	28	43	10	0	47	0	0	40	0	0		
364	3	10	111	10	0	131	14	0	106	0	0		
121	3	16	43	15	0	87	0	0	74	10	0	Provision has been made in this case as regards a labourer.	
13	1	10	—			34	0	0	30	0	0		
3	0	0	0	10	0	1	0	0	5	5	0		
41	1	17	43	13	0	35	13	0	34	0	0		
9	3	11	7	10	0	6	13	0	5	10	0		
61	1	26	35	0	0	34	11	0	27	0	0		
61	2	30	38	5	0	33	15	0	37	0	0		
197	3	18	13	10	0	13	0	0	11	0	0		
16	0	13	8	15	0	13	10	5	6	0	0		
6	1	30	3	0	0	3	15	3	3	0	0		
6	1	30	6	15	0	4	0	10	5	10	0		
6	3	10	3	0	0	0	0	6	3	0	0		
6	2	8	4	10	0	3	11	10	5	0	0		
6	2	4	4	10	0	4	10	0	4	0	0		
14	0	18	6	10	0	12	0	0	6	0	0		
14	2	38	5	15	0	15	0	0	12	0	0		
16	0	0	11	13	0	17	5	0	13	0	0		
60	2	11	38	0	0	48	11	8	46	17	5		
186	0	0	91	0	0	100	6	8	85	0	0		
8	3	14	6	0	0	7	0	0	5	18	0		
7	0	31	6	0	0	30	5	0	18	0	0		
2,014	0	7	3,191	17	6	3,520	11	8	6,240	0	5		

COUNTY OF

Names of Assistant Commissioners by whom Cases were decided.	No.	Name of Tenant.	Name of Landlord.	Townland.
Assistant Commissioners—				
L. Doyle (Legal). J. Hamilton. J. J. Gorry. J. T. Davys. G. H. Mitchell.	1228	Mary Hagans, ...	Reps. of late William Hagan,	[illegible], ...
	1229	Andrew Hagan, ...	Lord Plunket, ...	Drumone, ...
	1230	Samuel Hollinger, ...	do.	do. ...
	1231	Edward Smith, ...	Mrs. Fleming, ...	Glenish, ...
	1232	John Hanlon, ...	Mrs. M. Lees and others, ...	Kilmore, West, ...
	1233	Pat O'Hare, ...	Sir [illegible] Fowler, Bart., ...	Cloughbane, ...
	1234	Patrick Lennon, ...	John Dawson, ...	[illegible],
	1235	Patrick [illegible], ...	do.	do. ...
	1236	Hugh Boyland, ...	do.	do. ...
	1237	Redmond McMahon, ...	do.	do. ...
	1238	John McDonough, ...	do.	do. ...
	1239	Philip McGovern, ...	do.	do. ...
	1240	David Williamson, ...	do.	do. ...
	1241	Peter Conley, ...	do.	do. ...
	1242	Thomas Cleary, ...	do.	do. ...
	1243	James Stuart, ...	do.	do. ...
	1244	Do., ...	do.	do. ...
	1245	James McQuade, ...	Henry Crawford, Rep. of Henry Bewley,	[illegible], ...
	1246	Owen Brady, ...	do.	do. ...
	1247	Robert Dunne, ...	William R. Bradley, ...	Carragurt, ...
	1248	John McDonough, ...	do.	Moyrath, ...
	1249	Robert Hillis, ...	do.	Carragurt, ...
	1250	William Bradley, ...	do.	Drumroughill, ...
	1251	John McDonough, ...	do.	Moyrath, ...
	1252	Alexander Mulroy, ...	do.	Drumroughill, ...
	1253	Patrick McVey, ...	do.	Carragurt, ...
	1254	Charles Magill, ...	do.	do. ...
	1255	Charles Bradley, ...	do.	Drumroughill, ...
	1256	William Malarky, ...	do.	do. ...
	1257	John Miller, ...	do.	do. ...
	1258	Samuel Malarky, ...	do.	do. ...
	1259	Hugh Malarky, ...	do.	do. ...
	1260	Edward Gunning, ...	Most Rev. Lord Plunket, Bishop of Meath,	[illegible], ...

MONAGHAN.

Extent of Holding. Statute.	Poor Law Valuation.	Former Rent.	Judicial Rent.	Observations.	Value of Tenancy.
A. R. P.	£ s. d.	£ s. d.	£ s. d.	£ s. d.	£ s. d.
20 1 10	23 15 0	26 0 0	20 16 0		
13 0 0	28 0 0	10 18 6	15 7 1	Rent changed in 1867 from . . 14 19 9	
14 1 13	12 5 0	14 5 3	11 10 0		
6 3 10	6 0 0	8 0 0	5 10 0		
26 0 36	18 5 0	17 6 6	19 17 6		
23 1 36	19 10 0	21 3 3	16 7 6		
11 0 20	13 10 0	20 9 6	13 15 0		
16 0 34	11 0 0	14 1 0	10 15 0		
11 1 20	4 15 0	11 10 0	6 10 0		
5 0 25	3 10 0	4 0 0	3 11 6		
16 0 17	10 10 0	13 15 0	10 13 0		
6 0 1	1 18 0	3 17 9	2 15 0		
14 1 35	10 18 0	16 5 0	10 15 6		
11 1 0	8 0 0	16 10 0	5 0 0		
5 1 24	6 0 0	8 3 9	3 15 0		
6 2 30	5 0 0	6 1 0	8 5 0		
20 1 8	7 0 0	10 3 5	5 0 0		
13 1 9	0 10 0	10 15 0	5 0 0		
16 0 38	13 0 0	16 1 3	11 10 0		
4 2 15	3 5 0	3 13 7	3 0 0		
2 1 7	1 15 0	1 17 6	1 12 6		
4 1 24	3 0 0	4 1 1	3 10 0		
35 1 20	25 0 0	35 3 5	20 0 0		
4 1 3	3 15 0	4 10 0	3 0 0		
14 0 35	10 10 0	14 6 9	10 5 6		
16 0 17	8 5 0	11 18 10½	0 0 0		
11 0 6	7 16 0	10 5 8	6 3 8		
31 0 9	23 10 0	24 4 0	17 5 8		
15 1 30	9 0 0	12 3 8	9 10 0		
57 2 2	36 4 0	37 15 0	35 10 0		
14 2 18	10 13 0	14 6 6	11 0 0		
9 1 5	5 5 0	5 15 11	5 5 0		
13 3 17	14 0 0	15 2 8	11 12 6		

COUNTY OF

Names of Assistant Commissioners by whom Cases were decided.	No.	Name of Tenant.	Name of Landlord.	Townland.	
Assistant Commissioners—	1261	Robert Elliott, senior, ...	Most Rev. Lord Plunket, Bishop of Meath.	Drumbaghie,	...
L. Doyle (Legal).	1262	Andy Hagan, ...	do.	Umlaugh,	...
J. Fowler.					
J. J. Gooey.	1263	James McFarland, Rep. of Augustine McFarland.	do.	Killeen,	...
J. T. Davis.					
G. H. Mitchell.				Total,	...

COUNTY OF

Assistant Commissioners—					
Robert Fuller, Q.C. (Legal).	2354	Patrick Harron, ...	Mrs. Lowry, ...	Dungorone,	...
A. Blair.					
S. Byrne.	2355	James Duff, ...	Alexander G. Stuart, ...	Drumbarrick and others,	...
A. Montgomery.					
H. Sharkey.	2356	Robert Devine, ...	William Anderson, ...	Glenton,	...
	2357	Anne Alexander, ...	Robert H. Hamilton, ...	Aughnaclone,	...
	2358	James Reid, jun., ...	Mr. and Mrs. Montgomery, ...	Clenboro,	...
	2359	James McClean, ...	Rev. James Hamilton, ...	Cloggan,	...
	2360	Henry Duggin, ...	Joseph Goretony, ...	Tulnagel,	...
	2361	Mary Buckley, Rep. of Mathew Buckley,	Alexander G. H. McClelland,	Fenney,	...
	2362	William Steele, ...	Richard Close, ...	Kildress,	...
	2363	Duncan McAllister, ...	do.	do.	...
	2364	Robert Moneely, ...	Samuel Adams, ...	Cranghill,	...
	2365	John Dogherty, ...	Earl of Clanricarde, ...	Drumgeleny,	...
	2366	William Morgan, ...	Rev. James Hamilton, ...	Cloggan,	...
	2367	Thomas Henderson, ...	Oliver Sproule and others, Reps. of Charles Sproule,	Ballaghnes,	...
	2368	John Cheriston, ...	do.	do.	...
	2369	James Murray, ...	do.	do.	...
	2370	James Hogan, ...	Mr. and Mrs. Montgomery, ...	Glenbane,	...
	2371	William Kelly, ...	do.	Dohard,	...
	2372	Philip Hagan, ...	do.	Glenbane,	...
	2373	Bridget Cavanagh, ...	James Brown, ...	Syrvis,	...
	2374	Ferdinand Mallon, ...	do.	do.	...
	2375	James Long, ...	do.	Terrymullin,	...
	2376	Patrick McCabe, ...	do.	Drumramerd,	...
	2377	Edward Wilson, ...	do.	Terrymullin,	...
	2378	Thomas Dalson, ...	do.	Broughderry,	...
	2379	Alice Mallon, ...	do.	Syrvis,	...
	2380	Charles Barton, ...	do.	Garvaraham,	...

MONAGHAN—*continued.*

Extent of Holding, Statute.	Poor Law Valuation.	Former Rent.	Judicial Rent.	Observations.	Value of Tenancy.
A. R. P.	£ s. d.	£ s. d.	£ s. d.		£ s. d.
20 3 0	16 15 0	19 7 7	15 5 0		
73 1 31	37 10 0	29 13 8	18 10 0		
16 1 16	19 5 0	16 17 0	11 10 0		
396 2 37	407 7 0	500 0 6½	[illegible] 13 8		

TYRONE.

Extent of Holding, Statute.	Poor Law Valuation.	Former Rent.	Judicial Rent.	Observations.	Value of Tenancy.
				£ s. d.	
29 1 30	15 5 0	20 0 0	11 0 0	Rent changed in 1877 from 18 0 0; 1856 10 11 4	
18 1 0	8 15 0	11 12 0	8 10 0		
17 3 10	13 0 0	22 0 0	14 10 0		
14 2 25	11 5 0	11 15 0	10 15 0		
30 1 16	23 10 0	29 0 0	17 10 0	1867 22 0 0	
31 1 8	31 10 0	32 14 6	27 0 0		
10 0 0	—	13 10 0	0 0 0		
30 0 30	14 11 0	21 1 0	15 0 0		
67 0 0	31 0 0	33 0 0	27 0 0		
18 2 0	24 10 0	[illegible] 0 0	22 0 0		
11 2 0	5 5 0	11 17 6	5 10 0		
7 3 8	5 5 0	8 4 0	6 0 0		
14 2 0	11 5 0	16 15 0	11 10 0		
13 0 10	5 5 0	8 1 3	4 10 0		
24 2 30	7 0 0	10 16 3	7 0 0	1877 5 0 6	
30 2 10	6 15 0	13 15 0	8 10 0		
10 1 12	7 10 0	8 5 0	8 10 0	1865 6 16 7	
24 1 5	17 0 0	14 0 0	16 10 0		
16 0 30	10 10 0	19 17 0	7 5 0		
10 3 20	3 5 0	11 0 0	7 5 0	1877 9 0 0	
19 3 25	17 10 0	26 10 0	16 0 0	do. 17 10 0	
29 1 0	22 15 0	28 15 0	21 10 0	1874 24 10 0	
11 1 15	10 5 0	12 7 6	9 10 0	1867 10 16 0	
24 2 13	21 0 0	23 0 0	14 10 0	1875 22 17 2	
18 3 5	16 15 0	14 10 0	13 15 0	1877 15 1 8	
15 1 15	18 0 0	11 10 0	8 12 0	do. 10 5 0	
[illegible] 2 24	23 15 0	24 10 0	22 10 0	1878 31 0 0	

COUNTY OF

Names of Assistant Commissioners by whom Cases were decided.	No.	Name of Tenant.	Name of Landlord.	Townland.
Assistant Commissioners –				
[illegible], Q.C. (Legal). A. [illegible]. J. [illegible]. A. Montgomery. H. [illegible].	2381	Anne McLaughlin, ...	Rev. Christopher Irvine, ...	[illegible], ...
	2382	Michael McAnulty, ...	do.	do. ...
	2383	Charles Treacy, ...	Alexander G. S. [illegible],	Fearey, ...
	2384	Francis Teague, ...	do.	[illegible], ...
	2385	Edward Treacy, ...	do.	Fearey, ...
	2386	Thomas Harkin, ...	do.	do. ...
	2387	Peter Lennon, ...	Alexander G. Stewart, ...	Drumagil, ...
	2388	James McGlone, junior,	do.	do. ...
	2389	Bridget Kane, ...	do.	Derrymeen, ...
	2390	James McAleer, ...	do.	Drumagil, ...
	2391	Owen O'Neill, ...	do.	Derrymeen, ...
	2392	Patrick O'Neill, ...	do.	Dromore, ...
	2393	John Traynor, ...	do.	Derrymeen, ...
	2394	William Carry, ...	do.	do. ...
	2395	John [illegible], ...	do.	Dromore, ...
	2396	Francis McGuigan, ...	do.	[illegible], ...
	2397	Daniel McElroy, ...	John H. [illegible], ...	[illegible], ...
	2398	James O'Donnell, ...	do.	do. ...
	2399	Rev. Bernard Murphy, ...	Sir John M. Stewart, Bart., ...	[illegible], ...
	2400	Peter Corrigan, ...	do.	[illegible], ...
	2401	[illegible] McCluskey, ...	do.	[illegible], ...
	2402	Mary McCarron, ...	do.	do. ...
	2403	Michael McGarrity, ...	Henry E. H. Stewart, ...	[illegible], ...
	2404	Michael Rafferty, ...	do.	[illegible], ...
	2405	Michael Donnelly, ...	do.	Gortin, ...
	2406	Thomas Rafferty, ...	do.	[illegible], ...
	2407	Michael McCartan, ...	do.	do. ...
	2408	Terence McGarrity, ...	do.	do. ...
	2409	Patrick Rafferty, ...	do.	do. ...
	2410	Margaret Bradley, ...	do.	do. ...
	2411	John Rafferty, ...	do.	Gortin, ...
	2412	Mary Donnelly, Admx. of Patrick Donnelly.	do.	do. ...
	2413	James Nevin, ...	do.	[illegible], ...
	2414	John Loughran, ...	do.	Gortin, ...
	2415	Patrick Rafferty, ...	do.	[illegible], ...

TYRONE—*continued.*

Extent of Holding. Statute.	Poor Law Valuation.	Former Rent.	Judicial Rent.	Observations.		Value of Tenancy.
A. R. P.	£ s. d.	£ s. d.	£ s. d.		£ s. d.	£ s. d.
64 0 26	17 0 0	18 10 0	15 0 0			
17 0 0	9 12 0	11 0 2	9 10 0			
13 3 30	0 15 0	6 5 0	5 10 0			
65 0 0	18 0 0	28 0 0	19 0 0	Rent changed in 1866 from	23 10 0	
14 3 0	5 5 0	12 0 0	8 15 0			
67 1 30	17 5 0	20 0 0	16 15 0	1864	20 10 0	
11 1 26	8 10 0	9 16 0	7 15 0	1820	[illegible] 8 8	
10 3 11	10 0 0	10 15 0	8 0 0			
10 2 0	—	8 0 0	7 10 0			
7 2 20	6 0 0	8 15 0	6 15 0	1876	6 0 0	
8 1 0	—	6 18 0	5 15 0			
5 2 0	4 5 0	6 2 0	4 15 0			
20 1 8	—	15 16 0	11 10 0			
16 3 26	13 15 0	24 0 0	13 5 0	1836	13 17 [illegible]	
6 2 20	3 10 0	8 19 0	5 5 0			
7 0 19	7 10 0	8 0 0	6 5 0	do.	5 0 0	
30 3 4	19 15 0	30 0 0	15 0 0			
8 0 1	6 15 0	6 5 6	4 10 0			
19 1 25	11 10 0	16 0 0	7 8 0			
7 0 35	3 0 0	6 10 0	5 10 0			
14 0 30	5 5 0	10 0 0	7 5 0			
25 0 31	13 13 0	18 15 0	10 0 0			
18 2 20	9 15 0	17 0 0	7 15 0			
63 3 8	30 15 0	11 0 0	5 15 0	1874	20 0 0	
27 2 0	—	8 5 0	7 0 0	do.	5 5 0	
15 2 20	1 3 0	1 0 0	6 1 0	do.	7 8 0	
27 1 4	15 0 0	14 0 0	11 10 0	do.	17 6 8	
18 1 20	8 0 0	16 1 8	8 3 0	do.	7 17 6	
17 0 35	5 5 0	10 6 0	7 5 0	do.	7 15 0	
18 0 10	0 0 0	7 3 8	6 5 0	do.	6 12 0	
4 2 0	3 0 0	3 0 0	2 10 0	do.	1 10 8	
8 3 10	4 5 0	6 0 0	3 15 0	do.	4 11 —	
13 0 14	5 15 0	7 0 0	4 5 0	1873	4 3 0	
25 3 20	11 11 6	13 18 0	10 10 0			
14 3 35	5 7 0	9 17 0	8 0 0	1874	6 0 0	

COUNTY OF

Names of Assistant Commissioners by whom Cases were decided.	No.	Name of Tenant.	Name of Landlord.	Townland.
Assistant Commissioners—	2416	Michael Rafferty, ...	Henry B. H. Stewart, ...	Edenderry, ...
[illegible], Q.C. (Legal).	2417	Do., ...	do.	Gortin, ...
A. [illegible].	2418	Hugh Grimes, ...	do.	Edenderry, ...
S. Byrne.	2419	Patrick Hughes, ...	do.	do. ...
A. Montgomery.	2420	Michael Carney, ...	do.	Gortin, ...
H. Shearer.	2421	Bernard McCrory, ...	do.	Edenderry, ...
	2422	Peter McKernan, ...	R. F. Dale & others, Trustees of Martin's Estate,	Drumlamly, ...
	2423	Henry Charlton, ...	Francis McDon and others, ...	Tullyenney, ...
	2424	James Miller, ...	Edward E. Martin, ...	Lisnen, ...
	2425	Ellen Gamble & another,	John Love, ...	Edergoole, Upper,
	2426	Bridget McGurgan, ...	Alexander G. S. McCausland,	Cloughfin, ...
	2427	Patrick Toomey, ...	do.	Fanny, ...
	2428	Stephen McCormick, ...	do.	Cloghfin, ...
	2429	John McCullagh, ...	do.	do. ...
	2430	George Lambton, ...	Wm. Douglas and G. Douglas and others, Trustees of Charles W. Ogilby,	Lisnamlin, ...
	2431	Joseph Harkin, ...	Miss Rebecca Reynolds, ...	Skreen, ...
	2432	James Gill, ...	Martha Scott and another, ...	Aghindarragh, ...
	2433	Robert Henry, ...	Miss Maria S. Fleming, ...	Common Hall, ...
	2434	Hamilton S. Burrows, ...	do.	Roydstown, ...
	2435	Catherine Mallon, ...	James McGinty, ...	Cadney, ...
	2436	Dominick McAnespie, ...	do.	do. ...
	2437	Bridget Kelly, ...	Sarah Wilson, ...	Tullyvaryle, ...
	2438	John McAteer, ...	George H. Stack, ...	Mullaghmore, ...
	2439	Bernard McGovern, ...	do.	do. ...
	2440	William Forsey, ...	Mrs. Graham, ...	Killenaragh, ...
	2441	Michael Reid, ...	do.	do. ...
	2442	Patrick Reid, ...	do.	do. ...
	2443	William Gallen, ...	Major R. S. Hamilton, ...	Drumchimer, ...
	2444	Edward Slavin, ...	Donald H. Stewart, ...	Tullyclimagh, ...
	2445	Francis Rafferty, ...	Henry B. H. Stewart, ...	Edenderry, ...
	2446	John Maxwell, ...	John A. Galbraith, ...	Rosnarvey, ...
	2447	Mathew Brown, ...	Michael Gormley and another,	Gortmore, ...
	2448	Patrick McCusker, ...	Vincent Lifford, ...	Carr, ...
	2449	Hugh Sutherland, ...	Thomas Kerr, ...	Glenadrel, ...
	2450	Joseph Armstrong, ...	J. L. Manteith, ...	Glenkerrill, ...

TYRONE—*continued.*

Extent of Holding (Statute).	Poor Law Valuation.	Former Rent.	Judicial Rent.	Observations.	Value of Tenancy.
A. R. P.	£ s. d.	£ s. d.	£ s. d.	£ s. d.	£ s. d.
30 2 20	17 15 0	23 10 0	15 0 0	Rent changed in 1874 from . . 16 11 8	
12 1 25	5 5 0	6 5 0	4 15 0	do. 4 11 0	
14 2 0	5 15 0	8 0 0	5 10 0	do. 7 0 0	
8 0 5	5 5 0	4 0 0	2 15 0	do. 3 10 0	
11 0 25	6 5 0	4 10 0	5 0 0		
23 0 20	—	14 0 0	10 0 0		
8 1 12	6 15 0	6 10 0	5 10 0	By consent.	
15 3 24	14 5 0	16 0 0	14 5 0	do.	
41 1 25	29 5 0	35 0 0	31 5 0		
16 1 24	13 15 0	18 7 0	11 10 0		
25 0 30	11 0 0	18 13 0	14 1 0	Rent changed in 1863 from . . 16 15 0	
45 3 30	18 0 0	21 0 0	18 0 0		
40 2 0	2 5 0	4 4 0	3 2 6		
74 0 28	4 0 0	7 11 0	6 10 0		
86 0 7	17 10 0	20 0 0	15 10 0		
11 1 0	—	10 0 0	7 15 0		
20 2 15	—	12 2 6	12 0 0		
3 3 10	7 10 0	4 0 0	4 0 0		
18 0 27	26 17 0	28 13 0	27 10 0		
7 1 0	5 10 0	8 10 0	5 0 0		
6 1 20	5 15 0	7 10 0	6 11 0		
12 0 0	7 5 0	11 0 0	5 15 0	1881 10 0 0	
31 0 4	15 0 0	20 17 7	17 13 0		
4 3 35	4 10 0	11 0 0	7 10 0	1874 6 0 0	
11 1 8	9 10 0	10 10 0	7 10 0	do. 8 2 3	
15 0 23	13 5 0	14 5 0	11 5 0		
18 1 7	10 0 0	13 4 0	9 15 0		
11 0 28	5 15 0	9 0 0	7 3 6		
16 0 25	8 0 0	16 2 0	8 10 0	1880 7 0 0	
14 1 8	5 5 0	11 7 0	8 0 0	1874 9 15 0	
25 3 5	10 15 0	20 0 0	20 0 0	1870 20 0 0	
27 3 2	19 0 0	25 0 0	22 0 0		
20 0 24	26 15 0	27 10 0	21 0 0		
11 0 25	3 5 0	6 0 0	4 0 0		
70 0 20	33 0 0	43 0 0	30 10 0		

Names of Assistant Commissioners by whom Cases were decided.	No.	Name of Tenant.		Name of Landlord.	
Assistant Commissioners—					
[illegible] Fuller, q.c. (Legal). A. [illegible] S. Byrne. J. Montgomery. H. [illegible]	2151	Edward Connolly,	...	J. L. [illegible],	...
	2152	John McKeown,	...	Hon. [illegible] Thompson,	
	2153	Francis Dougherty,	...	do.	...
	2154	Michael McVeigh,	...	do.	...
	2155	Bridget McKinley,	...	do.	...
	2156	Patrick McManus,	...	do.	...
	2157	Hugh [illegible],	...	do.	...
	2158	Patrick [illegible],	...	do.	...
	2159	James Slavin,	...	do.	...
	2160	Neil Coulter, ...	...	Major R. S. Hamilton,	
	2161	Samuel Coulter,	...	do.	...
	2162	Edward McCusker, Rep. of John McCusker,		Mrs. [illegible],	...
	2163	John Downs,	...	John A. Galbraith,	
	2164	George McFarland,	...	do.	...
	2165	Margaret Chestnut,	...	do.	...
	2166	Robert Clarke,	...	do.	...
	2167	James Burt, ...	...	do.	...
	2168	Thomas Moyne,	...	William Johnston & an	
	2169	William McCracken,	...	do.	...
	2170	William Armstrong,	...	William Douglas and Trustees of G. W. Og	
	2171	James Teague,	...	do.	...
	2172	Nicholas Smith,	...	do.	...
	2173	William Smith, Admor. of Samuel Smith,		do.	...
	2174	William Gray, sen.,	...	do.	...
	2175	Joseph Gray, ...	...	do.	...
	2176	Margaret and Jane Gray,		do.	...
	2177	Daniel McBrien,	...	do.	...
	2178	Richard [illegible] and another,		do.	...
	2179	Thomas Johnston,	...	do.	...
	2180	John Cox, ...	...	do.	...
	2181	Robert [illegible],	...	do.	...

TYRONE—*continued.*

Extent of Holding. Statute.	Poor Law Valuation.	Former Rent.	Judicial Rent.	Observations.	Value of Tenancy.
A. R. P.	£ s. d.	£ s. d.	£ s. d.	£ s. d.	£ s. d.
44 2 30	33 0 0	18 0 0	11 0 0	Rent changed in 18[illegible] from . . . 18 0 0	
4 0 0	4 10 0	5 10 1	4 15 0		
17 1 36	31 15 0	23 14 10	10 10 0		
31 1 30	12 0 0	13 11 8	11 1 0		
11 1 4	7 3 0	7 5 0	6 12 6		
21 1 26	16 10 0	10 5 8	16 1 0		
16 2 20	11 5 0	11 0 3	8 5 0		
8 2 33	6 10 0	6 4 3	4 0 0		
40 2 36	35 5 0	27 10 0	27 15 0		
8 3 0	0 0 0	7 3 6	4 10 0		
39 0 29	20 0 0	28 0 0	20 0 0	1877 31 0 0	
10 2 31	10 4 0	16 10 0	13 10 0		
28 3 7	21 10 0	15 11 0	20 10 0		
10 0 16	6 15 0	6 12 0	8 0 0		
45 3 30	23 5 0	40 7 0	31 10 0		
8 2 21	8 10 0	8 0 0	5 7 6		
85 2 34	30 10 0	37 10 0	35 3 0		
5 2 15	4 5 0	5 0 0	5 12 6	1873 3 10 4	
19 2 11	7 5 0	10 0 0	7 0 0	1877 4 7 8	
43 1 20	26 0 0	25 0 0	23 0 0		
77 0 0	13 16 0	65 10 3	17 15 0		
37 0 2	21 15 0	35 0 0	27 10 0	1880 20 0 0	
30 0 10	31 10 0	84 17 10	27 10 0		
40 1 0	18 10 0	22 0 0	16 10 0		
40 1 15	30 0 0	33 4 0	25 4 0		
44 0 0	30 10 0	53 15 0	23 10 0		
44 0 0	19 10 0	37 10 0	30 10 0		
14 3 16	19 0 0	23 0 4	11 10 0	1880 12 4 0	
88 0 30	43 5 0	47 1 1	37 10 0		
18 3 23	16 10 0	18 10 0	14 0 0		
4 3 15	0 15 0	3 5 0	3 10 0		
19 1 0	8 10 0	10 5 0	6 3 0		
80 1 30	68 10 0	75 1 0	60 0 0		
60 3 15	67 0 0	40 13 4	44 0 0		
46 3 5	34 0 0	43 13 0	31 10 0		

[illegible]	William Dalton, ...	John A. [illegible],
[illegible]	John Cheshire, ...	Francis [illegible] and another
[illegible]	William Moore, ...	do.
[illegible]	John McKibbin, ...	Joseph Smith,
[illegible]	Hugh McIlwaine, ...	James Young,
[illegible]	William Chambers, ...	Joseph [illegible],
[illegible]	William Vale, ...	Mr. and Mrs. Montgomery,
[illegible]	[illegible], ...	Alexander H. Stewart,
[illegible]	James McIlroy, sen., ...	do.
[illegible]	[illegible], ...	Mrs. [illegible],
[illegible]	Edward McKay, ...	do.
[illegible]	James Kerr, jun., ...	William Douglas and other Trustees of [illegible] W. [illegible]
[illegible]	Patrick McIlroy, ...	Major R. H. Hamilton,
[illegible]	Arthur Woods, ...	William D'Arcy and others
[illegible]	Samuel Bunting, ...	The Earl of [illegible],
[illegible]	Thomas Campbell, ...	Catherine Hamilton & others
[illegible]	Hugh Cullen, ...	do.
[illegible]	James McFarland, ...	do.
[illegible]	William [illegible], ...	R. G. Johnston,
[illegible]	William McPeggy, ...	do.
[illegible]	John Farquhar, ...	Edward Chichester Knox,
2510	Margaret Brown, ...	do.
2511	William Brown, ...	do.
[illegible]	John Ballantine, ...	do.
2513	David Thompson, ...	do.
2514	William Ballantine, ...	do.
2515	Hugh Owen, ...	Captain Mervyn Archdale,

TYRONE—*continued.*

Area of Holding, Statute.	Poor Law Valuation.	Former Rent.	Judicial Rent.	Observations.	Valued Tenancy.
A. R. P.	£ s. d.	£ s. d.	£ s. d.		£ s. d.
44 1 0	33 5 0	44 8 9	32 10 0		
18 2 10	14 0 0	15 15 3½	11 0 0		
[illegible] 3 [illegible]	18 5 0	24 13 4	18 10 0		
10 1 5	6 5 0	8 13 0	6 13 0	By consent.	
23 0 3	17 10 0	22 0 0	17 15 0		
21 1 6	14 15 0	20 7 0	14 10 0		
23 3 0	16 5 0	21 3 6	16 0 0		
6 2 0	3 0 0	8 0 0	5 0 0		
30 1 24	24 0 0	30 0 0	23 10 0		
24 0 16	19 15 0	19 10 9	17 0 0	Rent changed in 18[illegible] from . . . £14 0 0	
70 1 1	48 10 0	60 0 0	52 0 0		
15 0 20	10 15 0	12 0 0	10 5 0	1856 11 17 0	
11 1 36	12 15 8	17 11 8	12 10 0		
8 0 23	5 14 11	7 12 5	6 15 0		
43 1 17	40 5 0	61 18 4	27 0 0		
21 0 [illegible]	10 0 0	10 1 6	11 12 6		
62 5 0	22 3 0	46 1 7	18 0 0	18[illegible] 17 0 0	
46 3 20	16 5 0	23 0 0	16 5 0	1851 7 0 0	
18 5 24	7 5 0	9 4 0	5 10 0		
10 3 10	8 5 0	10 0 6	5 10 0		
14 3 1	10 0 0	11 10 6	9 10 0		
51 0 15	32 0 0	34 19 3	29 16 0		
18 0 30	10 15 0	13 12 4	8 13 0	1867 11 5 0	
33 0 34	13 5 0	17 4 9	10 10 0	1867 7 14 6	
40 2 10	13 10 0	13 5 8	10 10 0	1866 7 14 1½	
25 1 13	9 5 0	12 8 4	7 5 0		
105 1 1	17 10 0	21 10 5	16 0 0	do. 12 13 3	
27 0 30	10 10 0	11 13 3	7 16 8	1867 7 14 1	
140 2 2	25 0 0	30 8 7	15 0 0	18[illegible] 17 13 3	
19 2 20	10 5 0	10 0 0	6 15 0		
4 1 17	3 10 0	4 0 0	3 8 4		
13 0 10	5 10 0	7 10 0	5 5 0	1867 10 0 0	
20 3 10	12 5 0	12 0 0	10 10 0		
8 0 30	5 0 4	10 0 0	4 15 0		
29 0 30	18 5 0	23 0 0	17 0 0	1868 15 3 7	

COUNTY OF

Names of Assistant Commissioners by whom Cases were decided.	No.	Name of Tenant.	Name of Landlord.	Townland.
Assistant Commissioners—				
[illegible], Q.C. (Legal). A. [illegible] S. [illegible] A. Montgomery. H. [illegible]	2521	David Lyons,	Captain Mervyn Archdale,	Galbally,
	2522	Patrick McLaughlin,	George G. Lambert,	Drumlaine,
	2523	Michael Gallagher,	do.	Moyfield,
	2524	Arthur Gallagher,	do.	Mullaghmore,
	2525	Patrick Gallagher,	do.	[illegible],
	2526	Michael Cox,	do.	do.
	2527	William Kelly,	do.	Drumlaine,
	2528	John McGrand,	do.	[illegible],
	2529	Do.	do.	Mullaghmore,
	2530	Thomas Sharkey,	do.	Drumlaine, and another.
	2531	Patrick [illegible],	do.	Mullaghmore,
	2532	James Durnan,	do.	Moyfield and another.
	2533	Rose McVey,	do.	do.
	2534	Thomas Sharkey,	do.	Drumlaine.
	2535	Thomas McIver,	do.	Lisbeg,
	2536	Patrick McKelvy,	do.	Lisbeg & another,
	2537	Ellen Kelly,	do.	do.
	2538	Mary McFadden,	do.	do.
	2539	Owen Stewart,	do.	Drumlaine,
	2540	Thomas McNabb,	do.	Lisbeg,
	2541	Patrick Keys (Myles), Rep. of Richard Morris.	Thomas A. Hope,	Crockanboy.
	2542	Mary Hegarty,	do.	Ferrall,
	2543	Michael McCullagh,	do.	do.
	2544	Michael Clarke,	do.	do.
	2545	Michael McCusk,	do.	do.
	2546	Bridget Keenan,	do.	do.
	2547	Mary Tracey, Rep. of late Andrew Tracey,	do.	do.
	2548	Peter [illegible] and another,	do.	do.
	2549	Paul Keenan,	do.	do.
	2550	Thomas Loughran,	do.	do.
	2551	James Morris, Rep. of Mary Morris.	do.	Crockanboy.
	2552	Dominick Bradley,	do.	Mountfield.
	2553	James Morris,	do.	Tremogue, West,
	2554	Charles McAleer,	do.	Mountfield,
	2555	Patrick McKenna,	do.	Aghnaveagh,

TYRONE—*continued.*

Extent of Holding. Statute.	Poor Law Valuation.	Former Rent.	Judicial Rent.	Observations.		Value of Tenancy.
A. R. P.	£ s. d.	£ s. d.	£ s. d.		£ s. d.	£ s. d.
20 3 25	16 15 0	20 0 0	15 0 0	Rent changed in 1867 Former .	13 3 0	
19 0 0	16 5 0	16 1 6	12 0 0			
8 3 1	7 5 0	7 17 0	6 0 0			
10 2 0	7 10 0	8 11 11	6 0 0			
10 0 17	5 10 0	6 5 4	5 0 0			
13 3 21	4 0 0	6 14 4	6 5 0	1873	7 10 6	
21 1 28	16 0 0	15 10 0	12 0 0			
17 0 0	11 0 0	13 3 10	9 10 0			
13 3 36	11 10 0	10 18 0	9 5 0			
10 1 0	7 18 0	8 17 8	6 13 6			
16 3 7	13 5 0	17 14 6	9 15 0			
25 0 0	27 0 0	10 15 5	15 0 0			
19 0 25	11 10 0	14 3 0	9 10 0			
22 3 13	16 5 0	21 8 6	16 0 0			
6 1 20	1 0 0	6 5 5	3 10 0			
20 3 5	14 10 0	16 14 5	13 10 0			
17 3 10	18 10 0	16 5 2	13 8 0			
12 2 0	9 10 0	9 18 11	7 15 0			
7 1 0	0 0 0	0 18 11	4 10 0			
13 0 30	9 0 0	9 18 11	8 0 0			
21 0 5	5 5 0	7 5 0	3 15 0	1881	6 10 0	
146 0 0	5 5 0	7 10 0	4 10 6			
120 1 30	7 15 0	8 10 0	5 10 0	do.	7 16 5	
30 0 10	7 5 0	6 5 0	4 15 0			
18 3 20	4 0 6	4 10 0	5 0 0	do.	1 0 0	
35 2 35	6 0 0	7 10 0	4 15 0			
84 0 0	6 5 0	6 8 0	3 0 0	do.	5 0 0	
52 2 26	5 5 0	10 0 0	5 15 0	do.	8 5 0	
15 2 10	7 10 0	8 5 0	4 15 0	do.	7 0 0	
345 1 30	13 0 0	20 0 0	16 0 0	do.	25 0 0	
36 0 8	5 13 0	10 10 0	7 0 0			
61 1 5	8 10 0	10 10 0	6 15 0	do.	8 4 4	
23 0 30	5 5 0	7 5 0	4 10 0	do.	6 5 0	
15 1 5	6 10 0	5 0 0	3 5 0	do.	5 5 6	
25 0 35	8 18 0	5 16 0	3 10 0	do.	9 13 5	

COUNTY OF

Names of Assistant Commissioners by whom Cases were [illegible]	No.	Name of Tenant.	Name of Landlord.	Townland.
Assistant Commissioners—				
Murrough O'Brien, Q.C. (Legal). A. Baker. W. Dyson. A. Montgomery. H. Ferguson.	2556	Peter McKeagh,	Thomas A. Hope,	Fernagh,
	2557	John Donnelly, Rep. of Peter Bradley.	do.	Monmurry,
	2558	Patrick McKenna, Admr. of Margaret McKenna.	do.	Crankanbey,
	2559	Owen Kane,	do.	Glenlark,
	2560	Francis McCullagh,	do.	do.
	2561	Cormack Bradley,	do.	do.
	2562	Christopher Mervin,	do.	Crunah,
	2563	Catherine McCrory,	do.	do.
	2564	Teague Devlin,	do.	do.
	2565	Catherine McCullagh,	do.	Aughnacavanny,
	2566	Michael Devlin,	do.	Glenlark,
	2567	Francis McNally,	do.	do.
	2568	Francis Fox,	do.	Fulness, West,
	2569	Andrew Fox,	do.	Fernagh,
	2570	Michael McDonagh,	do.	Aughnaclogh,
	2571	Charles Harvin,	do.	do.
	2572	Bridget Devlin,	do.	Glenlark,
	2573	James McKenna,	do.	do.
	2574	John Conway,	do.	do.
	2575	Peter McCullagh,	do.	do.
	2576	Mary McElhone,	do.	Crunah,
	2577	James McDonnell,	do.	Crankanbey,
	2578	Sarah McAleer,	do.	Monmurry,
	2579	Manus Fox,	do.	Fulness, West,
	2580	James Conway,	do.	Crankanbey,
	2581	Bryan Bradley,	do.	Glenlark,
	2582	Hannah Fox,	do.	do.
	2583	Patrick & Owen McCrory, Reps. of John McCrory.	do.	Crunah,
	2584	John [illegible],	do.	Aughnacavanny,
	2585	Cornelius McCann, Rep. of Pat McCann.	do.	do.
	2586	Toby O'Brien,	do.	Crunah,

TYRONE—continued.

Extent of Holding, Statute.	Poor Law Valuation.	Former Rent.	Judicial Rent.	Observations.		Value of Tenancy.
a. r. p.	£ s. d.	£ s. d.	£ s. d.		£ s. d.	£ s. d.
30 0 10	3 10 0	4 10 0	3 0 0	Rent changed in 1881 from	3 10 0	
18 0 25	6 15 0	6 15 0	4 10 0	do.	5 15 1	
15 3 0	8 0 0	8 10 0	5 7 0	do.	5 10 0	
22 3 10	5 10 0	9 18 0	4 8 6			
25 3 25	4 15 0	5 0 0	3 10 0			
56 0 15	4 0 0	3 15 0	3 5 0			
13 1 30	4 0 0	5 0 0	3 10 0	do.	3 14 0	
19 0 8	6 10 0	5 5 0	3 0 0	do.	1 8 1	
30 2 15	7 0 0	9 0 0	6 0 0	do.	7 3 0	
91 2 10	11 10 0	23 0 0	8 10 0	1880	10 5 0	
103 2 4	8 15 0	8 10 0	5 0 0	1881	7 17 0	
94 1 5	6 15 0	7 16 0	3 10 0	do.	7 0 0	
96 0 10	4 5 0	7 0 0	4 5 0	do.	1 11 0	
63 3 30	7 0 0	9 0 0	6 6 0			
25 3 23	4 0 0	3 10 0	3 5 0	do.	3 7 10	
39 1 25	6 13 0	5 10 0	4 7 6	do.	5 2 5	
51 3 13	5 15 0	0 17 6	9 13 0	do.	4 0 0	
30 2 20	7 15 0	8 0 0	6 7 6	do.	7 14 4	
124 2 25	13 0 0	13 15 0	9 8 0	do.	10 10 0	
34 0 16	14 5 0	18 10 0	11 8 0	do.	15 11 6	
13 0 10	3 0 0	3 10 0	2 5 0	do.	2 15 0	
31 2 17½	4 0 0	3 8 0	2 5 0	do.	1 10 0	
48 0 7	4 15 0	6 10 0	4 6 0			
38 0 23	17 5 0	22 15 0	14 15 0	do.	20 15 0	
34 2 33	7 10 0	9 18 6	6 12 0	do.	5 5 0	
64 1 20	8 16 0	12 10 0	7 0 0			
30 1 11	8 10 0	3 10 0	0 0 0			
15 2 10	6 15 0	5 5 0	3 10 0	do.	4 11 5	
17 0 17	5 3 0	7 0 0	4 0 0	1880	6 10 0	
18 1 20	4 0 0	5 10 0	3 5 0	do.	5 3 7	
14 1 20	6 0 0	8 0 0	5 10 0			
73 3 10	9 15 0	11 10 0	7 13 0			
30 0 25	4 13 0	3 10 0	3 13 0			
27 1 0	7 15 0	8 10 0	5 0 0			
107 1 10	11 5 0	13 18 0	9 15 0	do.	11 19 8	

COUNTY OF

Names of Assistant Commissioners by whom Cases were decided.	No.	Name of Tenant.	Name of Landlord.	Townland.
Assistant Commissioners—				
Edward Falkiner, Q.C. (Legal). A. Ellis. S. Byrne. A. MacNamara. H. Barton.	2491	Ellen Warnock, ...	Thomas A. Hope, ...	[illegible]
	2492	Patrick McCullagh, ...	do.	Glenlark, ...
	2493	Christopher Morris, ...	do.	Crouck, ...
	2494	Francis McCullagh, ...	do.	[illegible], ...
	2495	Susan Morris, Rep. of Myles Morris,	do.	do. ...
	2496	Margaret McKeown, ...	do.	[illegible], ...
	2497	James McCrory, ...	do.	Crouck, ...
	2498	Daniel McCrory, ...	do.	do. ...
	2499	Bell A. Morris, Rep. of Daniel Morris,	do.	do. ...
	2500	Peter Hegarty, ...	do.	[illegible], ...
	2501	Francis Kerr, ...	do.	do. ...
	2502	John McCullagh, ...	do.	Glenlark, ...
	2503	Bridget Morris, ...	do.	Crockanboy, ...
	2504	Myles McNally, ...	do.	[illegible], West, ...
	2505	Francis Bradley, junior,	do.	[illegible], ...
	2506	Sarah Morris, ...	do.	[illegible], West, ...
	2507	Jane Barry, ...	do.	Crockanboy, ...
	2508	John Bradley, ...	do.	do. ...
	2509	John Morris, ...	do.	[illegible], West, ...
	2510	John Bradley, Rep. of Dominick Bradley,	do.	[illegible], ...
	2511	Arthur Devlin, ...	do.	Glenlark, ...
	2512	Patrick Toy, ...	do.	do. ...
	2513	Neal Bradley, ...	do.	do. ...
	2514	John Mc[illegible], ...	do.	do. ...
	2515	John Bradley, ...	do.	do. ...
	2516	Rose Morris, ...	do.	[illegible], ...
	2517	Patrick Devlin, ...	do.	Glenlark, ...
	2518	Michael Walsh, ...	do.	do. ...
	2519	Owen & Michael McBride,	do.	[illegible], ...
	2520	Michael McGurk, ...	do.	[illegible], ...
	2521	Margaret Bradley, ...	do.	do. ...
	2522	Michael Morris, ...	do.	do. ...
	2523	Patrick Bradley, ...	do.	do. ...
	2524	Charles Morris, ...	do.	Crockanboy, ...
	2525	Patrick Kirk, senior and junior.	do.	[illegible], ...

TYRONE—*continued.*

Extent of Holding, Statute.	Poor Law Valuation.	Former Rent.	Judicial Rent.	Observations.	Value of Tenancy.
A. R. P.	£ s. d.	£ s. d.	£ s. d.	£ s. d.	£ s. d.
32 0 31	4 10 5	6 10 0	6 15 0	Rent changed in 1881 from 3 19 4	
19 2 5	3 10 0	5 15 0	3 7 6		
51 2 0	7 0 0	7 5 0	5 5 0		
36 0 5	7 5 0	8 15 0	5 5 0		
10 0 0	4 0 0	4 15 0	3 15 0	do. 4 5 0	
11 2 15	6 0 0	6 5 0	3 10 0		
27 0 0	5 10 0	5 4 0	2 15 0		
26 0 8	5 15 0	6 16 0	4 10 0		
51 2 5	5 15 0	6 15 0	4 10 0		
16 0 30	5 5 0	6 16 0	4 0 0	1880 5 12 4	
17 0 35	5 10 0	6 0 0	5 15 0	1881 5 0 0	
23 0 25	3 5 0	6 5 0	3 0 0		
20 0 35	4 15 0	5 10 0	5 15 0	do. 4 18 0	
23 2 0	10 15 0	22 15 0	9 0 0	do. 15 10 0	
8 2 20	3 5 0	6 7 4	2 15 0	do. 5 0 0	
10 1 8	5 0 0	5 5 0	5 10 0	do. 9 10 0	
13 3 22	12 0 0	22 10 4	6 0 0		
10 0 21	5 15 0	6 15 0	4 10 0	do. 5 16 0	
62 1 16	8 5 0	23 5 0	7 5 0	do. 8 16 5	
24 0 7	5 10 0	6 0 0	5 10 0		
31 0 27	4 5 0	5 0 0	5 0 0		
36 0 30	4 15 0	5 18 0	3 10 0		
31 0 18	4 16 0	5 0 0	5 0 0		
22 3 30	5 15 0	7 0 0	5 5 0	do. 5 0 0	
43 3 16	6 5 0	7 0 0	4 15 0		
20 3 11	5 0 0	8 0 0	2 15 0		
20 1 0	6 5 0	7 0 0	4 0 0	do. 4 17 6	
41 2 5	6 10 0	6 15 0	5 0 0		
28 3 15	7 0 0	8 0 0	5 0 0	do. 6 10 0	
20 1 25	8 0 0	10 10 0	5 5 0	do. 7 10 0	
11 5 34	5 5 0	6 10 0	5 0 0	1873 5 9 1	
5 1 13	5 17 0	6 12 0	6 5 0		
25 2 20	4 0 0	5 0 0	3 10 0	1881 3 15 0	
23 0 11	5 0 0	7 5 0	5 10 0	do. 5 7 6	
51 2 0	7 15 0	8 10 0	4 5 0	do. 7 5 0	

Names of Assistant Commissioners by whom Cases were decided.	No.	Name of Tenant.	Name of Landlord.	Townland.
Assistant Commissioners—				
Robert [illegible], Q.C. (Legal). A. [illegible]. S. [illegible]. A. [illegible]. H. [illegible].	2626	Ferdinand McIlroy, ...	Thomas A. Hope, ...	Glenlark, ...
	2627	James [illegible], ...	do.	do. ...
	[illegible]	Arthur McCrory, ...	do.	Formil, ...
	[illegible]	Patrick McNally (Peter),	do.	[illegible], West ...
	2630	John Keenan, ...	do.	do. ...
	2631	Arthur McNally, ...	do.	do. ...
	[illegible]	Edward Devlin, ...	Earl of Erne and another, ...	[illegible], ...
	[illegible]	Anne Devlin, ...	do.	[illegible], Upper,
	[illegible]	John Kilpatrick, ...	Mrs. J. M. Cooper, ...	[illegible], ...
	[illegible]	Margaret [illegible] and another.	Mrs. E. [illegible], by J. W. H. [illegible].	[illegible], ...
	[illegible]	Robert Irwin & others,	Catherine Hamilton & others,	[illegible] ...
	[illegible]	Robert Wilson, ...	John K. [illegible], ...	[illegible], ...
	[illegible]	Guy Clements, ...	Major G. P. McClintock, ...	[illegible], ...
	[illegible]	John [illegible], ...	R. M. Dale and others, ...	Drum, ...
	2640	James McCullagh, ...	John McFarland, ...	[illegible], ...
	2641	[illegible] Robinson, ...	do.	do. ...
	[illegible]	John [illegible], Admr. of Catherine [illegible].	Alexander G. Stuart, ...	[illegible], ...
	[illegible]	Francis [illegible], ...	Archibald Warnock, ...	[illegible], ...
	[illegible]	James [illegible], ...	Major A. G. Hamilton, ...	[illegible], ...
	[illegible]	George Thompson, ...	Captain M. Archdale, ...	[illegible], ...
	[illegible]	John [illegible], ...	Thomas A. Hope, ...	[illegible], West ...
	[illegible]	Edward [illegible], ...	do.	do. ...
	[illegible]	Patrick McNally, ...	do.	do. ...
	[illegible]	John [illegible], Rep. of T. Fox.	do.	[illegible], ...
	[illegible]	Patrick [illegible] (Michael),	do.	do. ...
	[illegible]	Denis Fox, ...	do.	[illegible], West ...
	[illegible]	Peter Donnelly, ...	do.	[illegible],
	[illegible]	Owen Keenan, ...	do.	[illegible], ...
	[illegible]	Laurence [illegible], ...	do.	[illegible], ...
	[illegible]	James [illegible], ...	do.	Formil, ...
	[illegible]	Owen McGurk, ...	do.	Mountfield, ...
	[illegible]	John [illegible], senior, ...	do.	[illegible], West ...
	[illegible]	Anne Bradley, Admx. of Francis Bradley.	do.	Mountfield, ...
	[illegible]	Bartholomew [illegible], ...	do.	[illegible], West ...
	[illegible]	John McAnenny, ...	do.	Glenlark, ...

TYRONE—*continued.*

Extent of Holding. Statute.	Poor Law Valuation.	Former Rent.	Judicial Rent.	Observations.		Value of Tenancy.
A. R. P.	£ s. d.	£ s. d.	£ s. d.		£ s. d.	£ s. d.
495 1 0	13 15 0	21 18 0	15 0 0	Rent changed in 1861 from . . .	19 10 0	
37 0 13	9 0 0	6 9 8	5 10 0			
73 0 30	6 10 0	8 18 0	5 5 0			
40 0 0	16 0 0	21 18 0	13 10 0	do.	18 10 0	
22 2 15	8 5 0	12 5 0	7 10 0	do.	10 17 0	
16 0 20	9 15 0	11 0 0	6 0 0			
27 0 30	13 10 0	16 17 0	11 5 0	1838	13 0 0	
20 1 30	4 10 0	5 17 6	5 5 0			
20 0 0	7 16 0	11 0 0	7 15 0			
44 0 16	12 5 0	15 10 0	11 10 0			
46 3 0	26 10 0	44 2 6	30 10 0			
43 0 0	17 15 0	46 17 9	30 0 0	By consent.		
75 2 8	61 10 0	64 2 6	45 0 0	do.		
23 2 18	14 0 0	14 0 0	11 16 0	do.		
9 1 10	2 10 0	5 0 0	3 0 0	Rent changed in 1866 from . . .	4 13 8	
36 0 0	12 5 0	17 0 0	10 0 0			
13 3 0	—	15 18 0	11 0 0			
60 0 0	24 10 0	30 0 0	23 10 0	1866	23 10 0	
17 2 10	8 10 0	8 4 4	6 10 0			
18 0 5	11 0 0	11 0 0	8 10 0	1879	10 5 0	
16 0 20	8 0 0	9 0 0	5 5 0	1861	8 0 0	
71 3 15	6 5 0	6 10 8	4 0 0			
22 0 38	5 5 0	7 10 0	4 10 0	do.	5 1 0	
40 0 30	4 15 0	7 10 0	5 10 0	By consent.		
22 0 10½	1 15 0	7 10 0	4 7 6	do.		
31 0 20	4 10 0	5 10 0	4 0 0	Rent changed in 1851 from . . .	6 6 0	
13 1 18	2 10 0	5 10 0	2 15 0	By consent.		
11 0 15	3 10 0	5 4 0	3 1 0	do.		
20 1 30	5 15 0	7 15 0	5 15 0	do.		
37 0 0	4 17 8	2 10 0	4 7 4	do.		
23 3 37	4 0 0	5 0 0	3 18 6	Rent changed in 1851 from . . .	3 5 0	
12 3 5	7 5 0	5 10 0	4 17 6			
9 2 33	5 10 0	4 10 0	3 13 4			
11 2 0	6 5 0	7 0 0	4 13 0	do.	6 10 0	
103 1 33	4 5 0	6 7 8	3 0 0			

COUNTY OF

Names of Assistant Commissioners by whom Cases were decided.	No.	Name of Tenant.	Name of Landlord.	Townland.
Assistant Commissioners—				
[illegible], Q.C. (Legal). A. Ellis. S. Byrne. A. Montgomery. H. [illegible].	2661	Joseph Ballentine, Admr. of William Ballentine,	Thomas A. Hope, ...	[illegible], ..
	2662	Myles Bradley, ...	do.	[illegible], ...
	2663	Daniel McAleer, ...	do.	[illegible], West, .
	2664	Patrick and James McMichael,	do.	Grange, ..
				Total, ...

PROVINCE OF

COUNTY OF

Assistant Commissioners—	783	James Agar, ...	Sir Maurice Fitzgerald, Bart.,	Ballymore, ...
R. R. Kane (Legal). Thomas Baldwin. J. G. Barry. J. H. Dwyer. P. Moran.	784	Robert Kirby, ...	do.	[illegible], ...
				Total, ...

COUNTY OF

Assistant Commissioners—	144	Joseph Harvey, ...	Lord Carysfort, ...	Carrickmines, ...
R. R. Kane (Legal). Thomas Baldwin. J. G. Barry. J. H. Dwyer. P. Moran.	145	Peter Travers, ...	Michael Neill, ...	Taylor's Grange.
				Total, ...

COUNTY OF

Assistant Commissioners—	531	Anastatia Hanrahan, ...	Francis Murphy and others,	[illegible], ...
R. R. Kane (Legal). Thomas Baldwin. J. G. Barry. J. H. Dwyer. P. Moran.	532	William Martin, ...	Frederick K. M. Reed, ...	Newtown [illegible], Lower.
	533	John Dunne, ...	Viscount Mountgarret, ...	Ballygurrey, ...
	534	William Dunne, ...	do.	do. ...
	535	William Fanning, ...	Samuel T. Grubb, ...	Ballymurreen, ...
	536	John Moore, ...	Viscount Mountgarret, ...	Lisdowney ...
	537	Michael Ryan, ...	do.	Ballyring, Lower,
				Total, ...

TYRONE—*continued.*

Extent of Holding. Statute.	Poor Law Valuation.	Former Rent.	Judicial Rent.	Observations.		Value of Tenancy.
a. r. p.	£ s. d.	£ s. d.	£ s. d.		£ s. d.	£ s. d.
17 0 12	5 5 0	7 0 0	[illegible] 5 0			
18 1 17	5 0 0	5 15 0	4 0 0			
18 0 17	7 10 0	6 0 0	5 10 0	Rent changed in 1881 from	7 10 0	
33 3 14	4 15 0	5 10 0	3 0 0	do.	3 3 11	
9,634 1 35	3,[illegible] 16 1	4,307 16 6½	3,15[illegible] 15 6			

LEINSTER.

CARLOW.

78 0 27	68 0 0	74 0 0	63 [illegible] 0	Rent changed in 1876 from	72 0 0	
83 1 4	61 0 0	55 0 0	57 5 0	1861	50 10 0	
161 1 31	[illegible] 0 0	129 0 0	[illegible] 0			

DUBLIN.

80 0 0	40 5 0	89 10 5	80 16 5	Rent changed in 1852 from	177 0 0	
33 1 31	15 10 0	80 0 0	25 5 0			
113 1 31	[illegible] 15 0	169 10 5	106 [illegible] 3			

KILKENNY.

186 3 16	113 10 0	145 3 5	125 0 0			
181 0 6	113 10 0	120 0 0	110 0 0	By consent.		
40 1 25	34 15 0	36 7 4	30 0 0	do.		
30 3 18	18 5 0	23 15 0	18 10 0	do.		
6 0 34	3 5 0	6 2 6	1 4 0	do.		
29 0 0	21 0 0	35 0 0	20 13 0	do.		
67 0 31	19 10 0	32 12 0	27 0 0	do.		
479 1 8	320 18 0	466 1 4	352 7 0			

COUNTY OF

Names of Assistant Commissioners by whom Cases were decided.	No.	Name of Tenant.	Name of Landlord.	Townland.
Assistant Commissioners—	330	Anne Garrigan, ...	James and Patrick Murphy,	[illegible], ...
R. R. Kane (Legal).	331	Anne Smith, ...	do.	do. ...
T. Baldwin	332	Hugh [illegible], ...	do.	[illegible], ...
J. G. Bagot.	333	Ellen Masterson, ...	do.	[illegible], ...
J. R. Dwyer.	334	Ellen Carey, ...	do.	do. ...
P. Moran.	335	Michael Corrigan, ...	do.	[illegible], ...
	336	Michael Masterson, ...	do.	[illegible], ...
	337	Patrick Corrigan, ...	do.	[illegible], ...
	338	James Carey, ...	do.	do. ...
	339	Philip Daly, ...	Lord [illegible], ...	[illegible], ...
	340	James Reilly, ...	do.	do. ...
	341	Do.	Mrs. E. [illegible], ...	Springtown, ...
	342	Matthew Mulligan, ...	do.	do. ...
	343	James Reynolds, ...	do.	do. ...
	344	Hugh Reilly, ...	do.	do. ...
	345	Charles Mullen, ...	do.	do. ...
	346	John [illegible], ...	do.	do. ...
	347	Bridget Brady, Admx. of Peter Brady,	do.	do. ...
	348	Patrick [illegible], ...	John E. Thompson, ...	[illegible], ...
	349	Bernard Reilly, ...	do.	do. ...
	350	Daniel Smith, ...	do.	do. ...
	351	James Miller, ...	Michael S. Fox, ...	[illegible], ...
	352	Do.	do.	[illegible], ...
	353	John [illegible], ...	[illegible] W. [illegible], ...	[illegible]
	354	Thomas McLoughlin, ...	Sir Walter Nugent, Bart., by his Assignees, G. H. [illegible] and [illegible] E. [illegible],	[illegible], ...
	355	Thomas [illegible], ...	do.	do. ...
	356	Patrick [illegible], ...	do.	do. ...
	357	Thomas [illegible], ...	do.	do. ...
	358	James [illegible], ...	do.	do. ...
	359	Felix McCabe, ...	do.	do. ...
	360	Thomas [illegible], ...	do.	do. ...
	361	James [illegible], ...	do.	do. ...
	362	John Brady, R. p. of [illegible] Brady	do.	[illegible], ...
	363	Patrick [illegible], ...	Major [illegible], ...	[illegible], ...
	364	Peter Flood, ...	do.	do. ...

£	s.	d.		£	s.	d.	£	s.	d.
64	5	0							
86	5	0							
72	0	0							
98	0	0	Rent changed in 1879 from . . .	30	10	0			
64	0	0							
45	0	0							
73	0	0							
17	0	0							
8	15	0							
17	10	0	1865	26	0	0			
6	0	0	1869	31	6	9			
10	0	0	do.	26	10	3			
8	0	0	do.	13	12	0			
12	15	0	do.	73	1	5			
25	10	0	do.	36	17	10			
14	0	0	do.	20	2	2			
9	0	0	1872	10	12	10			
5	16	0							
9	0	0	1866	10	0	4			
6	8	0							
8	10	0	do.	18	0	4			
34	0	0							
5	15	0							
13	0	0							
18	10	0							
7	13	0							
7	15	0							
10	10	0							
13	0	0							
12	0	0							
34	0	0							
42	16	0							
83	16	0							

COUNTY OF

Names of Assistant Commissioners by whom Cases were decided.	No.	Name of Tenant.	Name of Landlord.	Townland.
Assistant Commissioners—				
R. E. Kane (Legal). T. Baldwin. J. G. Barry. J. H. Dunne. F. Meehan.	[illegible]	James Early, ...	Major Robert Blackhall, ...	Ringowney, ...
	[illegible]	Catherine O'Brien, ...	do.	Cloon, ...
	[illegible]	Ellen Reilly, Admix. of Patrick Lowndes.	Algernon W. B. Greville, ...	Ballymanus, ...
	[illegible]	James McEoy, ...	do.	do. ...
	[illegible]	Pat. McKeon, ...	do.	do. ...
	370	Michael Boylan, ...	do.	Aghakeeran, ...
	371	Patrick Tierney, ...	do.	do. ...
	372	Thomas Monaghan, ...	do.	do. ...
	373	Peter Donnelly, ...	do.	Aghakeeran and others.
	374	James Fagan, ...	do.	Gaild, ...
	375	Anne Browne, ...	do.	Lettrim and ors.
	376	Michael Healy, ...	Francis F. Gregg and others, Reps. of Rev. Fras. Gregg.	Carrowmore, ...
	377	Mary Farrell, Rep. of Matthew Farrell	Thomas A. Garrett, ...	Cornagleragh, ...
	378	William Montgomery, Exors. of Alex. Harris.	Earl of Granard, ...	Clonmacthey, ...
	379	Mary Nelson, Rep. of Jas. Nelson, deceased.	Anthony Lefroy, ...	Corriskey, ...
	[illegible]	Cathrine Casey, ...	Tobias H. Peyton, ...	Cartronagh, ...
	[illegible]	Samuel Allen, ...	Lord Annaly, ...	Corry, ...
	[illegible]	Robert Mason, ...	do.	do. ...
	[illegible]	Robert Mason, ...	do.	Ballyglassin, ...
	384	Francis Dimond, ...	do.	Lisnagrill, ...
	[illegible]	Joseph Poe, ...	do.	Mohanlaun, ...
	[illegible]	John Rourke, ...	do.	Lisbane, ...
	387	Catherine Farrell, ...	do.	Killinure, ...
	[illegible]	Patrick Casey, ...	do.	Lisrevagh, ...
	[illegible]	Anne Christy, ...	Mary A. Archdall, ...	Cooperstown, ...
	[illegible]	Thomas Bennett, ...	do.	do. ...
	[illegible]	Alexander McVitty, ...	do.	do. ...
	[illegible]	James Savage, ...	do.	do. ...
	[illegible]	James Shaw, ...	Colonel E. R. King-Harman,	Abbeyshrule, ...
	[illegible]	Joseph Shaw, ...	do.	Drumlum, ...
	[illegible]	Thomas Goodwin, ...	do.	Ardagrie, ...
	396	Thomas Geraghty, ...	do.	Creevaghmore ...
	397	Richard J. Swift, ...	do.	Rosspark, ...
	[illegible]	Richard J. Swift, ...	do.	Clarygan, ...
	[illegible]	John Murray, ...	do.	Aughnacreevy.

LONGFORD—*continued.*

Extent of Holding. Statute.	Poor Law Valuation.	Former Rent.	Judicial Rent.	Observations.		Value of Tenancy.
A. R. P.	£ s. d.	£ s. d.	£ s. d.		£ s. d.	£ s. d.
23 0 10	20 18 0	21 7 6	19 0 0			
17 2 30	15 17 0	24 0 0	14 5 0			
16 1 8	8 18 3	10 0 0	8 10 0			
14 1 18	7 5 0	10 13 4	8 0 0			
18 0 27	7 10 0	10 15 8	7 10 0			
21 0 30	18 16 0	20 0 0	13 5 0	Rent changed in 1877 from - - -	15 4 0	
30 2 14	16 11 0	30 0 0	12 12 0	do.	18 0 0	
16 1 0	13 0 6	14 0 0	11 0 0	do.	10 18 0	
158 2 35	109 5 0	141 13 0	113 0 0			
27 1 0	24 10 0	32 6 8	26 5 0	1844	29 18 6	
23 1 0	21 0 0	28 5 11	23 0 0	1854	24 3 6	
33 1 14	27 13 0	36 10 4	32 0 0	1853	27 10 4	
17 3 7	8 5 0	11 0 0	7 0 0			
74 3 8	41 5 0	46 18 0	40 0 0			
23 0 5	21 15 6	27 15 0	23 14 0			
8 1 30	2 5 0	5 0 0	3 10 0			
111 3 25	118 0 0	150 0 0	132 0 0	1873	137 18 8	
32 0 5	27 0 0	30 0 0	28 15 0	do.	31 11 0	
15 1 16	16 5 0	20 0 0	16 10 0	do.	21 11 7	
22 2 28	30 0 0	35 0 0	23 0 0	do.	23 18 6	
35 1 37	33 0 0	46 0 0	33 10 0	do.	27 0 0	
16 1 29	10 18 0	13 10 0	10 0 0	1877	11 3 8	
24 1 3	12 10 0	22 0 0	15 13 0	do.	19 14 9	
18 0 33	6 10 0	6 0 0	6 0 0	1879	12 0 0	
64 1 20	31 15 0	37 16 0	24 12 0			
31 0 1	19 0 0	19 19 0	13 0 0			
—	14 0 0	22 10 6	17 0 0			
17 0 0	0 15 0	13 0 0	11 5 0			
9 1 38	13 5 0	18 12 0	14 13 0			
108 1 28	128 5 0	180 0 0	150 0 0	1876	165 6 6	
47 0 18	54 10 0	62 10 0	64 10 0			
53 0 10	25 0 6	40 13 10	33 0 0	1880	33 7 6	
71 3 11	31 10 0	45 4 6	33 10 0	1884	34 16 7	
17 1 25	9 0 0	10 14 5	10 4 0			
41 0 0	31 0 0	37 10 0	31 0 0			

COUNTY OF

Names of Assistant Commissioners by whom Cases were decided.	No.	Name of Tenant.	Name of Landlord.	Townland.
Assistant Commissioners—				
E. R. Kane (Legal). T. Baldwin. J. G. Barry. J. H. Doherty. P. Moran.	400	Peter Geraghan, ...	Colonel E. R. King-Harman,	[illegible], ...
	401	Do.	do.	Curry, ...
	402	Thomas Newman, ...	do.	Carrowmably and another,
	403	Bridget Geraghan, ...	do.	Loughill, ...
	404	Do.	do.	Clooncleaney, ...
	405	James McGarry, ...	do.	Abbeyglass, ...
	406	John Dowd, ...	do.	Curry, ...
	407	James Hogan, ...	do.	Knockavogan, ...
	408	Charles McGarry, ...	do.	do. ...
	409	James Ireland, ...	do.	Faygh, ...
	410	Edward Kelly, ...	do.	Cloonlyn & another,
	411	Peter Geraghan, ...	do.	Loughloony, ...
	412	Rossana Martin, ...	do.	do. ...
	413	Francis McGinn, ...	do.	Mauskavogan, ...
				Total, ...

COUNTY OF

Assistant Commissioners—	368	Anne Hurley, ...	Lord Rathdonnell, ...	Redbarn & another,
E. R. Kane (Legal). T. Baldwin. J. G. Barry. J. H. Doherty. P. Moran.	369	Bridget Murphy, otherwise Fitzgerald.	William H. Owens, ...	Curtinstown, ...
	370	Thomas Daly, ...	Percy Fitzgerald, ...	Tervanfarkin, ...
	371	Judith A. Kiernan, ...	Colonel J. K. Fortescue, ...	Ardloughan, ...
				Total, ...

COUNTY OF

LONGFORD—*continued.*

Extent of Holding. Statute.			Poor Law Valuation.			Former Rent.			Judicial Rent.			Observations.				Value of Tenancy.
A.	R.	P.	£	s.	d.	£	s.	d.	£	s.	d.		£	s.	d.	£ s. d.
30	0	33	33	10	0	39	12	6	35	0	0	Rent changed in 18[illegible] from . . .	19	5	1	
7	1	1	5	0	0	5	0	0	5	0	0					
39	2	16	30	0	0	34	6	5	33	0	0	1835	25	0	0	
81	0	27	35	5	0	46	7	8	44	7	0					
186	3	39	90	18	0	108	0	0	95	0	0	1876	17	1	0	
33	0	38	13	8	0	24	7	6	20	0	0					
16	3	12	12	15	0	16	6	0	13	0	0					
68	1	25	40	10	0	86	3	0	40	0	0					
47	0	36	34	10	0	34	17	6	28	0	0					
31	0	30	11	0	0	17	16	0	14	5	0					
40	3	1	27	10	0	38	11	6	32	0	0					
47	0	9	35	0	0	40	5	4	38	10	0					
13	3	17	0	15	0	11	10	6	10	10	0					
35	3	37	18	10	0	37	0	0	21	10	0					
8,030	1	25	9,484	3	0	2,608	18	0	2,330	5	9					

LOUTH.

140	3	10	121	0	0	135	0	0	120	0	0	By consent.	
77	1	6	11	15	0	16	1	9	10	17	6	do.	
39	0	7	15	0	0	20	11	8	18	10	0	do.	
101	3	28	71	0	0	85	18	4	76	10	0	do.	
358	3	10	218	15	0	257	1	8	225	17	0		

MEATH.

COUNTY OF

Names of Assistant Commissioners by whom Cases were Decided.	No.	Name of Tenant.	Name of Landlord.	Townland.
Assistant Commissioners—				
R. E. Kane (Legal).	352	John Higgins, ...	Earl of Darnley, ...	Corballis, ...
T. Baldwin.	353	Miles Reynolds, ...	do.	do. ...
J. G. Barry.	354	Do., ...	do.	do. ...
J. H. Dunne.	355	Daniel Mulvey, ...	do.	do. ...
P. Moran.	356	Thomas Dragan, ...	do.	do. ...
	357	Alice Higgins, ...	do.	do. ...
	358	James Nugent, ...	do.	do. ...
	359	Denis Higgins, ...	do.	do. ...
	360	Thomas Darby, ...	do.	do. ...
	361	William Bennett, ...	do.	do. ...
	362	Thomas Higgins, junior,	do.	do. ...
	363	Thomas Higgins, senior,	do.	do. ...
	364	Michael Dillon, ...	do.	Jamestown, ...
	365	Patrick Gill, ...	do.	do. ...
	366	Margaret Lynch, Admx. of Philip Lynch,	do.	do. ...
	367	Philip Smith, ...	do.	do. ...
	368	Lawrence Clarke, ...	do.	do. ...
	369	Michael Millea, ...	do.	do. ...
	370	Catherine Cassidy, ...	do.	Gilbertstown, ...
	371	Thomas Carey, senior, ...	do.	Crossmacole, ...
	372	Thomas Cummins, ...	do.	Portloman, ...
	373	Richard Keefe, ...	do.	do. ...
	374	Anne Daly, ...	do.	Mason, ...
	375	Thomas Darby, ...	do.	do. ...
	376	Mary Blight, ...	do.	do. ...
	377	Thomas Dunne, ...	do.	do. ...
	378	John Blight, ...	do.	do. ...
	379	Patrick Ging, ...	do.	do. ...
	380	Patrick Mc Manus, ...	do.	do. ...
	381	James Conlan, ...	Sir George Hutchinson Shuckburgh, Bart.	Cappagh, ...
	382	William Behan, ...	Michael Rafferty, ...	Piercetown, ...
	383	James Connolly, ...	John Daly, ...	Loggah, ...
	384	Jane Bell, ...	do.	do. ...
	385	John Traynor, ...	do.	do. ...
	386	Edward Moore, ...	Major H. G. Singleton, ...	Castlerea, ...

MEATH—continued.

Extent of Holding. Statute.	Poor Law Valuation.	Present Rent.	Judicial Rent.	Observations.		Value of Tenancy.
A. R. P.	£ s. d.	£ s. d.	£ s. d.		£ s. d.	£ s. d.
15 0 17	21 15 0	13 16 0	15 0 4	Rent changed in 1858 from . . .	13 17 0	
8 0 20	3 6 0	3 14 10	2 15 0	do.	8 10 0	
84 1 0	20 10 0	27 0 0	20 0 0	do.	15 0 0	
30 3 8	26 3 0	85 4 4	80 0 0	do.	20 3 6	
30 0 0	23 10 0	30 4 6	24 10 0	do.	27 16 4	
15 3 7	10 15 0	11 11 4	9 0 0	do.	6 10 0	
0 1 0	6 0 0	8 0 0	3 15 0	do.	3 15 0	
38 1 11	84 15 0	33 3 4	87 0 0	do.	96 7 7	
85 1 13	31 10 0	38 0 0	31 15 0			
19 0 33	11 3 0	17 6 0	11 10 0	do.	16 6 0	
10 1 21	12 0 0	18 6 8	11 15 0	do.	16 8 0	
23 3 8	17 15 0	20 13 4	10 16 0	do.	17 10 8	
9 0 0	0 15 0	1 12 1	1 13 1	do.	1 3 4	
18 3 0	11 15 0	12 12 3	11 10 0	do.	11 7 7	
8 1 1	2 15 0	3 17 0	5 0 0	do.	9 7 11	
3 1 20	3 15 0	7 18 8	1 13 1	do.	7 0 0	
17 3 21	10 10 0	13 9 6	13 13 0	do.	11 6 3	
23 0 27	16 10 0	18 0 0	19 0 0	do.	77 10 11	
7 1 20	4 5 0	4 10 8	4 0 0			
36 1 4	38 5 0	43 13 8	38 10 0	do.	39 13 11	
23 3 0	18 10 0	27 16 8	18 15 0			
84 0 0	78 0 0	80 0 0	78 0 0	1877	73 10 0	
16 3 37	6 15 0	11 15 3	8 0 0	1866	6 18 11	
66 0 33	38 5 0	50 8 4	46 9 0	do.	63 11 6	
9 1 37	3 0 0	7 4 0	8 13 0	do.	5 10 1	
40 0 27	30 20 0	37 3 3	33 5 0	do.	38 1 10	
8 0 31	3 5 0	8 10 4	5 13 0	do.	3 18 8	
30 0 13	16 10 0	25 19 0	31 3 0	do.	17 8 0	
10 3 4	6 0 0	8 17 0	8 10 0	do.	6 0 0	
23 1 10	37 0 0	44 0 0	46 0 0			
64 2 20	43 10 0	75 0 0	60 0 0			
1 2 25	3 18 0	3 18 6	8 10 0			
1 0 6	2 5 0	8 10 10	2 0 0			
1 3 0	2 0 0	3 15 3	2 10 0			
[illegible] 0 30	[illegible] 10 0	186 0 0	184 0 0	1873	187 10 0	

COUNTY OF

Names of Assistant Commissioners by whom Cases were decided.	No.	Name of Tenant.	Name of Landlord.	Townland.
Assistant Commissioners – R. R. Kane (Legal). T. Baldwin. J. G. Barry. J. H. Dorcy. P. Moran.	387	James Menahan, ...	John O'Neill, continued in the name of Patrick O'Neill, his Devisee.	Drynane, ...
	388	Patrick Leonard, ...	do.	do. ...
	389	Bridget Ridley, ...	Lord Headham and others, ...	Cornamona, Drinch,
	390	John Wogan, ...	Finlay Chester, ...	Drynane, ...
	391	James Wall, ...	do.	do. ...
	392	Peter Clarke, ...	Frances Sullivan, ...	Knockmoney, ...
	393	Michael Grandon, ...	do.	do. ...
	394	Patrick McQuaid, ...	do.	do. ...
	395	Patrick Cassidy, ...	Francis and M. J. Sullivan,	Higginstown, ...
	396	James McLoughlin, ...	do.	do. ...
	397	Christopher Flynn, ...	Frederick H. Langan, ...	Kilvarden, ...
	398	Patrick Coleway, ...	Patrick Kennedy, ...	Tevlaght, ...
	399	James Farrell, ...	do.	do. ...
	400	Luke Magrath, ...	Lieut.-Col. Francis Brodigan, devisee of Maria Kelly.	[illegible],
	401	Elizabeth O'Brien, ...	F. O'B. Murphy, ...	Whiteleysgrove, ...
	402	Patrick Dunne, ...	The Earl of Darnley, ...	Sheeran, ...
	403	Mathew Kavanagh, ...	do.	Cortalis, ...
	404	Elijah Lewis, ...	do.	Hayfield, ...
	405	Thomas Lewis, ...	do.	do. ...
	406	James Brady, ...	do.	Jamestown, ...
	407	Owen Murtagh, ...	do.	do. ...
	408	Thomas Brady, ...	do.	do. ...
	409	Patrick Clarke, ...	do.	do. ...
	410	Edward Cumisky, ...	do.	do. ...
				Total, ...

MEATH—*continued.*

Extent of Holding. Statute.	Poor Law Valuation.	Former Rent.	Judicial Rent.	Observations.		Value of Tenancy.
A. R. P.	£ s. d.	£ s. d.	£ s. d.		£ s. d.	£ s. d.
44 3 6	44 0 0	34 18 3	34 18 3	Rent changed in 1883 from	71 3 4	
45 3 31	41 15 0	34 15 9	44 13 9	do.	70 18 2	
36 3 21	30 5 0	35 0 0	35 0 0			
9 3 16	4 10 0	9 5 0	7 0 0			
21 0 25	20 0 0	21 7 0	17 0 0			
1 0 0	0 10 0	1 16 0	1 6 0	[illegible]	2 0 4	
19 0 18	10 5 0	13 0 0	13 0 0	do.	18 0 0	
0 0 32	3 10 0	4 3 0	3 17 0	do.	3 7 4	
7 3 20	3 10 0	7 10 0	5 10 0	1863	4 10 0	
8 3 31	4 10 0	8 0 0	6 0 0	do.	[illegible]	
25 3 34	13 0 0	30 10 0	27 0 0	1857	[illegible] 0	
77 2 17	30 5 0	75 11 0	64 0 0	1863	[illegible] 11 11	
60 3 23	40 0 0	65 0 8	41 0 0			
34 0 2	30 0 0	37 5 0	34 0 0	1856	31 10 0	
68 0 1	80 0 0	107 10 0	127 10 0	[illegible]	118 10 6	
45 2 0	18 10 0	25 13 10	25 10 0	1866	23 4 0	
16 0 16	0 13 0	10 13 8	7 15 0	do.	6 10 0	
61 3 16	45 0 0	55 19 0	45 0 0	do.	43 3 11	
122 0 8	115 0 0	135 0 4	117 10 0	1861	[illegible] 6 1	
14 3 10	7 0 0	11 3 6	9 10 0	1866	[illegible] 11	
11 3 0	8 0 0	9 18 4	8 5 0	do.	7 4 9	
11 1 10	7 15 0	5 18 4	7 15 0	do.	7 0 1	
0 1 36	0 13 0	0 0 4	2 7 0			
0 0 38	0 0 0	3 0 0	1 15 0	do.	2 1 0	
2,397 3 19	1,715 15 0	2,[illegible] 18 5	2,[illegible] 0 11			

COUNTY.

80 0 37	30 0 0	35 1 4	34 0 4		

COUNTY OF

Names of Assistant Commissioners by whom Cases were decided.	No.	Name of Tenant.	Name of Landlord.	Townland.
Assistant Commissioners—				
R. R. Kane (Legal). T. Baldwin. J. O. Barry. J. M. Dennis. P. Moran.	732	Robert [illegible], ...	[illegible], ...	[illegible], ...
	733	John [illegible], ...	A. J. [illegible], ...	[illegible], ...
	734	Michael [illegible], ...	Lord [illegible], ...	[illegible], ...
	735	Joseph Murray, ...	Lord [illegible] and another,	[illegible], ...
				Total, ...

PROVINCE OF

COUNTY OF

Assistant Commissioners—				
T. P. Lynch (Legal). Patrick Taaffe. E. L. Hunt. E. J. Kenny. P. O'Connell.	1858	Michael Kelly, ...	Richard French, ...	[illegible], ...
	1859	John Burke, ...	Edward [illegible], ...	[illegible], ...
	1860	William [illegible], ...	Joseph Fitzpatrick, ...	[illegible],
	1861	James Kenny, ...	do.	do. ...
	1862	Bridget Tuohy, successor to Peter Tuohy,	do.	do. ...
	1863	Thomas McKelly, ...	Rev. George [illegible], ...	[illegible], ...
	1864	Sally McDonagh, ...	R. W. Mervyn, ...	Dean Lodge, ...
	1865	Patrick Griffin, ...	Robert J. Martin, ...	[illegible], ...
	1866	Patrick Carey, ...	Colonel Clements, ...	[illegible], ...
	1867	Patrick Joyce, ...	do.	[illegible], ...
	1868	Barbara Coyne, Rep. of Stephen Coyne,	do.	[illegible], ...
	1869	John Reynolds, ...	do.	[illegible], ...
	1870	Thomas Holmes, ...	do.	do. ...
	1871	Tom Holmes, Rep. of Mary Holmes,	do.	[illegible], ...
	1872	Joseph Joyce, ...	do.	[illegible], ...
	1873	Mary Joyce, ...	do.	[illegible], ...
	1874	Martin Walsh, ...	do.	[illegible], ...
	1875	Mary Walsh, ...	do.	[illegible], ...
	1876	Mary Coyne, Rep. of Martin Coyne,	do.	[illegible], ...
	1877	John [illegible], ...	do.	do. ...
	1878	John [illegible], ...	Joseph Fitzpatrick, ...	[illegible], ...
	1879	Michael Burke, ...	Arthur Alexander, ...	[illegible], ...
	1880	Darby [illegible], ...	Henry de [illegible], ...	[illegible], ...

WEXFORD.

Extent of Holding Statute.	Poor Law Valuation.	Former Rent.	Judicial Rent.	Observations.	Value of Tenancy.
A. R. P.	£ s. d.	£ s. d.	£ s. d.		£ s. d.
21 3 17	12 6 0	20 0 0	17 13 0	By consent.	
42 1 16	20 10 0	26 15 1	20 0 0	do.	
52 3 15	20 0 0	20 7 6	24 13 0	do.	
61 0 11	20 0 0	25 16 0	20 0 0	do.	
186 1 20	67 15 0	103 18 7	71 0 0		

CONNAUGHT.

GALWAY.

11 3 0	—	6 0 0	8 0 0		30 0 0
92 3 5	9 13 0	18 0 0	15 10 0	By consent.	
—	2 0 0	3 10 0	1 8 0	do.	
—	1 0 0	3 15 0	3 7 0	do.	
—	7 0 0	17 15 0	6 4 5	do.	
11 7 26	3 10 0	3 19 0	3 19 0		
13 3 15	4 16 0	6 10 0	5 10 0		
13 0 0	3 0 0	5 5 6	3 15 0		
20 3 19	9 14 0	6 10 0	7 15 0		
4 3 0	1 0 0	3 10 0	7 0 0	do.	
26 2 16	1 13 0	4 18 0	6 0 0		
14 1 3	3 0 0	4 0 0	6 0 0		
39 1 33	8 10 0	4 0 0	8 6 0		
10 3 23	8 0 0	7 5 0	4 15 0		
16 3 12	8 0 0	3 15 0	6 15 0		
11 3 33	1 10 0	5 14 0	1 15 0		
613 0 13	16 0 0	22 0 0	60 0 0		
7 1 8	2 10 0	4 13 0	3 0 0		
7 6 20	3 0 0	4 10 0	3 10 0		
0 0 0	—	2 16 0	1 0 0		
3 0 0	6 0 0	6 5 0	4 0 0	do.	
28 0 30	11 10 0	20 14 0	13 10 0		
16 2 20	7 5 0	5 17 4	7 5 0		

Assistant Commissioners—

E. P. Lynch (Legal).
Patrick Taaffe.
R. L. Hunt.
R. G. Murray,
P. Gilhooly.

1881	Thomas Fitzpatrick, ...	William Bailey, a Minor, ...	Ollan, ...
1882	Patrick Mahony, ...	John M. Blake, ...	Carrowfield, ...
1883	Michael Whelan, ...	do.	do. ...
1884	Thomas Quinn, ...	Daniel Lahiff	Newtownmoyle & another.
1885	John Geraghty, ...	do.	Carheen, ...
1886	Michael Walsh, ...	do.	Fiddaun, ...
1887	Thomas Quinn, ...	do.	Castlequarter, ...
1888	Pat Kenny, ...	Francis Carey, ...	— ...
1889	Martin O'Toole, ...	do.	— ...
1890	William Kyne, ...	do.	— ...
1891	Bridget Mulkern, ...	do.	Doon, East, ...
1892	James Oliver, ...	Daniel Lahiff and another, ...	Knockanena, ...
1893	John Reilly, ...	James Blake, ...	Cloonbar, ...
1894	John Heneghan, ...	do.	Cloonan, ...
1895	Michael Devaney, ...	do.	Clooban, ...
1896	Thomas Lardiner, ...	do.	do. ...
1897	Margaret Mannion, ...	do.	do. ...
1898	Patrick Hennelly, ...	do.	do. ...
1899	Owen Reilly, ...	do.	do. ...
1900	John O'Flynn, ...	do.	Moor, ...
1901	John O'Neill, ...	do.	do. ...
1902	John Burke, ...	James Thompson, ...	Ballyvirack, South,
1903	Pat Flynn, ...	do.	do. ...
1904	Michael Connolly, ...	do.	Ballyvirack, North,
1905	Thomas Moran, ...	do.	do. ...
1906	Michael Loughrey, ...	Thos. E. Lahiff, a Lunatic, by James Lahiff, his Committee.	Seelan, ...
1907	John Keane, ...	do.	Ballybane, ...
1908	Michael Lamb, ...	do.	Seelan, ...
1909	Martin Lamb, ...	do.	Ballybeely, ...
1910	James Geoghegan, ...	do.	Ballybane, ...
1911	Patrick Lamb, ...	do.	Ballybeely, ...
1912	Patrick Geoghegan, ...	do.	Ballybane, ...
1913	Michael Martin, ...	do.	do. ...
1914	Patrick Lamb (Michael),	do.	Seelan, ...
1915	Do., ...	do.	Ballybeely, ...

GALWAY—*continued.*

Extent of Holding, Statute.	Poor Law Valuation.	Former Rent.	Judicial Rent.	Observations.	Value of Tenancy.
A. R. P.	£ s. d.	£ s. d.	£ s. d.	£ s. d.	£ s. d.
19 1 8	4 10 0	4 10 0	5 10 6		
25 0 33	8 10 0	19 10 0	11 15 0		80 0 0
34 0 34	3 15 0	11 4 6	16 0 0		75 0 0
156 1 8	53 15 0	80 0 0	64 0 0		
14 0 0	6 10 0	23 0 0	13 0 0		
11 0 0	1 15 0	13 5 0	8 10 0		
14 0 37	5 10 0	8 0 0	7 5 0		
35 2 33	4 0 0	12 9 0	7 11 0		45 0 0
15 1 18	3 10 0	5 10 0	4 13 0		40 0 0
17 1 25	1 10 0	4 10 0	3 17 6		30 0 0
34 0 25	1 10 0	7 10 0	8 18 0		45 0 0
18 1 14	6 0 0	8 0 0	4 0 0		
15 3 30	6 0 0	10 0 0	5 7 0		
25 3 30	9 3 0	15 0 0	13 0 0		
8 1 8	3 10 0	8 0 0	4 0 0		
18 2 38	6 0 0	10 0 0	7 15 0		
17 3 35	6 15 0	10 0 0	7 17 6		
16 0 37	5 10 0	10 0 0	7 17 6		
17 1 6	6 10 0	10 0 0	8 7 6		
10 0 0	5 5 0	10 0 0	7 15 0		
8 0 0	5 0 0	7 10 0	7 0 0		
71 0 30	6 10 0	16 0 0	8 10 0	Rent changed in 1857 from . . . 13 0 0	
87 0 30	8 15 0	30 10 0	11 0 0		
15 3 16	6 15 0	12 0 0	8 10 0	1860 10 0 0	
16 3 18	8 15 0	19 0 0	9 10 0	do. 10 0 0	
25 0 0	13 0 0	16 10 0	12 12 0		
13 0 0	8 10 0	5 2 4	6 18 0		
30 0 0	14 0 0	30 0 0	18 13 0	1865 16 15 0	
8 1 10	6 15 0	5 17 6	4 7 6		
20 0 18	18 0 0	24 5 8	11 5 0		
8 0 0	5 0 0	5 0 0	4 0 0		
37 1 0	18 0 0	37 10 0	21 0 0		
18 3 18	11 0 0	15 10 0	11 4 0		
16 3 16	4 10 0	7 10 0	6 15 0		
4 3 10	2 10 0	3 5 3	5 19 0		

COUNTY OF

Names of Assistant Commissioners by whom Cases were decided.	No.	Name of Tenant.	Name of Landlord.	Townland.
Assistant Commissioners—				
T. P. Lynch (Legal). Patrick Tracy. R. L. Hunt. E. J. Kiernan. F. Gunning.	1916	Thomas Dowdrick,	Wm. H. Lahiff, a Lunatic, by James Lahiff, his Committee,	Raheen,
	1917	Michael Fahaughey,	do.	do.
	1918	James Nee,	do.	do.
	1919	John Lamb,	do.	do.
	1920	Patrick Lamb,	do.	do.
	1921	John Mahon,	do.	do.
	1922	Patrick Garrick,	do.	do.
	1923	John Lamb (William),	do.	do.
	1924	Edmund McNamara,	do.	Glenbrack,
	1925	Thomas Kelly,	do.	Newton,
	1926	John Nolan,	R. J. M. de Burgh,	Gloonan,
	1927	Peter Dudy,	do.	do.
	1928	Bridget Burke,	do.	do.
	1929	Ulick Burke,	do.	do.
	1930	Robert Potter,	do.	Roganfield,
	1931	John Dunley,	do.	—
	1932	James Monaghan,	do.	Gloonan,
	1933	Edmund Lally,	Vincent Hough,	[illegible]
	1934	Anne Ryan,	do.	[illegible]
	1935	Patrick Cleary,	do.	do.
	1936	John Waters,	F. L. Geoghegan,	Loughane Beg,
	1937	John Fahy,	do.	do.
	1938	Thomas Hopkins,	do.	do.
	1939	John Dowling,	do.	Knock, South,
	1940	Kevin Waters,	do.	Loughane Beg,
	1941	Coleman Geary,	do.	Carrowmore, West,
	1942	Mary Fahy,	do.	do.
	1943	Peter Fahy,	do.	Carrowkeen, East,
	1944	Martin Fahy,	do.	Carrowmore,
	1945	Bartholomew Fahy,	do.	Loughane Beg,
	1946	Daniel Fahy,	do.	do.
	1947	Mary Kyne,	do.	do.
	1948	John Kyne,	do.	do.
	1949	Patrick Flaherty (Pat),	do.	do.
	1950	John Fahy,	do.	[illegible]

GALWAY—*continued.*

Extent of Holding. Statute.	Poor Law Valuation.	Former Rent.	Judicial Rent.	Observations.		Value of Tenancy.
A. R. P.	£ s. d.	£ s. d.	£ s. d.		£ s. d.	£ s. d.
8 0 0	4 0 0	4 4 0	3 10 0			
23 0 0	11 10 0	15 0 0	12 0 0	Rent changed in 1858 from . . .	15 0 0	
43 0 0	21 10 0	31 0 0	23 15 0	do.	29 1 10½	
60 0 0	27 13 0	33 0 0	28 0 0	do.	37 0 0	
26 0 0	20 15 0	18 10 0	13 0 0	do.	17 10 0	
40 0 0	18 13 0	22 0 0	14 3 0	do.	[illegible] 0 0	
8 0 0	5 15 0	4 4 0	3 11 0	do.	4 0 0	
26 0 0	13 0 0	18 0 0	13 0 0	do.	17 0 0	
41 1 0	8 13 0	10 0 0	7 13 0			
6 3 0	5 10 0	8 13 4	6 17 4			
16 0 23	8 9 0	13 0 0	10 4 0	By consent		
18 1 16	8 10 0	11 0 0	9 7 0	do.		
24 0 0	11 10 0	16 0 0	11 6 0	do.		
17 3 0	9 0 0	13 0 0	11 1 0	do.		
27 0 20	16 16 0	22 0 0	19 11 0	do.		
[illegible] 3 24	13 10 0	20 0 0	17 3 0	do.		
[illegible] 0 10	9 4 0	18 0 0	16 0 0	do.		
40 0 28	17 15 0	26 0 0	18 5 0			
65 3 34	27 15 0	32 0 0	28 0 0			
47 3 7	12 10 0	15 10 0	11 3 0			
11 0 [illegible]	3 8 0	5 17 6	4 15 0			32 0 0
6 0 [illegible]	5 0 0	6 6 0	3 11 0			[illegible] 0 0
5 0 6	3 10 0	5 10 0	1 0 0			[illegible] 0 0
10 0 0	7 0 0	11 10 0	9 4 0			40 0 0
14 0 8	6 2 0	8 0 0	7 4 0			60 0 0
7 0 16	2 17 0	2 15 0	5 0 0			30 0 0
15 0 10	4 5 0	7 17 6	6 0 0			40 0 0
31 1 0	2 5 0	5 5 0	8 17 6			25 0 0
11 0 0	3 18 0	4 0 10	3 15 0	Rent changed in 1859 from . . .	4 10 0	30 0 0
0 3 06	5 1 3	6 7 0	4 13 0			35 0 0
14 0 25	5 14 0	9 0 0	7 7 0			60 0 0
11 3 16	5 5 0	8 10 0	5 0 0			30 0 0
13 1 16	4 10 0	6 10 0	6 0 0			30 0 0
8 0 [illegible]	9 10 0	6 15 0	4 0 0			20 0 0
10 3 10	3 18 0	14 10 0	3 15 0			22 0 0

Names of Assistant Commissioners by whom Cases were decided.	No.	Name of Tenant.	Name of Landlord.	Townland.
Assistant Commissioners—				
T. P. Lynch (Legal). Patrick Taaffe. E. L. Hunt. R. J. Hinkman. P. O'Gallagher.	1851	Brian Hopkins, ...	F. L. Comyn, ...	Thoughmore, ...
	1852	John Folan, ...	do.	do. ...
	1853	Mary Cassidy, ...	do.	Knock, South, ...
	1854	Mark Commons, ...	do.	Gourane, East, ...
	1855	James Folan, ...	do.	Loughaun Beg, ...
	1856	Philip Flaherty, ...	Jerome Blagrave, Trustee and Exec. of Edward Mulchinock,	Fahanacleagh, ...
	1857	Denis Gallagher, ...	do.	do. ...
	1858	Bartholomew Lydon, ...	do.	do. ...
	1859	Thomas Lavelle, ...	do.	do. ...
	1860	Martin Sullivan, ...	do.	do. ...
	1861	Thomas Cooke, ...	do.	do. ...
	1862	Joseph Conroy, ...	do.	do. ...
	1863	John Dunnion, ...	Joseph Fitzpatrick, ...	Knockarasny,
	1864	James Acton, ...	do.	do. ...
	1865	Michael Tuck, ...	do.	do. ...
	1866	Catherine Dunnion, ...	do.	do. ...
	1867	Michael Keady, senior,	do.	do. ...
	1868	Michael Keady, junior,	do.	do. ...
	1869	Patrick McKay, ...	do.	do. ...
	1870	John Flaherty, ...	do.	do. ...
	1871	Thomas Farrell, ...	do.	do. ...
	1872	Martin Dowens, ...	John A. Dawson, ...	Kilmaclea, ...
	1873	Michael Kilkelly, ...	do.	Tooreen, ...
	1874	Patrick Clesham, ...	do.	do. ...
	1875	Darby O'Connor, ...	do.	Kinvarra, ...
	1876	Patrick Keane, ...	do.	Tooreen, ...
	1877	Richard Foley, ...	Patrick Cunnigan, ...	Lisheenagliss and Cappaghy.
	1878	Frank Montgomery, ...	John Lynch, ...	Bookelly, ...
	1879	Mary Kilbride, ...	do.	do. ...
	1880	Michael Keady, ...	do.	do. ...
	1881	Patrick Cunningham, ...	do.	Crannagh, ...
	1882	Thomas Walsh, ...	Michael Davis Keatinge, ...	Lisnavilly, ...
	1883	John McHugh, ...	George C. Lynch, ...	Cloonbeg, ...
	1884	Michael Francis, ...	Francis Comyn, ...	Ballyvaldrum,
	1885	Stephen Walsh, ...	do.	Loughaun Beg.

GALWAY—*continued.*

Extent of Holding. Statute.	Poor Law Valuation.	Former Rent.	Judicial Rent.	Observations.	Value of Tenancy.
A. R. P.	£ s. d.	£ s. d.	£ s. d.	£ s. d.	£ s. d.
6 0 35	2 0 0	3 5 0	3 10 0		20 0 0
11 1 9	6 0 0	6 15 0	8 5 0		10 0 0
16 1 0	7 12 0	13 0 0	10 10 0		45 0 0
15 3 8	5 0 0	7 17 6	5 17 6		35 0 0
11 0 0	3 0 0	8 0 0	6 10 0		40 0 0
16 1 7	4 10 0	8 14 0	6 15 0		
12 0 0	7 5 0	17 7 0	10 10 0		
8 0 1	9 15 0	5 17 0	3 15 0		
8 2 30	—	5 19 3	3 15 0		
5 3 28	2 15 0	5 17 0	3 10 0		
11 3 10	9 0 0	4 16 8	3 0 0		
13 3 11	5 16 0	8 12 0	6 5 0		
16 3 0	3 10 0	3 10 0	4 0 0		
12 3 13	8 0 0	10 14 0	8 10 0		
15 2 35	6 12 6	7 0 0	6 0 0		
7 3 18	4 10 0	5 5 0	4 15 0		
80 0 20	6 0 0	6 0 0	5 0 0		
35 1 28	5 7 6	5 0 0	5 0 0		
25 0 6	3 5 0	4 0 0	4 0 0		
64 3 5	9 0 0	2 0 0	3 10 0		
13 0 30	5 10 0	6 10 0	5 15 0		
9 3 0	1 12 0	6 10 0	3 15 0		
65 0 0	8 0 0	10 3 0	7 0 0		
10 3 14	3 10 0	7 17 0	5 0 0		
81 0 16	7 15 0	13 0 0	9 10 0		
13 3 0	4 1[illegible] 0	6 15 0	4 17 6	Rent changed in 1873 from . . 6 10 0	
76 1 25	21 10 0	21 0 0	25 10 0	1875 20 0 0	
25 3 26	10 5 0	12 2 0	11 10 0		
46 0 28	17 10 0	32 0 0	20 0 0		
80 1 3	12 15 0	23 0 0	17 0 0		
18 3 30	8 10 0	19 1 0	15 10 0		
10 0 17	2 15 0	4 0 0	3 11 0	By consent.	
8 0 8	3 5 0	3 0 0	5 15 0	do.	
30 1 30	7 10 0	13 0 0	8 10 0		45 0 0
9 1 22	5 0 0	6 17 0	3 10 0		80 0 0

COUNTY OF

Names of Assistant Commissioners by whom Cases were decided.	No.	Name of Tenant.	Name of Landlord.	Townland.
Assistant Commissioners— T. P. Lynch (Legal). Patrick Taaffe. E. L. Huff. F. J. Kirwan. P. Gillman.	1986	Pat Fahey	Francis Conyers, ...	[illegible], ...
	1987	Mary [illegible], .	Thomas E. Lalor, a Lunatic, by James Lalor, his Committee,	[illegible], ...
	1988	Michael Maley, ...	do.	Ballyb[illegible], ...
	1989	Walter Higgins ...	do.	do. ...
	1990	Patrick Hession, ...	do.	do. ...
	1991	Michael Hallinan, ...	do.	do. ...
	1992	Joseph Burke, ...	James Blakeney, ...	Ballyb[illegible], South,
	1993	John Glynn, ...	Arthur Alexander, ...	[illegible], ...
	1994	Michael Murray, ...	Thomas Gough, ...	[illegible], ...
	1995	Michael Howard, ...	Daniel Lalor & Mary Lalor, his Wife,	[illegible] and Ballyb[illegible],
	1996	William Robinson, ...	Earl of Clancarty, ...	[illegible], ...
	1997	Lawrence Heverty, ...	William Daly and another, Trustees of Lord Dunsandle,	[illegible] and another,
	1998	John Hallinan, ...	Edward Duggan, ...	Laggan, ...
	1999	Lawrence Mulloy, ...	Anthony Kelly, ...	Ballyw[illegible], ...
	2000	Pat Egan, ...	Lady Rogers, ...	[illegible], ...
	2001	Thomas Connor, junior,	Lord Dunsandle, ...	[illegible], ...
	2002	John Gilmore, ...	do.	do. ...
	2003	William Gilmore, ...	do.	do. ...
	2004	John Nolan, Rep. of Matthew Shiell,	do.	do. ...
	2005	Patrick Connor, ...	do.	do. ...
	2006	John Nolan, ...	do.	do. ...
	2007	John Shiell, ...	do.	do. ...
	2008	Francis J. Burke, a Lunatic, by [illegible], his Committee,	do.	[illegible], ...
	2009	James Walsh, ...	Sir Henry Burke, Bart., ...	[illegible], ...
	2010	Thomas Nevin, ...	do.	[illegible], ...
	2011	Edward Moran, ...	do.	do. ...
	2012	Thomas Cleary, ...	do.	Lagee, ...
	2013	John Tierney, ...	do.	Carragh, ...
	2014	Edward Cavanagh, ...	Hannah Lewis, ...	[illegible],
	2015	Thomas Mahon, ...	do.	[illegible], ...
	2016	William Stephens, ...	do.	[illegible], ...
	2017	Edward Cavanagh, ...	do.	[illegible], ...
	2018	Anne Dunne, ...	Susan McD. Lynch, ...	[illegible], ...
	2019	Thomas Hawkins, ...	Marquis of Clanricarde, ...	Killim[illegible], East,
	2020	Dominick Shiell, ...	do.	do. ...

GALWAY—*continued.*

Extent of Holding. Statute.	Poor Law Valuation.	Former Rent.	Judicial Rent.	Observations.	Value of Tenancy.
A. R. P.	£ s. d.	£ s. d.	£ s. d.	£ s. d.	£ s. d.
11 1 15	9 0 0	8 0 0	4 13 6		60 0 0
19 1 22	28 15 0	27 11 3½	20 0 0		
16 1 10	7 0 0	8 0 0	5 5 0		
18 0 29	8 10 0	9 16 7½	7 17 8		
6 1 35	4 5 0	5 0 0	4 10 0		
8 0 15	6 4 0	6 10 6	5 12 6		
35 1 11	8 0 0	15 0 0	11 10 8		
16 2 30	—	11 13 6	5 17 6		
47 2 10	15 10 0	19 18 0	12 10 0		80 0 0
19 2 10	4 10 0	11 6 8	8 0 0		
49 1 24	29 0 0	52 10 0	40 12 0		
48 2 15	17 5 0	27 16 8	22 0 0		120 0 0
5 2 35	0 16 0	3 7 6	3 10 0		
43 0 0	16 13 0	21 0 0	16 0 0		
36 2 21	14 15 0	25 7 8	23 0 0	Rent changed in 1854 from . . 20 6 0	
26 1 0	10 5 0	13 8 8	11 0 0	1861 16 8 8	60 0 0
27 3 37	20 5 0	24 0 0	15 0 0	do. 10 18 6	70 0 0
18 2 34	6 6 0	8 0 0	6 10 0	1879 8 10 6	60 0 0
29 3 38	8 15 0	14 0 0	11 10 0	1867 13 14 6	60 0 0
74 1 6	10 0 0	18 0 0	10 15 0	1880 10 5 8	70 0 0
14 2 37	8 10 0	8 0 0	6 0 0		35 0 0
23 2 29	16 0 0	13 5 8	10 17 4	1883 16 5 8	46 0 0
128 1 23	28 10 0	46 7 7	46 7 7		320 0 0
17 2 2	15 5 0	17 17 6	16 10 0		
104 1 16	63 0 0	57 6 6	46 0 0	1880 33 0 0	250 0 0
14 2 16	9 0 0	10 16 4	10 0 0		46 0 0
12 2 6	8 10 0	13 4 2	8 0 0		
10 3 12	4 15 0	5 0 0	5 0 0		65 0 0
46 2 22	35 0 0	51 6 6	40 0 0		200 0 0
35 0 30	11 12 0	20 10 0	16 10 0		75 0 0
18 0 0	4 10 0	6 6 8	6 15 0	1881 6 13 4	88 0 0
70 2 30	50 0 0	72 10 0	60 0 0		800 0 0
60 2 11	0 0 0	60 0 0	13 12 0		
10 2 20	14 10 0	20 15 0	18 5 0		
19 2 29	15 15 0	16 0 0	15 0 0		

COUNTY OF

Names of Assistant Commissioners by whom Cases were settled.	No.	Name of Tenant.	Name of Landlord.	Townland.
Assistant Commissioners—				
T. F. Lynch (Legal). Fitzgerald Taaffe. R. L. Hewe. E. J. Kinahan. F. [illegible].	2021	James Connell, ...	Marquis of Clanricarde, ...	[illegible], ...
	2022	John Forsyth, ...	do.	[illegible], ...
	2023	Do., ...	do.	[illegible], West
	2024	Bridget Kenny, ...	Sir Henry Burke, Bart., ...	[illegible], ...
	2025	Malachy Donnelly, ...	John K. Burke, ...	[illegible], ...
	2026	Francis Mullanney, ...	George S. Martin, ...	[illegible], ...
	2027	John Forty, ...	F. L. Dunne, ...	[illegible], North, ...
	2028	Michael Mahyes, ...	O. D. O'Clarke, ...	[illegible], ...
	2029	John Keane, ...	John A. Browne, ...	[illegible], ...
	2030	William Hardy, ...	James Macguire, Trustee and Exor. of Edward [illegible],	[illegible], ...
	2031	Thomas Walsh, ...	Joseph Fitzpatrick, ...	[illegible], ...
				Total, ...

COUNTY OF

Assistant Commissioners—	709	Patrick Cunningham, ...	G. C. B. Whyte, ...	[illegible], ...
Capt. [illegible] (Legal). M. F. Lynch. M. R. [illegible]. E. B. [illegible]. [illegible].	710	Patrick McGarry, ...	do.	[illegible], ...
	711	Thomas O'Connor, ...	do.	do. ...
	712	Martin Dolan, ...	do.	do. ...
	713	Peter Nolan, ...	do.	do. ...
	714	Lawrence Fearhy, ...	do.	[illegible], ...
	715	Michael McDaniel, ...	do.	do. ...
	716	James Fearhy (Owen),	do.	do. ...
	717	Patrick [illegible], ...	do.	[illegible], ...
	718	Do., ...	do.	[illegible],
	719	Patrick Fearhy, ...	do.	[illegible], ...
	720	William Robinson, ...	do.	[illegible], ...
	721	Bryan Cunningham, ...	do.	[illegible], ...
	722	James Dolan, ...	do.	[illegible], ...
	723	Michael Cunningham, ...	do.	do. ...
	724	James Dermott, ...	do.	[illegible], ...
	725	Mary [illegible], ...	do.	do. ...
	726	Michael Dolan, ...	do.	[illegible], ...
	727	Patrick Dolan, ...	do.	do. ...

GALWAY—*continued.*

Extent of Holding. Statute.	Poor Law Valuation.	Former Rent.	Judicial Rent.	Observations.	Value of Tenancy.
A. R. P.	£ s. d.	£ s. d.	£ s. d.	£ s. d.	£ s. d.
11 0 5	10 5 0	16 0 0	13 0 0		
110 5 0	171 10 0	173 1 0	125 10 0		
110 1 7	84 10 0	125 0 0	170 0 0		
13 1 19	3 5 0	7 0 0	3 10 0		
63 0 5	12 10 0	26 0 0	13 10 0		100 0 0
15 1 25	10 10 0	16 11 6	12 5 0		60 0 0
9 0 8	3 10 0	4 13 6	3 18 0		15 0 0
10 0 11	3 10 0	6 0 1½	1 10 0		
32 0 0	3 10 0	5 2 0	3 15 0		
15 0 31	7 0 0	14 7 0	8 0 0	Rent changed in 1860 from . . . 10 10 0	
18 0 7	7 0 0	10 10 0	8 13 0		
3,064 1 34	1,734 8 11	3,050 6 5½	2,313 7 4		

LEITRIM.

20 3 34	7 15 0	11 3 0	6 15 0	Rent changed in 1860 from . . 6 15 0	
14 3 23	6 13 0	8 6 0	7 0 0		
30 3 10	12 10 0	13 15 0	12 12 0	1860 13 7 6	
23 3 36	10 10 0	15 0 0	13 6 0	1871 11 0 0	
12 0 33	5 10 0	6 6 0	4 0 0		
15 0 0	4 15 0	7 0 0	6 0 0		
17 1 6	5 5 0	7 15 0	6 10 0		
13 0 0	4 13 0	7 0 0	5 0 0		
36 3 16	15 10 0	19 5 0	16 0 0		
27 1 5	11 0 0	16 0 0	13 10 0		
50 3 39	14 10 0	23 10 0	19 0 0	1875 17 13 0	
185 0 0	8 10 0	15 0 0	13 0 0		
13 3 27	5 0 0	8 5 0	6 0 0		
59 1 10	14 0 0	18 1 0	14 0 0		
14 0 0	7 5 0	8 0 0	6 10 0		
24 0 19	5 5 0	14 4 0	11 0 0		
15 9 10	4 0 0	6 0 0	0 10 0		
78 0 30	11 0 0	17 5 0	14 6 0		
25 3 0	7 5 0	13 16 0	10 0 0		

COUNTY OF

Names of Assistant Commissioners by whom Cases were decided.	No.	Name of Tenant.	Name of Landlord.	Townland.
Assistant Commissioners— Chas. Rogers (Legal). M. P. Lynch, [illegible]. [illegible]. [illegible].	728	Peter McLaughlin,	R. C. B. Whyte,	[illegible],
	729	William Long,	do.	[illegible].
	730	Patrick Kelly,	do.	[illegible],
	731	Martin McGarry,	do.	Cleary.
	732	William Kelly,	do.	[illegible],
	733	John O'Connor,	do.	[illegible],
	734	Michael McHugh,	do.	[illegible],
	735	Felix Harkin,	do.	do.
	736	Thomas Kerrigan,	do.	do.
	737	Gerard Fowley,	do.	[illegible],
	738	James Fowley (John),	do.	do.
	739	Patrick McGoldrick,	do.	do.
	740	Charles Cleary,	do.	[illegible],
	741	Bryan McTiernan,	do.	[illegible],
	742	Lawrence Cleary,	do.	[illegible],
	743	William Banks,	do.	[illegible],
	744	Patrick McGoldrick,	do.	do.
	745	Patrick McManus,	do.	do.
	746	James Kenny,	do.	[illegible],
	747	James Dolan,	do.	do.
	748	William Kenny,	do.	do.
	749	John Deery,	do.	do.
	750	Thomas Devany,	do.	[illegible],
	751	Dominick Gallagher,	do.	[illegible],
	752	Edward McGoldrick,	do.	do.
	753	Denis O'Hara,	do.	do.
	754	Andrew Feely,	do.	[illegible],
	755	Patrick Cunningham,	do.	[illegible],
	756	Philip Cunningham,	do.	[illegible],
	757	Thomas Feeley,	do.	do.
	758	John O'Connor,	do.	[illegible],
	759	John Cunningham,	do.	[illegible],
	760	Luke Kenny,	Thomas [illegible],	[illegible],
	761	Robert [illegible],	do.	[illegible],
	762	Thomas Kenny,	do.	do.

LEITRIM—continued.

Extent of Holding, Statute.			Poor Law Valuation.			Former Rent.			Judicial Rent.			Observations.				
A.	R.	P.	£	s.	d.	£	s.	d.	£	s.	d.			£	s.	d.
64	2	11	25	10	0	43	3	0	22	10	0					
56	0	7	13	0	0	17	5	0	13	10	0	Rent changed in 1865 from . . .		16	0	0
35	0	0	13	10	0	24	0	0	20	0	0					
97	0	37	20	5	0	33	16	0	30	0	0		1877	32	0	0
18	0	0	5	0	0	5	12	0	7	0	0					
[illegible]	2	0	20	15	0	30	5	0	26	0	0					
63	0	20	13	10	0	18	6	0	14	10	0					
42	3	7	13	15	0	21	4	0	16	10	0					
49	2	13	17	15	0	20	15	0	13	5	0					
94	0	33	7	0	0	9	15	0	8	5	0					
30	3	30	5	5	0	10	0	0	5	10	0					
23	0	0	4	15	0	9	13	0	8	0	0					
98	0	38	7	0	0	11	10	0	8	5	0					
83	1	20	33	5	0	31	0	0	28	10	0		1852	18	3	0
43	0	20	7	5	0	11	1	0	7	0	0		1865	9	14	0
10	0	15	7	5	0	4	0	0	4	15	0					
36	3	5	8	5	0	5	11	0	8	0	0					
11	3	28	0	0	0	0	4	0	5	10	0					
47	0	1	20	0	0	38	7	0	33	0	0					
84	3	5	21	0	0	36	2	0	23	18	0					
85	0	30	21	18	0	19	3	0	16	5	0					
87	3	27	25	5	0	23	16	0	15	0	0		1860	21	11	4
34	1	0	0	10	0	15	0	0	11	0	0		1860	14	7	0
50	0	0	11	5	0	13	0	0	10	5	0	By consent.				
30	0	20	13	4	0	16	10	0	15	0	0	do.				
63	3	23	17	10	0	18	0	0	14	0	0	do.				
8	3	0	3	15	0	4	13	0	3	15	0	do.				
30	1	23	13	10	0	18	15	0	16	0	0	do.				
32	0	9	4	4	0	5	10	0	6	10	0					
8	2	23	3	5	0	3	0	0	8	5	0	do.				
23	3	28	5	0	0	5	15	0	6	15	0	do.				
15	3	28	6	18	0	4	13	0	7	0	0	do.				
33	3	30	0	0	0	6	5	0	5	5	0					
15	2	1	6	18	0	9	5	0	4	15	0					
9	1	1	4	10	0	10	0	0	5	5	0					

Names of Assistant Commissioners by whom Cases were decided.	No.	Name of Tenant.	Name of Landlord.	Townland.
Assistant Commissioners—				
Chas. Roche (Legal). M. P. Lynch. H. B. [illegible]. R. B. [illegible]. Reginald Roche.	763	Mary Rooney, ...	Thomas Cromie[illegible], ...	[illegible], ...
	764	Patrick Flanagan, ...	do.	do. ...
	765	Patrick Rooney, ...	do.	do. ...
	766	Do., ...	do.	[illegible], ...
	767	Mathew Mallony, ...	do.	do. ...
	768	James Cromie[illegible], ...	do.	Cullenbane, ...
	769	Edward Fox, ...	do.	[illegible] and [illegible].
	770	John Burke, ...	[illegible] A. White, ...	Drumsay, ...
	771	Philip Cleary, ...	Adam White, ...	Bavagh, ...
	772	John Keaveny, ...	do.	Derrynaugher, ...
	773	Peter Gallagher, ...	James Tate and others, Reps. of Thomas Palmer.	Shanvill[illegible], ...
	774	Mary McNama, Admx. of Patrick McNama.	do.	do. ...
	775	Patrick O'Brien, ...	do.	do. ...
	776	Hugh McNama, ...	do.	do. ...
	777	Patrick McNulty, Rep. of John O'Hanly.	do.	do. ...
	778	James Harkin, ...	do.	do. ...
	779	Michael McHugh, ...	do.	[illegible], ...
	780	Patrick McNulty, ...	do.	do. ...
	781	Margaret McNulty, ...	do.	do. ...
	782	Bridget Kilbenny, ...	do.	do. ...
	783	Thomas Carty, ...	Francis La Touche, ...	Cagrade, ...
	784	Bridget Carty, ...	do.	do. ...
	785	Daniel Morton, ...	Lieutenant Colonel [illegible],	[illegible], ...
	786	James Drum, ...	do.	[illegible], ...
	787	Patrick Gilgan, ...	do.	Ross, ...
	788	Mary Cleary, ...	do.	[illegible], ...
	789	[illegible] Melanifi, Admx. of Thomas Melanifi.	do.	Cornamuck, ...
	790	Francis Kenny, ...	Archibald Collum, ...	Carn, ...
	791	Dominick Fallon, ...	John Palmer, ...	Cuilla [illegible], ...
	792	James [illegible], ...	Francis La Touche, ...	Carrigcliff, ...
	793	Patrick Lee, ...	Rev. Richard Tate, ...	[illegible],
	794	Patrick McGreevy, ...	Roger Perkins, ...	[illegible], ...
	795	Thomas Harte, ...	do.	do. ...
	796	William Doyle, ...	C. C. B. Whyte, ...	Moygara, ...
	797	Cormack Coffey, ...	A. L. Tottenham, ...	Ballyloy, ...

LEITRIM—continued.

Extent of Holding. Statute	Poor Law Valuation.	Former Rent.	Judicial Rent.	Observations.	Value of Tenancy.
A. R. P.	£ s. d.	£ s. d.	£ s. d.		£ s. d.
15 0 30	5 15 0	10 0 0	7 0 0		
21 2 22	7 10 0	10 3 1	7 15 0		
16 1 30	6 7 0	10 0 0	7 0 0		
11 0 24	8 0 0	12 3 4	13 10 0		
20 3 19	9 3 0	10 10 5	10 0 0		
12 1 0	6 0 0	13 0 0	8 0 0		
10 3 4	2 8 0	6 5 5	4 0 0		
17 3 16	4 5 0	10 0 0	8 0 0	By consent.	
23 2 7	19 10 0	15 18 7	13 5 0	do.	
16 3 37	4 10 0	9 0 0	7 10 0	do.	
14 3 27	6 0 0	12 0 0	8 0 0	do.	
4 0 7	3 0 0	5 8 7	4 0 0	do.	
11 3 27	5 15 0	11 10 0	6 10 0	do.	
3 2 30	2 4 0	7 0 0	3 10 0	do.	
3 0 26	0 15 0	3 3 0	1 10 0	do.	
9 1 23	3 10 0	6 0 0	3 8 0	do.	
9 1 34	5 10 0	8 0 0	5 15 0	do.	
13 1 33	7 10 0	6 10 0	7 0 0	do.	
13 2 20	6 0 0	10 0 0	6 0 0	do.	
13 0 26	5 0 0	6 10 0	5 0 0	do.	
20 3 0	7 15 0	9 3 6	7 15 0	do.	
8 1 9	0 10 0	1 11 0	1 6 0	do.	
22 0 23	11 16 0	23 5 0	13 5 0		
14 0 0	7 15 0	20 15 0	7 0 0		
21 3 14	14 0 0	23 0 0	15 0 0		
16 1 27	6 0 0	8 0 0	6 5 0		
25 3 20	6 14 0	10 0 0	8 0 0		
34 2 0	17 0 0	26 6 8	24 0 0	Rent changed in 1865 from . . . . £ s. d. 21 0 0	
4 2 1	2 10 0	5 0 0	4 0 0		
21 1 13	13 0 0	16 0 0	11 10 0		
8 2 30	—	10 0 0	8 8 0		
30 1 7	13 10 0	15 0 0	17 10 0		
20 0 4	13 15 0	18 3 0	15 15 0		
20 0 34	10 0 0	10 17 8	9 10 0		
45 0 0	5 10 0	8 0 0	7 0 0		

COUNTY OF

Names of Assistant Commissioners by whom Cases were decided.	No.	Name of Tenant.	Name of Landlord.	Townland.
Assistant Commissioners—				
Geo. [illegible] (Legal). M. F. Lynch. W. R. [illegible]. R. D. [illegible]. [illegible]	[illegible]	Anthony Callen, ...	A. L. [illegible], ...	[illegible], ...
	[illegible]	Patrick [illegible], ...	do. ...	[illegible] and another.
	[illegible]	Michael McManus, ...	do. ...	[illegible], ...
	601	John Kelly, Rep. of William Kelly.	do. ...	do. ...
	602	Bridget Maguire, Rep. of Francis Maguire.	do. ...	do. ...
	603	Tom Cullen, Rep. of [illegible] McCrudden.	do. ...	do. ...
	604	Christopher Stewart, ...	do. ...	[illegible], ...
	605	Michael Darcy, ...	C. C. B. Whyte, ...	[illegible], ...
	606	John Malloy, ...	do. ...	[illegible], ...
	607	Joseph McDermott, ...	do. ...	Larkam, ...
	608	Patrick Kelly, ...	Adam Whyte, ...	[illegible], ...
	609	James McDaniel, ...	C. C. B. Whyte, ...	[illegible], ...
	610	John [illegible], ...	Charles V. Peyton, ...	[illegible]
	611	Irwin Finlay, ...	John W. L. [illegible], ...	[illegible], ...
	612	John Dunny, ...	[illegible] Nixon, Admx. of William Nixon.	Mullane, ...
	613	Catherine McManus, Admx. of Jas. Kenny.	Arthur L. [illegible], ...	[illegible], ...
	614	Michael [illegible], ...	Sir Gilbert King, Bart., ...	[illegible], ...
	615	George Reid, ...	Francis Le Fanu, ...	[illegible] ...
	616	Robert Charlton, ...	do. ...	do. ...
	617	John Reynolds, ...	George E. G. [illegible], ...	[illegible], ...
	618	Daniel [illegible], ...	Charles Kelly, ...	[illegible], ...
	619	William McKeon, ...	do. ...	do. ...
	620	James Early, ...	do. ...	do. ...
	621	Martin Reynolds, ...	do. ...	do. ...
	622	Bridget [illegible], ...	do. ...	do. ...
	623	Anne Rourke, ...	do. ...	do. ...
	624	Michael [illegible], ...	do. ...	do. ...
	625	Charles [illegible], ...	Maurice Fitzgerald and another,	[illegible], ...
	626	Catherine Early, ...	do. ...	[illegible], ...
	627	Patrick [illegible], ...	do. ...	[illegible], ...
	628	James McLoughlin, ...	do. ...	[illegible], ...
	629	John McWeeny, ...	do. ...	[illegible], ...
	630	Charles Early, ...	do. ...	do. ...
	631	Michael McNicholas, ...	do. ...	[illegible], ...
	632	Francis McDermott, ...	do. ...	do. ...

LEITRIM—*continued.*

Extent of Holding. Statute.	Poor Law Valuation.	Former Rent.	Judicial Rent.	Observations.		Value of Tenancy.
A. R. P.	£ s. d.	£ s. d.	£ s. d.		£ s. d.	£ s. d.
9 3 25	5 5 0	7 0 0	6 0 0			
16 0 31	6 0 0	11 11 6	7 10 0			
27 2 32	7 5 0	17 10 0	11 15 0			
16 0 0	6 5 0	18 4 8	20 0 0			
20 1 19	13 13 9	15 18 6	14 0 0			
12 1 18	7 5 0	10 1 9	6 17 4			
20 0 1	6 0 6	14 7 0	11 0 0			
29 3 33	12 10 0	16 16 0	13 10 0			
234 0 0	18 10 0	25 18 0	20 10 0			
34 1 20	18 5 0	17 0 0	14 10 0	Rent changed in 1876 from . .	15 1 3	
65 1 18	23 0 0	35 0 6	23 0 0			
23 1 1	3 3 0	8 12 0	7 13 0	By consent.		
16 0 30	9 6 0	18 7 5	11 10 0			
25 0 34	13 18 0	18 10 7½	15 18 7½			
19 1 33	9 0 0	14 0 0	10 7 6			
11 3 11	5 5 0	6 0 0	6 10 0			
6 2 35	6 0 0	7 17 11	5 10 0			
6 3 20	5 10 0	6 0 0	4 0 0	do.		
17 2 0	10 0 0	11 0 0	5 0 0			
10 1 30	5 5 0	8 5 0	5 5 0	do.		
16 0 0	4 10 0	7 7 4	6 0 0			
20 1 6	8 7 6	9 10 7	5 10 0			
23 1 4	9 7 9	13 16 0	10 0 0			
15 1 4	5 7 0	9 10 7	8 15 0			
0 1 0	3 10 0	3 16 0	3 5 0			
3 2 20	1 10 0	3 4 4	2 0 0			
14 3 1	6 15 0	6 12 5	5 15 0			
16 1 8	6 15 0	10 0 0	7 0 0			
8 0 19	2 3 0	3 0 0	3 0 0			
9 3 14	3 10 0	6 18 0	6 0 0			
21 0 0	7 10 0	13 14 5	10 10 0			
23 0 16	11 12 0	18 18 0	15 10 0			
16 2 4	3 15 0	7 0 0	5 0 0			
15 3 32½	7 18 6	11 0 0	10 0 0			
18 2 32½	7 17 6	11 0 0	10 0 0			

Names of Assistant Commissioners by whom Cases were [illegible].	No.	Name of Tenant.	Name of Landlord.
Assistant Commissioners:—			
[illegible] (Legal).	833	[illegible], ...	Maurice Fitzgerald & ors.
M. F. [illegible].	834	William [illegible], ...	do. ...
[illegible].	835	Thomas [illegible], ...	do. ...
E. B. [illegible].	836	John Early, ...	do. ...
[illegible].	837	Francis [illegible], ...	do. ...
	838	William [illegible], ...	do. ...
	839	John [illegible], ...	do. ...
	840	Patrick [illegible],	M. M. D. [illegible],
	841	Ellen [illegible], ...	do. ...
	842	Michael Dwyer, ...	do. ...
	843	Patrick [illegible], ...	do. ...
	844	Do., ...	do. ...
	845	Charles Flynn, ...	John F. [illegible],
	846	Peter [illegible], ...	do. ...
	847	Michael [illegible], ...	do. ...
	848	William [illegible], ...	do. ...
	849	Thomas [illegible], ...	William [illegible],
	850	Patrick [illegible], ...	do. ...
	851	George [illegible], ...	do. ...
	852	Alexander [illegible], ...	do. ...
	853	John Taylor, ...	do. ...
	854	Michael [illegible], ...	do. ...
	855	James [illegible], ...	do. ...
	856	Patrick [illegible], ...	Earl of [illegible],
	857	Thomas [illegible], ...	do. ...
	858	Andrew [illegible], ...	do. ...
	859	Peter [illegible], ...	do. ...
	860	Mary [illegible], ...	do. ...
	861	Catherine Reynolds, Rep. of Henry Reynolds,	do. ...
	862	Patrick [illegible], ...	do. ...
	863	Michael [illegible], ...	do. ...
	864	James Mitchell, ...	do. ...
	865	John [illegible], ...	do. ...
	866	Patrick [illegible], ...	do. ...
	867	James [illegible], ...	do. ...

LEITRIM—continued.

Extent of Holding. Statute.	Poor Law Valuation.	Former Rent.	Judicial Rent.	Observations.	Value of Tenancy.
A. R. P.	£ s. d.	£ s. d.	£ s. d.		£ s. d.
14 3 0	5 10 0	6 10 6	7 10 0		
18 1 0	7 8 0	13 0 0	20 0 0		
15 0 31½	5 0 0	5 12 0	7 15 0		
16 0 0	5 0 0	7 13 0	7 0 0		
19 2 [illegible]	9 0 0	21 0 0	10 5 0		
16 0 22	6 0 0	9 [illegible] 0	7 15 0		
4 2 0	5 0 0	5 0 0	5 0 6		
10 0 31	3 0 0	1 7 4	5 0 0		
42 0 30	7 5 0	17 0 0	13 10 0		
16 0 20	4 5 0	[illegible] 4 6	6 0 0		
14 0 1	3 10 0	6 2 0	6 10 0		
14 0 0	5 0 0	7 13 0	8 5 0		
30 3 18	10 10 0	13 10 10	11 10 0		
96 0 14	11 5 0	14 17 6	13 0 0		
27 2 23½	0 15 0	13 5 0	11 5 0	Rent changed in 1878 from . . . £ s. d. 11 18 0	
30 0 13	6 5 0	6 16 6	6 16 0		
60 1 0	18 16 0	26 10 0	21 0 0	By consent.	
14 1 21	9 5 0	21 15 6	11 0 0	do.	
10 3 18	9 0 0	9 7 0	9 10 0	do.	
[illegible] 0 0	19 16 0	11 0 0	12 0 0	do.	
21 1 16	11 6 0	17 4 0	10 4 0	do.	
19 1 2	16 13 0	19 6 0	16 10 0		
86 2 0	10 10 0	10 13 0	9 0 0		
40 2 26	14 15 0	[illegible] 1 6	30 13 0	do.	
14 2 6	0 15 0	9 0 0	7 0 0	do.	
21 2 9	5 1 0	11 6 3	9 10 0	do.	
25 1 11	13 4 0	[illegible] 5 3	11 0 0	do.	
[illegible] 1 0	[illegible] 15 0	16 0 0	21 10 0	do.	
18 1 26	9 0 0	[illegible] 2 0	10 12 0	do.	
13 1 14	0 10 0	5 10 0	5 10 0	do.	
11 1 [illegible]	4 15 0	9 0 0	7 0 0	do.	
10 0 34	6 1 0	9 0 0	7 0 0	do.	
37 0 20	14 10 0	[illegible] 0 0	15 16 0	do.	
11 0 13	4 10 0	9 5 0	6 10 0	do.	
17 0 10	20 5 0	15 4 5	11 0 0	do.	

COUNTY OF

Names of Assistant Commissioners by whom Cases were decided.	No.	Name of Tenant.	Name of Landlord.	Townland.
Assistant Commissioners—				
[illegible] (Legal). M. F. Lynch. [illegible]. [illegible]. [illegible].	868	James [illegible], ...	Earl of [illegible], ...	[illegible], ...
	869	Owen [illegible], ...	do.	[illegible], ...
	870	Peter McW[illegible], ...	do.	[illegible], ...
	871	Mary [illegible], ...	do.	[illegible], ...
	872	Bridget [illegible], ...	do.	do. ...
	873	Thomas McK[illegible], ...	do.	[illegible], ...
	874	John Early, ...	do.	[illegible], ...
	875	Thomas [illegible], junior, ...	do.	[illegible], ...
	876	Patrick [illegible], ...	do.	[illegible] & anr.,
	877	Dominick [illegible], ...	do.	[illegible], ...
	878	[illegible], ...	do.	[illegible], ...
	879	Patrick [illegible], ...	do.	[illegible], ...
	880	Peter [illegible], ...	do.	[illegible], ...
	881	Cornelius [illegible], ...	do.	do. ...
	882	William [illegible], ...	do.	[illegible], ...
	883	John [illegible], ...	do.	do. ...
	884	Michael [illegible], ...	do.	do. ...
	885	Arthur [illegible], ...	Francis O'Brien, a Minor, by Ellen O'Brien, his Guardian.	[illegible],
	886	Do.	do.	[illegible], ...
	887	Terence [illegible], ...	do.	[illegible], ...
	888	Thomas [illegible], ...	do.	[illegible], ...
	889	Do.	do.	[illegible],
	890	Anne [illegible] and another, Reps. of [illegible],	do.	[illegible], ...
	891	Michael Ward, ...	do.	do. ...
	892	Bernard [illegible], ...	do.	[illegible], ...
	893	Patrick [illegible], ...	do.	do. ...
	894	Thomas [illegible], ...	do.	do. ...
	895	Matthew [illegible], ...	do.	[illegible],
	896	Patrick [illegible], ...	do.	do. ...
	897	Bernard Clarke, ...	do.	do. ...
	898	Thomas Clarke, ...	do.	do. ...
	899	Francis [illegible], ...	do.	do. ...
	900	Bernard McW[illegible] and [illegible].	do.	[illegible], ...
	901	[illegible], ...	do.	do. ...
	902	James [illegible], ...	do.	do. ...

LEITRIM—*continued.*

Extent of Holding. Statute.	Poor Law Valuation.	Former Rent.	Judicial Rent.	Observations.		Value of Tenancy.
A. R. P.	£ s. d.	£ s. d.	£ s. d.		£ s. d.	£ s. d.
14 1 20	17 10 0	22 0 0	13 0 0	By consent.		
10 0 30	7 0 0	11 3 0	8 5 0	do.		
18 2 20	6 15 0	13 0 0	8 0 0	do.		
15 3 10	8 14 0	11 5 0	9 5 0	do.		
22 0 30	5 15 0	7 0 0	6 5 0	do.		
5 3 0	3 10 0	4 10 0	3 10 0	do.		
20 0 20	9 0 0	11 17 0	8 0 0	do.		
9 2 5	4 10 0	7 0 4	5 15 0	do.		
16 0 0	6 15 0	10 1 5	7 10 0			
13 1 16	5 17 0	7 0 0	6 0 0			
4 0 0	5 0 0	8 5 0	7 0 0			
19 1 16	11 15 0	16 10 0	13 10 0			
12 2 5	5 7 0	8 13 0	7 10 0			
10 0 0	7 15 0	10 5 0	8 10 0			
13 1 9½	5 5 0	7 10 0	4 0 0			
13 1 9½	5 0 0	7 10 0	4 0 0			
15 0 0	7 0 0	10 12 0	7 10 0			
7 0 0	4 0 0	6 10 0	6 13 0			
21 0 4	11 5 0	22 15 11	17 0 0	Rent changed in 1841 from . .	15 0 0	
18 1 10	5 15 0	11 5 0	11 5 0			
5 0 0	3 0 0	5 0 9	5 5 0	1857	1 2 7	
10 3 15	3 15 0	20 10 11	13 10 0			
7 3 33	3 15 0	6 6 3	5 10 0			
10 0 9	3 0 0	7 7 0	5 5 0			
10 0 0	7 15 0	11 7 8	8 0 0			
64 1 10	23 14 0	30 4 0	35 0 0	1858	27 11 9	
35 0 14	15 5 0	21 10 7	17 0 0			
30 0 3½	9 3 0	27 4 0	23 0 0	do.	10 15 11	
12 1 32	14 10 0	20 4 4	18 0 0			
21 1 30	13 5 0	23 0 9	18 0 0			
20 2 10	10 0 0	19 0 6	13 10 0	do.	10 10 0	
26 1 25	9 10 0	22 0 0	15 0 0	do.	12 16 0	
13 0 17	6 15 0	21 1 9	7 15 0			
18 3 10	5 15 0	13 10 0	5 5 0	1859	0 0 0	
25 0 0	11 0 0	18 10 0	13 15 0			

COUNTY OF

Names of Assistant Commissioners by whom Cases were decided.	No.	Name of Tenant.	Name of Landlord.	Townland.
Assistant Commissioners— Chas. Hogan (Legal). W. F. Lynch. H. H. Montgomery. H. B. Hamilton. Hammond Baker.	903	Patrick Duignan, ...	Francis O'Beirne, a Minor by Edward O'Beirne, his Guardian,	Tully, ...
	904	James McKeon, ...	do.	Drumlougher, ...
	905	John Flanagan, ...	do.	Corranacreeve,
	906	do.	do.	do. ...
	907	Thomas Costello, ...	do.	Aughnaclidomard,
	908	Bernard Brien, ...	do.	Mucknagh, ...
	909	Rose Conroy, ...	do.	Drumshanbo, ...
	910	do.	do.	Carbeagh, ...
	911	Patrick McKeon, ...	do.	Moneyconn, ...
	912	John Farry, ...	do.	Drumsheriff Barry,
	913	Richard Gibbs, ...	do.	do. ...
	914	William Mulloy, ...	do.	Cornelwell, ...
	915	George Flynn, ...	do.	Ballinamuck, ...
	916	John Morris, ...	do.	do. ...
	917	Dan Tuohill, ...	do.	do. ...
	918	John Flynn, ...	do.	do. ...
	919	Bridget Connolly, Admix. of Peter Connolly,	do.	Tully, ...
	920	John Waters, ...	Charles C. S. Whyte and Ferdinando Whyte,	Ballinamoney, ...
	921	James Farrell, ...	do.	Aughaloby, ...
	922	Leonard Forsyth, ...	do.	Aughgarry, ...
	923	Bernard Kelly, ...	Anne E. Grattan, ...	Drumdick, ...
	924	John Coleman, ...	Captain W. H. White, ...	Drumgowragh, ...
	925	John Reynolds, ...	do.	do. ...
	926	Patrick Hester, ...	do.	do. ...
	927	Patrick McKiernan, ...	do.	do. ...
	928	James McPartland, ...	do.	do. ...
	929	Mark Carr, ...	do.	Mullaghbrack, ...
	930	Margaret McCabe and Michael McCabe,	do.	Drumshane, ...
	931	John Mitchel, ...	William Lefroy, ...	Ardrum, ...
	932	Isabella Lee, Exx. of Thomas Lee,	Captain J. Barley, ...	Carrigeen, ...
	933	Bartholomew Brien, ...	Colonel Robert Marshall, ...	Tonagh, ...
	934	Bridget Moran, ...	do.	do. ...
	935	Peter Gallagher, ...	do.	do. ...
	936	Patrick McWeeny, Rep. of James McWeeny,	Lord Harlech, ...	Derrywillow, ...
	937	James Conlon, ...	do.	do. ...

LEITRIM—*continued.*

Extent of Holding, Statute.	Poor Law Valuation.	Former Rent.	Judicial Rent.	Observations.		Value of Tenancy.
A. R. P.	£ s. d.	£ s. d.	£ s. d.		£ s. d.	£ s. d.
14 0 37	6 5 0	10 16 5	8 10 0	Rent changed in 1856 from	8 10 0	
14 0 31	7 5 0	11 3 10	10 10 0	1861	9 5 8	
13 3 20	4 15 0	6 6 7	7 0 0			
10 3 25	3 15 0	6 1 11	5 6 0			
20 0 31	9 5 0	22 5 5	11 10 0	1870	10 0 0	
34 1 0	16 0 0	25 3 5	16 0 0			
6 1 13	3 10 0	4 1 3	4 15 0			
7 1 29	3 5 0	6 10 10	5 10 0			
7 0 3	3 0 0	4 3 0	6 0 0			
15 3 11	5 15 0	10 3 1	7 5 5	1877	6 14 1	
17 1 23	6 5 0	11 5 3	8 0 0	do.	7 10 0	
11 0 25	5 5 0	7 17 5	6 0 0	1865	7 3 8	
31 1 13	10 16 0	15 13 8	13 0 0	1857	11 6 0	
21 0 23	12 0 0	16 7 6½	12 5 0			
20 2 3	12 0 0	16 3 7	15 10 0	1866	9 17 0	
41 2 16	23 15 0	32 11 1	26 0 0	1857	23 14 9	
46 1 5	30 15 0	65 11 0	40 0 0	1856	45 10 0	
9 2 1	6 14 0	9 15 0	9 15 0			
6 3 4	4 15 0	7 10 0	8 0 0			
19 1 30	8 10 0	17 15 0	13 10 0	By consent.		
19 1 20	11 13 0	15 0 0	13 0 0	do.		
24 1 10	11 10 0	13 0 0	13 0 0	do.		
14 0 30	4 15 0	6 0 0	5 0 0	do.		
23 0 15	7 0 0	9 16 0	9 0 0	do.		
19 1 23	5 5 0	8 13 6	8 0 0	do.		
10 0 8	3 15 0	8 15 0	7 15 0	do.		
11 1 14	5 5 0	5 0 0	5 0 0			
14 0 16	4 15 0	7 10 0	6 0 0	do.		
20 1 27	13 10 0	19 0 0	14 0 0	do.		
35 2 34	21 5 0	37 10 0	24 0 0	do.		
30 0 8	18 10 0	19 13 8	15 10 0	do.		
25 3 30	10 16 0	15 15 3	12 10 0	do.		
16 1 16	9 16 0	19 4 10	10 5 0	do.		
24 3 34	13 10 0	28 10 5	19 10 0	do.		
17 0 24	8 10 0	20 15 6	9 0 0	do.		

COUNTY OF

Names of Assistant Commissioners by whom Cases were decided.	No.	Name of Tenant.	Name of Landlord.	Townland.
Assistant Commissioners—				
[illegible] (Legal). M. F. Lynch. M. B. [illegible]. E. H. [illegible]. [illegible].	938	Adam Hall, ...	Archibald [illegible], ...	Rowan, ...
	939	John [illegible], ...	William A. O'Brien, ...	Mullaghmore, ...
	940	Anne Brady, ...	do.	do. ...
	941	James Hagan, ...	do.	do. ...
	942	William Brady, ...	do.	do. ...
	943	James Egan, ...	do.	do. ...
	944	Anthony Brady, ...	do.	do. ...
	945	George Dobson, junr., ...	Captain A. M. [illegible], ...	Ballygowan,
	946	Farrell McWeeney, ...	do.	Clonloughill, ...
	947	Edward Glynn, ...	do.	Curraun, ...
	948	George Dobson, senr., ...	do.	[illegible], ...
	949	David O'Brien, ...	do.	Aghamore, ...
	950	Patrick [illegible], ...	do.	Lands, ...
	951	John Lanaghan, ...	Henry Allen, ...	[illegible], ...
	952	[illegible] Moffett, ...	do.	Adrum, ...
	953	Thomas Moffett, ...	do.	Drumnagrave, ...
	954	Thomas Dunne, ...	do.	[illegible], ...
	955	Mary Lewis, ...	Henry Allen and Miss Allen,	Clonfeakle, ...
	956	Michael Lewis and Anne Lewis.	do.	[illegible], ...
	957	Matthew Gaffney, ...	do.	Drumman, ...
	958	William Tuthill, ...	John Vernon Tuthill, ...	Gortangillan, ...
	959	Francis Donohoe and Bernard O'Reilly,	do.	do. ...
	960	John [illegible], ...	do.	do. ...
	961	Peter Lynch, ...	[illegible] V. Lowder, a Minor, and others.	[illegible], ...
	962	Mary Curtis, ...	William G. B. [illegible], ...	Annaduff (Glebe,
	963	Do.	do.	do. ...
	964	John Lavin, ...	do.	[illegible] Glebe
	965	Francis Walsh, ...	do.	do. ...
	966	John McCann, ...	do.	do. ...
	967	Thomas Conroy, Admor. of Mary Conroy.	do.	Annaduff Glebe,
	968	James Burke, ...	do.	do. ...
	969	James Mann, ...	do.	do. ...
	970	Do.	do.	do. ...
	971	John Farrell, ...	Elizabeth M. Carter and anor., Reps. of Richard D. Carter.	[illegible] & [illegible] Early.
	972	John Lawrence, ...	Colonel H. T. Clements, ...	Townparks, ...

LEITRIM—continued.

Extent of Holding (Statute)	Poor Law Valuation	Former Rent	Judicial Rent	Observations		Value of Tenancy
A. R. P.	£ s. d.	£ s. d.	£ s. d.		£ s. d.	£ s. d.
7 1 8	5 0 0	5 5 0	5 8 0	By consent.		
16 0 24	6 10 0	10 10 0	7 10 0	Rent changed in 1879 from	£ s. d.	
65 3 33	19 5 0	37 0 0	28 15 0	1857	18 14 3	
66 1 35	17 5 0	35 15 0	33 18 0	1866	15 5 0	
17 1 13	0 0 0	9 10 0	7 5 0			
30 3 35	10 10 0	15 10 0	13 0 0			
11 0 3	3 5 0	7 12 5	6 10 0			
23 5 20	10 15 0	26 0 8	23 0 0			
7 1 7	4 8 0	5 3 2	5 4 0			
5 3 17	8 10 0	4 11 8	3 10 0			
40 0 34	20 5 0	22 0 6	20 3 0			
100 3 35	45 0 0	75 18 2	70 0 0			
33 2 5	12 10 0	15 8 10	14 10 0			
36 1 30	18 3 0	18 0 0	12 0 0			
11 1 10	3 5 0	7 10 0	6 10 0			
17 0 13	9 0 0	13 3 0	11 0 0			
30 3 30	10 15 0	13 6 4	13 5 0			
41 1 10	19 5 0	27 0 0	24 0 0			
30 2 1	9 0 0	18 6 8	13 0 0			
15 0 35	10 0 0	12 6 0	11 10 0			
23 0 11	3 5 0	15 10 0	10 0 0			
60 1 20	24 0 0	19 18 0	15 10 0			
16 2 14	5 10 0	7 7 0	7 0 0	1879	5 0 0	
60 1 08	44 1 0	42 10 0	44 10 0			
9 0 10	4 0 0	8 14 0	5 14 8			
9 1 28	5 0 0	6 15 0	6 18 0			
14 1 0	7 10 0	14 5 0	11 10 0			
56 3 9	9 15 0	17 15 0	16 10 0			
18 1 8	6 10 0	0 5 0	8 10 0			
4 2 33	5 10 0	8 15 4	5 10 0			
61 3 31	26 0 0	37 15 4	35 0 0			
30 1 7	14 0 0	24 13 0	16 8 0			
37 3 12	21 15 0	22 5 0	27 0 0			
30 0 0	13 12 0	17 10 6	18 10 0			
29 1 18	13 15 0	20 1 6	16 10 0	1881	19 0 0	

COUNTY OF

Names of Assistant Commissioners by whom Cases were decided.	No.	Name of Tenant.	Name of Landlord.	Townland.
Assistant Commissioners—				
Cecil Roche (Legal). M. F. Lynch. H. R. Marsden. R. B. Hamilton. Edmund Roche.	973	John Sheedy, ...	Col. H. T. Clements, ...	[illegible]
	974	Michael Reilly, ...	do.	do. ...
	975	Thomas Faughnan, ...	do.	do. ...
	976	Thomas Reynolds, ...	do.	do. ...
	977	Edward Dairer, ...	do.	Ordnal, ...
	978	Elizabeth McGovern, ...	R. M. D. Duckworth, ...	Gowney, ...
	979	Bridget Pyer, ...	do.	do. ...
	980	Thomas Smyth, ...	Francis and Ellen O'Beirne, ...	Rossagone, ...
				Total, ...

COUNTY OF

Assistant Commissioners—				
William Rowan (Legal). A. B. Nolan. E. O'Brien. R. R. Davis. H. G. Gregory.	3466	John Sheridan, ...	Rev. T. S. Carter, ...	Fahies, ...
	3467	Frank Gibbons, ...	do.	Tonaglass, West,
	3468	Hugh Maguire (John),	do.	Derrygeran, ...
	3469	Michael Gallagher, ...	Maguire & R. Dickson, ...	Mountain, ...
	3470	Nancy Gallagher, ...	do.	do. ...
	3471	Owen Gallagher (Neal)	do.	do. ...
	3472	Patrick O'Malley (Red),	do.	Ballyglass and another,
	3473	Bridget Gallagher (Terry)	do.	[illegible], ...
	3474	Anne Patton, ...	do.	Mountain, ...
	3475	Mary Gallagher, ...	do.	do. ...
	3476	Edward Moran, ...	do.	do. ...
	3477	Michael Gilmartin, ...	do.	do. ...
	3478	Martin Patton, ...	do.	do. ...
	3479	Patrick Gilmartin, ...	do.	Mountain, ...
	3480	Patrick Joyce, ...	do.	Ballyglass, ...
	3481	Thomas Campbell, ...	do.	do. ...
	3482	Bridget Lynch, ...	do.	Tonaglass, East,
	3483	Patrick Lynch, ...	do.	do. ...
	3484	Michael Lynch, sen.	do.	do. ...
	3485	Daniel Oliver, ...	do.	do. ...
	3486	Michael Moran, ...	do.	Ballyglass, ...
	3487	Edward Joyce, ...	do.	Ballyglass, ...

LEITRIM—continued.

Extent of Holding. Statute.	Poor Law Valuation.	Former Rent.	Judicial Rent.	Observations.	Value of Tenancy.
A. R. P.	£ s. d.	£ s. d.	£ s. d.	£ s. d.	£ s. d.
6 2 2	6 0 0	8 0 0	6 0 0	Rent changed in 1858 from - - 6 0 0	
15 1 34	8 0 0	14 10 0	10 0 0	1871 12 0 0	
23 2 1	10 0 0	18 0 0	12 0 0	1880 13 0 0	
17 3 22	8 0 0	18 0 0	9 10 0	1872 16 0 0	
33 1 16	15 0 0	21 0 0	22 0 0		
36 0 30	7 0 0	15 0 0	11 0 0		
27 3 28	7 8 0	18 16 0	10 0 0		
31 3 16	13 10 0	19 13 7	17 10 0		
6,750 2 37½	2,446 11 3	3,735 16 5	2,903 11 10½		

MAYO.

7 0 0	3 7 0	2 13 0	2 11 0		
7 0 0	1 16 0	5 5 0	2 3 0		
3 3 14	1 10 0	2 6 0	1 11 0		
14 0 5	3 13 0	5 16 10½	3 7 6		
12 0 6	1 6 0	3 14 5	1 13 0		
12 3 16	1 6 8	3 16 5	1 15 0		
6 0 18½	1 10 0	3 5 8	1 18 0		
6 3 12½	1 10 0	3 3 3	1 12 0		
12 0 31	1 15 0	3 5 3	1 16 0		
10 0 8	3 0 0	1 15 6	1 10 0		
10 0 0	0 15 0	2 0 0	1 12 0		
5 1 33½	1 5 0	2 10 0	1 15 0		
13 2 21	1 6 0	2 4 3	1 18 0		
9 1 20½	1 6 6	3 10 0	1 15 0		
9 0 29	1 0 0	3 15 0	2 4 0		
11 0 7	1 10 0	4 18 5	2 10 0		
3 1 4	—	1 0 0	0 13 0		
4 1 0	0 18 0	1 5 5	0 17 0		
10 0 7	0 5 0	2 0 0	1 5 0		
8 0 33	2 0 0	2 0 8	1 5 0		
5 3 8	1 5 0	3 0 4	1 18 0		
8 0 20	0 16 0	3 2 3	1 6 6		

COUNTY OF

Names of Assistant Commissioners by whom Cases were decided.	No.	Name of Tenant.	Name of Landlord.	Townland.
Assistant Commissioners— Wm. Barton (Legal). A. B. Nolan. E. O'Kelly. R. E. Bayly. H. C. Gormley.	[illegible]	Joseph McDermott,	Charles S. S. Dickens,	Tonragee, East,
	[illegible]	Michael Gallagher,	do.	do.
	[illegible]	James Conway,	do.	Tonragee, West,
	8451	Michael Gormaly,	do.	do.
	[illegible]	Charles Patten,	do.	Knockvillen,
	[illegible]	Mathew Gallagher,	do.	do.
	8454	John Garvey,	Patrick Malley,	Dooniver,
	[illegible]	John Lavelle,	do.	do.
	[illegible]	Bridget Kilbane,	do.	do.
	[illegible]	Patrick Gannon,	do.	do.
	[illegible]	Michael Lavelle,	do.	do.
	[illegible]	Daniel Calleary, junior,	Trustees of the Achill Mission,	Salsey,
	[illegible]	Myles Sweeney,	do.	Lyonbeen,
	[illegible]	Catherine Calleary (Pat) and another,	do.	Pulravey,
	[illegible]	Patrick Murphy,	do.	do.
	[illegible]	Patrick Calleary,	do.	do.
	[illegible]	James Calleary,	do.	do.
	[illegible]	Daniel Calleary,	do.	do.
	[illegible]	Michael Calleary,	do.	do.
	[illegible]	James Lynchehaun,	do.	do.
	[illegible]	James Calleary,	do.	do.
	[illegible]	Neal Lynchehaun,	do.	do.
	[illegible]	Patrick Corrigan,	do.	do.
	[illegible]	Michael Kilbane,	Richard Pike,	Doogort,
	[illegible]	Anthony Malley,	do.	do.
	[illegible]	Anne [illegible],	do.	do.
	[illegible]	Margaret Corrigan,	do.	do.
	[illegible]	Martin Patten,	do.	do.
	[illegible]	Nancy Conway,	do.	do.
	[illegible]	Mary McLoughlin,	do.	do.
	[illegible]	James Gallagher,	do.	do.
	[illegible]	Peter O'Donnell & anor.,	Colonel A. W. E. Gore,	Doughloy,
	[illegible]	John Malley and another,	do.	do.
	[illegible]	Hugh Corrigan & anor.,	do.	do.
	[illegible]	Darby Geary and others,	do.	do.

MAYO—*continued.*

Extent of Holding. Statute.	Poor Law Valuation.	Former Rent.	Judicial Rent.	Observations.	Value of Tenancy.
A. R. P.	£ s. d.	£ s. d.	£ s. d.		£ s. d.
8 0 0	1 10 0	3 0 0	1 15 0		
5 0 2	0 5 0	1 15 0	1 1 0		
10 1 8	1 5 0	8 15 6	8 0 0		
6 2 19	0 12 0	2 13 8	1 8 0		
7 1 29½	3 0 0	8 12 10	3 7 8		
11 2 24	0 15 0	1 10 0	1 10 0		
8 0 0	—	3 0 0	1 0 0		
3 0 16	—	8 0 0	1 0 0		
3 2 20	—	1 0 0	0 15 0		
6 0 0	—	3 10 0	1 15 0		
3 2 13	—	2 7 6	1 5 0		
7 0 0	2 10 0	5 0 0	2 5 0		
65 2 10	12 0 0	20 0 0	13 0 0		
12 2 0	5 10 0	8 0 0	7 15 0		
7 0 0	0 11 0	2 0 0	1 0 0		
6 0 0	1 0 0	3 0 0	1 13 0		
8 1 0	1 5 0	3 0 0	1 5 0		
7 0 0	0 11 0	1 10 0	1 0 0		
6 0 0	1 13 0	4 0 0	2 5 0		
16 1 8	1 13 0	3 0 0	3 3 6		
7 0 0	0 11 0	2 0 0	1 0 0		
25 0 0	2 10 0	4 10 0	3 17 6		
4 0 0	1 7 0	1 10 0	1 5 0		
3 0 21	0 15 0	1 15 0	1 0 0		
7 2 20	0 13 0	1 16 0	1 10 0		
3 2 22	0 13 0	1 19 0	1 5 0		
3 3 28	0 14 0	2 10 0	1 6 0		
8 0 2	1 0 0	3 6 0	1 10 0		
4 1 20	1 0 0	3 3 0	1 4 0		
6 2 7	0 15 0	3 5 6	0 18 0		
4 1 20	1 1 0	2 16 0	1 16 0		
7 0 10	4 0 0	6 5 6	4 0 0		
7 1 10	2 10 0	6 13 4	4 0 0		
8 2 0	4 15 0	7 12 6	5 0 0		
7 0 20	5 5 0	6 8 4	4 5 0		

COUNTY OF

Names of Assistant Commissioners by whom Cases were decided.	No.	Name of Tenant.	Name of Landlord.	Townland.
Assistant Commissioners—				
William Rowan (Legal). A. R. Nolan. M. O'Keary. E. B. Bayly. H. G. Garrett.	[illegible]	Martin Patten and another,	Col. A. W. K. Gore,	Dooghbeg,
	3524	John Mason and another,	do.	do.
	3525	Patrick Masterson,	Richard Pike,	Derreen,
	3526	Owen McNulty,	do.	Saula,
	3527	Bridget McTigue,	do.	do.
	3528	James Kilbane,	do.	do.
	3529	John McLaughlin,	do.	do.
	3530	Patrick Sweeny,	do.	Derreen,
	3531	Charles McKay,	do.	do.
	3532	Owen Kilbane,	do.	Gloshane,
	3533	Edward Cleary,	do.	Derreen,
	3534	Nancy McCann,	do.	do.
	3535	Phelim McCann,	do.	do.
	3536	John Patten (Martin),	do.	do.
	3537	Honor Kilroy,	do.	Dooega,
	3538	Patrick Reily,	do.	do.
	3539	Honor Dever,	do.	do.
	3540	Michael McNamara,	do.	do.
	3541	Mary Johnson,	do.	do.
	3542	Martin McNamara,	do.	do.
	3543	Thomas McNamara,	do.	do.
	3544	Owen Masterson,	do.	do.
	3545	John Evans,	Thomas F. O'Reilly,	Claremork,
	3546	Daniel Gallagher,	Trustees of the Achill Mission,	Dugort, Achill Island,
	3547	Patrick McNulty,	do.	Cashel,
	3548	Anthony Gallagher (Michael),	do.	Cassie, Achill Island,
	3549	John English (Pat),	do.	do.
	3550	Ellen Reddy,	do.	Dugort, Achill Island,
	3551	Michael Burns,	do.	do.
	3552	Thomas English (Pat),	do.	Cassie, Achill Island,
	3553	Michael Gaughan,	do.	Dugort,
	3554	Hugh Gallagher (Dan),	do.	Doeghinnelly, Achill Island,
	3555	Denis Lavell,	do.	Dugort, Achill Island,
	3556	Bryan McNamara (John),	do.	Dugort, Achill Island,
	3557	Michael Lavelle (Bryan),	do.	do.

MAYO—*continued.*

Extent of Holding—Statute.	Poor Law Valuation.	Former Rent.	Judicial Rent.	Observations.	Term of Tenancy.
A. R. P.	£ s. d.	£ s. d.	£ s. d.		£ s. d.
0 3 10	5 0 0	1 3 1	4 [illegible] 0		
6 3 30	4 10 0	0 13 4	4 3 0		
6 0 7	1 0 0	1 4 0	1 [illegible] 0		
11 1 13	3 5 0	4 15 0	3 0 0		
12 0 1	6 0 0	5 14 0	4 0 0		
0 0 [illegible]	3 0 0	4 15 0	1 10 0		
0 3 [illegible]	1 15 0	4 17 0	3 0 0		
3 0 15	1 0 0	1 0 0	1 5 0		
5 0 13	0 10 0	1 4 0	1 0 0		
5 1 10	0 10 0	1 0 0	1 0 0		
0 3 17	1 5 0	1 5 0	1 0 0		
4 3 [illegible]	1 10 0	4 3 0	1 15 0		
5 0 10	0 15 0	9 4 0	1 4 0		
4 0 20	0 13 0	5 1 0	1 12 0		
3 3 [illegible]	0 8 0	3 3 0	0 17 6		
4 3 [illegible]	0 0 0	7 0 0	1 0 0		
0 1 [illegible]	0 0 0	0 0 0	1 6 0		
3 2 [illegible]	0 0 0	0 0 0	0 10 0		
4 2 30	0 0 0	0 0 0	1 1 0		
3 1 [illegible]	0 5 0	3 3 0	0 15 0		
4 3 0	0 13 0	3 5 0	0 0 0		
4 3 [illegible]	0 5 0	0 0 0	1 1 0		
4 0 0	5 0 0	7 7 0	4 19 0		
6 1 [illegible]	—	0 13 0	3 0 0		
4 1 12	1 10 0	5 0 0	1 10 0		
5 1 12	3 0 0	3 10 0	1 13 0		
0 2 0	1 15 0	3 5 0	1 3 0		
2 3 [illegible]	—	5 10 0	0 17 6		
5 0 0	—	5 7 1	0 16 0		
4 3 13	2 0 0	4 10 0	1 5 0		
3 1 11	0 17 0	5 0 0	1 4 0		
4 0 0	—	5 10 0	2 3 0		
5 2 0	1 13 0	5 5 0	2 0 0		
3 3 0	2 0 0	2 10 0	1 0 0		
4 0 0	0 7 0	1 0 0	0 12 6		

COUNTY OF

Names of Assistant Commissioners by whom Cases were decided.	No.	Name of Tenant.	Name of Landlord.	Townland.
Additional Commissioners—				
William Reeves (Legal). A. R. Nolan. E. O'Reilly. F. R. Bayly. H. G. Gibbons.	2554	Patrick Lavell (Vesty),	Trustees of the Achill Mission,	Dugort, Achill Island.
	2556	Anthony Lavell (Vesty),	do. — —	do. —
	2560	Thady Vesty, —	do. — —	do. —
	2561	John McNamara (Tom),	do. — —	do. —
	2562	Terence McNamara, —	do. — —	do. —
	2563	Widow Kate McNamara,	do. — —	Slievemore, Achill Island.
	2564	James McHale, —	do. — —	Dugort & Slievemore.
	2565	Patrick Weir, —	do. — —	Slievemore, ..
	2566	Anthony Henning, —	do. — —	do. —
	2567	Widow Cafferky (John),	do. — —	Cashel, Achill Island.
	2568	John Cummins, —	do. — —	Dugort, Achill Island.
	2569	Patrick Cafferky, —	do. — —	do. —
	2570	John Ferry, —	do. — —	do. —
	2571	Widow McGinty (Andy),	do. — —	Cashel, Achill Island.
	2572	Lawrence McNulty, —	do. — —	do. —
	2573	John Gallagher, —	do. — —	Cashel, —
	2574	Lawrence McNulty and Michael Lavelle.	do. — —	Dooagh & Slievemore, Achill Island.
	2575	Patrick Ferry and Co.,	do. — —	Dooagh, Achill Island.
	2576	Patrick Burke, —	do. — —	Slievemore, Achill Island.
	2577	Owen Gallagher (Hugh),	do. — —	Cashel, Achill Island.
	2578	Biddy Lavell, —	do. — —	Slievemore, Achill Island.
	2579	Patrick Cox, —	do. — —	Pollagh, Slievemore.
	2580	John Lavell (Trumpet),	do. — —	Dooagh, Slievemore, Achill Island.
	2581	Michael Lavell (Weaver),	do. — —	Slievemore, Achill Island.
	2582	Daniel Corran, —	do. — —	Dookinella, Calvey and Thulis.
	2583	John Gallagher (Anthony),	do. — —	Dookinella, Calvey,
	2584	Edmond Calvey, —	do. — —	do. —
	2585	Michael English, —	do. — —	Slievemore, —
	2586	Lackey Malley, —	do. — —	do. —
	2587	Patrick Lavelle (Tom), —	do. — —	do. —
	2588	Bryan Malley, —	do. — —	do. —
	2589	John Lavelle (Brown), —	do. — —	do. —
	2590	Anthony Mangan, —	do. — —	do. —
	2591	Kate Ferry, —	do. — —	do. —
	2927	Anthony Cafferky (Owen),	do. — —	do. —

MAYO—*continued.*

Extent of Holding, Statute.	Poor Law Valuation.	Former Rent.	Judicial Rent.	Observations.	Value of Tenancy.
A. R. P.	£ s. d.	£ s. d.	£ s. d.		£ s. d.
6 2 [illegible]	—	3 0 0	1 8 0		
4 0 17	2 0 0	3 10 0	1 5 0		
2 0 0	1 2 6	2 5 0	0 18 0		
9 2 [illegible]	5 15 0	5 16 0	2 14 0		
8 3 30	3 0 0	4 0 0	2 5 0		
8 0 0	9 15 0	8 0 0	3 16 0		
15 0 0	8 0 0	10 0 0	7 0 0		
1 1 0	0 2 0	0 8 3	0 5 0		
3 0 0	—	0 15 0	0 10 0		
4 1 12	3 0 0	3 6 0	1 6 0		
5 1 [illegible]	0 15 0	1 0 0	0 12 6		
8 1 0	—	1 0 0	0 10 0		
6 0 7	0 10 0	3 0 0	1 5 0		
4 1 18	1 16 0	2 5 0	1 8 6		
4 1 22	1 3 8	2 8 6	1 3 0		
4 1 19	1 10 0	2 0 0	1 2 6		
10 1 30	4 0 0	1 10 0	3 8 0		
7 2 0	3 10 0	3 0 0	3 6 0		
8 2 30	1 14 0	2 0 0	1 14 0		
4 1 18	2 5 0	5 0 0	1 8 0		
1 0 0	0 10 0	0 15 0	0 10 0		
8 0 0	1 0 0	1 10 0	1 0 0		
5 0 0	1 7 0	1 15 0	1 6 0		
7 1 [illegible]	1 5 0	2 10 0	1 12 0		
7 2 0	3 10 0	5 18 7	2 11 0		
7 2 0	3 10 0	8 15 0	2 15 0		
7 2 0	2 5 0	4 3 6	3 13 6		
7 2 0	2 15 0	3 10 0	2 0 0		
7 2 0	2 15 0	3 10 0	3 5 0		
4 3 0	1 13 0	1 12 6	1 6 0		
3 1 9	0 18 0	1 7 6	0 17 8		
8 2 0	5 2 0	2 15 0	1 13 6		
8 3 0	1 13 0	2 7 6	1 15 6		
7 3 0	2 18 0	3 10 0	2 2 0		
7 3 0	2 10 0	3 0 0	3 2 0		

COUNTY OF

Names of Assistant Commissioners by whom Cases were decided.	No.	Name of Tenant.	Name of Landlord.	Townland.
Assistant Commissioners—				
William Bowen (Legal). A. B. Nolan. E. O'Brien. E. B. Bayly. H. C. Gibney.	3793	Patrick Lavelle (Brian),	Trustees of the Achill Mission,	[illegible] —
	3794	Edward Patten, —	do. — —	do. —
	3795	Thomas English, —	do. — —	do. —
	3796	John Kelly, — —	do. — —	do. —
	3797	Patrick Malley (Owen),	do. — —	do. —
	3798	Bridget Lavelle, —	do. — —	do. —
	3799	Anthony Barrett, —	do. — —	do. —
	3800	Michael Lavelle (Ned), —	do. — —	do. —
	3801	Anthony Lavelle, —	do. — —	do. —
	3802	Edward English, —	do. — —	do. —
	3803	Martin Vesey, —	do. — —	do. —
	3804	Anthony Peters, —	do. — —	do. —
	3805	John Gealy, —	do. — —	do. —
	3806	Patrick Gallagher, —	do. — —	Cashel, —
	3807	Hon. Anne McDowell, —	do. — —	Bal, Dookinelly, Valley, Keel E., and Dugort W.
	3808	Owen Gloty (Pat), —	Charles S. B. Dickson, —	Tonragee, East, —
	3809	Patrick Costigan, —	do. — —	[illegible], —
	3810	Anne Lafferty, —	Trustees of the Achill Mission,	Mulranny, Lyminhan,
	3811	Thomas Lavell (Davey),	do. — —	Dugort, Achill Island.
	3812	Patrick Patten (Tom),	do. — —	do. —
	3813	Mary McAlinney, —	do. — —	Doonbrenda, Tiskin.
	3814	Owen O'Donnell, —	Richard Pike, — —	[illegible], —
	3815	Julia [illegible], —	do. — —	do. —
	3816	Patrick O'Donnell (Mary),	do. — —	do. —
	3817	Patrick McKeown (William),	do. — —	Dooega, —
	3818	Manus Conway, —	do. — —	[illegible], —
	3819	Patrick Malloy, —	do. — —	Dooega, —
	3820	Mary Fury, — —	do. — —	do. —
	3821	Edward Fury, —	do. — —	do. —
	3822	John Sweeney, —	do. — —	Dooega, —
	3823	Sarah Sweeney, —	do. — —	Dooega, —
	3824	Michael Lavelle (John),	do. — —	do. —
	3825	Anne Barrett, —	do. — —	do. —
	3826	Hugh Corrigan, —	do. — —	do. —
	3827	Patrick McNamara (Peter),	do. — —	do. —

MAYO—*continued.*

Extent of Holding Statute.	Poor Law Valuation.	Former Rent.	Judicial Rent.	Observations.	Value of Tenancy.
A. R. P.	£ s. d.	£ s. d.	£ s. d.		£ s. d.
3 2 0	1 5 0	1 10 0	1 0 0		
5 0 0	1 7 0	1 15 0	1 6 0		
5 3 20	3 0 0	2 18 0	1 13 0		
4 1 30	1 13 0	1 18 4	1 8 0		
7 3 0	2 13 0	3 10 0	3 0 0		
2 2 0	1 5 0	1 18 0	1 0 0		
7 2 0	2 10 0	3 10 0	2 0 0		
7 2 0	2 13 0	3 10 0	3 0 0		
4 0 30	2 7 0	1 15 0	1 6 0		
4 0 30	2 0 0	1 15 0	1 5 6		
3 3 5	0 14 0	0 17 6	0 13 0		
0 3 36	2 3 0	2 12 6	1 13 0		
7 3 0	3 18 0	5 10 0	3 2 0		
9 1 23	2 5 0	3 0 0	1 14 0		
73 0 0	13 1 0	13 0 0	4 8 0		
0 3 13	3 10 0	2 4 0	2 0 0		
17 0 0	5 10 0	6 15 0	3 7 6		
11 0 0	0 17 0	2 0 0	1 3 0		
3 3 0	0 18 0	3 0 0	1 8 0		
3 0 0	1 17 0	1 10 0	1 1 0		
5 2 0	2 0 0	3 5 10	1 0 3		
6 3 35	0 18 0	2 8 0	1 9 0		
5 1 8	1 0 0	1 9 0	1 3 8		
8 0 31	1 10 0	4 8 0	1 17 6		
6 0 18	0 5 0	2 7 8	1 7 6		
4 0 0	0 10 0	1 16 0	1 8 6		
3 3 30	0 5 6	2 6 0	0 13 0		
5 3 0	1 8 0	3 16 0	1 10 6		
5 3 0	1 8 6	3 16 0	1 10 8		
8 3 20	0 10 0	2 10 0	1 4 6		
3 0 7	0 17 0	5 17 0	1 0 6		
3 3 36	1 11 0	3 17 0	1 13 0		
8 0 16	0 6 0	5 4 0	0 16 6		
8 0 18	0 10 0	2 8 0	1 5 6		
2 3 8	0 5 0	2 8 8	0 17 6		

COUNTY OF

Names of Assistant Commissioners by whom Cases were decided.	No.	Name of Tenant.	Name of Landlord.	Townland.
Assistant Commissioners—				
William Roper (Legal). A. R. Nolan. E. O'Kelly. E. R. Bayly. H. G. Gammon.	3628	Frank Malley, ...	Richard Pike, ...	Dooega, ...
	3629	Michael McNamara, ...	do.	do. ...
	3630	Michael Gormally (Neal),	do.	do. ...
	3631	John Carton, ...	do.	do. ...
	3632	Michael Gallagher, ...	do.	do. ...
	3633	James Dever, ...	do.	do. ...
	3634	Peggy Furey, ...	do.	do. ...
	3635	Michael McLoughlin, ...	do.	Derreens, ...
	3636	Thomas McLoughlin, ...	do.	do. ...
	3637	Nancy O'Donnell, ...	do.	Srahmore, ...
	3638	Michael Duggan, ...	do.	Dooega, ...
	3639	Thomas Weir, ...	do.	do. ...
	3640	Denis Curran, ...	do.	do. ...
	3641	Anthony Killeen, ...	do.	do. ...
	3642	Anthony Gallagher, ...	do.	do. ...
	3643	Margaret Killeen, ...	do.	do. ...
	3644	Michael Malley, ...	do.	do. ...
	3645	Judy Killeen, ...	do.	do. ...
	3646	Patrick Killeen, ...	do.	do. ...
	3647	John Malley, ...	do.	do. ...
	3648	John Patten, ...	do.	do. ...
	3649	Patrick Malley, ...	do.	do. ...
	3650	Patrick Malley, ...	do.	do. ...
	3651	Mary Malley, ...	do.	do. ...
	3652	John M'Ginty (Kate), ...	do.	do. ...
	3653	Mathew Gallagher, ...	Earl of Cavan, ...	Tonatanvally, Achill Island.
	3654	Bernard Patten, ...	do.	Tonatanvally, ...
	3655	Hugh Gallagher, ...	Charles S. R. Holmes, ...	Tonragee, East, Achill.
	3656	Terence Gormly, ...	do.	Tonragee, West,
	3657	Anthony Ginty, ...	do.	Tonragee, East, ...
	3658	Patrick Campbell (Neal),	do.	Ballyglass, ...
	3659	Anthony Patten, senior,	Richard Pike, ...	Derreen, ...
	3660	Patk. O'Donnell (Bernard),	do.	do. ...
	3661	Manus Malley, ...	do.	do. ...
	3662	James O'Donnell, ...	do.	do. ...

MAYO—*continued.*

Extent of Holding. Statute.	Poor Law Valuation.	Former Rent.	Judicial Rent.	Observations.	Value of Tenancy.
A. R. P.	£ s. d.	£ s. d.	£ s. d.		£ s. d.
3 1 0	—	3 11 0	1 1 0		
3 3 0	0 9 0	1 13 0	0 18 0		
4 3 0	0 11 0	4 18 0	1 4 0		
5 3 0	1 13 0	3 10 0	1 10 0		
3 0 10	1 0 0	3 7 0	1 8 0		
4 3 8	0 [illegible] 0	2 13 6	1 6 0		
4 3 13	1 0 0	5 3 6	1 10 0		
3 1 20	0 15 0	3 8 0	1 3 0		
5 3 20	1 0 0	3 13 0	1 6 0		
4 3 16	0 15 0	1 18 0	1 6 0		
4 3 7	0 8 6	2 17 0	1 3 0		
2 3 20	0 5 0	3 5 0	1 8 0		
6 3 [illegible]	2 8 0	4 8 0	1 16 0		
5 0 16	1 0 0	2 1 0	1 0 0		
5 2 20	1 17 6	3 17 8	1 12 0		
5 3 [illegible]	1 13 0	4 7 0	2 0 0		
3 0 10	1 4 0	3 3 0	1 0 0		
7 2 0	0 3 0	5 7 0	1 0 0		
3 0 36	1 8 0	2 5 0	0 18 0		
7 2 [illegible]	2 0 0	4 5 0	2 3 0		
4 0 10	1 18 0	5 5 0	2 1 0		
3 1 23	1 2 0	3 2 0	1 5 6		
5 3 0	1 10 0	4 8 6	1 15 0		
4 3 [illegible]	2 0 0	3 12 0	1 17 0		
4 0 [illegible]	1 10 0	2 5 0	1 13 0		
3 3 10	0 13 0	1 17 11	1 19 6	By consent.	
4 0 0	0 16 0	8 10 1	3 7 3	do.	
8 0 0	—	3 8 8	3 5 0	do.	
8 0 8	1 0 0	1 0 0	1 5 0	do.	
4 0 27	1 6 0	1 16 1	1 6 7	do.	
7 3 31	2 18 0	4 7 8	3 1 8	do.	
4 0 [illegible]	1 0 0	3 4 0	1 10 0		
9 2 [illegible]	1 0 0	5 1 0	0 16 8		
1 3 36	1 8 0	2 16 0	1 7 6		
3 3 20	1 0 0	3 5 0	0 18 0		

COUNTY OF

Names of Assistant Commissioners by whom Cases were decided	No.	Name of Tenant	Name of Landlord	Townland	
Assistant Commissioners:—					
William Barton (Legal). A. D. Nolan. R. O'Malley. E. B. Bayly. H. C. Gregory.	2663	Patrick Corrigan (Biddy),	Richard Pike,	Derreen,	—
	2664	Catherine McGloughlin,	do.	do.	—
	2665	Anthony McGinty,	do.	Dooega,	—
	2666	Bridget Lavelle (Tom),	do.	do.	—
	2667	Rowly Killeen,	do.	do.	—
	2668	Edward Killeen,	do.	do.	—
	2669	Anthony Corrigan,	do.	do.	—
	2670	Bridget Mulvenna,	do.	do.	—
	2671	Anthony Malley,	do.	do.	—
	2672	Matilda Malley,	do.	do.	—
	2673	John Gallagher (Owen),	do.	do.	—
	2674	Patrick Ginnelly,	do.	do.	—
	2675	Patrick Lavelle (Bridget),	do.	do.	—
	2676	Anthony Gallagher,	do.	do.	
	2677	Martin Lavelle (Weaver),	do.	do.	—
	2678	James Johnston,	do.	do.	—
	2679	Owen Gallagher,	do.	do.	—
	2680	Patrick Killeen,	do.	do.	—
	2681	Daniel Gallagher,	do.	do.	—
	2682	Anne Lavelle,	do.	do.	—
	2683	Mary Lavelle (Widow),	do.	do.	—
	2684	Michael Cafferty,	do.	do.	—
	2685	Michael Lavelle (Martin),	do.	do.	—
	2686	John Lavelle (Martin),	do.	do.	—
	2687	Owen Patten,	do.	do.	—
	2688	Bridget Ginnelly,	do.	do.	—
	2689	James McKeown,	do.	do.	—
	2690	Bryan Johnston,	do.	do.	—
	2691	John Gallagher (Pat),	do.	do.	—
	2692	Patrick Geraghty,	Charles S. N. Dickens,	Tonragee, East,	—
	2693	James O'Hara,	do.	do.	—
	2694	Michael O'Hara,	Sir Charles J. K. Gore, Bart.,	Ballaghanisla,	—
	2695	Mary Brennan,	do.	Carrowkeribly,	—
	2696	Thomas Wade,	do.	do.	—
	2697	Thomas Kearney,	do.	Rathnacreeva,	—

MAYO—*continued.*

Extent of Holding. Statute.	Poor Law Valuation.	Former Rent.	Judicial Rent.	Observations.	Value of Tenancy.
a. r. p.	£ s. d.	£ s. d.	£ s. d.		£ s. d.
3 1 30	0 15 0	1 16 0	1 9 0		
2 0 23	0 15 0	1 3 0	0 16 6		
3 0 34	0 8 0	2 7 6	0 17 8		
4 1 25	0 13 0	2 4 0	1 5 6		
3 1 20	0 15 0	2 2 0	1 5 0		
3 1 6	1 0 0	3 5 0	1 10 6		
3 1 0	0 16 0	2 15 0	1 8 6		
8 0 0	1 8 0	0 4 0	1 14 0		
4 0 0	0 10 0	2 7 0	1 7 8		
3 0 0	0 16 0	2 4 0	1 6 6		
3 3 20	0 19 0	2 6 8	0 13 0		
0 0 38	1 8 0	4 3 0	2 2 0		
3 2 36	0 10 0	2 8 0	1 4 0		
5 3 0	1 19 0	4 6 0	3 3 0		
0 1 36	2 0 0	1 8 0	3 [illegible] 0		
4 3 31	0 13 0	3 4 0	1 [illegible] 0		
5 0 20	1 14 0	3 14 0	2 0 6		
8 0 16	1 10 0	6 0 0	3 0 0		
8 0 31	1 19 0	4 15 0	2 5 0		
4 3 19	0 18 0	3 13 0	1 10 0		
8 3 4	1 14 0	5 5 0	2 14 0		
1 1 28	1 10 0	3 7 6	1 16 6		
2 1 30	0 18 0	2 2 0	1 3 6		
6 1 3	1 6 0	3 1 0	1 10 0		
8 3 16	1 8 0	3 4 0	1 3 6		
8 3 20	0 16 0	3 1 0	1 4 0		
3 3 25	1 0 0	2 7 0	1 5 0		
8 1 0	0 15 0	8 3 0	1 4 0		
4 0 0	1 0 0	2 3 0	1 8 0		
6 0 28	2 0 0	5 9 3	3 16 0	By consent.	
7 0 30	—	1 13 3	1 1 0	do.	
8 3 34	2 18 0	4 0 0	4 0 0		
18 0 33	3 0 0	7 10 0	7 10 0		
16 0 10	7 0 0	10 3 0	6 3 0		
10 3 17	10 15 0	12 0 0	10 0 0		

COUNTY OF

Names of Assistant Commissioners by whom Cases were decided.	No.	Name of Tenant.	Name of Landlord.	Townland.
Assistant Commissioners—				
William Reeves (Legal). A. D. Nolan. E. O'Kelly. R. E. Bayly. H. G. Gresham.	3676	Thomas O'Hara, ...	Sir Charles J. K. Gore, Bart.,	Rathnarrow, ...
	3435	John Kenny, ...	do.	do. ...
	3700	Margaret McDonagh, ...	do.	Carrowkeeran, ...
	3701	Patrick D. Mulhern, ...	do.	do. ...
	3702	Patrick Cunningham, ...	do.	do. ...
	3703	Michael Brennan, ...	do.	do. ...
	3704	Michael Morgan, ...	do.	[illegible], ...
	3705	Bartholomew Higgins, ...	do.	do. ...
	3706	Patrick Barrett, ...	do.	Cuffsley, ...
	3707	Andrew Hardy, ...	do.	do. ...
	3708	Patrick Smyth, ...	do.	Mullahowney, ...
	3709	John Smyth, ...	do.	do. ...
	3710	Mathew Costello, ...	do.	Demesk, ...
	3711	Peter O'Hara, ...	do.	[illegible],
	3712	James Hunter, ...	do.	Ardnaglass, ...
	3713	James Gallagher, ...	do.	do. ...
	3714	Patrick Lavin, ...	do.	do. ...
	3715	Thomas Quinn, ...	do.	do. ...
	3716	John Moore, ...	do.	do. ...
	3717	James Lavin, ...	do.	do. ...
	3718	Anthony Hannahan, ...	do.	do. ...
	3719	Mathew Flanagan, ...	Francis J. Campe, ...	Rathmurrcash-Do,
	3720	James Joyce, ...	R. Vesey Stoney, ...	Rengarrow, ...
	3721	Do. ...	do.	do. ...
	3722	Patrick Waldron, ...	Maude Knox, ...	Tullygorm, ...
	3723	Patrick Walsh, sen., ...	do.	do. ...
	3724	Patrick Walsh, jun., ...	do.	do. ...
	3725	Anne Murray, ...	do.	do. ...
	3726	Michael McLoughlin, ...	do.	do. ...
	3727	William Pope, ...	O. V. Jackson, ...	Ballydrung, ...
	3728	John O'Hara, ...	do.	do. ...
	3729	Thomas Doherty, ...	do.	do. ...
	3730	William Mellon, ...	do.	Carrowcrin, ...
	3731	Patrick Lafferty, ...	Robert W. Thompson, ...	Glenree, ...
	3732	Michael Lavelle, ...	do.	Carrowmaglough

MAYO—*continued.*

Extent of Holding. Statute.	Poor Law Valuation.	Former Rent.	Judicial Rent.	Observations.	Value of Tenancy.
A. R. P.	£ s. d.	£ s. d.	£ s. d.		£ s. d.
52 0 0	12 0 0	24 0 0	20 10 0		
17 3 0	6 5 0	5 0 0	3 18 0		
13 3 0	5 0 0	11 5 0	6 10 0		
19 0 9	5 10 0	15 10 0	9 15 0		
49 0 37	20 [illegible] 0	24 8 8	19 0 0		
29 1 25	6 10 0	13 0 0	9 8 0		
8 1 0	6 5 0	5 5 0	4 7 0		
46 3 15	20 0 0	27 0 0	20 10 0		
23 0 31	5 0 0	8 0 0	6 0 0		
24 2 35	4 10 0	7 8 8	7 0 0		
9 3 0	4 5 0	5 14 0	4 18 0		
13 2 0	8 0 0	7 10 0	5 5 0		
15 0 19	6 15 0	8 19 0	5 0 0		
22 2 5	5 5 0	7 10 0	6 0 0		
31 1 0	14 15 0	23 1 5	15 0 0		
31 1 0	16 16 0	23 1 2	13 4 0		
7 0 14	3 15 0	7 13 4	5 13 0		
25 0 16	13 0 0	17 0 0	14 10 0		
13 1 25	8 10 0	11 10 0	9 0 0		
11 3 10	7 15 0	8 16 8	7 15 5		
7 0 14	4 0 0	7 0 0	5 15 0		
28 0 25	7 10 0	9 5 0	7 10 0		
9 0 20	1 15 0	3 8 5	5 10 0		
1 0 35	0 10 0	1 0 0	0 15 0		
8 3 0	6 3 0	8 16 0	3 13 0		
14 0 0	8 0 0	8 2 0	5 7 0		
9 3 0	5 3 0	5 0 0	4 8 0		
5 1 0	4 5 0	6 17 0	5 0 0		
5 3 0	4 0 0	4 5 0	8 13 0		
21 2 9	8 0 0	12 18 0	10 15 0		
10 2 25	4 15 0	8 5 0	6 5 0		
23 5 0	11 5 0	17 0 0	12 0 0		
11 0 35	5 5 0	6 0 0	7 0 0		
9 0 20	3 15 0	3 10 8	3 0 0		
12 3 0	4 11 0	6 5 0	5 16 0		

COUNTY OF

Names of Assistant Commissioners by whom Cases were decided.	No.	Name of Tenant.	Name of Landlord.	Townland.
Assistant Commissioners—				
William Reeves (Legal). A. R. Nolan. R. O'Kelly. E. R. Bayly. H. C. Gaisford.	2730	Edward Evans,	Robert W. Thompson,	Carrowmaghagh,
	2731	Patrick Judge,	do.	Seeinish,
	2732	Richard Farrell,	Earl of Arran,	Ternaverekle,
	2735	Mary Carroll,	do.	Leighnane,
	2737	Martin Durkan,	do.	Carrowreagh,
	2738	Mary Judge,	do.	do.
	2739	William Carr,	do.	Leighnane,
	2740	James Boyd,	do.	Ballytrebury,
	2741	John Bailey,	John T. Kirkwood,	Carlin,
	2742	Mary Malloh,	Mervyn Pratt,	Ballinlough and another.
	2743	Anthony Kelbourgh,	do.	do.
	2744	Henry Gordon,	do.	Tobernavy,
	2745	John McAndrew,	do.	Pullathaby,
	2746	William Holmes,	do.	Gortmanh,
	2747	Michael Moore,	do.	do.
	2748	Anthony McAndrew,	do.	do.
	2749	Mary Cains,	do.	do.
	2750	James Robinson,	do.	Ballinlougham,
	2751	Marcus McNamara,	Sir R. W. H. Palmer, Bart.,	Cartronsim,
	2752	Bridget Sheahy,	Trustees of the Achill Mission,	Dooega, Achill Island.
	2753	Martin Gandy,	Wm. S. Nicholson & another,	Clarick,
	2754	James Gordon,	Robert W. Thompson,	Carrowkilde,
	2755	James Lalor,	do.	Carrowmaghagh.
	2756	Bridget Moran,	do.	do.
	2757	Laurence Reddy,	George T. N. Carter,	Feltagh,
	2758	Patrick Hughes,	Sir Charles J. K. Gore, Bart.,	Carrickmoreh,
	2759	Michael Kerr,	do.	Ardnaglass,
	2760	Martin Gallagher,	Patrick Gallagher,	Mongore,
	2761	Thomas Henry,	Miss M. A. Thompson,	Carrowmaghagh,
	2762	John Barrett,	Earl of Arran,	Ballymulvey,
	2763	Bridget Gordon,	do.	Carrowkelly,

MAYO—*continued.*

Extent of Holding. Statute.	Poor Law Valuation.	Former Rent.	Judicial Rent.	Observations.	Value of Tenancy.
A. R. P.	£ s. d.	£ s. d.	£ s. d.		£ s. d.
15 0 0	4 0 0	4 13 6	4 4 0		
26 0 0	6 0 0	7 0 8	5 5 0		
30 0 0	14 10 0	15 6 8	13 4 6		
61 3 31	28 5 0	25 3 0	23 9 0		
21 2 0	2 6 0	11 19 8	16 10 0		
11 1 20	4 10 0	8 3 0	4 10 5		
20 2 6	11 0 0	18 1 0	13 . 0		
46 0 25	27 15 0	32 17 0	30 0 0		
17 6 0	1 0 0	3 0 0	1 8 4		
75 0 13	20 15 0	24 0 0	21 15 0		
72 0 10	18 15 0	20 0 0	25 0 0		
60 3 23	32 0 0	38 10 0	35 15 0		
36 8 0	6 18 0	6 0 0	4 10 0		
126 3 28	7 0 0	8 10 0	7 10 5		
112 1 4	6 0 0	4 0 0	4 5 0		
346 1 20	7 0 0	8 0 8	8 8 0		
121 5 24	4 10 0	4 0 0	4 5 0		
80 1 11	5 15 0	6 0 0	6 0 0		
65 0 33	26 10 0	24 10 0	25 15 0		
1 2 6	1 2 0	1 5 0	6 12 0		
30 0 15	3 0 0	10 7 8	6 15 0		
10 0 0	6 15 0	5 3 6	5 2 0	By consent.	
0 2 5	3 18 0	5 6 6	3 2 6	do.	
14 0 0	6 16 0	5 0 8	4 0 2	do.	
7 0 0	3 10 0	6 0 0	6 8 0		
14 1 35	0 10 0	7 15 0	6 0 0		
32 1 27	9 10 0	18 16 8	13 17 6	do.	
100 0 0	5 10 0	8 10 0	8 11 9	do.	
24 0 0	8 15 0	12 4 6	12 4 8	do.	
40 0 24	15 0 0	16 5 6	14 10 0	do.	
13 2 1	7 10 0	7 5 0	7 6 0	do.	
27 1 18	9 15 0	18 7 0	20 0 0	do.	
30 1 1	16 5 0	19 15 0	14 14 0	do.	
15 0 35	9 0 0	20 15 6	9 5 0	do.	
17 0 0	7 5 0	7 13 10	6 18 6	do.	

COUNTY OF

Names of Assistant Commissioners by whom Cases were decided.	No.	Name of Tenant.	Name of Landlord.	Townland.
Assistant Commissioners—				
William [illegible] (Legal). A. B. Nolan. R. O'Reilly. E. R. Bayly. H. G. Gregory	2768	James [illegible],	Earl of Arran,	[illegible],
	2769	Mary Gallagher,	do.	[illegible],
	2770	Peter Harrison,	do.	[illegible],
	2771	Lewis Loving,	do.	[illegible],
	2772	Michael McLoughlin,	John T. [illegible],	[illegible],
	2773	John Kelly,	do.	do.
	2774	Patrick Melvin,	do.	do.
	2775	Michael Weir,	do.	do.
	2776	Peggy Melvin,	do.	do.
	2777	Patrick Fleming, senior,	do.	[illegible],
	2778	Michael [illegible],	do.	[illegible],
	2779	Thady [illegible],	do.	[illegible],
	2780	Luke Geary,	do.	do.
	2781	Michael Geary,	do.	do.
	2782	William Geary,	do.	do.
	2783	Patrick Geary,	do.	do.
	2784	Charles [illegible],	Edward H. C. Perry,	[illegible],
	2785	Michael Dempsey,	do.	[illegible],
	2786	Patrick Clarke (Mat),	do.	[illegible],
	2787	Patrick Clarke (James),	do.	[illegible],
	2788	Thomas Clarke,	do.	[illegible],
	2789	Patrick [illegible],	do.	[illegible],
	2790	[illegible] Hughes,	do.	[illegible],
	2791	Thomas Coleman,	do.	[illegible],
	2792	John Clarke (Mat),	do.	[illegible],
	2793	Patrick Hawley, Rep. of Mary [illegible],	do.	[illegible],
	2794	Owen McNaly,	do.	do.
	2795	Daniel Hegarty,	do.	do.
	2796	Michael Browne (Martin),	do.	[illegible],
	2797	John [illegible],	do.	[illegible],
	2798	Peter Dempsey,	do.	do.
	2799	Dominick [illegible],	do.	[illegible],
	2800	John [illegible],	do.	[illegible],
	2801	Ellen Brown,	do.	do.
	2802	John Boyle,	do.	[illegible],

MAYO—*continued.*

Extent of Holding. Statute.	Poor Law Valuation.	Tenant Rent.	Judicial Rent.	Observations.	Value of Tenancy.
A. R. P.	£ s. d.	£ s. d.	£ s. d.		£ s. d.
7 1 0	5 5 0	3 7 6	4 0 0	By consent.	
44 1 30	11 0 0	17 2 6	13 0 0	do.	
32 2 30	21 5 0	23 1 0	20 0 0	do.	
13 0 20	7 10 0	10 2 6	8 0 0	do.	
18 0 0	6 0 0	7 11 0	6 0 0	do.	
6 2 0	5 10 0	3 15 0	3 0 0	do.	
7 0 0	5 10 0	2 16 0	3 0 0	do.	
11 2 0	6 10 0	7 12 0	6 5 0	do.	
9 2 0	3 10 10	4 18 0	3 10 0	do.	
6 2 0	4 5 0	6 17 6	5 5 0	do.	
15 3 0	6 10 0	5 0 0	3 10 0	do.	
12 0 4	6 2 6	7 0 0	5 14 0	do.	
8 2 0	6 12 6	5 16 0	4 17 0	do.	
5 0 0	4 2 0	4 10 0	4 0 0	do.	
9 3 0	6 12 0	4 16 0	4 0 0	do.	
17 2 0	4 15 0	5 18 0	6 17 0	do.	
12 0 30	6 10 0	8 10 0	6 12 6		
9 0 26	2 5 0	4 4 0	2 18 0		
9 0 22	6 0 0	7 0 0	3 18 0		
18 2 10	9 15 0	14 18 0	12 10 0		
16 1 33	8 10 0	10 0 0	7 10 0		
22 0 30	8 10 0	13 0 0	10 10 0		
[illegible] 2 30	9 0 0	10 16 0	7 0 0		
27 2 16	18 15 0	19 0 0	15 0 0		
11 2 0	7 15 0	9 5 0	7 1 0		
9 1 5	3 0 0	3 10 0	3 0 0		
10 3 20	4 18 0	6 0 0	3 5 0		
10 0 0	6 16 6	9 18 0	7 0 0		
8 0 20	6 15 0	8 10 0	7 3 6		
6 3 20	3 16 0	5 15 0	2 5 0		
10 0 10	4 15 0	6 5 0	5 0 0		
24 1 0	15 0 0	17 0 0	13 0 0		
13 3 25	5 0 0	6 16 0	4 10 0		
14 0 20	8 15 0	10 5 0	5 4 0		
16 1 10	8 10 0	8 4 0	7 11 0		

COUNTY OF

Names of Assistant Commissioners by whom Cases were decided.	No.	Name of Tenant.	Name of Landlord.	Townland.	
Assistant Commissioners—					
William Meyler (Legal). A. B. Nolan. E. O'Neill. R. R. Bayly. H. H. Gregory.	2903	James Teslin, ...	Edmund H. C. Perry, ...	Church Clonghan,	
	2904	Patrick Lluris (John), ...	do.	Clonghan,	—
	2905	John Brown, ...	do.	Kilbeltel,	—
	2906	Peter Kelly, ...	do.	do.	—
	2907	Margaret Thills, ...	do.	do.	—
	2908	John Keon, ...	do.	do.	—
	2909	Bridget Kelly, ...	do.	do.	—
	2910	Mary Kelly, ...	do.	Clonghan, Kilbeltel,	Kil.
	2911	Thomas Geraghty, ...	do.	Kilbeltel,	—
	2912	Richard Mallon, ...	Robert Kelly, ...	Knockleagh,	—
	2913	Martin Clarke, ...	Edmund H. Perry, ...	Kilbeltel,	—
Assistant Commissioners—					
Charles Hamilton (Legal). J. Bain. A. Gerty. R. Kelly. W. C. Connell.	2914	John Brangan & another,	Thomas Lorimh, ...	Shancally,	—
	2915	Anthony Foley, ...	do.	Trevalred,	—
	2916	Michael Foley (Mark),	do.	do.	—
	2917	Patrick McNelty (Mary),	Robert Crean, ...	Bradallagh,	—
	2918	Patrick Walsh (Reggin),	do.	do.	—
	2919	Peter Walsh (Nicholas),	do.	do.	—
	2920	Martin Mack, ...	Lord Dillon, ...	Drummakery,	—
	2921	Lawrence Finn, ...	Michael F. Trenton, ...	Ballyveeghan,	—
	2922	Martin Mulory, ...	do.	Gleantown,	—
	2923	Michael Costello, ...	do.	Knockaveeghan,	—
	2924	Martin Rogers, ...	do.	Glenmore,	—
	2925	Patrick Duffy, ...	John Birmingham, ...	Knockatrean,	—
	2926	Catherine Hughes, Rep. John Hughes.	George Vesey, ...	Carraghalan,	—
	2927	Michael Hughes, ...	do.	do.	—
	2928	Michael Geary, ...	do.	do.	—
	2929	John Hughes (McDonagh), Rep. Pat Hughes.	do.	Carraghalan,	—
	2930	Pat Hughes (John), ...	do.	do.	—
	2931	Thomas Hughes, ...	do.	do.	—
	2932	Thomas Kelly, ...	do.	do.	—
	2933	John Reilly, ...	do.	Ballybrackan,	—
	2934	Patrick Connor, ...	do.	Ballybrackan, Carraghalan	—
	2935	Peter Carraher, ...	do.	do.	—

MAYO—*continued.*

Extent of Holding. Statute.	Poor Law Valuation.	Former Rent.	Judicial Rent.	Observations.	Value of Tenancy.
a. r. p.	£ s. d.	£ s. d.	£ s. d.		£ s. d.
17 0 10	8 5 0	11 0 0	9 5 0		
13 1 30	5 5 0	7 10 0	6 0 0		
6 3 15	4 5 0	8 5 0	4 10 0		
5 0 8	7 0 0	7 10 0	6 10 0		
3 0 0	3 15 0	6 5 0	5 5 0		
7 3 15	0 4 0	6 15 0	5 7 6		
8 3 30	2 10 0	3 10 0	3 5 0		
11 0 38	5 10 0	5 0 0	6 15 0		
21 1 10	10 0 0	12 0 0	10 0 0		
10 0 0	—	8 4 0	5 0 0		
18 3 18	7 18 0	9 15 0	8 5 0		
10 0 34	6 0 0	4 5 0	3 0 0	By consent.	
6 3 33	4 10 0	5 10 0	3 0 0	do.	
23 0 8	4 5 0	6 3 9	5 7 6	do.	
11 3 30	5 0 0	7 0 0	6 0 0	do.	
7 2 10	3 15 0	5 0 0	3 15 0	do.	
4 0 0	8 0 0	4 10 0	3 10 0	do.	
30 3 31	11 7 0	18 8 4	13 7 0		
9 2 35	4 5 0	8 8 8	6 0 0	do.	
7 3 20	5 15 0	7 8 5	8 8 9	do.	
7 1 0	4 15 0	20 7 0	5 8 8	do.	
9 2 0	1 15 0	5 0 0	3 4 8	do.	
10 1 30	5 15 6	9 13 6	7 0 0	do.	
18 0 33	8 17 0	13 0 0	10 10 0		
64 3 14	19 10 0	27 0 0	23 10 0		
13 3 10	0 10 0	13 14 0	8 15 0		
19 0 23	7 15 0	9 0 0	7 18 0		
18 3 25	8 3 0	21 0 0	9 15 0		
71 1 10	15 8 0	16 0 0	13 10 0		
18 0 30	8 0 0	10 0 0	8 5 0		
14 0 33	7 8 0	18 1 0	9 0 0		
23 3 13	9 18 0	14 9 4	11 18 0		
8 3 10	8 14 0	4 8 0	3 10 0		

COUNTY OF

Names of Assistant Commissioners by whom Cases were decided.	No.	Name of Tenant.	Name of Landlord.	Townland.
Assistant Commissioners—				
Charles Hawkins (Legal). J. Hill. A. Craig. R. Kelly. W. G. Connell.	[illegible]	Mary Kelly, Rep. of James Kelly,	George Vesey, ...	[illegible], ...
	[illegible]	John [illegible], ...	do.	Ballybeakan, ...
	[illegible]	John Brett, ...	Lord Clanmorris, ...	[illegible], ...
	2839	William Judge, ...	[illegible] Moore O'Farrell, ...	Farnane, ...
	2840	Mary McPhale, ...	Thomas Philip Irwin, a Lunatic,	Castle, ...
	2841	Mary McDonnell and Peter McDonnell,	Stephen Gibbons, ...	Loughbrury, ...
	[illegible]	James Loftus, ...	Ignatius Kelly, ...	Rathdane, Upper,
	[illegible]	Michael Kelly (Tom), ...	Robert Dunn, ...	Derbolagh, ...
	[illegible]	Patrick Phillips, ...	C. R. Seymour, ...	[illegible], ...
	[illegible]	James Walsh, ...	do.	Kilduane, ...
	[illegible]	Thomas Gallagher, senior,	do.	do. ...
	[illegible]	Thomas A. Gallagher, ...	do.	do. ...
	[illegible]	Thomas O'Hara, ...	do.	Ardmore, ...
	[illegible]	Michael Hession, ...	Court of Chancery, ...	Ahymurragh, ...
	[illegible]	John McNulty, ...	Matthew F. Gallagher and Samuel H. Gallagher,	do. ...
	[illegible]	John Mulligan, ...	Rev. William Jackson, ...	[illegible], ...
	[illegible]	Pat Loftus, ...	do.	Lenaboy, ...
	[illegible]	Thomas Durkin, ...	Sir Charles J. K. Gore, Bart.,	[illegible], ...
	[illegible]	Michael McFadden, ...	do.	do. ...
	[illegible]	Anthony Joy, ...	do.	do. ...
	[illegible]	Patrick Kelly, ...	do.	do. ...
	[illegible]	William Keary, ...	do.	Parkyhill, ...
	[illegible]	Patrick Gorman, ...	George Vesey, ...	Carraghadoony, ...
	[illegible]	Thomas Cunningham, ...	Michael P. Tuohy, ...	Carrygarrighan, ...
	[illegible]	Thomas Dunne, ...	Charles L. Fitzgerald, ...	Tawnyglebe, Lisnamanagh, and [illegible]
	[illegible]	Patrick Logan, ...	John Irwin, a Lunatic, ...	Bygrand, ...
	[illegible]	Patrick Moran, ...	James Nixon, ...	Mountmask, Upr.,
	[illegible]	Anthony Moran, Rep. of John McHale,	do.	do. ...
	[illegible]	Thomas Lynskey, ...	Christopher J. P. Irwin, a Lunatic,	Park, ...
	[illegible]	Richard Garvey, ...	Ignatius Kelly, ...	Rathdane, Upper,
	[illegible]	Catherine Garvey, widow,	do.	do. ...
	[illegible]	Patrick Daly, ...	do.	do. ...
	[illegible]	Thomas Sevanick, ...	do.	do. ...
	[illegible]	Patrick Sevanick, ...	do.	do. ...
	2870	Michael Glynn, ...	George Harlow, ...	Lisheeaugh, ...

MAYO—*continued*

Extent of Holding. Statute.	Poor Law Valuation.	Former Rent.	Judicial Rent.	Observations.	Value of Tenancy.
A. R. P.	£ s. d.	£ s. d.	£ s. d.		£ s. d.
14 1 11	10 15 0	11 18 0	11 0 0		
10 0 11	5 10 0	6 12 0	1 6 0		
62 1 20	24 15 0	42 10 0	22 10 0		
104 0 0	15 16 0	46 0 0	20 0 0		
11 0 0	3 15 0	6 0 0	5 10 0	By consent.	
43 3 23	30 0 0	45 0 0	42 0 0	do.	
16 0 0	6 10 0	11 7 4	9 7 6	do.	
3 0 0	2 10 0	4 0 0	3 0 0	do.	
11 0 34	7 0 0	13 0 0	8 5 0		
10 0 0	5 15 0	9 16 0	7 15 0		
12 0 20	7 0 0	10 19 0	8 15 4		
19 0 20	9 0 0	23 0 0	9 10 0		
13 3 1	8 10 0	6 6 0	7 5 0		
—	3 16 0	4 6 8	3 0 0		
17 1 18	8 15 0	6 4 10	5 5 0		
16 0 31	7 0 0	10 19 8	9 0 0		
4 0 16	2 0 0	5 10 0	1 0 0		
3 0 1	2 0 0	4 0 0	3 10 0		
17 1 0	6 15 0	8 4 0	7 15 0		
0 3 27	2 5 0	4 0 0	3 18 4		
14 2 13	6 3 0	8 18 0	7 3 0		
14 1 33	0 0 0	23 0 0	10 0 0		
24 1 36	—	30 0 0	8 10 0		
21 3 0	4 10 0	5 1 8	5 15 0	do.	
6 1 0	2 10 0	5 7 6	3 13 4	do.	
7 0 20	3 16 0	1 0 0	3 13 6	do.	
16 1 20	3 0 0	4 7 0	1 16 0	do.	
20 0 0	0 0 0	1 15 0	1 0 0	do.	
11 2 33	0 1 0	9 16 0	6 0 0	do.	
0 0 0	4 7 0	0 9 3	5 5 0	do.	
5 0 0	4 6 0	0 9 2	5 5 0	do.	
5 0 0	4 4 0	6 0 2	5 0 0	do.	
9 0 0	4 0 0	0 0 0	3 0 0	do.	
7 2 0	6 10 0	8 13 5	7 10 0	do.	
7 0 0	4 5 0	0 2 0	4 16 0		

COUNTY OF

Names of Assistant Commissioners by whom Cases were decided.	No.	Name of Tenant.	Name of Landlord.	Townland.
Assistant Commissioners—				
CHARLES HAMILTON (Legal). J. RICE. A. CURTIS. E. KELLY. W. C. CONNELL.	3871	Edmund McNicholas, ...	George Harkan, ...	Lishaleagh, ...
	3872	Thomas Doyle, ...	do.	do. ...
	3873	Mary Keating, ...	Anthony O. Kearey, ...	do. ...
	3874	John Gallagher, ...	Reps. of George Harkan, deceased.	do. ...
	3875	John Walsh, ...	Charles L. Fitzgerald, ...	Lugmoremoney, ...
	3876	John Barrett, ...	Earl of Arran, ...	Trough, ...
	3877	Thomas Fitzmaurice, ...	Charles Lister, ...	Cloongowragh, ...
	3878	John McNicholas, ...	Nicholas Lynch, ...	Cuiltemoghtan, ...
	3879	James Doyle, ...	Luke Harkan, ...	Lisheery, ...
	3880	Margaret Flynn, ...	Gen. Sir Roger Palmer, Bart.,	Tawnaroy, ...
	3881	Pat. Burns (Tom), ...	do.	do. ...
	3882	Edward Gillen, ...	do.	do. ...
	3883	Pat. O'Brien, ...	do.	do. ...
	3884	Bryan Lackan, ...	do.	do. ...
	3885	Michael Burns (Pat), ...	do.	Tawnagreeny, ...
	3886	John Lackan (John), ...	do.	do. ...
	3887	Patrick McGlynn, ...	do.	Cloonalleagh, ...
	3888	John Gibbons, ...	do.	Tonroalleagh, ...
	3889	Ellen Glavally (Ned), ...	do.	Tawnagreeny, ...
	3890	Morris Cawley, ...	do.	Toonalleagh, ...
	3891	Michael Lavelle, ...	do.	do. ...
	3892	Michael Murray, ...	do.	do. ...
	3893	James Cawley, ...	do.	Cloonalleagh, ...
	3894	James Carraven, ...	do.	Loonalleagh, ...
	3895	Anthony Cawley, ...	do.	do. ...
	3896	Ellen Burns (Widow),	do.	Tawnagreen, ...
	3897	John Tonlan, ...	do.	do. ...
	3898	Edward Glavally (Ned,)	do.	do. ...
	3899	Thomas Burns, ...	do.	do. ...
	3900	Morris Geran, ...	do.	do. ...
	3901	Ellen Glavally (Michael),	do.	Tawnameany, ...
	3902	Bessie Loftus, ...	Lady Sarah White, ...	Carrowmore, ...
	3903	John Murtagh, ...	do.	Caghtown, ...
	3904	Pat Moran, ...	do.	—
	3905	Honor Gordon, ...	do.	Carrynacurrin, ...

MAYO—*continued.*

Extent of Holding. Statute.	Poor Law Valuation.	Former Rent.	Judicial Rent.	Observations.	Value of Tenancy.
A. R. P.	£ s. d.	£ s. d.	£ s. d.		£ s. d.
5 0 0	4 10 0	6 15 0	5 5 0		
12 0 0	5 18 0	8 16 0	7 10 0		
9 0 10	4 10 0	9 0 0	6 10 0		
18 0 0	6 11 0	9 17 3	7 15 0		
13 0 0	11 15 0	15 16 9	11 0 0	By consent.	
30 0 0	4 0 0	4 10 0	4 0 0	do.	
4 0 0	—	6 10 0	3 10 0	do.	
18 2 0	2 10 0	7 0 0	6 10 0	do.	
13 0 0	7 3 0	10 14 6	8 17 6		
23 3 0	4 0 0	7 0 0	5 14 0		
10 0 20	3 0 0	8 8 0	3 13 6		
15 1 25	6 6 0	6 15 0	4 10 0		
18 1 10	2 10 0	4 10 0	5 15 0		
7 1 18	3 10 0	2 5 0	1 16 0		
26 1 8	3 5 0	5 15 0	4 15 0		
1 0 20	2 0 0	3 10 0	1 10 0		
20 1 20	2 10 0	4 18 0	3 15 0		
19 2 15	2 0 0	9 10 0	3 3 0		
7 3 0	9 10 0	4 5 0	4 5 0		
16 1 0	4 0 0	7 0 0	6 7 6		
8 1 30	3 0 0	3 1 0	3 15 0		
20 1 20	4 10 0	5 0 0	6 0 0		
17 2 17	3 5 0	5 15 0	3 2 0		
15 1 18	2 10 0	4 5 0	5 5 0		
10 0 20	2 15 0	5 5 0	2 5 0		
4 3 14	1 10 0	2 10 0	3 7 6		
5 2 26	2 5 0	5 15 0	3 0 0		
17 2 0	3 5 0	4 0 0	3 5 0		
9 1 30	1 14 0	2 12 0	3 5 0		
7 3 38	3 5 0	4 0 0	3 7 6		
9 3 0	2 10 0	6 10 0	2 13 6		
18 3 11	7 15 0	12 0 0	10 10 0	do.	
25 0 36	10 12 0	18 10 0	13 10 0	do.	
11 0 35	8 10 0	9 7 10	6 0 0	do.	
26 0 0	11 10 0	26 10 0	14 0 0	do.	

COUNTY OF

Names of Assistant Commissioners by whom Cases were decided.	No.	Name of Tenant.	Name of Landlord.	Townland.	
Assistant Commissioners—					
CHARLES HAMILTON (Legal).	[illegible]	John McDonnell, ...	Lady Sarah White, ...	Carrycastle,	...
E. BATE.	[illegible]	Catherine Loftus, Rep. of Thomas Loftus	do.	Cumbrine,	...
A. COTTY.	[illegible]	Catherine Murtagh, ...	do.	Carrowcastle,	...
E. KELLY.	[illegible]	Pat Flannery, ...	do.	do.	...
W. G. GRENALL.	3010	John Moran, ...	do.	do.	...
	3011	Patt Durkan, ...	do. ...	do.	...
	3012	Michael Colsey, ...	do.	do.	...
	3013	James Phillips, ...	do.	Ougheteem,	...
	[illegible]	John Walsh, ...	do.	Cloonacastle,	...
	3015	Thomas Corcoran, ...	do.	do.	...
	3016	John Reid, ...	do.	Ougheteem,	...
	3017	Patrick Mulroy, ...	do.	do.	...
	3018	Pat Dunleavy, ...	do.	do.	...
	3019	John O'Neal, ...	do.	do.	...
	3020	James Dunleavy ...	do.	do.	...
	3021	Henry Dunleavy, ...	do.	do.	...
	[illegible]	Darby Moran, ...	do.	Carrycastle,	...
	[illegible]	Thomas Dunleavy, ...	do.	Ougheteem,	...
	[illegible]	Thomas Walsh, ...	do. ...	Carrowcastle,	...
				Total,	...

COUNTY OF

Assistant Commissioners—	[illegible]	John Farrell, ...	Miss Anne Neville, ...	Derrylush,	...
C. ROBERTS (Legal).	969	John Ford, ...	do.	do.	...
M. F. LYNCH.	970	Andrew O'Hara, ...	James Grove and others, ...	Callowhinny,	...
H. B. HARRISON.	971	Owen Grey, ...	Alexander Nixon, ...	Cloonbarry,	...
R. B. MEREDITH.	972	Elizabeth Spellman, Rep. of Michael Spellman,	Catherine O'Connor, ...	Bunborough,	...
EDMOND ROGERS.	973	Thomas Spellman, ...	do.	do.	...
	974	Catherine Gaffney, ...	do.	Rahery,	...
	975	Patrick Conlish, ...	Arthur O'Connor and others, ...	Derrymurry,	...
	976	Peter McGuinness, ...	do.	do.	...
	977	Thomas Brennan, ...	do.	do.	...
	978	Patrick Gaffney, Rep. of Thomas Gaffney,	do.	do.	...

MAYO—*continued.*

Extent of Holding. Statute.	Poor Law Valuation.	Former Rent.	Judicial Rent.	Observations.	Term of Tenancy.
A. R. P.	£ s. d.	£ s. d.	£ s. d.		£ s. d.
21 0 0	10 10 0	16 10 0	12 10 0	By consent.	
9 2 10	6 18 0	9 0 0	7 13 9	do.	
18 1 25	7 9 0	11 10 0	10 0 0	do.	
11 1 10	7 6 0	10 0 0	9 10 0	do.	
9 1 33	4 0 0	6 8 0	5 5 0	do.	
11 0 3	6 0 0	8 0 0	5 16 0	do.	
18 0 33	8 10 0	12 15 0	10 10 0	do.	
11 1 16	5 0 0	7 18 0	6 17 6	do.	
10 2 20	6 0 0	7 10 0	6 11 3	do.	
10 1 30	7 10 0	10 0 0	8 10 0	do.	
12 3 30	6 3 0	8 12 6	7 5 0	do.	
9 3 23	6 5 0	5 0 0	7 0 0	do.	
13 0 33	8 0 0	11 16 0	10 0 0	do.	
18 1 24	8 10 0	13 0 0	10 8 0	do.	
6 1 16	5 0 0	8 14 0	8 16 0	do.	
11 1 11	6 13 0	9 8 0	8 0 0	do.	
10 0 5	5 5 0	8 0 0	6 15 0	do.	
13 3 23	0 0 0	8 12 6	7 5 0	do.	
16 3 25	0 15 0	14 10 0	13 10 0	do.	
6,308 1 31½	2,030 6 10	3,230 0 8½	2,589 0 8		

ROSCOMMON.

Extent of Holding.	Poor Law Valuation.	Former Rent.	Judicial Rent.	Observations.		Term of Tenancy.
					£ s. d.	
77 2 31	25 5 0	29 3 10	27 0 0			
23 3 21	7 10 0	14 17 6	11 0 0	Rent changed in 1877 from . . .	7 16 0	
26 1 13	—	19 0 10	11 0 0			
19 0 0	8 0 0	14 0 0	20 0 0	1865	7 0 0	
6 0 38	4 0 0	6 13 9	4 0 0	1880	3 10 0	
12 3 0	6 0 0	7 0 0	6 0 0			
38 1 10	19 5 0	13 11 9	12 0 0	1863	11 10 0	
13 0 10	6 13 0	12 5 0	9 0 0			
19 0 20	8 10 0	13 2 0	8 5 0			
5 0 20	4 5 0	6 19 4	6 5 0	1885	5 1 0	
26 1 30	6 0 0	13 14 6	9 0 0			

COUNTY OF

Names of Assistant Commissioners by whom Cases were decided.	No.	Name of Tenant.	Name of Landlord.	Townland.
Assistant Commissioners—				
Const. Reeves (Legal). M. P. Lynch. H. B. [illegible]. R. B. Hamilton. Edward Roche.	979	John [illegible], ...	Arthur O'Connor and others,	Drumcarey, ...
	980	Patrick Healy, ...	do.	do. ...
	981	Paul Gaffney, ...	do. ...	[illegible], ...
	982	Mary Moran, Rep. of John [illegible].	Hugh McKiernan, ...	[illegible], ...
	983	Martin [illegible], ...	do.	do. ...
	984	Christopher McMorrow, Rep. of Kelly McMorrow,	do.	[illegible],
	985	John [illegible], ...	do.	[illegible], ...
	986	John Cavanagh, ...	do.	do. ...
	987	William and Pat Lewis,	do.	do. ...
	989	William Cullen, ...	do.	do. ...
	989	Andrew Gaffney, ...	do.	do. ...
	990	Michael McManus, ...	do.	do. ...
	991	Thomas [illegible], ...	do.	do. ...
	992	Thady Gaffney, ...	do.	do. ...
	993	Wm. McDonagh & anor., Reps. of Pat McDonagh.	Arthur O'Connor and others, Minors, by Guar. O'Connor.	Drumcarey, ...
	994	Mary [illegible], ...	Robert E. [illegible], ...	[illegible], ...
	995	John Doyle, ...	Sir Gilbert King, Bart. ...	[illegible],
	996	Michael Lloyd, ...	do.	[illegible], ...
	997	James Kelly, ...	[illegible] McDonnell, ...	Rockport, ...
	998	Patrick [illegible], ...	Richard Keogh and Another,	Lodge, ...
	999	Michael [illegible], ...	do.	Drummond, ...
	1000	Bernard Dolan and anor.,	do.	Lodge, ...
	1001	Edward [illegible], ...	do.	do. ...
	1002	Bridget & William Boyd, Admors. of Pat Boyd.	do.	[illegible], ...
	1003	Ellen [illegible], ...	[illegible] Whyte, ...	[illegible], ...
	1004	John Beirne (Byrne), ...	William [illegible] and others,	[illegible]
				Total, ...

COUNTY OF

Assistant Commissioners—	1299	Michael Callaghan, ...	William A. [illegible], ...	[illegible], ...
Const. Reeves (Legal). M. P. Lynch. H. B. [illegible]. R. B. Hamilton. Edward Roche.	1300	Hugh [illegible], ...	Cornelius A. Keogh, ...	[illegible],
	1301	Michael Dowd, ...	do.	[illegible],
	1302	Daniel [illegible], ...	do.	[illegible],

ROSCOMMON—*continued.*

Extent of Holding. Statute.			Poor Law Valuation.			Former Rent.			Judicial Rent.			Observations.			
A.	R.	P.	£	s.	d.	£	s.	d.	£	s.	d.		£	s.	d.
27	1	0	11	15	0	20	0	0	13	0	0				
20	1	0	12	0	0	17	1	6	14	0	0	Rent changed in 1849 from . . .	6	17	6
21	0	11½	11	10	0	15	3	6	11	15	0	do.	6	17	0
11	1	10	4	15	0	6	0	0	0	0	0	1878	7	0	0
11	1	0	5	0	0	0	0	0	4	0	0				
43	2	0	16	10	0	40	0	0	25	0	0				
21	0	0	6	2	0	9	10	0	7	0	0				
9	1	27	4	5	0	7	0	0	5	10	0	do.	6	0	0
13	1	31	3	0	0	0	0	0	6	15	0	do.	0	0	0
6	2	6	3	0	0	6	5	0	3	15	0	do.	4	0	0
18	0	20	4	0	0	0	10	0	0	0	0	do.	0	0	0
5	0	27	1	0	0	3	15	0	0	10	0	do.	6	10	0
11	0	7	4	0	0	8	0	0	0	5	0	do.	6	10	0
6	2	5½	0	0	0	5	5	0	4	0	0	do.	4	0	0
35	1	6	0	0	0	14	15	0	10	15	0				
12	1	25	7	15	0	15	10	0	9	0	0				
20	0	27	15	10	0	10	13	4	17	0	0	By consent.			
17	2	7	11	5	0	18	3	3	18	0	0				
16	0	10	7	15	0	11	5	3	0	0	0				
11	3	19	5	10	0	10	4	4	9	10	0				
22	0	0	11	10	0	20	0	0	15	10	0				
14	1	20	10	0	0	12	10	0	10	10	0				
17	0	20	15	0	0	23	4	0	16	10	0	Rent changed in 1856 from . . .	18	2	3

COUNTY OF

Names of Assistant Commissioners by whom Cases were decided.	No.	Name of Tenant.	Name of Landlord.	Townland.
Assistant Commissioners—				
Cecil Roche (Legal). M. F. Lynch. M. R. [illegible]. J. D. [illegible]. [illegible]	1303	James [illegible],	Cornelius A. Keogh,	[illegible],
	1304	Fortley Fahy,	do.	[illegible] & [illegible]
	1305	Margaret Maguire,	do.	[illegible],
	1306	Michael Reilly, junior,	do.	do.
	1307	Mary Rellan,	do.	[illegible],
	1308	Thomas McTernan,	do.	do.
	1309	Catherine Clerkin,	do.	do.
	1310	Bartholomew Morahan,	do.	do.
	1311	Timothy McDonagh,	Colonel King-Harman,	Corbel,
	1312	Thomas Kenny,	do.	do.
	1313	James Kenny,	do.	do.
	1314	Patrick Quinnan,	do.	do.
	1315	John McDonagh,	do.	do.
	1316	Bridget McDonagh, Rep. of Brian McDonagh,	do.	do.
	1317	Bartholomew McDonagh,	do.	do.
	1318	Bridget McDonagh,	do.	do.
	1319	Patrick Rush,	do.	[illegible],
	1320	[illegible], Admr. of John Kelly,	do.	do.
	1321	Owen Laing,	Ulick A. Kent,	[illegible],
	1322	John Clarke,	do.	do.
	1323	Michael McTiernan,	do.	do.
	1324	Michael Fallon,	do.	do.
	1325	Patrick Fallon,	do.	do.
	1326	Thady Laing,	do.	do.
	1327	John Redfern,	do.	do.
	1328	Thomas Fahy,	do.	do.
	1329	Patrick Lynch,	do.	do.
	1330	Bernard Cannon,	do.	do.
	1331	Anne Quinlan, Admx. of Thomas Quinlan,	do.	do.
	1332	Catherine Harte,	do.	do.
	1333	John McManus,	Captain Hewitson,	[illegible],
	1334	William Adams,	Sir Gilbert King, Bart.,	[illegible],
	1335	Do.,	do.	[illegible],
	1336	Margaret Connolly, Admx. of Patrick [illegible],	R. G. Weir and William Fry,	[illegible],
	1337	James Coggins,	Sir Chas. J. Knox-Gore, Bart.,	[illegible],

SLIGO—*continued.*

Extent of Holding. Statute.	Poor Law Valuation.	Former Rent.	Judicial Rent.	Observations.	Value of Tenancy.
A. R. P.	£ s. d.	£ s. d.	£ s. d.	£ s. d.	£ s. d.
11 2 27	4 5 0	10 0 0	7 0 0	By consent.	
23 1 33	10 5 0	14 0 0	12 0 0	do.	
16 3 5	4 15 0	6 0 0	5 0 0	do.	
18 1 0	6 5 0	10 0 0	5 0 0	do.	
27 2 26	3 10 0	5 0 0	4 11 0	do.	
23 1 32	16 15 0	24 16 0	10 11 0	Rent changed in 1871 from . . 9 0 0	
17 2 23	10 5 0	14 13 6	11 10 0	1856 15 0 6	
30 0 10	5 15 0	16 0 0	13 10 0	1876 15 0 0	
24 2 33	8 15 0	9 15 0	7 0 0	do. 6 1 4	
23 2 13	10 18 0	17 10 0	14 0 0	1876 6 8 10	
18 2 14	4 10 0	8 15 0	6 0 0	do. 4 6 10	
17 0 23	4 15 0	9 5 0	5 0 0	do. 4 5 4	
40 1 10	18 0 0	25 18 6	21 0 0	By consent.	
18 0 15	6 16 0	6 11 0	5 4 0	do.	
7 1 15	9 16 0	3 18 0	2 15 0	do.	
23 0 4	4 10 0	8 0 0	5 7 0	do.	
21 2 18	6 15 0	9 1 0	7 1 0	do.	
23 0 25	5 0 0	10 5 0	8 5 0	Rent changed in 1875 from . . . 6 16 9	
23 1 16	14 15 0	12 0 0	10 0 0		
26 0 28	16 10 0	25 10 0	20 10 0		
73 3 28	16 0 0	31 0 0	27 0 0		
63 0 27	0 16 0	19 5 0	10 5 0		
43 0 8	10 0 0	31 17 0	20 9 0		
129 3 25	40 10 0	63 0 0	41 10 0		
11 1 10	8 15 0	10 6 0	8 14 0		
164 3 27	13 10 0	19 10 0	15 5 0	1869 15 0 0	
16 3 10	9 15 0	25 0 0	18 10 0		
73 1 12	20 19 0	25 0 0	21 0 0		
23 1 0	9 13 0	15 0 0	10 0 0		
14 3 23	10 0 0	10 0 0	8 0 0		
17 0 11	31 0 0	45 15 0	34 0 0	1876 13 15 0	
10 1 0	8 10 0	7 15 0	6 15 0		
61 1 24	27 10 0	33 0 0	26 10 0		
55 2 20	16 5 0	23 10 0	18 5 0		
18 2 18	6 10 0	11 10 0	9 0 0		

COUNTY OF

Names of Assistant Commissioners by whom Cases were decided.	No.	Name of Tenant.	Name of Landlord.	Townland.
Assistant Commissioners—				
[illegible] (Legal).	1338	John Grady, jun., ...	John Grady, ...	Mahanagh, ...
M. F. Lynch.	1339	John Grady, Rep. of Patrick Grady	Mrs. Fleming, ...	do. ...
H. M. [illegible].	1340	Thomas, Admon. of John Quinn	Rt. Hon. R. [illegible] Flanagan,	[illegible], ...
E. R. Hamilton.	1341	John Hession, ...	do.	do. ...
Edmund Roche.	1342	Andrew McIlroy, ...	do.	do. ...
	1343	Thomas Wynne, ...	do.	do. ...
	1344	Patrick Early, ...	Reps. of Meredith Thompson,	Christiantown, ...
	1345	Bridget Hardy, ...	Frances A. Thompson, ...	do. ...
	1346	Daniel Kilpatrick, ...	Wensley Palmer, Exor of Wm. J. Griffith	Cullentra, ...
	1347	Daniel Costen, ...	do.	do. ...
	1348	Michael Kierans, ...	do.	do. ...
	1349	Thomas Raycroft, ...	do.	do. ...
	1350	James Kilpatrick, ...	do.	do. ...
	1351	Thomas McDonagh, ...	Colonel King Harman, ...	Corlea, ...
	1352	Do. ...	do.	do. ...
				Total, ...

PROVINCE OF

COUNTY OF

Assistant Commissioners—				
R. Reeves, Q.C. (Legal).	1372	Michael Fahy and anor., Admons. of Pat. Fahy.	T. H. Kenny, ...	Moyvannan, North,
C. O'Keeffe.	1373	[illegible] Geary, ...	John Smith, ...	[illegible], ...
E. G. McCarthy.	1374	Charles O'Donnell, ...	do.	do. ...
H. G. Nash.	1375	Thomas Sexton (Michael),	do.	do. ...
E. G. Pery.	1376	Thomas King, ...	Timothy Mahaghan?, ...	[illegible], ...
	1377	Peter [illegible], ...	do.	do. ...
	1378	Mary Curtin, Rep. of Cornelius Curtin.	John Bland?, ...	[illegible], West, ...
	1379	Patrick Carey, ...	Henry V. [illegible], ...	Ballykeevagh, ...
	1380	Thomas Costello, ...	Thomas S. Dove?, ...	Tullerue?, ...
	1381	Patk. Magrath, ...	do.	do. ...
	1382	Michael Halpin, ...	do.	do. ...
	1383	Michael Gilligan, ...	do.	do. ...

SLIGO—*continued.*

Extent of Holding. Statute.	Poor Law Valuation.	Former Rent.	Judicial Rent.	Observations.	Value of Tenancy.
A. R. P.	£ s. d.	£ s. d.	£ s. d.	£ s. d.	£ s. d.
4 0 0	—	3 0 0	1 13 0		
38 1 9	13 0 0	20 0 0	15 0 0	[illegible] 1860 from . . 16 0 0	
16 3 0	4 14 0	5 4 0	5 1 0		
7 2 11	3 5 0	4 5 0	4 5 0		
21 1 8	5 11 0	9 0 0	7 10 0	[illegible] 2 7 0	
18 0 35	6 15 0	8 10 0	6 10 0	[illegible] 4 0 0	
18 0 0	7 15 0	14 14 0	5 7 0	By consent	
16 3 37	4 10 0	14 0 0	7 16 0	do.	
16 1 20	5 16 0	13 0 0	8 0 0		
31 3 34	10 15 0	23 0 0	13 10 0		
10 3 23	10 1 0	23 0 0	15 8 0		
18 3 29	9 1 0	18 0 0	13 10 0		
51 3 5	14 1 0	27 3 6	17 0 0		
21 1 2	6 13 0	8 13 0	5 10 0	1878 4 3 8	
23 2 20	4 0 0	5 0 0	5 0 0	do. 1 11 [illegible]	
1,[illegible] 2 16	218 12 0	244 11 6	[illegible] 13 8		

MUNSTER.

CLARE.

14 2 18	9 10 0	20 0 0	16 10 0		
124 1 20	87 8 0	128 0 0	87 11 0	By consent.	
16 0 20	19 10 0	20 0 0	23 10 0	do.	
17 1 13	8 15 0	11 0 0	8 10 0	do.	
44 1 17	8 0 0	20 0 0	14 0 0	do.	
30 0 6	8 15 0	14 0 0	9 4 0	do.	
18 2 17	10 10 0	20 0 0	8 0 0		73 0 0
23 2 13	10 10 0	18 0 0	11 0 0	do.	
14 0 28	6 0 0	8 5 0	6 15 0	do.	
11 3 28	6 15 0	7 15 0	7 0 0	do.	
40 2 34	15 8 0	28 2 0	19 0 0	do.	
18 3 6	7 15 0	15 0 0	13 0 0	do.	

1390	James Collins, ...	do. ...
1391	Edmund Carey, ...	do. ...
1392	Simon Halloran, ...	do. ...
1393	Patrick McMahon, ...	do. ...
1394	Patrick Scanlon, ...	do. ...
1395	Bridget Dwyer, ...	do. ...
1396	John Pilkington and another.	James Tyrrell, a Minor,
1397	John Leahy, ...	H. V. MacNamara,
1398	William Hopkins, ...	Wainwright T. Crowe,
1399	Martin Keane, ...	Marquis of Conyngham,
1400	Patrick Kelly, ...	Lord Leconfield, ...
1401	Michael Byrne, ...	do. ...
1402	James Irwin, ...	do. ...
1403	Francis Egan, ...	Michael Casey and others,
1404	Thomas Keatley, ...	do. ...
1405	Michael Ryan, ...	do. ...
1406	John Dowse, ...	George F. Roughan,
1407	John Vaughan, ...	Mrs. E. M. Hickes,

CLARE—continued.

Extent of Holding. Statute.	Poor Law Valuation.	Present Rent.	Judicial Rent.	Observations.	Value of Tenancy.
A. R. P.	£ s. d.	£ s. d.	£ s. d.		£ s. d.
30 0 15	12 5 0	21 0 0	15 15 0	By consent.	
21 3 17	18 8 0	13 17 0	14 0 0	do.	
4 0 20	5 0 0	4 13 0	2 15 0	do.	
24 0 21	9 5 0	17 10 0	13 10 0	do.	
2 1 20	—	2 5 0	1 11 0	do.	
5 0 0	1 0 0	4 0 0	3 0 0	do.	
2 1 0	1 0 0	4 14 0	4 14 0	do.	
52 0 20	13 10 0	23 0 0	24 10 0	do.	
6 3 17	0 5 0	3 5 0	2 14 0	do.	
8 1 0	2 5 0	4 5 0	5 0 0	do.	
8 1 0	0 10 0	3 11 0	2 13 6	do.	
89 2 13	18 15 0	60 0 0	53 0 0	do.	
91 0 35	30 13 0	45 0 0	35 0 0	do.	
16 1 20	10 10 0	14 14 0	11 10 0	do.	
204 0 0	40 0 0	85 0 0	60 0 0	do.	
20 1 14	10 13 0	13 10 0	11 12 0		100 0 0
38 1 28	25 15 0	30 10 0	20 15 0		150 0 0
67 2 20	53 18 0	60 12 0	25 0 0		200 0 0
84 1 21	46 0 0	40 13 10	40 13 10		270 0 0
7 1 8	4 15 0	5 0 0	3 0 0		30 0 0
10 5 20	5 0 0	20 0 0	13 13 0		80 0 0
7 3 30	5 13 0	5 10 0	6 5 0		30 0 0
7 0 24	1 5 0	0 3 5	5 13 0		80 0 0
60 0 25	21 5 0	25 0 0	25 0 0		
4 3 15	3 0 0	5 10 0	5 0 0		
25 1 0	8 0 0	14 10 0	11 0 0		
13 2 8	4 5 0	7 10 0	6 15 0		
16 1 21	8 10 0	15 10 2	4 10 0		
2 3 20	1 15 0	3 0 0	3 0 0		
1 2 22	—	3 0 0	1 0 0		
1 1 0	—	4 10 0	2 10 0		
24 3 16	10 15 0	25 10 0	16 0 0		100 0 0
15 1 0	6 0 0	11 10 0	5 15 0		40 0 0
23 0 11	10 13 0	25 0 0	21 10 0		
61 1 7	11 10 0	23 0 0	21 0 0		

Names of Assistant Commissioners by whom Cases were decided.	No.	Name of Tenant.	Name of Landlord.	Townland.
Assistant Commissioners—				
R. Reeves, Q.C. (Legal). C. O'Keeffe. H. G. MacCarthy. H. C. Nash. E. G. Price.	1419	Nicholas M. Lillis,	The Misses Caldwell,	Ferrane, West,
	1420	John O'Neill,	Hector S. Vandeleur,	[illegible]
	1421	Michael Walsh,	do.	do.
	1422	Thomas Shea,	do.	do.
	1423	Simon McGrath,	do.	do.
	1424	William Stoddert, Rep. of Thomas Stoddert,	do.	Carrowmore,
	1425	John McDonnell,	Mrs. Abbey Mahony,	Carrowmore, [illegible]
	1426	John Cunningham,	do.	do.
	1427	Simon Cunningham,	do.	do.
	1428	Michael Creighton,	do.	do.
	1429	Nicholas M. Lillis,	William H. W. Fitzgerald,	Ferrane, West,
	1430	Michael Maxwell (John),	John F. Stoddert,	Brugh,
	1431	Thomas Hough,	do.	do.
	1432	Patrick Hough,	do.	do.
	1433	Simon McEnna,	O. W. J. Studdert and mother, Minors,	Gowerane,
	1434	Patrick Hamilton,	Mrs. Jane Sampson and others,	Tullabrack,
	1435	Stephen Cahany,	do.	do.
	1436	Simon Fitzgerald,	do.	do.
	1437	Simon Kelly,	do.	do.
	1438	John Killeen,	do.	do.
	1439	Michael Purcell,	do.	do.
	1440	Edmund Purcell,	do.	do.
	1441	Catherine Talty,	do.	do.
	1442	Francis Gorman,	do.	Furrihy,
	1443	James Gorman,	do.	do.
	1444	Simon McGrath,	do.	do.
	1445	Joseph Kett,	do.	Furrihy & [illegible]
	1446	James Hough, junior,	do.	Carrowblough [illegible]
	1447	John Walsh (James),	do.	do.
	1448	Edmund Mahony,	do.	do.
	1449	Michael Hough (Ed.),	do.	do.
	1450	Michael Hough (John),	do.	do.
	1451	Michael Donohoe,	do.	do.
	1452	Patrick Walsh,	do.	do.
	1453	Michael Gorman,	do.	do.

CLARE—*continued.*

Extent of Holding. Statute.	Poor Law Valuation.	Former Rent.	Judicial Rent.	Observations.	Value of Tenancy.
A. R. P.	£ s. d.	£ s. d.	£ s. d.		£ s. d.
150 3 31	80 10 0	80 0 0	60 0 0		180 0 0
31 2 13	13 0 0	16 0 0	16 0 0		140 0 0
16 3 20	8 13 0	13 0 0	13 0 0		100 0 0
23 1 14	10 0 0	10 0 0	10 0 0		180 0 0
18 2 13	9 10 0	13 0 0	11 5 0		100 0 0
130 0 37	83 10 0	93 0 0	75 0 0		500 0 0
6 2 31	—	4 7 2	5 6 0		18 0 0
20 1 1	8 15 0	16 18 4	16 10 0		110 0 0
18 3 6	8 10 0	13 0 0	9 10 0		90 0 0
40 1 34	14 10 0	27 10 0	20 0 0		140 0 0
17 0 8	5 0 0	8 0 0	6 0 0		50 0 0
18 0 11	5 10 0	9 7 0	7 10 0		60 0 0
16 3 20	5 5 0	9 10 0	7 0 0		60 0 0
13 3 8	6 0 0	12 0 0	9 15 0		100 0 0
5 2 14	5 0 0	7 0 0	3 10 0		
83 3 15	27 0 0	43 9 4	43 0 1		300 0 0
130 1 1	55 10 0	42 0 0	46 0 0		220 0 0
13 1 10	3 0 0	10 0 0	8 10 0		90 0 0
6 1 0	1 5 0	5 0 0	3 0 0		15 0 0
67 2 0	55 0 0	37 0 0	34 0 0		200 0 0
18 1 25	3 5 0	5 10 0	7 0 0		80 0 0
70 1 19	17 10 0	35 5 0	30 5 0		180 0 0
14 2 15	3 15 0	6 0 0	5 5 0		35 0 0
64 0 3	51 14 0	63 17 6	57 10 0		160 0 0
21 2 7	11 10 0	20 0 0	16 10 0		110 0 0
4 3 8	2 10 0	5 5 0	4 5 0		45 0 0
25 1 30	11 5 0	13 1 8	11 10 0		160 0 0
38 3 23	14 10 0	18 5 0	16 0 0		120 0 0
61 0 10	26 0 0	18 18 0	19 10 0		130 0 0
30 3 10	9 10 0	13 18 0	12 15 0		120 0 0
78 2 6	27 10 0	36 10 0	34 10 0		270 0 0
31 1 16	13 15 0	15 11 10	15 10 0		100 0 0
18 0 35	5 0 0	11 0 0	8 0 0		35 0 0
51 3 8	9 5 0	15 10 0	14 5 0		130 0 0
61 2 35	10 5 0	34 8 5	24 8 9		180 0 0

COUNTY OF

Names of Assistant Commissioners by whom Cases were decided.	No.	Name of Tenant.	Name of Landlord.	Townland.
Assistant Commissioners—				
R. Reeves, Q.C. (Legal). G. O'Keeffe. E. G. McCarthy. H. C. Nash. E. G. Pitt.	1454	Thomas Kent, ...	Mrs. Jane Stacpoole and others,	Carrowblough...
	1455	Simon Downes, ...	do.	Carrowmore, Sth.,
	1456	John Downes, ...	do.	do. ...
	1457	James Barton, ...	do.	do. ...
	1458	Mary Hough, ...	do.	do. ...
	1459	Thomas Downes, ...	do.	do. ...
	1460	Thomas Egan, ...	W. F. Green, ...	Cloonygarvan, ...
	1461	Martin Cotter, ...	do.	do. ...
	1462	Mary Kelly, ...	do.	do. ...
	1463	John Gorman, ...	do.	do. ...
	1464	Michael O'Brien, Rep. of Patrick O'Brien.	do.	do. ...
	1465	Michael Cleary, Rep. of Cornelius Lynch.	do.	do. ...
	1466	Martin Egan, ...	do.	do. ...
	1467	Michael Kilmartin, ...	do.	do. ...
	1468	John Houlihan, ...	do.	do. ...
	1469	Simon Walsh, ...	do.	do. ...
	1470	Martin Walsh, ...	do.	do. ...
	1471	David Walsh, ...	do.	do. ...
	1472	John McMahon, ...	do.	Carrowmore, Nth.,
	1473	Stephen Cotter, ...	do.	do. ...
	1474	Patrick O'Keefe, ...	do.	do. ...
	1475	Michael O'Keefe, ...	do.	do. ...
	1476	Johanna Egan, ...	do.	do. ...
	1477	Daniel McInerney, ...	Morgan Walsh, ...	Scragh, ...
	1478	Martin Downes, ...	do.	do. ...
	1479	Richard Ryan, ...	do.	do. ...
	1480	John McInerney, ...	do.	do. ...
	1481	Patrick Barry, ...	John Tymons, by the Rev. F. Tymons, his Guardian.	Ballykett, ...
	1482	Nicholas M. Lillis, ...	do.	Dalton, West, ...
	1483	John Mulqueen, ...	do.	Moyadda Beg, ...
	1484	Ellen Mulligan, ...	do.	do. ...
	1485	Anthony McNamara, ...	E. P. Westby, ...	Frangrove, ...
	1486	Martin Collins, ...	do.	Doonagore, ...
	1487	Thomas Russell, ...	do.	do. ...
	1488	Patrick Walsh, ...	do.	do. ...

CLARE—*continued.*

Extent of Holding (Statute).	Poor Law Valuation.	Former Rent.	Judicial Rent.	Observations.	Value of Tenancy.
A. R. P.	£ s. d.	£ s. d.	£ s. d.	£ s. d.	£ s. d.
31 0 26	11 10 0	20 0 0	18 0 0		100 0 0
40 2 16	16 17 0	11 10 0	11 0 0		180 0 0
30 3 4	9 5 0	11 5 0	11 5 0		80 0 0
23 1 0	3 3 0	10 5 0	9 0 0		70 0 0
23 1 30	10 15 0	15 1 0	15 2 0		80 0 0
30 0 34	9 7 0	16 0 0	12 18 0		80 0 0
36 1 8	13 13 0	21 17 0	19 0 0		130 0 0
48 0 30	25 0 0	23 14 3	20 5 0		200 0 0
17 0 4	8 17 0	10 0 12	7 16 0		76 0 0
30 1 27	21 10 0	20 15 0	20 0 0		130 0 0
64 0 29	5 10 0	11 8 4	9 10 0		120 0 0
16 1 30	5 0 0	5 3 2	7 2 6		40 0 0
55 0 15	24 10 0	21 14 4	27 10 0		180 0 0
[illegible] 1 0	11 15 0	17 16 1	18 16 0		120 0 0
15 0 23	7 17 0	9 0 5	7 10 0	Rent changed in 1865 from 7 8 8	80 0 0
36 1 1	14 15 0	16 8 2	16 1 5		120 0 0
18 0 16	5 7 0	7 0 5	5 12 0		70 0 0
54 1 30	17 13 0	16 18 7	14 15 0		110 0 0
16 3 34	5 15 0	8 18 6	8 12 6		100 0 0
10 1 23	7 3 6	18 0 0	8 0 0		100 0 0
16 0 31	9 5 0	13 0 0	10 0 0		100 0 0
29 0 30	15 10 0	23 10 0	11 2 0		65 0 0
9 1 35	6 0 0	6 0 0	8 10 0		50 0 0
5 1 16	—	5 1 0	8 4 0		14 0 0
7 0 0	—	6 15 0	3 15 0		20 0 0
3 0 [illegible]	—	1 10 0	1 10 0		10 0 0
8 0 30	—	9 5 0	2 5 0		15 0 0
46 1 20	34 0 0	44 0 0	41 0 0		150 0 0
12 0 23	6 0 0	9 0 0	5 0 0		60 0 0
30 2 2	16 13 0	24 4 0	21 0 0		300 0 0
80 2 31	46 10 0	68 17 0	60 0 0		240 0 0
49 0 0	36 10 0	35 10 0	31 0 0		250 0 0
53 0 0	17 0 0	20 0 0	15 0 0		150 0 0
27 0 14	10 5 0	13 0 0	23 0 0		100 0 0
58 0 19	17 0 0	26 0 0	18 0 0		170 0 0

COUNTY OF

Names of Assistant Commissioners by whom Cases were decided.	No.	Name of Tenant.	Name of Landlord.	Townland.
Assistant Commissioners—				
R. Reeves, Q.C. (Legal). C. O'Keeffe. E. C. McGildowney. H. C. Hamm. E. G. Penn.	1489	James Mangan, —	E. P. Westby, — —	Dromin, —
	1490	Mary McInerney, Admx. of Michael McInerney.	do. — —	do. —
	1491	Mary Tuey, — —	do. — —	do. —
	1492	Denis Tuey, — —	do. — —	do. —
	1493	Connor Hough, —	do. — —	do. —
	1494	Michael Ranin, —	do. — —	do. —
	1495	Bartholomew Scanlan, —	do. — —	do. —
	1496	Patrick Connolly, —	do. — —	do. —
	1497	Thomas Crawford, —	do. — —	do. —
	1498	Bridget Mulvihill, —	do. — —	do. —
	1499	Hugh Maguire, —	do. — —	do. —
	1500	John Maguire, —	do. — —	do. —
	1501	Honor Collins, —	do. — —	do. —
	1502	James Tuey (Pat), —	do. — —	Dromin, East and West.
	1503	Anthony Roche, —	do. — —	do. —
	1504	John Daly, — —	Mary Foley, — —	Dromin, —
	1505	Thomas Keogh. —	Mary Ryan, — —	Castlesomerard, —
	1506	Michael Reidy, —	do. — —	do. —
	1507	Michael Hanrahy, —	do. — —	do. —
	1508	Mary Hannahy, —	do. — —	do. —
	1509	Joseph O'Dea, —	do. — —	do. —
	1510	Michael Fahey, Rep. of Martin Fahey.	Col. W. E. A. MacDonnell, —	Knockgow, —
	1511	Do. — —	do. — —	Fortlough, —
	1512	Pat McNamara, —	John Collinson, — —	Kilmo Ballymullen Beg.
	1513	James Shanahan, —	R. B. M. Johnston & another,	Toonagh, East, —
	1514	William Carey, —	James J. Carey, — —	Quilty, West, —
	1515	James Hennessy, —	Thomas Killeen, — —	Ballymaclea Beg.
	1516	Patrick Ryan, —	Ernest Simpson, — —	Kilbeggypuring
	1517	James Cumming, —	do. — —	do. —
	1518	Thomas Cumming (Sen.),	do. — —	do. —
	1519	James Ryan, —	do. — —	do. —
	1520	Michael Cumming (Big),	do. — —	do. —
	1521	John Egan, — —	Thomas M. Cregan, —	Cloughatoule, —
	1522	James Ryan, —	George Ingram, — —	Fornaght, —
	1523	Hannah Shaughnessy, —	Marquis of Conyngham, —	Clonmoney, —

A.	R.	P.	£	s.	d.	£	s.	d.	£	s.	d.
8	1	33	—			8	0	0	3	10	0
54	1	30	25	0	0	87	0	0	81	0	0
90	0	0	21	0	0	95	0	0	23	0	0
16	1	7	10	0	0	12	0	0	10	0	0
96	3	27	23	0	0	[illegible]	0	0	29	0	0
13	1	8	6	10	0	8	0	0	8	8	0
11	0	30	5	0	0	6	10	0	5	10	0
90	2	6	10	10	0	12	0	0	11	0	0
25	0	13	13	0	0	13	0	0	10	10	0
8	1	16	4	15	0	8	0	0	5	0	0
53	1	31	29	10	0	25	0	0	[illegible]	0	0
47	3	25	18	10	0	83	0	0	23	0	0
30	1	12	18	0	0	85	0	0	30	0	0
62	1	30	16	0	0	34	0	0	22	0	0
28	0	0	23	0	0	86	0	0	22	0	0
7	3	26	2	15	0	7	0	0	6	0	0
71	1	30	9	0	0	80	0	0	14	0	0
96	1	20	14	10	0	45	0	0	24	0	0
40	0	0	5	0	0	13	15	0	30	0	0
96	2	30	5	5	0	10	5	0	12	0	0
64	3	6	7	10	0	18	0	0	13	0	0
67	3	23	12	0	0	77	0	0	22	15	0
60	1	11	14	15	0	30	0	0	[illegible]	0	0
38	0	0	12	0	0	25	0	0	10	10	0
9	1	4	1	5	0	4	5	0	2	10	0
7	2	23	2	15	0	9	5	0	8	5	0
3	2	23	0	7	.0	6	10	0	2	15	0
[illegible]	0	0	45	10	0	70	0	0	25	0	0
18	3	39	10	15	0	35	5	0	11	15	0
84	0	23	25	10	0	25	0	0	20	0	0
122	3	30	26	0	0	85	15	6	38	0	0
65	2	10	13	15	0	15	10	0	11	10	0
48	0	0	12	5	0	10	12	0	13	0	0
41	1	24	5	15	0	30	0	0	13	0	0
37	1	23	13	10	0	13	0	0	11	0	0

COUNTY OF

Names of Assistant Commissioners by whom Case was decided.	No.	Name of Tenant.	Name of Landlord.	Townland.
Assistant Commissioners—				
R. Reeves, Q.C. (Legal). G. O'Keeffe. R. O. McCausland. M. G. Nash. E. G. Finn.	1524	Patrick Maloney, ...	Marquis of Conyngham, ...	[illegible], ...
	1525	John Walsh, ...	do.	do. ...
	1526	John Speight, ...	do.	do. ...
	1527	Michael Cunning, ...	Daniel Walsh, ...	[illegible], ...
	1528	Patrick Dillon, ...	Rev. H. J. Taylor, ...	Ardning, ...
	1529	John Hoskins, ...	do.	do. ...
	1530	Anne Lane, ...	do.	do. ...
	1531	James Downes, ...	Mrs. Jane Hargrave and Richard Hargrave,	Carrowmore, &c.,
	1532	John Glabney, ...	do.	Carrowkilnaglenon,
	1533	John Talty, ...	do.	do. ...
	1534	John Talty, Admst. of Hugh Talty,	do.	do. ...
	1535	Patrick Boyle, ...	James Joseph Geary, ...	Quilty, West, ...
	1536	Michael O'Brien, ...	Hector R. Vandeleur, ...	Onderfrankish, ...
	1537	Johanna Maloney, ...	Rev. Aldery Maloney, ...	Carrowmore, &c.,
	1538	John O'Dea, Rep. of John O'Dea,	John F. Stackford, ...	Hough, ...
	1539	John Cassey, Rep. of Martin Morrison,	do.	do. ...
	1540	Patrick Mungan and others,	Dennis Sampson, ...	Ballycorban East.
	1541	Anne Cunning, ...	do.	Killmurrygeeny,
	1542	Michael Keogh, ...	Thomas McAdam, ...	Rosmuckle, ...
	1543	John Curtis, ...	Dr. Pollock, ...	Glenagalone, ...
	1544	Benjamin Ryan, ...	do.	do. ...
	1545	Thomas Kingsley, ...	do.	do. ...
	1546	James Slattery, ...	do.	do. ...
	1547	James Cunning, ...	do.	do. ...
	1548	James McNamara, ...	do.	do. ...
	1549	John Roland, ...	R. H. Bailey, ...	Ballybank, ...
	1550	James Barton, ...	do.	do. ...
	1551	Patrick Roland, ...	do.	do. ...
	1552	Michael Hillane (Cooney),	George Macquern, ...	Cloontoraloe, ...
	1553	James Ryan, ...	do.	Cloneen, ...
	1554	Michael Fitzgerald, ...	Thomas MacMahon Cregan, ...	Cloughleels, ...
	1555	David Fitzgerald, ...	do.	do. ...
	1556	Bridget McInerney, ...	do.	do. ...
	1557	Ignatius and Matthew Ryan,	do.	do. ...
	1558	Michael McInerney, ...	do.	do. ...

CLARE—*continued.*

Extent of Holding, Statute.	Poor Law Valuation.	Former Rent.	Judicial Rent.	Observations.	Value of Tenancy.
A. R. P.	£ s. d.	£ s. d.	£ s. d.		£ s. d.
89 3 19	16 10 0	33 10 0	23 0 0	By consent.	
194 1 [illegible]	[illegible] 0 0	106 0 0	75 0 0	do.	
68 0 6	20 16 0	36 0 0	25 0 0	do.	
14 3 33	7 10 0	18 0 0	13 15 0	do.	
71 2 5	73 5 0	90 0 0	77 5 0	do.	
69 3 17	57 5 0	90 0 0	70 16 0	do.	
35 1 20	26 10 0	84 5 0	57 5 0	do.	
29 1 23	21 0 0	27 0 0	27 0 0		180 0 0
17 1 6	7 10 0	13 0 0	9 10 0		60 0 0
10 2 0	16 5 0	10 10 0	10 10 0		100 0 0
25 2 20	16 5 0	19 10 0	16 5 0		170 0 0
4 2 18	3 5 0	1 10 0	5 15 0		
30 3 28	11 15 0	20 0 0	16 5 0		130 0 0
2 3 25	2 0 0	4 15 0	4 12 6		35 0 0
13 3 3	5 15 0	12 9 4	11 10 0		110 0 0
23 0 37	7 1 0	15 5 0	13 13 0		100 0 0
307 1 36	2 5 0	7 16 0	7 10 0	do.	
125 1 30	45 0 0	60 0 0	40 0 0	do.	
38 3 17	16 0 0	33 1 1	27 0 0		500 0 0
107 0 11	8 15 0	16 0 0	13 0 0		50 0 0
49 2 9	11 10 0	14 19 0	10 10 0		80 0 0
21 3 17	11 0 0	15 1 0	11 0 0		100 0 0
45 0 11	10 15 0	30 17 0	23 0 0		180 0 0
20 0 7	6 10 0	14 17 0	10 10 0		65 0 0
65 3 8	12 10 0	31 5 0	16 0 0		190 0 0
37 2 10	8 10 0	6 15 0	5 5 0		40 0 0
68 0 0	18 15 0	27 0 0	20 0 0		160 0 0
17 2 20	4 16 0	8 13 0	8 5 0		35 0 0
60 3 18	7 15 0	23 10 0	15 12 0		180 0 0
28 0 18	10 0 0	41 1 3	36 3 0		180 0 0
16 0 0	3 5 0	9 15 9	6 3 0		
21 2 8	5 15 0	6 10 0	4 13 0		
16 0 6	3 7 0	4 0 0	3 13 0		
14 3 25	3 15 0	6 1 0	4 2 0		
16 0 0	2 13 8	5 5 0	3 5 0		

COUNTY OF

Names of Assistant Commissioners by whom Cases were decided.	No.	Name of Tenant.	Name of Landlord.	Townland.
Assistant Commissioners—				
R. Reeves, Q.C. (Legal). G. O'Keeffe. R. G. McCausland. H. G. Nash. E. G. Pery.	1839	James Ryan, ...	Thomas MacMahon Cregan, ...	Cloughleafin, ...
	1840	Michael Ryan, ...	do. ...	do. ...
	1841	Anne, Admx. of Martin O'Brien.	do.	do. ...
	1842	Margaret, Admx. of Patrick Fitzgerald.	do.	do. ...
	1843	Thomas Ryan, ...	do.	do. ...
	1844	Roger, Admor. of James Maloney.	do.	do. ...
	1845	Michael Crotty, ...	Richard Going and others, ...	[illegible]
	1846	Denis Nunan, ...	Col. J. W. O'Donnell, ...	[illegible], West, ...
	1847	Patrick O'Brien, ...	John C. Delmege, ...	Glenagross, ...
	1848	Mathew Nolan, ...	Charles W. Smith, ...	Rathcoole, ...
	1849	William Bourke, ...	do.	do. ...
	1850	Mary Donohue, ...	Colonel McAdam, ...	Ballykilleen, ...
				Total, ...

COUNTY OF

Assistant Commissioners—	2081	Patrick Daly, ...	John O'Brien, ...	[illegible]
E. O. MacDevitt (Legal). T. Walshe. P. Hanbury. F. O. Griffin. F. Maxwell Carroll.	2082	Daniel Driscoll, ...	do.	[illegible], ...
	2083	John Collins, ...	do.	[illegible]
	2084	Denis Daly, Rep. of Hannah Daly.	Daniel MacSweeny, ...	[illegible], ...
	2085	Jerry Mahony, ...	do.	[illegible], ...
	2086	Ellen Kiely, ...	do.	[illegible], East,
	2087	Patrick Sweeny, ...	do.	[illegible], ...
	2088	John Sweeney, junior, ...	do.	do. ...
	2089	Mary McCarthy, ...	Richard Beamish, ...	[illegible], ...
	2090	Peter Hayes, ...	John Morris, ...	[illegible], ...
	2091	John Jennings, ...	Captain Murragh, ...	[illegible],
	2092	Jeremiah Coghlan, ...	[illegible] Life Assurance Company and others.	Derryconnell, ...
	2093	William S. Bateman, ...	John S. Lucas, ...	[illegible], ...
	2094	Thomas Kelly, Rep. of Catherine Kelly.	Daniel McInerney, ...	[illegible], East,
	2095	Denis Connelly, ...	Robert H. E. Whyte, ...	do. ...
	2096	Timothy Sullivan, Rep. of Daniel Sullivan.	Earl of Bantry, ...	[illegible],
	2097	Thomas Donovan, ...	W. S. Starkie, ...	[illegible], ...
	2098	Michael Walsh, ...	Samuel Hawkins, ...	[illegible], ...

CLARE—continued.

Extent of Holding Statute.			Poor Law Valuation.			Former Rent.			Judicial Rent.			Observations.
A.	R.	P.	£	s.	d.	£	s.	d.	£	s.	d.	
10	0	0	1	10	0	4	0	0	3	0	0	
70	3	[illegible]	3	5	0	6	10	0	4	10	0	
37	1	[illegible]	8	0	0	4	15	0	3	10	0	
41	0	0	1	10	6	5	3	8	5	6	8	
16	0	0	8	8	0	7	10	0	6	0	0	
18	3	0	3	2	8	7	5	3	6	3	0	

Names of Assistant Commissioners by whom Cases were decided.	No.	Name of Tenant.		Name of Landlord.	
Assistant Commissioners—					
E. G. MacDermott (Legal). T. Walpole. P. Mahony. F. O. Grady. F. Maxwell Carroll.	2069	Cornelius Regan,	...	Callaghan McCarthy,	
	2070	Mary Foun,	...	Henry B. Dumerah,	
	2071	Michael Crowley,	...	Rev. James Forde and	
	2072	Daniel McCarthy,	...	Patrick McCarthy,	
	2073	James Barry,	...	do.	...
	2074	Edmund Barry,	...	do.	...
	2075	Jeremiah Mahony,	...	Earl of Kenmare,	
	2076	Timothy Hanington,	...	do.	...
	2077	John Long,	...	George Lucas,	...
	2078	John Sheehy, Admr. of Patrick Sheehy,		do.	...
	2079	James Hayes,	...	Mrs. I. H. Ogeary,	
	2080	Patrick Hayes,	...	do.	...
	2081	Jerry McCarthy,	...	do.	...
	2082	Do., ...	...	do.	...
	2083	John McCarthy,	...	do.	...
	2084	Cornelius Fitzpatrick,	...	do.	...
	2085	Mrs. Bridget Fitzpatrick,		Horace P. Townsend,	
	2086	James Brien,	...	do.	...
	2087	Daniel Fitzpatrick,	...	do.	...
	2088	Derby Hayes,	...	William Judge Sheehy,	
	2089	Margaret Dillon,	...	do.	...
	2090	Denis Mahony,	...	do.	...
	2091	William Mahony,	...	do.	...
	2092	James Dempsey,	...	do.	...
	2093	Daniel McCarthy,	...	Edinburgh Life As Company and others.	
	2094	James Sellar,	...	do.	...
	2095	Michael Leary,	...	Samuel N. Hutchins a	
	2096	James Crowley,	...	Mrs. Power,	...
	2097	John Rice,	...	Captain W. C. Collis,	
	2098	Do., ...	...	do.	...
	2099	John White,	...	do.	...
	2100	Maurice Rice,	...	do.	...
	2101	William Flynn,	...	do.	...
	2102	Maurice Lenmanny,	...	do.	...
	2103	Catherine Rice,	...	do.	...

CORK—continued.

Extent of Holding. Statute.	Poor Law Valuation.	Former Rent.	Judicial Rent.	Observations.	Value of Tenancy.
A. R. P.	£ s. d.	£ s. d.	£ s. d.		£ s. d.
30 0 0	33 13 0	37 0 0	33 4 0	By consent.	
10 0 30	8 10 0	13 14 5	10 16 5	do.	
40 3 0	23 10 0	33 0 0	30 0 0	do.	
15 0 0	6 5 8	11 0 0	9 0 0	do.	
7 3 0	3 0 0	5 10 0	4 10 0	do.	
7 2 0	3 0 0	5 10 0	4 10 0	do.	
21 0 0	7 10 0	9 0 0	8 0 0		
461 3 33	33 10 0	39 0 0	30 3 0		
41 0 0	25 15 0	41 0 0	33 0 0	do.	
65 1 4	33 16 0	54 0 0	31 0 0	do.	
16 0 0	10 10 0	17 0 0	13 10 0	do.	
31 0 0	7 0 0	18 0 0	14 10 0	do.	
5 0 0	4 10 0	5 17 0	7 0 0	do.	
4 3 0	5 0 0	5 5 0	4 0 0	do.	
10 0 0	3 10 0	12 3 4	9 0 0	do.	
5 3 0	4 0 0	8 14 5	7 0 0	do.	
25 0 0	16 0 0	25 0 0	19 0 0		165 0 0
21 0 0	12 15 0	24 0 0	10 0 0		118 0 0
13 0 0	9 5 0	18 10 0	10 10 0		73 10 0
30 0 0	23 0 0	41 0 0	34 0 0	do.	
11 0 0	3 0 0	6 0 0	4 0 0	do.	
18 0 0	7 0 0	14 0 0	8 19 0	do.	
10 0 5	6 16 0	15 0 0	10 10 0	do.	
10 0 0	5 10 0	15 0 0	6 10 0	do.	
23 0 37	15 10 0	15 7 6	13 10 0		
25 0 0	7 5 0	9 16 0	8 10 0		
10 1 0	7 5 0	15 5 0	9 5 8		
14 0 30	7 15 0	11 17 6	9 0 0		
10 1 0	4 15 0	8 10 0	6 0 0	do.	
47 0 0	12 0 0	15 0 0	13 5 0	do.	
56 0 0	21 0 0	35 0 0	34 0 0	do.	
152 3 30	50 0 0	80 0 0	73 0 0		
30 0 0	5 15 0	7 7 0	6 0 0	do.	
40 0 0	16 15 0	23 3 0	18 5 0	do.	
35 0 0	8 0 0	20 1 3	14 10 0	do.	

COUNTY OF

Names of Assistant Commissioners by whom Cases were decided.	No.	Name of Tenant.	Name of Landlord.	Townland.
Assistant Commissioners—				
E. G. MacDermott (Legal). T. Walpole. P. Mahony. F. G. Griffith. F. Maxwell Gamble.	2104	Ellen McCarthy, ...	Captain W. G. Chute, ...	[illegible],
	2105	John Fitzgerald, ...	do.	[illegible], ...
	2106	Ellen Hales, ...	John Olaf McCall, ...	Ballyhooly, ...
	2107	Mary Hegarty, ...	do.	do. ...
	2108	Daniel Ahern, ...	do.	do. ...
	2109	Do., ...	do.	do. ...
	2110	James Daly, ...	Rev. William H. Neane, ...	Garryduff, ...
	2111	John Collins, ...	do.	do. ...
	2112	John Reardon, ...	Mrs. A. E. Carroll, ...	[illegible], ...
	2113	Jeremiah Donegan, ...	George A. Wood, ...	Farran, ...
	2114	Jane Leahy, Admx. of Philip Leahy,	Earl of Listowel, ...	[illegible], ...
	2115	Timothy Regan, ...	Richard Roberts, ...	Tullig, ...
	2116	John Duggan, ...	James Matt. Murragh, ...	[illegible], ...
	2117	Patrick Browne, ...	do.	do. ...
	2118	Daniel Dwyer, ...	do.	do. ...
	2119	Mrs. Catherine Collins,	R. N. Hutchins and others, ...	[illegible], ...
	2120	William Collins, ...	do.	do. ...
	2121	John McCarthy, ...	do.	do. ...
	2122	Patrick Hennessy, ...	do.	[illegible], ...
	2123	Catherine Driscoll, Admx. of William Driscoll,	Sir H. W. Becher, Bart., ...	[illegible], ...
	2124	Honora [illegible], ...	Richard Beamish, ...	[illegible], ...
	2125	Thomas Jermyn, ...	Daniel McSweeney, ...	[illegible], ...
	2126	Jeremiah Sullivan, ...	Maria J. Lawrence, ...	[illegible],
	2127	Thomas Barry, ...	Anthony John Cliffe, ...	[illegible], ...
	2128	John Murphy, Admr. of Patrick Murphy, decd.,	Sir Henry W. Becher, Bart.,	[illegible] ...
	2129	John McCarthy, ...	do.	do. ...
	2130	Denis Collins, ...	do.	do. ...
	2131	Bat. Dulligan, ...	do.	do. ...
	2132	Daniel McCarthy, ...	do.	do. ...
	2133	Owen Leonard, ...	do.	do. ...
	2134	Do., ...	do.	do. ...
	2135	Denis Scully, ...	Earl of Kenmare, ...	Maughanasilly,
	2136	Thomas Sheehan, ...	John O'Brien, ...	[illegible], ...
	2137	Mathew Sweeney, ...	R. W. Long, ...	[illegible], ...
	2138	Ellen McCarthy, ...	Sir H. W. Becher, Bart., ...	[illegible], ...

CORK—*continued.*

Extent of Holding. Statute.	Poor Law Valuation.	Former Rent.	Judicial Rent.	Observations.	Value of Tenancy.
A. R. P.	£ s. d.	£ s. d.	£ s. d.		£ s. d.
84 0 0	8 0 0	14 0 0	13 13 0	By consent.	
40 0 0	10 5 0	16 10 0	13 0 0	do.	
44 1 20	60 15 0	84 12 5	71 13 0	do.	
64 1 0	40 0 0	50 11 5	42 0 0	do.	
70 0 22	34 0 0	73 13 0	60 14 0	do.	
67 3 10	50 0 0	84 16 9	71 9 4	do.	
84 0 0	34 10 0	40 0 0	43 0 0		
9 0 0	—	10 0 0	36 0 0		
132 0 28	63 10 0	83 10 0	70 0 0	do.	
65 0 21	63 10 0	80 0 0	75 0 0	do.	
25 1 10	18 0 0	33 0 0	32 0 0		
35 1 31	8 15 0	11 5 0	10 0 0		
73 0 27	37 15 0	50 0 0	38 0 0	Proceedings have been made as regards a holding in this case.	120 0 0
76 2 30	45 0 0	63 5 7	42 0 0		100 0 0
32 0 24	11 10 0	23 11 0	16 0 0		130 0 0
43 0 0	18 10 0	31 0 0	22 0 0		
45 0 0	25 0 0	30 13 0	30 0 0		
50 0 0	14 13 0	30 0 0	22 0 0	do.	
60 0 0	10 10 0	27 0 0	27 0 0	do.	
38 1 6	15 0 0	30 0 0	17 0 0		130 0 0
32 0 0	13 0 0	30 0 0	24 10 0		155 0 0
63 1 10	16 5 0	32 10 0	24 0 0		
18 1 31	9 15 0	14 0 0	18 10 0		
77 1 28	34 18 0	41 0 3	41 0 3		230 0 0
72 3 0	4 5 0	10 0 0	4 0 0		80 0 0
25 0 6	18 0 0	16 0 0	15 0 0		115 0 0
21 0 7	7 13 0	19 0 0	10 0 0		80 0 0
60 1 20	18 15 0	25 0 0	23 10 0		140 0 0
21 0 19	9 15 0	12 0 0	10 0 0		80 0 0
27 0 14	12 16 0	17 0 0	14 0 0		100 0 0
46 0 37	19 0 0	25 13 10	23 0 0		150 0 0
313 0 30	16 0 0	20 0 0	25 0 0		
44 3 3	6 5 0	25 0 0	13 0 0		
16 0 0	8 0 0	20 10 0	15 0 0		
7 1 20	5 10 0	10 0 0	8 0 0		60 0 0

COUNTY OF

Names of Assistant Commissioners by whom Cases were decided.	No.	Name of Tenant.	Name of Landlord.	Townland.
Assistant Commissioners—				
E. C. MacDevitt (Legal). T. Walpole. F. Mahony. F. G. Grattan. F. Maxwell Gardiner.	2139	Timothy Driscoll,	Sir H. W. Becher, Bart.,	[illegible]
	2140	Patrick McCarthy,	do.	[illegible]
	2141	William Barrett,	do.	do.
	2142	Mrs. Abbey Mulhane,	do.	do.
	2143	John Mahony, jun.,	do.	Ringarogy,
	2144	Patrick Mahony,	do.	Ringarogy and islands.
	2145	Daniel Mahony,	do.	Ringarogy,
	2146	John McCarthy,	do.	do.
	2147	Michael Cadogan, Admor. of James Cadogan.	do.	do.
	2148	Patrick Cadogan,	do.	Ringarogy and [illegible].
	2149	Timothy Cadogan,	do.	Turkhead,
	2150	Denis Cadogan,	do.	do.
	2151	Mrs. Ellen Mulhane,	do.	Horse Island,
	2152	John Young,	do.	do.
	2153	Jeremiah Cadogan,	do.	do.
	2154	John Nolan,	do.	do.
	2155	Mrs. Ellen Kealeher,	William J. Kingsley,	[illegible]
	2156	John Baron,	do.	do.
	2157	Thomas Smyth,	do.	do.
	2158	John Connell,	George H. Newman,	[illegible]
	2159	Patrick Hegarty,	do.	do.
	2160	Jeremiah Mahony,	do.	do.
	2161	Timothy Mahony,	Daniel [illegible],	[illegible]
	2162	Patrick Regan,	Maria and Lizzie O'Grady,	[illegible]
	2163	Florence McCarthy,	Rev. James Forbes and anor.,	[illegible]
	2164	John Sullivan,	Thomas B. Whitney,	[illegible]
	2165	Johanna Hurley,	do.	do.
	2166	Timothy Donovan,	Earl of Bandon,	[illegible]
	2167	James Walsh,	do.	do.
	2168	Jeremiah McCarthy,	do.	[illegible]
	2169	John McCarthy,	do.	do.
	2170	Timothy Sexton, Admor. of John Sexton.	John A. Jagoe,	Lyre,
	2171	Neil Hurley,	John R. H. Becher,	[illegible]
	2172	Mathew J. Sweetnam,	W. L. M. McVeigh,	Aughadown, &c.
	2173	Edmund Kennelly,	Captain William C. Collis,	[illegible]

CORK—*continued.*

Extent of Holding, Statute.	Poor Law Valuation.	Former Rent.	Judicial Rent.	Observations.	Value of Tenancy.
A. R. P.	£ s. d.	£ s. d.	£ s. d.		£ s. d.
60 3 15	18 15 6	18 5 0	15 5 0		120 0 0
48 3 30	32 0 0	33 0 0	[illegible] 0 0		188 0 0
25 0 18	10 5 0	13 0 0	12 0 0		50 0 0
67 0 0	9 15 6	15 0 0	12 0 0		80 0 0
[illegible] 1 17	8 15 0	11 10 0	11 0 0		[illegible] 0 0
27 1 8	11 0 0	27 0 0	17 0 0		315 0 0
36 0 17	8 0 0	13 0 0	11 10 0		85 0 0
19 3 31	8 5 0	15 10 0	13 10 0		80 0 0
72 3 38	16 0 0	23 15 0	21 0 0		145 0 0
40 0 20	25 0 0	47 1 10	33 0 0		163 0 0
36 0 0	19 10 0	30 8 8	18 0 0		150 0 0
13 3 0	8 6 0	16 0 8	12 0 6		80 0 0
56 0 0	21 0 0	35 4 0	30 0 0		160 0 0
18 0 0	25 5 0	17 10 0	16 0 0		[illegible] 0 0
86 1 8	7 15 0	10 0 0	6 0 0		60 0 0
51 9 1	14 10 0	17 7 0	15 0 0		120 0 0
50 0 0	11 16 0	23 0 0	16 0 0	By consent.	
6 0 0	4 5 0	10 0 0	4 15 0	do.	
68 0 0	16 16 0	25 0 0	20 0 0	do.	
16 0 3	5 15 0	8 14 0	6 10 0		
34 0 36	5 0 0	13 17 0	12 11 0		
67 3 38	7 15 0	13 17 0	13 17 0		
44 0 0	15 0 0	17 7 0	13 0 0		80 0 0
156 0 0	40 0 0	67 0 0	57 0 0	Provision has been made as regards labourers.	
18 0 0	5 0 0	8 15 0	5 0 0		
[illegible] 0 25	26 10 0	70 0 0	20 0 0		
56 0 25	10 0 0	60 0 0	34 0 0		
63 0 0	11 0 0	16 15 6	15 16 4		150 0 0
30 1 0	4 5 0	4 15 4	3 12 4		80 0 0
43 0 0	20 7 0	30 7 0	25 0 0		148 0 0
43 0 0	23 0 0	38 7 0	30 0 0		165 0 0
62 0 15	13 16 0	30 0 0	21 0 0		
86 3 10	18 10 0	36 0 0	22 0 0		
36 2 36	34 16 0	56 0 0	36 0 0		
46 0 0	18 0 0	31 0 0	19 0 0	By consent.	

COUNTY OF

Names of Assistant Commissioners by whom Cases were decided.	No.	Name of Tenant.	Name of Landlord.	Townland.
Assistant Commissioners—				
E. G. MacDevitt (Legal). T. Wallace. P. Hamilton. P. G. Griffin. F. Maxwell Cassidy.	2174	Kian Smith, ...	John G. McCall, ...	Ballybrady, South,
	2175	Dan Collins, ...	Sir Henry W. Becher, Bart.,	Gurteen, ...
	2176	Patrick McCarthy, ...	Mary S. Hungerford, ...	[illegible], ...
	2177	Denis Murphy, ...	James Whelan, ...	[illegible], ...
	2178	Daniel Daly, ...	Henry Freeman, ...	Ballymacmoran, ...
	2179	Benjamin Harper, ...	Richard H. Galway and anor.,	Dundeady, ...
	2180	Denis Donovan, otherwise Fachtna,	do.	do. ...
	2181	Daniel Dempsey, ...	Thomas Beamish, ...	Clogagh, North,
	2182	Laurence Leary, ...	Callaghan McCarthy, ...	Dunworley, ...
	2183	John Hurley, ...	The Earl of Bandon, ...	Lissaneane, ...
	2184	Michael Madden, ...	do.	do. ...
	2185	Richard Lewis, ...	Daniel McSweeney, ...	Skeaman, West,
	2186	Patrick Sullivan, ...	Samuel N. Hutchins and ors.,	Ardnagashel, ...
	2187	Daniel Hagan, ...	William James Glanger, ...	Mossy Gurney,
	2188	Timothy Leary, ...	Augustus Travers, ...	Timoleague, ...
	2189	Johanna Kashane, ...	Mrs. Elizabeth Longfield and others	Ballyhalwick, ...
	2190	William Smith, ...	do.	do. ...
	2191	Denis Scollan, ...	Robert Travers, ...	Timoleague, ...
	2192	Denis Mahony, ...	Mrs. Louisa Gregory, ...	Ballinamough, ...
	2193	John T. Mahony, ...	do.	do. ...
	2194	Cornelius Daly, ...	Patrick McCarthy, ...	Bawnbeg, ...
	2195	Jeremiah Fahily, ...	do.	do. ...
	2196	French Daly, senior, ...	do.	do. ...
	2197	John Fern, ...	Margaret Sharkey and others,	Lissane, ...
	2198	John Donovan, ...	do.	Lisnabeg, ...
	2199	James Donovan, ...	do.	Ballyshane, ...
	2200	Do.	do.	Dunmore, ...
	2201	James Regan, ...	do.	do. ...
	2202	Timothy Donovan, Rep. of John Donovan.	do.	do. ...
	2203	Michael Mahony, ...	do.	do. ...
	2204	John Mahony, ...	do.	do. ...
	2205	Thomas Callanan, ...	do.	do. ...
	2206	James Barrett, ...	William F. Hume Jones, ...	Islandbeg, ...
	2207	Patrick Crotty, ...	do.	do. ...
	2208	Thomas O'Leary, ...	do.	Aghaleary, ...

CORK—*continued.*

Extent of Holding Statute.			Poor Law Valuation.			Former Rent.			Judicial Rent.			Observations.	Value of Tenancy.
A.	R.	P.	£	s.	d.	£	s.	d.	£	s.	d.		£ s. d.
34	1	11	38	5	0	49	10	0	45	0	0	By consent.	
71	2	31	11	0	0	20	0	0	14	10	0		100 0 0
31	0	0	22	15	0	34	0	0	45	0	0		
63	0	0	24	0	0	45	0	0	35	0	0		
27	0	0	13	0	0	26	0	0	25	0	0		
33	1	17	20	15	0	30	0	0	30	0	0		
29	0	28	14	0	0	19	10	0	16	0	0		
46	0	0	23	10	0	41	12	0	30	0	0		
20	1	0	29	0	0	63	0	0	30	5	0	do.	
28	1	14	4	0	0	13	1	0	12	[illegible]	0		100 0 0
35	0	0	7	10	0	30	0	0	19	0	0		90 0 0
48	3	10	27	0	0	43	0	0	37	0	0		
09	1	26	85	10	0	70	0	0	63	10	0		
100	0	0	80	15	0	123	0	0	119	12	0	do.	
4	2	5	8	0	0	17	0	0	14	10	0	do.	
35	0	0	27	0	0	30	0	0	30	0	0	do.	
67	0	0	26	0	0	67	0	0	45	4	0	do.	
32	3	21	22	0	0	35	10	6	30	0	0	do.	
6	1	0	3	10	0	9	13	0	7	18	6		
8	1	19	3	5	0	4	12	0	3	14	0		
26	0	10	7	10	0	15	13	0	12	12	0		
40	0	20	6	5	0	11	10	0	14	0	0		
28	2	26	6	17	0	9	10	0	8	10	6		
18	1	34	13	15	0	16	11	11	14	0	0		
29	1	0	21	0	0	30	16	6	22	0	0		
25	2	11	21	0	0	30	4	10	26	0	0		
5	3	30	10	15	0	13	9	7	10	0	7		
17	0	0	15	0	0	31	17	6	17	14	0		
18	0	09	19	15	0	22	19	9	19	0	0		
35	3	20	18	15	0	33	3	10	21	0	0		
8	3	0	3	5	0	4	4	0	4	4	0		
16	0	10	11	10	0	19	16	5	15	0	0		
73	1	6	30	10	0	43	15	0	30	0	8		
60	1	37	22	15	6	61	0	0	37	0	0		
65	0	6	36	10	0	46	0	0	46	0	0		

COUNTY OF

Names of Assistant Commissioners by whom Cases were decided.	No.	Name of Tenant.	Name of Landlord.	Townland.
Assistant Commissioners—				
E. O. MacDevitt (Legal). T. Walpole. P. Mahony. H. G. Griffith. F. Maxwell Carroll.	2209	Samuel Kingston, ...	William F. Bence-Jones, ...	Cloghroe, ...
	2210	Mary Collins, ...	Hon. James Pratt and another,	Coolnahane, ...
	2211	John Walsh, ...	do.	do. ...
	2212	Patrick Mahony, ...	do.	do. ...
	2213	John Callanan, ...	do.	Cahirbeg, ...
	2214	James Barrett, ...	James Butler, ...	Fahalane, ...
	2215	Patrick Riordan, ...	Col. and Mrs. Grant, ...	Gneeves, ...
	2216	Cornelius Donovan, ...	Margaret Stawley and others,	Dromore, ...
	2217	Patrick Kelly, ...	Mrs. Elizabeth Brophy, ...	Clogher, ...
	2218	Denis Callaghan, ...	Rev. Richard Hanrahan, ...	Ardagh, ...
	2219	Michael Robinson, Rep. of Stephen Downey.	Col. William Nash and anor., Trustees of Mrs. Nettles.	Gurteen, ...
	2220	John Murray, ...	M. A. R. Dunbar and another,	Inchidaniel, ...
	2221	Michael Murphy, ...	do.	do. ...
	2222	Timothy Driscoll, ...	The Earl of Bandon, ...	Knocknacurra, ...
	2223	Achilles Ward, ...	Henry W. Baldwin, ...	Knockane, ...
	2224	William Coleman, ...	Earl of Donoughmore, ...	Tooreen, ...
	2225	Ellen Murphy, ...	James McC. Kavanagh, ...	Bromanbarragh,
	2226	Honora Twomey, Rep. of John Twomey.	Rev. George Herrick, ...	Knockaunagh, ...
	2227	Owen Dunne, ...	Patrick McCarthy, ...	Dunkillo, ...
	2228	James Green, ...	Thos. Fuller a Minor, by Joseph H. Fuller, his next friend.	Lisheen, ...
	2229	Daniel Leary, ...	Mrs. Elizabeth Brophy, ...	Lackabawn, ...
	2230	Stephen Mangan, ...	do.	Clogher, ...
	2231	Robert Scofield, ...	Richard Donovan and another,	Cherry Crowley,
	2232	Honora Hughes, ...	Mrs. Elizabeth Brophy, ...	Clogher, ...
	2233	Maurice Ahern, ...	do.	do. ...
	2234	John McCarthy, ...	Sir H. W. Becher, Bart., ...	Farranmacteige, ...
	2235	Andrew Shanahan, ...	St. L. S. M. Tighe, ...	[illegible], ...
	2236	Daniel Crowley, ...	Thomas Whitney, ...	Derrylugga, ...
	2237	Jeremiah Connolly, ...	do.	do. ...
	2238	John Brien, junior, ...	John W. Glavin, ...	Clounmahon, ...
	2239	Denis Dempsey, ...	do.	do. ...
	2240	Daniel Foley and another,	Frederick D. Cornwall & others, Repts. of George Cornwall.	Maulnarouga, ...
	2241	Denis Hegarty, ...	Miss Anne Gillman and others,	Inchidaniel, ...
	2242	Jeremiah Connor, ...	Rev. Edward Barry, ...	Tullig, ...
	2243	Benjamin Haslam, ...	The Duke of Devonshire, ...	Tooreen, ...

CORK—*continued*.

Extent of Holding. Statute.	Poor Law Valuation.	Former Rent.	Judicial Rent.	Observations.	Value of Tenancy.
A. R. P.	£ s. d.	£ s. d.	£ s. d.		£ s. d.
72 0 0	[illegible] 10 0	112 0 0	[illegible] 4 0		
[illegible] 0 0	11 0 0	17 0 0	17 0 0		
118 0 10	45 0 0	85 0 0	[illegible] 0 0		
17 0 0	6 15 0	10 17 0	8 10 0		
64 3 15	12 15 0	18 0 0	17 0 0		
[illegible] 1 0	21 0 0	[illegible] 0 0	[illegible] 0 0		
63 1 15	14 5 0	[illegible] 0 0	15 0 0	By consent.	
15 0 7	10 8 0	15 11 6	12 14 5		
61 1 [illegible]	9 10 0	18 18 0	13 0 0		
13 0 0	8 0 0	10 0 0	[illegible] 4 0		
14 0 0	7 0 0	9 0 0	6 0 0	Provision has been made in this case as regards a labourer.	
46 0 0	15 0 0	22 10 0	26 10 0		
41½ 0 0	15 18 0	21 0 0	18 13 0		
56 1 20	40 10 0	57 0 0	[illegible] 0 0		
180 0 0	63 18 0	[illegible] 0 0	[illegible] 0 0	do.	
[illegible] 0 18	118 0 5	127 11 0	107 1[illegible] 0		
46 1 37	17 5 0	[illegible] 0 0	35 0 0		
117 0 24	11 0 0	18 0 0	15 0 0		
10 0 0	8 0 0	15 0 0	13 0 0		
31 3 20	16 6 0	27 4 0	19 0 0		
72 0 6½	16 0 0	[illegible] 17 0	19 0 0		
56 1 9½	10 0 0	18 0 0	11 16 0		
77 0 0	65 15 0	83 13 0	63 15 0		
45 0 0	5 10 0	10 0 0	7 0 0		
61 0 24	9 13 0	15 10 0	13 0 0		
7 0 0	6 0 0	4 10 0	5 10 0		[illegible] 0 0
16 0 18	11 18 0	18 15 0	13 10 0		
42 3 3	8 5 0	18 0 0	16 0 0		
61 1 15	12 5 0	17 0 0	17 0 0		
82 3 [illegible]	7 0 0	19 13 4	16 16 0		
41 2 0	15 10 0	[illegible] 6 8	18 0 0		
46 0 0	10 0 0	34 0 0	[illegible] 0 0	By consent.	
77 3 13	17 10 0	[illegible] 0 0	71 0 0	do.	
118 0 20	34 15 0	65 0 0	35 0 0	do.	
[illegible] 0 0	30 8 0	70 0 0	[illegible] 0 0	do.	

COUNTY OF

Names of Assistant Commissioners by whom Cases were decided.	No.	Name of Tenant.	Name of Landlord.	Townland.
Assistant Commissioners—				
E. C. MacDevitt, (Legal.) T. Walpole. F. [illegible] P. G. [illegible] F. Maxwell [illegible]	2244	John Sheehan (John),	The Duke of Devonshire,	[illegible]
	2245	Cornelius [illegible],	Michael A. R. Barker and others,	[illegible]
	2246	Mary Donoghue,	do.	Lettergorman,
	2247	Cornelius Horgan,	do.	[illegible]
	2248	Charles McCarthy Downing,	Frederick D. Cornwall and others, Reps. of Ann Cornwall,	[illegible]
	2249	Ellen Leary, Admx. of John Leary	Augusta Travers,	[illegible]
	2250	Timothy Buckley,	Sir James L. Cotter, Bart.,	[illegible]
	2251	John Murphy,	Sir James L. Cotter, Bart., and another,	[illegible]
	2252	Denis Connell,	Julia [illegible],	Greenhill,
	2253	Maurice Connell,	do.	do.
	2254	Timothy Mahony,	J. A. E. Newman,	Dromy, West, and another,
	2255	Jeremiah Leary,	do.	[illegible]
	2256	Edmund Barry,	do.	[illegible]
	2257	Catherine Cronin,	Michael F. Barry,	[illegible]
	2258	Daniel Murphy,	do.	do.
	2259	Catherine [illegible],	Francis Lyons,	[illegible]
	2260	Maurice Healy,	do.	do.
	2261	Julia Murray, Admx. of John Murray,	do.	[illegible]
	2262	William Murphy,	do.	do.
	2263	John Leary,	Rev. George [illegible],	[illegible]
	2264	Richard Cronin,	do.	[illegible]
	2265	James Cronin,	do.	[illegible]
	2266	Jeremiah Leary,	do.	do.
	2267	Honora Leary, Admx. of Jeremiah Leary,	do.	do.
	2268	John Cronin,	do.	do.
	2269	Michael Sullivan,	Mrs. Eliza O'Callaghan,	Lahane,
	2270	Do.	do.	do.
	2271	John Hurley,	Anne [illegible] and others,	Lettergorman,
	2272	John Cunningham,	do.	[illegible]
	2273	Michael Healy,	do.	do.
	2274	Jeremiah Mahony,	The Earl of Bandon,	[illegible]
	2275	Denis Sweeny and others,	John A. E. Newman,	[illegible]
	2276	Peter Leonard, senr.,	Sir Henry W. Becher, Bart.,	[illegible]
	2277	Denis Driscoll,	do.	[illegible]
	2278	John Sullivan, Rep. of Julia Sullivan,	E. J. Gumbleton and another,	[illegible]

CORK—*continued.*

Extent of Holding. Statute.	Poor Law Valuation.	Former Rent.	Judicial Rent.	Observations.	Value of Tenancy.
A. R. P.	£ s. d.	£ s. d.	£ s. d.		£ s. d.
60 2 1	81 10 0	28 0 0	13 10 0	By consent.	
45 0 0	35 0 0	40 0 0	[illegible] 0 0	do.	
13 0 25	6 0 0	17 0 0	8 0 0	do.	
46 3 26	17 0 0	32 0 0	23 0 0	do.	
1[illegible] 0 0	86 15 0	105 4 0	80 0 0	do.	
33 3 0	37 5 0	55 0 0	45 10 0	do.	
45 0 0	7 10 0	10 0 0	8 0 0	do.	
33 [illegible] 0	6 0 0	5 10 0	6 10 0	do.	
18 0 0	11 10 0	22 5 5	18 0 0		
12 0 0	13 0 0	18 0 0	14 0 0		
40 0 0	8 10 0	19 0 0	10 16 0	do.	
1 3 0	0 5 0	3 10 0	3 5 0	do.	
[illegible] 3 19	41 10 0	50 0 0	43 0 0	do.	
[illegible] 1 25	[illegible] 10 0	47 15 10	35 0 0	Provision has been made in this case as regards a labourer.	
[illegible] 0 0	67 0 0	48 13 10	33 0 0		
107 3 13	39 15 0	[illegible] 0 0	67 10 0		
120 1 26	44 16 0	138 0 0	[illegible] 0 0		
123 0 [illegible]	19 18 0	[illegible] 0 0	[illegible] 0 0		
64 0 0	11 10 0	77 0 0	12 0 0		
69 1 31	10 18 0	70 0 0	14 0 0		
164 0 0	27 0 0	35 0 0	88 0 0	Provision has been made in this case as regards a labourer.	
87 1 22	19 0 0	30 0 0	25 0 0		
[illegible] 1 31	10 15 0	39 0 0	14 0 0		
106 2 7	31 0 0	40 0 0	31 0 0		
66 [illegible] 20	0 5 0	14 0 0	12 10 0		
1 0 0	—	8 0 0	2 0 0	By consent.	
3 0 0	0 10 0	1 10 0	1 10 0	do.	
[illegible] 3 [illegible]	13 10 0	94 15 0	17 0 0	do.	
10 [illegible] [illegible]	6 5 0	8 10 0	7 0 0	do.	
23 1 30	13 5 0	16 0 0	17 4 0		
67 2 5	18 0 0	16 13 4	10 15 4		116 0 0
60 0 0	8 15 0	9 0 0	6 0 0	do.	
35 1 27	10 0 0	20 0 0	17 0 0		150 0 0
26 6 30	20 10 0	23 15 0	22 18 0		160 0 0
6 0 0	9 15 0	4 0 0	3 0 0		

COUNTY OF

Names of Assistant Commissioners by whom Cases were decided.	No.	Name of Tenant.	Name of Landlord.	Townland.
Assistant Commissioners—				
E. O. MacDevitt (Legal). T. Walpole. P. Mahony. P. G. Griffin. F. Maxwell [illegible].	1279	Thomas Sullivan, ...	R. J. [illegible] and another,	[illegible], ...
	1280	William [illegible], ...	do.	do. ...
	1281	Michael Neill, ...	do.	do. ...
	1282	Paul [illegible], ...	Arthur John [illegible] [illegible],	[illegible], ...
				Total, ...

COUNTY OF

Assistant Commissioners—				
J. G. MacCarthy (Legal). J. [illegible]. J. J. O'Shaughnessy. P. Newton. G. Adams.	1328	David Casey, ...	Daniel O'B. Corkery, ...	[illegible], ...
	1329	John Baron, ...	do.	do. ...
	1330	Bridget Daniel, ...	do.	do. ...
	1331	James Moriarty, ...	do.	do. ...
	1332	John Leary, ...	do.	do. ...
	1333	Honoria Dwyer, ...	do.	do. ...
	1334	Johanna Curran, ...	do.	do. ...
	1335	Cornelius Moriarty, ...	do.	[illegible], ...
	1336	Patrick Sullivan, ...	do.	do. ...
	1337	Daniel Sullivan, ...	do.	do. ...
	1338	Michael Sullivan, ...	do.	do. ...
	1339	John Clifford, ...	do.	do. ...
	1340	Thomas Fitzgerald, ...	do.	do. ...
	1341	Jeremiah Moran, ...	do.	do. ...
	1342	James Sullivan, ...	do.	do. ...
	1343	Thomas [illegible], ...	do.	do. ...
	1344	Ellen MacGillicuddy, ...	do.	[illegible], ...
	1345	Patrick Kelly, ...	do.	do. ...
	1346	Jeremiah Leary, ...	do.	do. ...
	1347	Denis Sullivan, ...	do.	do. ...
	1348	John Sullivan, D., ...	do.	do. ...
	1349	David Casey, ...	do.	Glenbeigh, ...
	1350	Patrick Sullivan, ...	do.	Glenbeigh, Lower,
	1351	Patrick Sullivan, ...	do.	do. ...
	1352	Michael Moriarty, ...	do.	do. ...
	1353	Darby Sullivan, D., ...	do.	Glenbeigh, Upper,

CORK—*continued.*

Extent of Holding, Statute.			Poor Law Valuation.			Former Rent.			Judicial Rent.			Observations.
A.	R.	P.	£	s.	d.	£	s.	d.	£	s.	d.	
10	0	0	3	10	0	6	6	8	4	4	0	
18	1	0	6	0	0	8	10	0	6	10	0	
6	0	0	3	15	0	4	4	0	3	17	8	
92	1	24	40	0	0	75	10	5	64	0	0	By consent.
10,655	1	3	4,163	10	10	6,894	3	7	5,523	8	11	

KERRY.

18	3	20	3	10	0	3	7	0	3	7	0	
14	1	20	1	10	0	3	5	8	2	5	0	Rent changed in 1865 from . . .
41	2	13	6	15	0	9	0	0	7	0	0	By consent.
54	1	0	7	5	0	12	7	6	9	0	0	do.
17	0	27	3	10	0	4	18	0	4	0	0	do.
53	2	23	7	13	0	13	10	0	10	16	0	do.
19	1	1	4	13	0	7	17	6	6	0	0	do.
18	1	27	0	0	0	24	0	0	18	0	0	Rent changed in 1873 from . . . 1878
8	3	1	2	14	0	0	0	0	5	10	0	
16	3	1	3	0	0	0	0	0	6	0	0	By consent.
9	0	0	5	13	0	9	0	0	8	10	0	do.
30	2	3	4	5	0	10	0	0	10	0	0	do.
14	0	0	5	16	0	16	0	0	12	0	0	do.
10	3	0	2	5	6	4	10	0	3	10	0	do.
10	0	5	3	5	0	6	10	0	4	5	0	do.
10	3	6	0	3	6	4	10	0	3	10	0	do.
10	0	8	4	0	0	16	0	0	0	0	0	do.
10	1	31	3	15	0	4	10	0	5	13	0	Rent changed in 1866 from . . .
14	2	10	3	5	0	8	15	0	5	10	0	1869
74	1	33	14	0	0	19	0	0	14	0	0	1866
41	2	17	0	18	0	12	15	0	10	0	0	
28	1	30	0	5	0	12	3	0	10	15	0	1873
34	1	0	3	10	0	18	0	0	14	0	0	
30	0	14	3	0	0	8	10	0	7	0	0	1860
37	1	30	4	10	0	10	10	0	6	0	0	
49	0	36	11	10	0	13	13	0	13	16	0	[illegible]

COUNTY OF

Names of Assistant Commissioners by whom Cases were decided.	No.	Name of Tenant.	Name of Landlord.	Townland.
Assistant Commissioners—				
J. G. McCarthy (Legal). J. Haughton. J. J. O'Shaughnessy. P. Newton. G. Abraham.	1254	Daniel Hallihey, ...	Daniel O'B. Corkery, ...	Glenlough, Upper,
	1255	John Mullviney, ...	do.	Drummondough,
	1256	Peter Heaney, ...	do.	do. ...
	1257	Patrick Sullivan, ...	do.	do. ...
	1258	Julia Sullivan, ...	do.	do. ...
	1259	John & Timothy Kirby,	do.	do. ...
	1260	Larry Sullivan, ...	do.	do. ...
	1261	Michael McCarthy, ...	do.	do. ...
	1262	Honoria Sullivan, ...	do.	do. ...
	1263	Patrick Harney, ...	do.	Rahanagran, ...
	1264	Thomas Sullivan, ...	do.	do. ...
	1265	Catherine Brown, ...	do.	do. ...
	1266	Thomas Fitzgerald, ...	do.	do. ...
	1267	John Crowley, ...	do.	do. ...
	1268	John Leary, ...	do.	do. ...
	1269	James Fitzgerald, ...	do.	Skelp, ...
	1270	John Dunphy, ...	do.	do. ...
	1271	Edward Fitzgerald, ...	do.	do. ...
	1272	Patrick Quinlan, ...	do.	do. ...
	1273	James Fitzgerald, ...	do.	do. ...
	1274	Maurice Fitzgerald, ...	do.	do. ...
	1275	Daniel Kelliher, ...	Dr. Adrian Taylor, ...	Gurrahill, ...
	1276	Patrick Kelliher, ...	do.	do. ...
	1277	Johanna Leary, ...	do.	do. ...
	1278	Michael Lehane, ...	do.	do. ...
	1279	Joseph Rice, ...	do.	Dunlahive, ...
	1280	John Quane, ...	do.	Derrylahan, ...
	1281	George Rice, ...	do.	do. ...
	1282	John Sweeny, ...	do.	Doughill, ...
	1283	Hugh Twomey, ...	Rev. W. Lowe, ...	Garrygarry, ...
	1284	Patrick Daly, ...	Marquis of Lansdowne, ...	Inislee, ...
	1285	Michael Shea, ...	do.	Ballyneville, ...
	1286	James Shea, ...	do.	Drumanahow, ...
	1287	Jeremiah Harrington, ...	do.	do. ...
	1288	Daniel Brennan, ...	Colonel Trevor Goff, ...	Knocknamanagh, ...

KERRY—continued.

Extent of Holding. Statute.	Poor Law Valuation.	Former Rent.	Judicial Rent.	Observations.		Value of Tenancy.
A. R. P.	£ s. d.	£ s. d.	£ s. d.		£ s. d.	£ s. d.
104 2 18	7 3 0	10 0 0	8 12 0	Rent changed in 1856 from	8 0 0	62 0 0
16 0 21	9 5 0	8 15 0	5 5 0	By consent.		
25 0 23	6 5 0	5 9 4	5 5 0	do.		
21 3 39	4 10 0	5 9 4	5 5 0	do.		
29 0 13	6 10 0	7 5 5	6 0 0	do.		
30 3 20	7 10 0	4 14 4	4 0 0	do.		
47 2 12	6 10 0	6 15 0	5 10 0	do.		
13 0 10	8 10 0	5 3 0	4 5 0	do.		
19 3 27	4 0 0	6 13 0	6 15 0			60 0 0
17 1 23	6 5 5	9 0 0	8 0 0	Rent changed in 1866 from	5 0 0	80 0 0
13 0 8	1 0 0	3 0 0	3 0 0	1878	0 10 0	20 0 0
89 0 0	10 15 0	18 11 0	13 10 0	1868	16 0 0	90 0 0
611 2 14	23 10 0	48 0 0	30 10 0	1878	30 0 0	230 0 0
62 0 16	3 15 0	8 15 0	1 12 0	1881	6 7 8	40 0 0
23 2 45	8 10 0	5 8 10	4 15 0	By consent.		
48 5 35	5 0 0	10 5 0	8 0 0	Rent changed in 1871 from	9 13 6	80 0 0
23 2 36	5 0 0	11 0 0	8 15 0	1865	8 0 0	80 0 0
28 0 35	4 15 0	10 0 0	7 10 0	1874	8 1 0	60 0 0
30 3 33	8 17 0	18 0 0	6 10 0	do.	9 4 0	60 0 0
80 0 30	16 10 0	40 0 0	35 0 0			150 0 0
41 3 23	9 13 0	30 0 0	15 0 0			120 0 0
120 1 38	10 0 0	26 0 0	18 0 0	1883	15 0 0	180 0 0
126 3 36	23 10 0	47 0 0	34 0 0	1868	30 0 0	270 0 0
101 2 30	8 10 0	30 0 0	16 4 0	1863	15 0 0	150 0 0
155 0 1	5 10 0	25 0 0	21 10 0	1866	21 0 0	150 0 0
21 0 15	3 6 0	9 4 4	6 15 0	By consent.		
85 3 16	9 15 0	27 18 4	15 5 0	Rent changed in 1866 from	22 0 0	125 0 0
74 1 37	8 15 0	27 13 4	13 10 0	do.	22 0 0	120 0 0
80 0 0	5 5 0	13 10 0	10 0 0			80 0 0
107 1 8	15 15 0	38 0 0	25 0 0			
63 1 25	11 10 0	30 5 0	23 5 0			
51 2 30	5 13 0	8 10 0	5 10 0	1870	8 0 0	40 0 0
81 2 12	10 5 0	17 10 0	12 10 0			60 0 0
40 3 27	5 0 0	10 0 0	6 10 0			50 0 0
34 0 0	8 10 0	22 0 0	17 10 0	By consent.		

Names of Assistant Commissioners by whom Cases were decided.	No.	Name of Tenant.	Name of Landlord.	Townland.
Assistant Commissioners—				
J. G. MacCarthy (Legal). J. Hallowell. J. J. O'Shaughnessy. F. Newton. G. Arabin.	1289	Michael Sheehan, ...	Colonel Thomas Hoff, ...	[illegible], ...
	1290	John Harrington, ...	do. ...	do. ...
	1291	Anne Coffey, ...	do. ...	do. ...
	1292	John Moriarty, ...	do. ...	[illegible], ...
	1293	Patrick & John Moriarty,	do. ...	[illegible], ...
	1294	Daniel Leary, ...	Alexander McCarthy, ...	Gortahoma, ...
	1295	John Moriarty, ...	do. ...	do. ...
	1296	Martin Brennan, ...	do. ...	do. ...
	1297	Michael Sullivan, ...	do. ...	do. ...
	1298	Jeremiah Sullivan, ...	do. ...	do. ...
	1299	John Sullivan, ...	do. ...	do. ...
	1300	Jeremiah Sullivan, ...	Elizabeth Susan Jermyn, ...	Lios, ...
	1301	John Sullivan, ...	do. ...	do. ...
	1302	Michael Connell, ...	do. ...	do. ...
	1303	Mylas Moriarty, ...	do. ...	do. ...
	1304	Florence McCarthy, ...	do. ...	do. ...
	1305	Daniel Shea, ...	do. ...	do. ...
	1306	Michael Moriarty, ...	do. ...	do. ...
	1307	Patrick McAuliffe, ...	do. ...	do. ...
	1308	John Callaghan, ...	Elizabeth A. Palmer and others, Reps. of Edward G. Palmer,	Adrigole, ...
	1309	Daniel McCarthy, ...	Richard Aldwell, ...	[illegible], ...
	1310	Michael Sullivan, ...	John E. Maybury, ...	[illegible]
	1311	John Sullivan (J.), ...	Francis C. Bland, ...	[illegible], ...
	1312	Patrick Sullivan (T.), ...	do. ...	do. ...
	1313	John Sullivan, ...	do. ...	do. ...
	1314	James Sullivan, ...	do. ...	do. ...
	1315	Eugene Sullivan, ...	do. ...	Gortdrum, ...
	1316	Patrick Sullivan, ...	do. ...	Derreen, ...
	1317	Thomas Cunningham, ...	do. ...	do. ...
	1318	John Sullivan, ...	do. ...	Derreen, West, ...
	1319	Timothy Sullivan, ...	do. ...	Derreen, East, ...
	1320	Mary Neill, ...	do. ...	Dromoderig, ...
	1321	Philip Shea, ...	do. ...	do. ...
	1322	Eugene Sullivan, ...	do. ...	Anhabane, East,
	1323	Mary Neill, ...	do. ...	Lettershinnagh, ...

KERRY—continued.

Extent of Holding. (Statute.)	Poor Law Valuation.	Former Rent.	Judicial Rent.	Observations.	
A. R. P.	£ s. d.	£ s. d.	£ s. d.		£ s. d.
135 0 37	10 10 0	36 0 0	30 10 0	By consent.	
19 1 0	4 0 0	10 0 0	8 10 0	do.	
163 3 10	37 10 0	[illegible] 0 0	67 0 0	Rent changed in 1877 from . . .	83 10 0
30 0 1	15 0 0	23 0 0	23 4 0	By consent.	
124 0 34	13 0 0	[illegible] 0 0	44 0 0	do.	
13 3 [illegible]	6 15 0	8 11 8	8 13 0		
62 2 36	21 10 0	17 5 0	13 0 0	Rent changed in 1862 from . . .	16 0 0
12 2 16	4 6 0	8 15 0	6 15 0	1866	8 0 0
78 0 15	8 15 0	16 3 0	12 13 0	do.	15 0 0
[illegible] 0 0	13 5 0	35 17 4	15 10 0	do.	23 10 0
27 0 15	10 0 0	18 4 0	11 0 0	do.	15 0 0
5 1 0	3 5 0	6 0 0	3 15 0	By consent.	
4 1 [illegible]	1 0 0	3 10 0	2 7 4	do.	
8 0 34	2 5 0	5 11 4	5 0 0		
16 3 0	4 12 0	10 0 0	7 0 0		
31 2 20	10 10 0	23 3 0	18 10 0		
14 0 0	5 18 0	10 3 0	7 5 0		
6 2 [illegible]	1 5 0	2 6 0	2 5 0	Rent changed in 1862 from . . .	2 0 0
18 3 [illegible]	5 0 0	11 3 8	8 0 0		
37 1 [illegible]	5 0 0	11 0 0	11 0 0		
64 0 0	6 15 0	26 0 0	24 0 0		
16 0 10	2 0 0	12 0 0	8 10 0	By consent.	
[illegible] 0 0	5 10 0	13 10 0	10 5 0	do.	
11 0 0	6 7 0	19 10 0	9 15 0	do.	
100 0 0	4 0 0	18 10 0	30 5 0	do.	
12 0 0	5 15 0	18 13 0	[illegible] 0 0	do.	
162 0 0	6 13 0	10 0 0	7 10 0	do.	
41 0 0	10 0 6	24 18 0	11 10 0	do.	
64 0 0	2 0 0	4 0 0	5 10 0	do.	
97 0 0	10 0 0	18 10 0	12 0 0	do.	
138 0 30	5 0 0	10 14 0	3 5 0	do.	
133 0 0	8 0 0	13 4 0	11 0 0	do.	
[illegible] 0 0	4 1 0	5 13 0	1 0 0	do.	
12 0 0	6 15 0	20 0 0	5 0 0	do.	
15 0 0	7 0 0	9 18 0	2 5 0	do.	

COUNTY OF

Names of Assistant Commissioners by whom Cases were decided.	No.	Name of Tenant.	Name of Landlord.	Townland.
Assistant Commissioners— J. O. Mulhallen (Legal). J. Hamilton. J. J. O'Shaughnessy. F. Newton. G. Abraham.	1324	James Brown, ...	Francis C. Bland, ...	Mohagh[illegible], ...
	1325	Jeremiah Sheehan, ...	Samuel T. Hewitt, ...	Gortagown, ...
	1326	Cornelius Sheehan, ...	do.	do. ...
	1327	Patrick Sheehan, ...	do.	do. ...
	1328	Richard Brown, ...	do.	Tulla, ...
	1329	Denis Foley, ...	Thomas E. Sullivan, ...	Kerry, ...
	1330	Daniel Harrington, ...	do.	do. ...
	1331	Hannah Bowler, ...	Daniel O'B. [illegible], ...	Meelan, ...
	1332	Darby Brown, ...	do.	[illegible], ...
	1333	Michael Dwyer, ...	do.	[illegible], ...
	1334	John Sullivan, ...	Elizabeth A. Palmer & others, Exors. of E. H. Palmer.	Ashgrove, ...
	1335	Denis [illegible], ...	Dr. Adrian Taylor, ...	[illegible], North,
	1336	Mathew Tuomey, ...	do.	[illegible], ...
	1337	Timothy Halloran, ...	Richard P. [illegible], ...	[illegible], ...
	1338	Patrick Carey, ...	do.	Tullig, ...
	1339	Eugene O'Sullivan, ...	do.	Trugh, ...
	1340	Thomas O'Sullivan, ...	Marquis of Lansdowne, ...	[illegible], ...
	1341	William [illegible], ...	do.	do. ...
	1342	Ellen Kelly, ...	do.	do. ...
	1343	Catherine Dailey, ...	do.	do. ...
	1344	Timothy Sugrue, ...	do.	do. ...
	1345	John Daley, ...	do.	do. ...
	1346	James Guerin, ...	Provost, Fellows, and Scholars of Trinity College, Dublin.	Doon[illegible], ...
	1347	Luke Crowley, ...	do.	[illegible], ...
	1348	Jeremiah Sullivan, ...	do.	Killorough and another,
	1349	Do.	do.	Gurrane, ...
	1350	James Keating, ...	do.	do. ...
	1351	James Kelly, ...	Thomas A. Stoughton, ...	[illegible], ...
	1352	Daniel O'Connor, ...	do.	[illegible] and another,
	1353	Patrick Casey, ...	do.	[illegible], ...
	1354	Roger Linehan, ...	do.	[illegible], ...
	1355	Michael Linehan, ...	do.	do. ...
	1356	Patrick Casey, ...	do.	do. ...
	1357	Do.	do.	[illegible], ...
	1358	Denis Casey, ...	do.	do. ...

KERRY—continued.

Extent of Holding, Statute.	Poor Law Valuation.	Former Rent.	Judicial Rent.	Observations.	Value of Tenancy.
A. R. P.	£ s. d.	£ s. d.	£ s. d.		£ s. d.
37 0 0	5 5 0	6 10 0	4 0 0	By consent.	
25 0 0	5 15 0	11 1 0	10 0 0	do.	
17 3 7	6 10 0	7 15 11	4 15 0	do.	
25 0 0	10 5 0	15 16 0	13 15 0	do.	
25 0 [illegible]	7 0 0	13 0 0	10 0 0	do.	
18 0 16	9 0 0	23 0 0	10 0 0	do.	
18 [illegible] [illegible]	10 15 0	15 0 0	13 10 0	do.	
22 1 34	3 5 0	8 0 0	4 15 0	Rent changed in 1875 from £ s. d. 6 5 0	26 0 0
[illegible] 0 20	[illegible] 0 0	6 10 0	4 10 0		
100 0 0	7 0 0	13 7 0	8 13 0	1848 11 10 0	100 0 0
31 3 0	6 15 0	9 0 0	9 0 0		70 0 0
77 3 37	10 5 0	22 0 0	23 0 0		100 0 0
214 2 15	10 0 0	30 0 0	17 0 0		140 0 0
58 0 23	8 0 0	15 0 0	10 10 0	1856 10 3 5	75 0 0
105 0 0	15 15 0	30 0 0	27 10 0	1858 30 0 0	220 0 0
[illegible] 0 12	11 15 0	23 17 6	18 10 0	1872 16 17 3	182 0 0
43 0 0	19 5 0	30 0 0	30 0 0	1874 15 5 0	[illegible] 0 0
25 0 0	19 1 0	27 10 0	15 15 0	do. 14 0 0	145 0 0
13 0 23	4 18 0	7 10 0	6 7 0	do. 5 15 0	65 0 0
43 0 0	16 10 0	30 13 0	23 15 0	do. 24 10 0	120 0 0
34 3 23	8 4 0	14 5 0	10 0 0	do. 11 4 6	185 0 0
60 1 16	10 15 0	17 4 0	17 5 0	do. 13 16 0	172 0 0
81 3 37	5 5 0	9 10 0	6 10 5	By consent.	
35 0 30	5 10 0	8 5 0	5 18 5	do.	
73 1 0	5 15 0	14 0 0	11 5 0	do.	
35 1 25	5 15 0	13 11 0	9 18 0	do.	
120 3 0	7 10 0	15 10 0	13 10 0	do.	
63 0 0	16 5 0	15 11 0	11 15 0		50 0 0
172 1 25	5 0 0	13 6 5	13 10 0	Rent changed in 1860 from 10 0 0	50 0 0
270 1 37	5 0 0	10 0 0	10 0 0		75 0 0
35 0 0	5 5 0	10 10 0	6 0 0		50 0 0
50 3 5	6 15 0	6 10 0	7 0 0		80 0 0
35 3 0	15 0 0	22 10 0	15 0 0		150 0 0
8 3 0	3 5 0	8 15 5	5 15 0		30 0 0
50 0 0	12 10 0	21 10 0	17 0 0		140 0 0

COUNTY OF

Names of Assistant Commissioners by whom Cases were decided.	No.	Name of Tenant.	Name of Landlord.	Townland.
Assistant Commissioners—				
J. G. McCarthy (Legal). J. Harrington. J. J. O'Shaughnessy. P. Newton. G. Adamson.	1359	Michael Sullivan, junior,	Thomas A. Stoughton, ...	Meelagarbane, ...
	1360	Timothy Shea, ...	do. ...	Lisvane, ...
	1361	Daniel Curran, ...	do.	do. ...
	1362	Maurice Leary, ...	do.	Killagarriv, ...
	1363	John and Daniel Foley,	The MacGillicuddy, ...	Carrowgarrow, ...
	1364	Bartholomew Doherty, ...	do.	Coughling, ...
	1365	Maurice & Patrick Keating,	Charles Segrave, ...	Ballard, ...
	1366	Cornelius Shea, ...	do.	do. ...
	1367	Daniel McCarthy, ...	do.	do. ...
	1368	Cornelius McCarthy, ...	do.	do. ...
	1369	Mathew McCarthy, ...	do.	Pallasgrenie, ...
	1370	Michael Shea, ...	do.	do. ...
	1371	John Connell, ...	do.	do. ...
	1372	Timothy Riordan, ...	do.	do. ...
	1373	John McCarthy, ...	do.	do. ...
	1374	Cornelius & Denis Segrave,	do.	do. ...
	1375	Patrick Shea, ...	do.	do. ...
	1376	Do.	do.	do. ...
	1377	James Keating, ...	do.	do. ...
	1378	Michael King, ...	do.	do. ...
	1379	Martin Shea, ...	do.	do. ...
	1380	James Brennan, ...	Brother F. A. Fitzgerald, ...	Cummins Prior, ...
	1381	Jeremiah Shea, ...	do.	do. ...
	1382	John Sullivan, ...	do.	do. ...
	1383	Patrick Segrave, ...	do.	do. ...
	1384	Mary English, ...	John H. Segrave, ...	Kinnaird, East, ...
	1385	James Fitzgerald, ...	do.	do. ...
	1386	Michael Walsh, ...	do.	do. ...
	1387	Christopher Segrave, ...	do.	do. ...
	1388	John Walsh, ...	do.	do. ...
	1389	Maurice Walsh, ...	do.	do. ...
	1390	Bartholomew English, ...	do.	do. ...
	1391	William Cregan, ...	do.	Caghmore, ...
	1392	Mary and John Shea, ...	do.	do. ...
	1393	Daniel Segrave, ...	do.	Carraghmore, ...

KERRY—*continued.*

Extent of Holding (statute).	Poor Law Valuation.	Tenancy Rent.	Judicial Rent.	Observations.		Value of Tenancy.
A. R. P.	£ s. d.	£ s. d.	£ s. d.		£ s. d.	£ s. d.
60 2 0	9 10 0	16 0 0	15 0 0			180 0 0
80 0 0	12 10 0	22 12 0	18 0 0			120 0 0
40 0 0	7 0 0	11 2 0	10 0 0			70 0 0
50 3 0	8 10 0	13 13 0	10 0 0			70 0 0
102 0 0	14 10 0	22 15 0	11 10 0			150 0 0
28 0 0	12 15 0	16 14 4	14 10 0			140 0 0
285 0 13	15 15 0	45 0 0	23 0 0	Rent changed in 1867 from	40 0 0	200 0 0
60 1 17	3 15 0	11 0 0	6 0 0			85 0 0
30 1 11	4 0 0	15 0 0	8 0 0			80 0 0
41 3 36	6 5 0	9 0 0	7 11 0	1850	4 8 0	80 0 0
60 3 16	8 0 0	16 10 0	16 10 0	1828	19 1 0	125 0 0
80 1 0	5 5 0	13 0 0	8 5 0	1850	10 0 0	60 0 0
36 3 10	3 10 0	20 0 0	11 5 0			100 0 0
33 1 10	5 10 0	14 10 0	9 10 0			70 0 0
68 3 30	7 16 0	20 10 0	15 2 0			85 0 0
101 3 16	20 0 0	46 0 0	37 12 0			200 0 0
63 2 0	9 0 0	25 0 0	14 15 0			120 0 0
62 1 20	17 15 0	31 16 0	27 10 0			200 0 0
64 0 10	6 16 0	17 0 0	9 0 0	1853	15 0 0	16 0 0
19 0 0	15 3 0	52 10 0	34 10 0			200 0 0
89 0 4	8 0 0	16 5 0	13 10 0	1861	15 0 0	100 0 0
47 0 33	6 15 0	18 5 0	8 15 0			71 0 0
30 3 33	4 0 0	18 0 0	7 0 0	1864	9 0 0	40 0 0
21 1 6	3 0 0	3 0 0	[illegible]			40 0 0
47 0 23	4 0 0	9 17 0	7 0 0			45 0 0
34 2 0	3 0 0	15 0 0	8 0 0	1866	0 0 0	63 0 0
58 1 14	1[illegible] 15 0	28 0 0	19 0 0			170 0 0
83 0 1	18 10 0	36 0 0	22 0 0	do.	20 0 0	200 0 0
19 3 7	3 15 0	7 10 0	7 14 0	do.	0 0 0	63 0 0
20 3 15	6 14 0	11 0 0	8 0 0	do.	13 5 0	30 0 0
21 0 0	7 10 0	12 0 0	10 10 0	do.	14 10 0	75 0 0
27 1 30	8 0 0	13 0 0	9 0 0	do.	9 0 0	45 0 0
66 0 0	13 10 0	24 0 0	30 0 0	1864	24 0 0	140 0 0
71 1 20	4 10 0	10 0 0	8 10 0			80 0 0
39 0 0	6 10 0	8 0 0	4 5 0			55 0 0

1399	Patrick Sugrue, —	do. —
1400	Jeremiah Flaherty, —	do. —
1401	John Murphy, —	do. —
1402	Maurice Curran, —	do. —
1403	Florence Sullivan, —	do. —
1404	Michael Sugrue, —	do. —
1405	Humphrey Leary and another.	do. —
1406	Martin Coffey, —	Daniel C. O'Connell,
1407	Bartholomew Connor, —	do. —
1408	Denis Shea, — —	Catherine Hussey,
1409	Cornelius Shea, —	Robert H. Palmer,
1410	John Sullivan, —	do. —
1411	Cornelius O'Connor, —	Sir Maurice O'Connell
1412	Michael Griffin, —	do. —
1413	Thomas Cooper —	do. —
1414	William Garvey, —	do. —
1415	Mary Walsh, —	do. —
1416	John Casey, — —	do. —
1417	Humphrey and Johanna Keating.	do. —
1418	Denis Connor, —	do. —
1419	Gabby Shea, — —	John F. Fitzgerald,
1420	Patrick P. Kelly, —	do. —
1421	Daniel Brown, —	do. —
1422	Patrick Coffee, —	do. —

KERRY—*continued.*

Extent of Holding. Statute.	Poor Law Valuation.	Former Rent.	Judicial Rent.	Observations.		Value of Tenancy.
A. R. P.	£ s. d.	£ s. d.	£ s. d.		£ s. d.	£ s. d.
[illegible] 1 0	5 10 0	23 4 4	10 10 0	Rent changed in 1869 from	11 4 8	95 0 0
41 0 5	10 15 0	21 13 1	19 0 0	1858	13 0 0	100 0 0
11 1 9	4 8 0	8 16 0	7 15 0			85 0 0
21 0 0	6 10 0	12 0 0	9 10 0			72 0 0
18 1 20	6 10 0	9 10 0	7 5 0			80 0 0
14 3 0	5 0 0	10 10 0	7 15 0			60 0 0
17 1 0	6 10 0	10 10 0	7 0 0			60 0 0
22 1 0	6 5 0	10 0 0	8 0 0			78 0 0
22 3 3	5 0 0	8 0 0	6 10 0			55 0 0
6 3 20	3 10 0	5 0 0	4 5 0			45 0 0
13 1 0	5 10 0	12 10 0	9 15 0			70 0 0
17 2 14	6 15 0	10 0 0	9 0 0			70 0 0
[illegible] 1 0	3 5 0	12 0 0	9 0 0	1873	9 15 9	
161 1 20	10 0 0	34 0 0	18 0 0			
15 1 30	0 5 0	1 16 0	1 8 0			
13 0 7	1 10 0	5 10 0	3 10 0	By consent.		
19 1 20	4 13 0	10 4 0	8 5 0	Rent changed in 1860 from	9 8 8	
43 0 0	7 8 0	10 9 0	8 0 0			70 0 0
57 1 35	18 0 0	36 18 0	16 5 0			200 0 0
38 0 0	18 17 0	30 13 4	16 8 0			155 0 0
93 1 27	12 6 0	36 15 0	15 17 6	By consent.		
18 3 0	6 16 0	16 19 0	10 0 0			80 0 0
30 0 0	7 3 0	18 1 0	10 0 0			100 0 0
44 3 16	8 0 0	15 16 0	10 0 0			70 0 0
115 0 0	21 5 0	42 0 0	37 10 0	Rent changed in 1875 from	28 4 8	220 0 0
51 1 1	7 10 0	25 0 0	15 0 0	do.	18 10 0	110 0 0
38 0 4	6 5 0	15 0 0	11 10 0	1859	13 0 0	80 0 0
52 0 0	16 0 0	37 10 0	30 0 0	By consent.		
75 3 15	8 0 0	34 0 0	18 10 0	Rent changed in 1850 from	19 13 6	150 0 0
10,875 1 36	1,455 11 0	4,020 17 0	2,325 6 0			

COUNTY OF

Names of Assistant Commissioners by whom Cases were decided.	No.	Name of Tenant.	Name of Landlord.	Townland.
Assistant Commissioners—				
T. D. Hallinan (Legal). John Gibson. Thomas Rice. W. C. Hemsworth. William Evans.	908	John Leonard, ...	Horace S. O'Brien, ...	Parkmore, ...
	909	James Ryan, ...	Colonel Thomas Lloyd, ...	Newtownballynabola,
	910	William Bourke, ...	Lady De Burgho, ...	Portavaha, ...
	911	Patrick McMilligan, ...	Henry Westropp, ...	Knockanacraky, ...
	912	John Ryan, ...	Governors Erasmus Smith's Schools,	Garryvalla, ...
	913	John Bourke, ...	do. ...	Kilduff, ...
	914	Michael Mahony, ...	Charles S. Pennington & anor., Trustees of Lucy Woolley,	Parkaree, ...
	915	Jeremiah Mahony, ...	William de S. Filgate & others, Trustees of Count de Salis,	Ballymalone, ...
	916	John Kirby, ...	E. C. Villiers and others, ...	Marlbrook, ...
	917	Mary Connell, ...	Dr. Lyons, ...	Ploughland, ...
	918	Thomas W. Bennett, ...	Sir John Nordi, Bart., & others,	Glengar, ...
	919	Charles Markey, ...	Mountifort W. Gavin, ...	Bawnanevern, ...
	920	Kate Dwyer, Admx. of Patrick Dwyer,	Michael M. L. Apjohn, ...	Drumwatley, ...
	921	John Hanragan, ...	Rev. Thomas Walker, ...	Ballylangford, ...
	922	Michael Field, ...	Edward J. Dunphy, ...	Shanacloon, ...
	923	John O'Brien, ...	Lord Lansfield, ...	Bawnroe, ...
	924	Bridget Ryan, ...	do. ...	do. ...
	925	Timothy Tuohy, ...	do. ...	Pennington, ...
	926	Jeremiah Lynch, ...	Lord Langford, ...	Upper Dallas, ...
	927	Mary Lynch and another,	do. ...	Lower Dallas, ...
	928	Thomas Lynch, ...	do. ...	do. ...
	929	Edward Hennessy, ...	Patrick J. McTiernan, ...	Shanbally and another,
	930	John Hennessy, ...	do. ...	Newtown, ...
	931	Thomas Naughton, ...	Edward T. Maxey, ...	Capparoe, ...
	932	John Nash, ...	do. ...	Fort, ...
	933	Michael Gleeson (Kin),	Horace S. O'Brien, ...	Kyle, ...
	934	James Doyle, ...	do. ...	Balliesmore, ...
	935	Timothy Gleeson, ...	do. ...	do. ...
	936	William Ryan, ...	do. ...	do. ...
	937	John Doyle, ...	do. ...	do. ...
	938	Mary Fogarty, ...	do. ...	Parkmore, ...
	939	Denis O'Meally, ...	do. ...	do. ...
	940	Michael Godfrey, ...	do. ...	Kyle, ...
	941	John McGrath, ...	Governors of Erasmus Smith's Schools,	Tullabeg and another,
	942	Jeremiah Ryan, ...	do. ...	Ballybeddy, ...

LIMERICK.

Extent of Holding. Statute.	Poor Law Valuation.	Former Rent.	Judicial Rent.	Observations.	Value of Tenancy.
A. R. P.	£ s. d.	£ s. d.	£ s. d.		£ s. d.
40 2 [illegible]	[illegible] 10 0	23 0 0	27 0 0		
[illegible] 3 38	62 0 0	62 0 0	60 0 0		
11 0 0	5 0 0	7 0 0	6 15 0		
194 0 6	87 0 0	111 0 0	170 0 0		
[illegible] 1 [illegible]	12 0 0	23 13 6	18 16 8		
17 3 [illegible]	10 0 0	15 0 7	13 0 0		
30 0 0	19 0 0	30 0 0	17 5 0		
12 9 0	8 16 0	12 0 0	11 15 0		
37 1 23	73 18 0	45 0 5	84 0 0		
81 3 26	61 0 0	76 0 0	63 0 0		
40 3 0	43 10 0	83 15 3	73 0 0		
22 3 27	16 13 0	31 0 0	71 0 0		
61 3 [illegible]	48 13 0	107 3 4	34 0 0		
30 0 23	[illegible] 5 0	27 0 0	[illegible] 16 0		
87 2 [illegible]	23 10 0	30 7 6	87 0 0		
19 3 30	33 0 0	15 0 0	60 0 0		
61 1 41	61 0 0	70 0 0	63 0 0		160 0 0
[illegible] 1 21	25 0 0	57 0 0	56 0 0		[illegible] 0 0
63 1 30	68 0 0	60 4 0	47 0 0		
22 1 18	23 16 0	17 16 0	13 20 0		
100 1 17	63 15 0	78 0 0	73 0 0		
48 9 15	36 0 0	60 5 0	48 0 0		
36 3 19	94 5 0	45 7 3	[illegible] 0 0		
[illegible] 3 [illegible]	37 8 0	87 13 10	30 0 0		
64 3 6	[illegible] 10 0	144 0 0	200 0 0		
62 0 0	23 10 0	38 0 0	30 0 0		
19 3 13	[illegible] 0 0	22 0 0	[illegible] 0 0		
24 3 23	13 7 6	17 0 0	16 0 0		
30 0 1	16 0 0	25 0 0	13 16 0		
48 3 19	[illegible] 9 6	29 0 0	30 0 0		
19 1 [illegible]	8 15 0	10 5 0	6 5 0		
15 0 0	8 15 0	13 0 0	13 0 0		
26 0 15	9 5 0	11 0 0	11 9 0		
36 3 31	42 0 0	46 0 0	40 13 0	By consent.	
33 0 25	14 10 0	25 0 7	19 18 0	do.	

COUNTY OF

Names of Assistant Commissioners by whom Cases were decided.	No.	Name of Tenant.	Name of Landlord.	Townland.
Assistant Commissioners—				
T. D. Rearden (Legal). John Gallagher. Thomas Rourke. W. C. Hornsall. William Bryan.	943	Patrick Mulcahy, ...	Governors of [illegible] Schools,	[illegible] ...
	944	William Crowley, ...	Lady De Burgho,	Clashenly, ...
	945	Michael Murphy, ...	do.	[illegible] ...
	946	William Higgins, ...	William De Salis, Fitzgerald and another,	Ballysallagh, ...
	947	Honora Fitzgerald, ...	Mary L. Smith and others, ...	Tullow, ...
	948	Denis Ryan, ...	Hector R. O'Brien, ...	Cappamore, ...
	949	Patrick Sullivan, ...	do.	Parkmore Fresh. lin.
	950	William Darby, ...	Col. R. [illegible], Reps. of Col. Smith,	Garlandstown, ...
	951	Edward Dwyer, ...	do.	Mongarvan, ...
	952	Patrick Cassidy, ...	do.	[illegible], ...
	953	Patrick Galvey, ...	Robert Henry, ...	Burghead, ...
	954	John Casey, Admor. of D. Donovan,	do.	do. ...
	955	Edmund Lawlor, ...	do.	do. ...
	956	Michael Mulcahy, ...	do.	do. ...
	957	Do.	do.	do. ...
	958	John Fitzgibbon, ...	do.	do. ...
	959	John Moran, ...	Robert Fleming, ...	[illegible], ...
	960	John Meagher, ...	do.	do. ...
	961	Michael Reddy, ...	Rev. W. W. O'Grady & others,	Ballyduhig, ...
	962	John Noonan, ...	do.	do. ...
	963	Cornelius Casey, ...	do.	do. ...
	964	Margaret Lynch, ...	do.	do. ...
	965	Bridget Noonan, ...	do.	do. ...
	966	Michael Noonan, ...	do.	do. ...
	967	Patrick Naughton, ...	Earl of Dunraven, ...	Castle Roberts, ...
	968	Owen Fowley, ...	Rev. John Fry, ...	[illegible], ...
	969	Terence O'Brien, ...	do.	do. ...
	970	John Ryan, ...	do.	do. ...
	971	William Mulqueen, ...	do.	do. ...
	972	Maurice Carey, ...	Reps. of Holmes White, ...	Drumkeen, ...
	973	Catherine Walsh, ...	Peter M. Sweetman, ...	Ballydawn, ...
	974	Ellen Fitzgerald, ...	do.	Knockanoney, ...
	975	John Kavanagh, ...	Col. M. Westropp, ...	Patrickswell, ...
	976	Thomas O'Dea, ...	Col. Walter Hallo, ...	Felorny, ...
	977	John Kirby, ...	Lady Emily Pigott, ...	Kilfinnagh, ...

LIMERICK—*continued.*

Extent of Holding. Statute.	Poor Law Valuation.	Former Rent.	Judicial Rent.	Observations.	Value of Tenancy.
a. r. p.	£ s. d.	£ s. d.	£ s. d.		£ s. d.
52 2 27	17 0 0	[illegible] 4 6	30 0 0		
66 3 4	37 10 0	45 11 3	43 0 0		
19 0 0	—	10 18 0	6 13 0		
16 3 [illegible]	19 10 0	37 0 0	33 14 0		
44 0 7	16 10 0	36 0 0	23 15 0		
[illegible] 0 0	23 10 0	[illegible] 0 0	[illegible] 14 0		
[illegible] 0 30	6 10 0	8 0 0	8 0 0	By consent.	
37 1 4	[illegible] 0 0	[illegible] 6 8	[illegible] 5 0		
37 2 6	[illegible] 5 0	37 0 0	30 0 0		
10 3 [illegible]	8 10 0	13 5 6	11 0 0		
1 3 0	4 5 0	6 [illegible] 6	5 0 0		
31 0 14	31 10 0	[illegible] [illegible] 0	[illegible] 0 0		
6 2 0	15 0 0	31 7 6	[illegible] 10 0		
3 0 [illegible]	4 5 0	0 5 6	5 10 0		
7 1 4	19 15 0	19 1 0	16 15 0		
8 0 5	14 0 0	30 0 0	21 10 0		
30 0 7	24 0 0	36 15 0	30 0 0		[illegible] 0 0
32 1 10	23 0 0	40 13 0	30 0 0		180 0 0
43 0 13	16 5 0	37 0 0	22 0 0		
61 3 0	38 10 0	65 10 0	37 10 0		
38 0 35	23 15 0	43 0 0	35 0 0		
103 1 11	74 10 0	117 10 0	80 0 0		
73 1 [illegible]	68 15 0	[illegible] 3 8	75 0 0		
18 0 0	33 0 0	58 7 6	40 0 0		
128 0 [illegible]	75 10 0	106 18 0	90 0 0		
40 1 [illegible]	53 5 0	61 1 6	53 10 0		
71 1 8	64 10 0	110 3 2	87 0 0		
47 3 5	46 5 0	74 10 0	62 0 0	Provision has been made as regards a labourer in this case.	
32 0 10	[illegible] 10 0	54 7 6	25 15 2	By consent.	
0 3 10	3 5 0	4 0 0	3 5 0		
43 1 33	58 15 0	87 12 4	67 13 4	do.	
73 3 23	75 15 0	116 0 0	107 0 0		
65 1 7	65 10 0	80 0 0	70 0 0		
38 3 30	38 13 0	34 10 0	30 10 0		
14 2 10	19 0 0	33 10 4	18 10 0		

F. D. Baldwin (Legal).
John Goldsmith.
Thomas Roche.
W. C. Hemphill.
William Evans.

978	John Ryan,	...	Robert Hogan, ...
979	Patrick Barry,	...	John Massy Graham, a by Viscount Massy,
980	Laurence Dillon,	...	do. ...
981	Mary Hogan,	...	Robert Smithwick,
982	Anne Maher, Admx. of Daniel Maher,		William Lane Joynt,
983	Patrick Sweeney,	...	B. H. Stewart,
984	Do., ...	...	Mrs. Ellen Gough,
985	John Hogan,	...	Heffernan Considine,
986	James Ryan,	...	do. ...
987	John Cormack,	...	do. ...
988	John McGrath,	...	do. ...
989	James Byrne,	...	do. ...
990	John Power,	...	Cornelius Madden,
991	John Lenahan,	...	Colonel R. G. Hare,
992	Jeremiah O'Grady,	...	H. A. S. Pigott,
993	James Cummins,	...	H. B. M. Lyons and a Trustee of Edward George Bury, ...
994	James Lynch,	...	
995	Sarah Sheehan,	...	Charles Coppinger,
996	Patrick O'Donnell,	...	William G. Murphy,
997	Patrick Halpin,	...	do. ...
998	John Keogh,	...	Lord Clancarty,
999	Patrick Lanigan,	...	do. ...
1000	Michael Mulcahy,	...	Colonel C. H. Vereker,
1001	Patrick Ryan,	...	do. ...
1002	John Shea,	...	do. ...
1003	Patrick Barry,	...	do. ...
1004	James Kirby,	...	do. ...
1005	Charles O'Neill,	...	do. ...
1006	Michael Keenan,	...	do. ...
1007	Michael Meehan,	...	do. ...

LIMERICK—*continued.*

Extent of Holding. Statute.	Poor Law Valuation.	Former Rent.	Judicial Rent.	Observations.	Value of Tenancy.
A. R. P.	£ s. d.	£ s. d.	£ s. d.		£ s. d.
7 0 37	—	7 0 0	6 15 0		
5 2 18	5 10 0	11 0 0	8 10 0		
14 3 0	13 0 0	15 0 0	13 15 0		
15 0 31	11 0 0	17 10 0	15 10 0		
65 0 0	33 0 0	70 0 0	48 0 0		
13 1 8	16 10 0	23 0 0	24 0 0		
14 3 8	11 5 0	23 13 6	20 0 0		
19 2 23	27 0 0	26 7 6	22 0 0		
17 0 7	26 0 0	31 1 4	27 10 0		
37 0 18	40 0 0	70 2 6	61 0 0		
71 2 36	69 0 0	165 6 8	125 0 0		
61 2 0	125 10 0	41 16 2	90 0 0		
3 0 6	—	1 13 0	1 17 0		
54 0 29	37 18 0	55 0 0	45 0 0		
46 3 0	38 15 0	58 0 0	45 0 0		
51 0 3	87 0 0	48 15 0	30 0 0		100 0 0
20 0 6	7 5 0	20 5 8	18 15 0		
13 0 10	6 0 0	4 18 6	6 10 0		70 0 0
45 0 78	45 15 0	66 18 10	35 0 0		
38 1 0	—	34 17 6	30 0 0		
74 2 4	67 18 0	120 0 0	85 0 0		
44 0 37	47 10 0	42 0 0	45 0 0		
8 0 16	13 5 0	17 13 3	10 0 0	By consent.	
36 1 33	38 0 0	67 6 5	53 0 0	do.	
80 3 4½	33 15 0	48 8 8	38 10 0	do.	
7 1 5	6 15 0	10 18 1	6 10 0	do.	
61 0 23	40 18 0	64 18 9	60 0 0	do.	
57 0 17	42 10 0	86 5 8	62 0 0	do.	
27 0 5	17 16 0	36 17 10	20 0 0	do.	
44 2 7	33 0 0	70 17 5	65 0 0	do.	
8 2 26	10 15 0	13 3 4	11 15 0	do.	
10 1 27	14 15 0	35 14 6	17 15 6	do.	
5 0 8	5 8 0	5 0 8	3 18 6	do.	
8 1 9	15 0 0	27 0 2	14 0 0	do.	
53 1 37	18 5 0	30 0 0	38 0 0	do.	

COUNTY OF

Names of Assistant Commissioners by whom cases were decided.	No.	Name of Tenant.	Name of Landlord.	Townland.
Assistant Commissioners—				
E. D. Bailey (Legal). John Gibbons. Thomas Roche. W. G. Heffernan. William Evans.	1013	[illegible]	Lord [illegible],	[illegible],
	1014	John Curtin,	Sir Croker Barrington, Bart.,	[illegible],
	1015	Benjamin Nelson,	Richard E. Lloyd,	Farranmeel,
	1016	John Kirby,	Rev. R. J. C. Studdert,	Killeagh,
	1017	Edmund O'Brien,	Lady Louisa Fitzgibbon,	Kilshin,
	1018	John Walsh,	Robert T. Webber,	Curraw,
	1019	David Walsh,	Lord Longford,	Clogher,
	1020	Patrick Flaherty,	do.	East Clogher,
	1021	John Barry,	Thomas F. H. De Burgh,	Ballyphilip,
	1022	Timothy Magrath,	Michael O'Shaughnessy,	Bruree,
	1023	Patrick Lyons,	Mrs. Maria Baker, and Christopher J. Carleton,	Ballyfookeen,
	1024	Mary Murphy,	do.	Clashroe,
	1025	John Lyons,	do.	Ballyfauna, and Clashroe,
	1026	John Regan,	do.	Ballyfookeen,
	1027	John O'Rourke,	do.	do.
	1028	James Mahony,	Usher Williamson,	Knockane,
	1029	Thomas Wall,	Robert Maxwell,	Ballygibbin North,
	1030	James Carroll,	do.	do.
	1031	John Fitzgerald,	Lord [illegible],	[illegible],
	1032	Michael Condon,	do.	do.
	1033	John Fitzgerald,	do.	do.
	1034	John Donovan,	do.	do.
	1035	Patrick O'Brien,	do.	[illegible] or [illegible],
	1036	Charles Bailey,	Rev. John McCarthy, and Rev. P. D. O'Regan,	Spittle, Upper,
	1037	Thomas Thompson,	Mrs. Frances Marshall, Executrix of W. J. H. Marshall, and R. W. Marshall, a minor, by Frances Marshall his guardian,	Spittle,
	1038	John Foley,	do.	do.
	1039	Patrick Mullins,	Nathaniel Buckley,	Knockmanagh,
	1040	James Hegarty,	do.	Carrigane, and Carrigane [illegible],
	1041	Daniel Hayes,	Col. F. G. T. [illegible],	[illegible],
	1042	Michael Casey,	Michael Hickey,	South [illegible],
	1043	William Lyons,	Thomas A. Franks,	Mount Eagle,
	1044	James Lyons,	do.	do.
	1045	Johanna McCarthy,	do.	[illegible],

LIMERICK—continued.

Extent of Holding. Statute.	Poor Law Valuation.	Former Rent.	Judicial Rent.	Observations.	Value of Tenancy.
A. R. P.	£ s. d.	£ s. d.	£ s. d.		£ s. d.
47 0 [illegible]	41 0 0	61 0 0	54 0 0	By consent.	
[illegible] 0 0	48 10 0	84 0 0	70 0 0	do.	
[illegible] 2 0	15 5 0	21 0 0	14 0 0	do.	
30 0 [illegible]	61 0 0	45 10 5	[illegible] 6 2	do.	
4 3 [illegible]	0 5 0	10 12 0	0 [illegible] 0	do.	
70 3 6	30 5 0	43 11 0	[illegible] [illegible] 0		[illegible] 0 0
26 2 [illegible]	61 5 0	[illegible] 0 0	31 0 0		
64 1 [illegible]	66 10 0	47 13 0	67 0 0		
[illegible] 0 [illegible]	64 5 0	[illegible] 10 8	41 0 0		[illegible] 0 0
8 1 0	4 0 0	5 10 0	4 10 0		
11 0 16	[illegible] 0 0	[illegible] 0 0	[illegible] 0 0		
45 0 [illegible]	61 16 0	50 0 0	41 0 0		
[illegible] 2 11	61 0 0	87 14 0	44 0 0		
8 0 15	10 13 0	11 0 0	10 10 0		
50 2 14	66 0 0	[illegible] 0 0	[illegible] 0 0		
107 0 0	104 0 0	120 0 0	120 0 0		
41 0 0	84 10 0	44 15 0	40 0 0		
97 1 8	100 5 0	137 10 0	107 0 0		
17 1 6	26 0 0	[illegible] 13 0	[illegible] 0 0		
14 3 [illegible]	16 10 0	76 7 5	[illegible] 0 0		
[illegible] 2 27	40 10 0	67 16 4	45 0 0		
[illegible] 0 0	[illegible] 15 0	[illegible] 17 4	[illegible] 0 0		
10 1 [illegible]	8 10 0	15 0 0	18 0 0		
108 0 0	67 15 0	[illegible] 7 0	70 0 0		
[illegible] 0 20	11 0 0	43 10 2	[illegible] 0 0		
10 7 16	13 0 0	30 14 6	31 10 0		
43 2 15	10 10 0	15 0 0	13 6 0		156 0 0
[illegible] 1 5	8 10 0	5 0 0	7 10 0		
54 1 11	5 5 0	13 10 0	11 10 0		
1 2 0	5 0 0	5 10 0	4 0 0		
[illegible] 1 [illegible]	[illegible] 10 0	100 11 0	87 0 0		
[illegible] 3 20	78 0 0	105 11 2	[illegible] 0 0		
51 0 [illegible]	7 15 0	[illegible] 11 0	16 0 0		

COUNTY OF

Names of Assistant Commissioners by whom Cases were decided.	No.	Name of Tenant.	Name of Landlord.	Townland.
Assistant Commissioners—				
T. D. [illegible] (Legal). John [illegible]. Thomas Rowe. W. G. [illegible]. William Evans.	1046	John Cronin, ...	Thomas J. Franks, ...	Cullane, North, ...
	1047	David Walsh, ...	Morgan D. O'Connell, ...	Forty Acres, ...
	1048	Edward Casey, ...	John Monck Croker, a minor,	Ballingarde (part), Oakhampton.
	1049	Michael O'Donnell, ...	Graham William J. Norreys, and Thomas John Franks.	Tully, ...
	1050	Daniel Mannix, ...	Rev. George Quaile, ...	Crogane, ...
	1051	Cornelius O'Connor, ...	Thomas Sanders, ...	Foxhall, ...
	1052	Michael Riordan, ...	Mary M. Bevan, ...	Newtown Oxaun or Ballyvonda,
	1053	Edmond Casey, ...	Colonel Robert Maunsell, ...	Fanstown, Kilmallock.
	1054	John Mahony, ...	C. S. Cooper, and others, ...	Knockfeang, West.
				Total, ...

LIMERICK—*continued.*

Extent of Holding. Statute.	Poor Law Valuation.	Former Rent.	Judicial Rent.	Observations.	Value of Tenancy.
A. R. P.	£ s. d.	£ s. d.	£ s. d.		£ s. d.
35 1 25	16 5 0	35 0 0	27 0 0		
33 1 24	37 0 0	56 15 6	44 0 0		
340 3 33	391 8 0	473 18 0	420 0 0		
35 1 0	32 0 0	36 1 6	30 0 0		
50 1 21	—	80 0 0	75 0 0		
103 3 10	100 10 0	170 0 0	145 0 0		
14 2 10	13 10 0	34 11 0	25 0 0		
41 0 2	11 5 0	71 13 10	60 0 0		
383 2 30	296 15 0	483 16 7	425 0 0		
4,725 0 31½	3,884 6 0	7,028 11 7	6,613 0 3		

CIVIL BILL COURT.

SUMMARY

Of Cases in which Judicial Rents have been Fixed by the Civil Bill Courts and notified to the Irish Land Commission during the month of July, 1892.

	Number of Cases in which Judicial Rents have been fixed.	Acreage.	Tenement Valuation.	Former Rent.	Judicial Rent.
		Statute Acres. A. R. P.	£ s. d.	£ s. d.	£ s. d.
Ulster—					
Cavan, ...	4	54 2 0	67 6 0	89 10 0	66 5 0
Fermanagh, ...	3	56 0 38	8 10 0	26 15 0	21 5 0
Total, ...	7	110 2 38	75 16 0	116 5 0	87 10 0
Leinster—					
Meath, ...	1	14 1 3	6 5 0	8 16 0	6 0 0
Connaught—					
Galway, ...	4	148 1 4	64 15 0	64 12 5	86 0 0
Roscommon, ...	60	963 1 11	446 10 6	656 14 10	505 12 0
Total, ...	64	1,111 2 15	511 5 6	721 7 3	591 12 0
Munster—					
Cork, ...	7	723 0 7	178 15 0	231 5 0	208 5 0
Limerick, ...	1	7 3 30	7 15 0	14 9 4	10 10 0
Tipperary, ...	24	827 0 20	465 15 0	615 8 3	483 7 0½
Total, ...	32	1,557 3 17	650 5 0	877 14 6	700 2 0½

IRELAND.

ULSTER, ...	7	110 2 38	75 16 0	116 5 0	87 10 0
LEINSTER, ...	1	14 1 3	6 5 0	8 16 0	6 0 0
CONNAUGHT, ...	64	1,111 2 15	511 5 6	721 7 3	591 12 0
MUNSTER, ...	32	1,557 3 17	650 5 0	877 14 6	700 2 0½
TOTAL, ...	104	2,794 1 33	1,243 16 6	1,728 4 11	1,385 4 0½

PROVINCE OF

COUNTY OF

County Court Judge.	No.	Name of Tenant.	Name of Landlord.	Townland.
George Waters, Q.C.	443	James McCann, ...	Augustine and Alice Henshall,	Drumaine, ...
	444	James Flood, ...	Richard Atkinson & another, Trustees of Anne C. Hogg,	Killdarragh, ...
	445	Elizabeth Turner, ...	Andrew C. Montgomery, ...	Lisboy, ...
	447	Richard Jennings, ...	Earl Annesley, ...	[illegible], ...
				Total, ...

COUNTY OF

P. J. Blakeney, Q.C.	60	Cornelius McCaffrey, ...	Earl of [illegible], ...	[illegible], ...
	61	Terence McManus, ...	do.	[illegible], ...
	64	Rev. Daniel [illegible], ...	Francis Graham, ...	[illegible],
				Total, ...

PROVINCE OF

COUNTY OF

John C. [illegible], Q.C.	34	James [illegible], ...	Earl of Dunraven, ...	[illegible], ...

PROVINCE OF

COUNTY OF

T. R. [illegible], Q.C.	1	Thomas [illegible], ...	Catherine Baldwin, ...	[illegible], ...
	2	James Lenihan, ...	do.	do. ...
	3	William [illegible], ...	do.	do. ...
	4	John Burke, ...	do.	do. ...
				Total, ...

ULSTER.

CAVAN.

Extent of Holding. Statute.	Poor Law Valuation.	Former Rent.	Judicial Rent.	Observations.	Value of Tenancy.
A. R. P.	£ s. d.	£ s. d.	£ s. d.		£ s. d.
—	7 5 0	7 15 0	8 5 0		
13 2 17	10 0 0	14 0 0	14 0 0		
31 3 24	21 10 0	23 15 0	19 0 0		
39 0 39	28 16 0	34 0 0	27 0 0		
84 2 0	67 5 0	89 10 0	66 5 0		

FERMANAGH.

18 0 5	5 3 0	16 0 0	13 0 0		
3 1 1	4 5 0	8 15 0	1 10 0		
4 3 30	—	9 0 0	6 15 0		
26 0 36	8 10 0	33 15 0	21 5 0		

LEINSTER.

MEATH.

14 1 3	6 3 0	5 10 0	6 0 0		

CONNAUGHT.

GALWAY.

55 0 33	23 0 0	34 5 3	33 0 0		
38 2 20	11 5 0	14 3 0	16 0 0		
26 0 30	11 15 0	15 2 6	16 0 0		
34 1 25	18 15 0	24 0 0	25 0 0		
153 1 6	64 15 0	94 19 9	95 5 0		

COUNTY OF

County Court Judge.	No.	Name of Tenant.	Name of Landlord.	Townland.
Arthur Hamill, Q.C.	261	Thomas McMahon, ...	Thomas C. MacDermott, Esq.,	Drumore, ...
	262	Margaret Tansey, ...	Bernard Sweeny, ...	Cuilt, ...
	263	Hartley Conlon, ...	James Carroll, ...	Gildown, ...
	264	Michael Barrett, ...	Henry Boyd, ...	Bridge Corrow,
	265	James Nicholson, ...	do.	do. ...
	266	Patrick Fox, ...	Charles M. O'Conor, ...	Ballyrushy, ...
	267	Hugh Armstrong, ...	Captain Walsh, ...	Annaghking, ...
	268	Patrick Tonkin, ...	Dr. Thomas Lyons, ...	Cregganeen, ...
	269	Patrick Flanagan, ...	do.	do. ...
	270	Michael McLoughlin, ...	do.	do. ...
	271	Daniel Flood, ...	do.	do. ...
	272	Anne Reilly, ...	do.	do. ...
	273	Thomas Hale, ...	Lucy O'Grady, ...	Carrowgarvaleigh,...
	274	Michael Keane, ...	do.	do. ...
	275	John Ross, ...	do.	do. ...
	276	Anne Campbell, ...	do.	do. ...
	277	Ellen Morrison, ...	do.	do. ...
	278	Tobias Evans, ...	do.	do. ...
	279	Winifred Loughery, ...	do.	do. ...
	280	Andrew Carney, ...	do.	do. ...
	281	Michael Hodges, ...	do.	do. ...
	282	Thomas Cafferkey (John),	do.	do. ...
	283	Ellen Cafferkey, ...	do.	do. ...
	284	Patrick Cafferkey, ...	do.	do. ...
	285	John Cox, ...	do.	do. ...
	286	Thomas McDermott, ...	do.	do. ...
	287	John McDermott, ...	do.	do. ...
	288	Thos. and John Corrigan,	do.	do. ...
	289	Thomas Kearney, ...	do.	do. ...
	290	William Kearney (Tom),	do.	do. ...
	291	John Cafferkey, Rep. of James Cafferkey,	do.	do. ...
	292	Michael Keating, ...	do.	do. ...
	293	Thos. Kearney, (William),	do.	do. ...
	294	Thady Duffy, ...	do.	do. ...
	295	Michael Feeny, ...	Captain P. Gally, ...	Gard, ...

ROSCOMMON.

Extent of Holding. Statute.	Poor Law Valuation.	Former Rent.	Judicial Rent.	Observations.	Value of Tenancy.
a. r. p.	£ s. d.	£ s. d.	£ s. d.		£ s. d.
20 0 30	6 0 0	11 7 6	8 15 0		
2 0 30	2 0 0	1 0 0	2 10 0		
15 1 30	9 10 0	16 15 0	9 12 6		
20 3 8	13 0 0	11 0 0	15 15 0		
12 3 33	4 10 0	7 0 0	5 13 4		
25 3 34	23 10 0	25 0 0	20 0 0		
23 3 17	18 5 0	23 18 6	18 10 0		
8 1 10	2 0 0	3 0 6	2 8 0		
1 1 25	1 15 0	4 0 0	2 18 0		
7 1 23	3 16 0	6 10 0	1 8 0		
6 1 35	3 5 0	6 5 0	4 5 0		
0 0 13	3 15 0	9 8 0	6 5 0		
15 3 11	4 10 0	4 15 0	4 10 0		
10 3 33	3 15 0	8 0 0	3 15 0		
11 1 16	2 10 0	4 15 0	3 15 0		
16 1 8	2 15 0	4 15 6	3 14 0		
17 1 36	2 17 6	7 0 0	3 10 0		
7 3 25	2 0 0	1 5 0	1 15 0		
12 3 13	2 10 0	3 10 0	3 10 0		
8 3 20	3 5 0	7 10 0	4 4 0		
16 3 9	4 0 0	4 10 0	4 10 0		
18 3 4	4 15 0	4 11 0	5 0 0		
13 1 8	3 13 0	7 5 0	6 0 0		
12 0 20	0 16 0	7 5 6	6 0 0		
6 0 38	3 13 0	5 15 0	3 10 0		
9 0 5	2 3 6	4 14 0	3 10 0		
8 0 1	2 5 6	4 14 0	3 10 0		
18 3 30	5 5 0	8 5 6	6 14 0		
7 3 20	5 0 0	6 0 0	5 5 0		
10 1 13	2 5 0	7 0 0	5 6 0		
18 3 25	6 0 0	6 16 0	6 10 0		
16 1 25	4 16 8	7 5 0	5 0 0		
8 1 16	5 5 0	7 5 0	5 0 0		
18 0 24	4 13 0	6 14 0	5 0 0		
30 3 25	15 10 0	24 11 6	20 0 0		

County Court Judge.	No.	Name of Tenant.	Name of Landlord.	Townland.
Arthur Hamill, Q.C.	296	Michael Conroy, ...	Captain F. Balfe, ...	Carrickmore, ...
	297	William Irwin, ...	do	Annaduling, ...
	298	Peter Davis, ...	do	do ...
	299	Patrick Gill, ...	do	do ...
	300	Peter Gill, ...	do	do ...
	301	Thomas Connor, ...	do	do ...
	302	Abraham Lyons, ...	do	do ...
	303	Thomas Tighe, ...	do	do ...
	304	Patrick Ferris, ...	do	do ...
	305	James Walker, ...	do	do ...
	306	Bernard Kelly, ...	do	do ...
	307	Peter Reilly, ...	T. G. McConnell, ...	Ardagh, ...
	308	Michael Hogan, ...	do	Cloon, ...
	309	Michael Flynn, ...	do	Tullynure, ...
	310	John Daly, ...	do	do ...
	311	Mary Glynn, ...	do	do ...
	312	James McElhone, ...	do	Drumillagh, ...
	313	Patrick Carey, ...	do	Cloon, ...
	314	Michael Carey, ...	do	do ...
	315	Thomas Gallagher, Rep. of Pat Doyle	do	do ...
	316	Dominick Carey, ...	do	do ...
	317	Bernard McDermott, ...	Dr. Thomas Lyons, ...	Cargaren, ...
	318	Anne Davis, Rep. of Peter & Bridget Davis	Rep. of Michael Quinn, decd.	Ballyduane, ...
	319	Catherine Flanagan, ...	Charles Brodrick, ...	Drumlough, ...
	320	Mary Halden, ...	do	Bruming, ...
				Total, ...

ROSCOMMON—continued.

Extent of Holding. Statute.	Poor Law Valuation.	Former Rent.	Judicial Rent.	Observations.	Value of Tenancy.
A. R. P.	£ s. d.	£ s. d.	£ s. d.		£ s. d.
[illegible] 3 [illegible]	15 10 0	14 11 0	16 0 0		
7 1 5	3 5 0	5 7 2	3 5 0		
16 2 0	17 16 0	[illegible] 5 0	[illegible] 0 0		
[illegible] 1 4	18 0 0	16 7 4	13 15 0		
15 1 [illegible]	0 15 0	27 1 2	20 0 0		
6 3 5	2 0 0	5 17 10	3 15 0		
7 [illegible] [illegible]	8 0 0	3 14 1	[illegible] [illegible] 0		
20 1 [illegible]	15 5 0	17 16 0	16 5 0		
12 [illegible] 0	5 15 0	6 [illegible] [illegible]	5 10 0		
12 [illegible] [illegible]	[illegible] 5 0	9 16 4	7 10 0		
13 [illegible] [illegible]	7 10 0	9 [illegible] [illegible]	[illegible] [illegible] 0		
76 0 16	13 [illegible] 0	15 1 0	16 10 0		
72 2 0	18 16 0	14 14 [illegible]	10 0 0		
[illegible] 1 37	[illegible] 0 0	25 10 0	22 [illegible] 0		
[illegible] [illegible] 34	[illegible] [illegible] [illegible]	13 5 5	11 [illegible] 0		
[illegible] 0 0	17 15 0	20 3 0	13 10 0		
17 0 0	6 10 0	[illegible] 5 0	7 15 0		
21 2 [illegible]	11 5 0	17 18 10	11 10 0		
15 1 6	10 16 0	10 [illegible] 0	[illegible] [illegible] [illegible]		
18 3 31	5 15 0	7 3 0	6 10 0		
10 0 0	4 5 0	5 1 [illegible]	[illegible] [illegible] 0		
109 0 0	[illegible] 0 0	[illegible] 7 [illegible]	[illegible] [illegible] [illegible]		
15 1 7	10 0 0	11 0 0	4 5 0		
10 0 [illegible]	1 15 0	7 14 [illegible]	5 [illegible] 0		
17 1 [illegible]	3 15 0	[illegible] 5 0	9 0 0		
[illegible] 1 13	446 10 0	[illegible] 15 10	[illegible] 13 0		

PROVINCE OF

COUNTY OF

County Court Judge.	No.	Name of Tenant.	Name of Landlord.	Townland.
[illegible], Q.C.	[illegible]	Cornelius [illegible], ...	Mrs. Mary M. Brown and ors.,	[illegible], ...
	53	James Cronin, ...	do.	[illegible], ...
	54	Timothy Kenny, ...	Captain F. J. Woodley, ...	[illegible], ...
	55	Do.	do.	[illegible], ...
	56	Samuel Jagoe, ...	John A. Jagoe, ...	[illegible], ...
	57	Denis Sheehy, ...	Adam Newman, ...	[illegible], ...
	58	James Lynch, ...	do.	[illegible], ...
				Total ...

COUNTY OF

T. A. [illegible], Q.C.	75	Cornelius McNamara, ...	William L. Joyce, ...	[illegible], ...

COUNTY OF

J. A. [illegible], Q.C.	2	[illegible], ...	Richard E. [illegible], ...	[illegible], ...
	3	Thomas [illegible], ...	do.	[illegible], ...
	4	John [illegible], ...	do.	[illegible] ...
	5	James [illegible], ...	Mrs. Harriet [illegible], ...	[illegible], ...
	6	Richard [illegible], ...	Rev. J. W. [illegible] and others,	[illegible], ...
	7	Bartholomew Carroll, ...	Miss A. F. [illegible] and others,	[illegible], ...
	8	John Brennan, ...	Earl of [illegible], ...	[illegible], ...
	9	Cornelius Hogan, ...	Mrs. Mary [illegible], ...	[illegible], ...
	10	Edward [illegible] (Fox), ...	[illegible] and others, ...	[illegible], ...
	11	Mary McKeogh, ...	do.	[illegible], ...
	12	Catherine McCormack, ...	do.	[illegible], ...

MUNSTER.

CORK.

COUNTY OF

County Court Judge.	No.	Name of Tenant.	Name of Landlord.	Townland.
J. A. Wall, Q.C.	13	Michael Hogan, ...	Joseph Griffith, ...	Gregan Beg, ...
	14	Martin Glasson, ...	M. G. K. [illegible] and another, Minors,	Carrighaunady,
	15	William Glasson, ...	do.	do. ...
	16	James Walsh, ...	do.	do. ...
	17	John Glasson, ...	do.	do. ...
	18	John Brien, ...	do.	do. ...
	19	Philip Kennedy, ...	do.	do. ...
	20	John Brien, ...	do.	do. ...
	21	Michael Butler, ...	Mrs. Louisa O'Reilly, ...	Cloughleaning, ...
	22	Michael Ryan, ...	George M. Finch, ...	Ballywilliam, ...
	23	Thomas Barry, ...	Miss Susan Jones, ...	Ballyseeman, ...
	24	Michael Glasson, ...	Bevan Donnelly, ...	Gonaduff, ...
	25	James Hyland, ...	Richard W. Smith, ...	Keyleng, ...
				Total, ...

TIPPERARY—*continued.*

Extent of Holding. Statute.	Poor Law Valuation.	Former Rent.	Judicial Rent.	Observations.	Value of Tenancy.
A. R. P.	£ s. d.	£ s. d.	£ s. d.		£ s. d.
63 1 13	28 15 0	37 0 0	31 0 0		
14 1 19	16 10 0	19 10 0	16 0 0		
29 3 38	17 0 0	21 5 0	17 0 0		
16 0 33	19 10 0	19 10 0	10 0 0		
45 2 15	30 0 0	60 0 0	54 0 0		
40 1 35	37 0 0	42 8 8	37 5 4		
10 0 31	15 10 0	11 10 0	9 18 8		
10 2 4	8 5 0	10 14 6	9 8 6		
43 0 15	15 5 0	77 10 0	19 10 0		
48 0 16	21 3 0	30 3 4	30 0 0		
33 0 28	25 0 0	30 10 0	23 5 1½		
21 3 0	13 5 0	23 4 5	15 15 0		
18 2 0	7 10 0	11 5 7	5 0 0		
607 0 10	465 13 0	613 5 7	483 7 0½		

SUMMARY

Showing, according to Counties and Provinces, the Number of Cases in which Judicial Rents have been Fixed, upon the Reports of Valuers appointed by the Irish Land Commission, on the Joint Applications of Landlords and Tenants.

	Number of Cases in which Judicial Rents have been Fixed.	Acreage.	Tenement Valuation.	Former Rent.	Judicial Rent.
		Statute Acres	£ s. d.	£ s. d.	£ s. d.
CONNAUGHT—					
Galway, ...	17	816 3 34	99 5 0	125 18 0	130 15 0
MUNSTER—					
Clare, ...	8	737 3 11	91 7 0	204 4 0	181 10 0
Tipperary, ...	85	4,117 1 19	2,468 3 0	3,130 7 10	2,731 16 10
Total, ...	93	4,854 5 30	2,559 10 0	3,334 11 10	2,923 6 10

IRELAND.

CONNAUGHT, ...	17	816 3 34	99 5 0	125 18 0	130 15 0
MUNSTER, ...	93	4,854 5 30	2,559 10 0	3,334 11 10	2,923 6 10
TOTAL, ...	110	5,671 0 24	2,658 15 0	3,460 9 10	3,054 1 10

Rents fixed upon the Report of Valuers appointed by the Irish Land

PROVINCE OF

COUNTY OF

Number.	Name of Tenant.	Name of Landlord.	Townland.
1	Bridget Flanagan,	Richard Bolton,	Kockill,
2	Michael Finn,	do.	do.
3	Philip Walsh,	do.	do.
4	James Cunningham,	do.	do.
5	Hugh Collins, and John Collins,	do.	do.
6	John Kyne,	do.	do.
7	Denis Clarke,	do.	[illegible],
8	James Kyne,	Elizabeth Kirwan,	Keekill,
9	Patrick Kyne,	do.	do.
10	Ellen Walsh,	Henrietta Kirwan,	do.
11	Mark Rabbitt,	do.	do.
12	John (late Michael Walsh), and Alice Walsh.	do.	do.
13	Patrick Hardiman,	[illegible] G. Richardson,	Lacamore,
14	Michael Gallagher,	do.	Aghafaddo,
15	Patrick Lyons (Young),	do.	Lacamore,
16	John Martin,	do.	do.
17	John Hynes,	do.	do.
			Total,

PROVINCE OF

COUNTY OF

1	James O'Keeffe,	Edward A. Gore,	Knockbrennaghan,
2	Patt Doherty, & Margaret Doherty,	do.	[illegible],
3	Timothy Fitzpatrick,	do.	[illegible],
4	Ellen Connell,	do.	[illegible],
5	James McMahon, and Samuel Williams,	do.	[illegible],
6	Denis Sheehan,	do.	Ballyvarra,
7	Do.	do.	Donagore,
8	Michael Clancy,	do.	[illegible],
			Total,

Commission on the Joint Application of Landlord and Tenant.

CONNAUGHT.

GALWAY.

Extent of Holding, Statute.	Poor Law Valuation.	Former Rent.	Judicial Rent.
A. R. P.	£ s. d.	£ s. d.	£ s. d.
1 3 19	1 5 0	1 7 0	1 0 0
22 3 20	5 15 0	6 15 0	5 5 0
23 3 20	5 15 0	6 15 0	5 8 0
40 1 30	10 0 0	8 10 6	5 15 0
45 2 23	13 10 0	13 10 8	10 0 0
35 0 1	9 15 0	10 7 0	6 10 0
70 3 30	14 15 0	21 0 0	17 0 0
51 2 35	11 15 0	14 3 0	10 8 0
45 1 20	11 10 0	11 18 0	9 10 0
20 3 30	5 8 0	7 6 0	3 8 0
20 3 38	5 3 0	7 4 0	5 5 0
20 3 20	5 8 0	7 6 0	3 5 0
80 2 27	—	—	11 5 0
8 2 25	—	—	1 7 0
20 3 5	—	—	9 10 0
18 0 10	—	—	6 0 0
15 0 18	—	8 10 0	3 2 0
518 3 24	99 5 0	135 15 0	120 15 0

MUNSTER.

CLARE.

COUNTY OF

Number.	Name of Tenant.	Name of Landlord.	Townland.
1	Mary Creagh,	Vincent Meredith,	Gurteen,
2	Robert Graves,	do.	Ballinagraph,
3	Joseph Ryan,	do.	Gurtavoh,
4	John Ryan,	do.	Coolleeven,
5	Thomas Conroy,	do.	Cobbingardon,
6	Andrew Ryan,	do.	do.
7	Edward Lanby,	do.	Cashmemaer,
8	Lawrence Ryan,	do.	Cashel,
9	William Creagh (Tim),	do.	Gurteen,
10	Johnson Carroll,	do.	Gurtavoh, Lower,
11	Mary Ryan,	do.	Garrane,
12	Patrick Slattery,	do.	do.
13	James Bazza,	do.	do.
14	Margaret Creagh,	do.	do.
15	John Rourke,	do.	Fennerville & Meadowmount,
16	Cornelius O'Brien,	do.	Kilpatrick,
17	Daniel Breen,	do.	Garrard,
18	William Dwyer (Port),	do.	Cobbingardon,
19	Julia Butler,	do.	Gerryduff, East,
20	Timothy Ryan,	do.	Gurtavoh, Lower,
21	John Lovison,	do.	Gurtavoh,
22	George Taylor,	do.	do.
23	Michael Taylor,	do.	Gurteard,
24	Anne Burke,	do.	Meadowmount,
25	William Connors,	do.	Coolleeven,
26	James Reilly,	do.	Reading,
27	Cornelius Ryan,	do.	Reading and Meadowmount,
28	Adam Curtis,	do.	Garrane,
29	William Creagh (Owen),	do.	do.
30	Alice Murphy,	do.	Coolleeven,
31	John Fraley,	do.	Meadowmount,
32	Jeremiah Dwyer,	do.	Kilpatrick and Coolfin,
33	Thomas Fennessy,	do.	Cashmemaer,
34	Edmund Moriarty,	do.	do.
35	Edmund Carew,	do.	Coolleeven,

TIPPERARY.

Extent of Holding, Statute.	Poor Law Valuation.	Former Rent.	Judicial Rent.	Observations.
A. R. P.	£ s. d.	£ s. d.	£ s. d.	
27 2 21	14 16 0	30 10 6	29 16 0	
73 3 34	81 0 0	[illegible] 0 0	78 0 0	
61 3 [illegible]	16 0 0	11 18 8	11 13 4	
60 0 27	46 0 0	78 18 4	67 0 0	
86 3 31	83 15 8	146 18 8	93 0 0	
38 3 30	37 15 0	44 12 0	37 10 0	
75 1 37	63 1 0	91 18 6	75 0 0	
33 1 [illegible]	18 10 0	17 2 8	14 5 0	
41 1 24	24 15 0	27 6 6	29 10 0	
23 3 16	5 0 0	9 8 8	8 0 0	
10 1 3	8 10 0	9 17 3	9 7 7	
33 3 24	15 0 0	22 11 6	13 0 0	
29 3 23	4 6 0	5 0 0	7 5 6	
37 3 6	24 0 0	30 0 0	24 0 0	
18 0 12	7 16 0	7 10 0	7 6 8	
40 3 36	40 5 8	43 16 1	40 0 0	
43 1 13	34 15 8	33 13 0	35 0 0	
73 0 25	68 15 0	74 11 8	67 0 0	
16 1 38	18 10 0	10 11 4	8 10 0	
26 0 33	10 10 0	11 16 9	9 10 8	
24 0 6	16 5 0	83 7 4	28 0 0	
79 1 8	62 10 0	75 3 0	63 10 0	
16 2 5	5 10 0	10 18 8	6 15 0	
37 3 [illegible]	10 15 0	26 17 8	26 0 0	
20 1 7	12 0 8	13 1 4	13 0 5	
39 0 1	17 10 0	23 6 5	28 0 0	
43 0 6	24 19 0	32 7 0	21 7 0	
18 1 6	18 18 0	28 16 4	23 10 0	
24 1 24	17 0 0	24 14 0	21 14 0	
8 0 10	5 0 0	8 10 8	6 10 0	
103 0 14	83 13 0	90 15 0	80 15 0	
38 0 33	38 5 8	49 11 6	48 0 0	
8 1 16	7 16 0	8 16 10	10 10 0	
19 3 38	17 18 0	22 4 6	18 0 0	
5 0 5	4 15 0	6 7 0	5 10 0	

COUNTY OF

Number.	Name of Tenant.	Name of Landlord.	Townland.
36	Mary Hayes,	Viscount Hawarden,	Attyrick,
37	Patrick Canny,	do.	Goldengarden and Kilpatrick,
38	John Ryan (Lawrence,)	do.	Garrane,
39	James Ryan,	do.	do.
40	Lawrence Ryan,	do.	[illegible],
41	William Murphy,	do.	Goldengarden,
42	Edward Ryan (Mary),	do.	[illegible],
43	James Fraley,	do.	[illegible],
44	John Ryan (Edmund),	do.	[illegible] and [illegible],
45	Edmond Reilly,	do.	[illegible], Upper,
46	Mathew Gilbert,	do.	[illegible] and Dunrick,
47	Thomas Furlong,	do.	Carrow,
48	William Carew,	do.	do.
49	Thomas Lonergan,	do.	Clare,
50	Cornelius Dwyer,	do.	Carrow,
51	Mary Ahern,	do.	do.
52	Edmond Tuohy,	do.	do.
53	Mary Carroll,	do.	do.
54	John Ryan ([illegible]),	do.	do.
55	Patrick Dwyer (Paul),	do.	[illegible],
56	Daniel Breen,	do.	Carrow,
57	Daniel Ryan (James),	do.	do.
58	Patrick Fogarty,	do.	do.
59	Robert Bennett,	do.	[illegible],
60	Joseph Ryan,	do.	Carrow,
61	Johanna Connell,	do.	do.
62	James Carroll,	do.	do.
63	Michael Carew,	do.	do.
64	Malachy Dwyer (Mat),	do.	Dunrick and [illegible],
65	James Maher,	do.	[illegible], Upper,
66	James Byrne,	do.	[illegible], Lower and Upper,
67	John Byrne,	do.	[illegible],
68	Philip Reilly,	do.	Dunrick,
69	Bridget Ryan,	do.	[illegible] & [illegible],
70	Jeremiah Cooper,	do.	Dunrick,

TIPPERARY—*continued.*

Extent of Holding. Statute.	Poor Law Valuation.	Former Rent.	Judicial Rent.	Observations.
A. R. P.	£ s. d.	£ s. d.	£ s. d.	
18 3 36	13 10 0	17 14 0	14 0 0	
78 0 19	[illegible] 15 0	73 3 2	[illegible] 0 0	
84 3 39	18 0 0	18 0 0	15 0 0	
49 0 4	19 0 0	20 0 0	[illegible] 0 0	
11 3 21	11 15 0	16 1 0	13 0 0	
3 1 10	3 10 0	4 15 0	4 5 0	
[illegible] 1 22	67 10 0	[illegible] 0 0	65 0 0	
175 2 0	126 0 0	167 10 6	135 0 0	
60 1 6	40 5 0	63 15 0	49 0 0	
26 3 [illegible]	19 15 0	16 15 0	16 15 0	
77 1 19	[illegible] 0 0	37 0 0	[illegible] 0 0	
46 1 1	[illegible] 10 0	[illegible] 0 0	27 5 0	
[illegible] 3 27	[illegible] 15 0	82 10 5	[illegible] 10 0	
110 0 17	97 0 0	122 9 0	112 0 0	
127 2 16	79 10 0	64 15 0	34 0 0	
77 0 [illegible]	32 0 0	22 15 0	[illegible] 10 0	
49 0 29	17 10 0	16 14 0	[illegible] 14 6	
41 0 31	27 5 0	21 15 0	[illegible] 0 0	
23 1 24	15 15 0	19 17 0	16 0 0	
72 0 8	[illegible] 5 0	[illegible] 1 0	45 0 0	
17 0 [illegible]	7 15 0	6 4 9	6 4 5	
56 0 6	27 0 0	39 4 0	37 10 0	
43 1 13	[illegible] 15 0	[illegible] 14 4	[illegible] 14 4	
63 2 0	45 10 0	[illegible] 1 6	52 0 0	
180 0 0	51 0 0	49 18 6	48 [illegible] 6	
40 2 34	27 13 0	[illegible] 18 0	22 [illegible] 0	
[illegible] 0 4	16 0 0	23 10 0	21 0 0	
47 1 5	29 10 0	[illegible] 11 3	30 14 0	
47 0 20	19 5 0	[illegible] 12 0	25 0 0	
15 3 6	3 10 0	8 6 0	7 0 0	
[illegible] 1 18	[illegible] 0 0	108 1 0	102 1 0	
60 2 36	47 0 0	61 6 0	47 0 0	
38 0 22	18 15 0	14 0 4	12 5 0	
36 1 22	31 0 0	25 10 0	16 0 0	
65 0 6	[illegible] 5 0	41 3 0	[illegible] 0 0	

COUNTY OF

Number.	Name of Tenant.	Name of Landlord.	Townland.
71	William Perkins, ...	Viscount Hawarden, ...	Coolanga, Upper, ...
72	Cornelius Ryan, ...	do.	[illegible], ...
73	Edmund Ryan (Martin), ...	do.	[illegible], ...
74	Philip Ryan, ...	do.	Glenough, Lower, and Foragh,
75	Thomas Dwyer, ...	do.	[illegible], ...
76	Catherine Gorman, ...	do.	Coolanga, Upper, ...
77	John Ryan, ...	do.	Garrigeen, ...
78	Michael Kelly, ...	Arthur F. O. Tollemache, ...	[illegible], ...
79	Thomas Doyle (Larry), ...	Rev. J. W. Barlow and others, ...	Birchhill, ...
80	Michael Leahy, ...	do.	do. ... ...
81	John Doyle (Larry), ...	do.	do. ... ...
82	Denis Dwyer, ...	do.	do. ... ...
83	John Doyle (Davy), ...	do.	do. ... ...
84	Thomas Doyle (Davy), ...	do.	do. ... ...
85	Patrick Daly, ...	O. E. & Henry Dawson, ...	[illegible], ...
			Total, ...

TIPPERARY—*continued.*

Extent of Holding. Statute.	Poor Law Valuation.	Former Rent.	Judicial Rent.	Observations.
a. r. p.	£ s. d.	£ s. d.	£ s. d.	
[illegible] 3 [illegible]	11 0 0	17 7 8	14 0 0	
14 3 14	11 0 0	15 4 6	10 5 0	
[illegible] 1 11	[illegible] 0 0	[illegible] 14 0	23 0 0	
84 3 [illegible]	61 10 0	[illegible] 16 0	[illegible] 0 0	
101 1 [illegible]	64 0 0	75 0 0	75 0 0	
14 1 [illegible]	8 10 0	9 4 4	7 10 0	
[illegible] 1 34	[illegible] 10 0	[illegible] 1 0	[illegible] 0 0	
18 2 19	4 10 0	9 0 0	9 0 0	
43 3 10	19 5 0	[illegible] 11 0	[illegible] 0 0	
[illegible] 1 4	[illegible] 10 0	37 0 0	24 0 0	
43 1 [illegible]	33 15 0	37 5 6	[illegible] 0 0	
[illegible] 1 37	18 5 0	18 0 0	16 10 0	
[illegible] 2 27	17 5 0	19 17 6	17 0 0	
16 3 25	10 0 0	15 0 0	13 0 0	
24 1 27	5 15 0	11 0 0	9 5 0	
4,317 1 18	[illegible] 5 0	[illegible] 7 10	[illegible] 15 10	

Dublin: Printed by Alex. Thom & Co., 87, 88, & 89, Abbey-street,
The Queen's Printing Office,
For Her Majesty's Stationery Office.

www.ingramcontent.com/pod-product-compliance
Lightning Source LLC
Chambersburg PA
CBHW020103030726
47498CB00006B/1932
* 9 7 8 3 7 4 2 8 0 6 0 8 6 *